What Readers Are Saying About
Siege Of The Capital

"Although laced throughout with fiction, Mr. Tevelin's book captures the essential elements of Mr. Khaalis' takeover, and the drama of those thirty-nine hours. He managed to make the complexity of the incident into a very readable story." *Earl Silbert, U.S. Attorney for the District of Columbia during Khaalis' siege*

"Dave Tevelin vividly captured the horror of the Khaalis slayings, and the drama of his takeover of the three buildings in D.C. He nailed Khaalis' voice, and compellingly laid out the web of factors that led to both the murders of his family and his actions four years later. I recommend this book highly." *Henry Schuelke, former Assistant U.S. Attorney for the District of Columbia who prosecuted the murderers of Khaalis' family*

"Siege of the Capital, a blend of fiction with real time events, is a great read! Its account brought back memories of a life-changing event for those involved in the 1977 hostage siege and the dramatic trial that followed. For me, as the federal prosecutor involved in the case, Dave Tevelin's account of those days -- and Khaalis' back story -- is well researched, vivid, and compelling." *Mark Tuohey, former Assistant U.S. Attorney, District of Columbia*

"Dave Tevelin weaves a taut drama filled with over-the-top characters in an fantastic series of events, all of which are based in fact! A terrific retelling of a bizarre chapter of Washington history that is both authentic and gripping." *Tim Murray, former D.C. pretrial official and Executive Director of the Pretrial Justice Institute*

SIEGE OF THE CAPITAL
A Jake Katz Novel
Dave Tevelin

SIEGE OF THE CAPITAL

Hamaas Abdul Khaalis recognized it as soon as the needle hit the groove. Sonny Rollins' *Oleo*. He put his palms together and nodded at Omar.

"You have exquisite taste, my friend."

"I thought you'd like it."

He did more than like it. He loved it, and when he was Ernest McGhee, he loved to play it, especially that three-minute drum solo that raced along so fast and smooth it felt like only three seconds when he finished. Omar must have been paying attention when he told him the story about the night he sat in on it with Sonny at the Five-Spot, down in the Bowery in '59, and how the whole house gave him a standing O when he finally settled back into the groove. Now he only drummed his fingers on the arm of Omar's shabby easy chair but the feeling was still there, all the rhythm jumping through him one more time.

Omar sat cross-legged on his bed, the only other place to sit in the apartment, and slapped the mattress in time to Hamaas.

"Hamaas still got that Ernie in him!," he howled.

Hamaas didn't hear him. He was listening to Max Roach bang the skins on the record and thinking one more time about that night he kept right up.

"You miss it, huh?" Omar asked.

Hamaas shrugged. "It'll always be in me," he said, "but like Sonny used to say, the jazz business is always bad. And as much as I loved it, I love Allah more."

"I know you do, and I thank you again for showing me the way, brother." Omar lifted his palms and nodded. "Shokran."

A little shiver ran through Hamaas. He thought about asking Omar to raise the heat but he knew the brother was on hard times, so he kept his coat on and rubbed his hands. He dropped by for a reason so he got to it, in his way.

"So, how are things now with you and Salimah?," he asked.

1

"They're good, man, good," Omar said. "She's a righteous woman. I am blessed to have her in my life, truly." He took a moment to think on it a little longer, then shook his head at Hamaas.

"It's just me, man. A man's a man, right? I'm out and about, I see things, women, you know? I know you know what I'm sayin'."

"I know," Hamaas said, "and Allah knows. That's why the Qur'an says the sisters have to cover up their temptations. Surah 24, The Light, right? That's why it says women are not to display their charms in public, not even to 'swing their legs when walking', huh?, gotta draw their hijabs over their breasts. Allah knows what you're going through and that's why he said a righteous sister shouldn't put you through it. You need to stay away from those harlots on the street, get your mind straight, not your dick, huh?"

"Yeah, but that's a tough thing, man, at least for me it is. Shit, you got a wife, you got two wives, man. Whole different thing for you."

"Fair enough," Hamaas said, "but let me ask you, brother, how's your business doin'?"

"My business? I thought we talkin' about pussy, man," Omar said.

"Hold on a minute. Surah 4 tells you why. An-Nisaa, Women? If you can afford 'em, you can marry two women, three women, even four women if you want. But if you don't think you can provide for more than one, then that's all you marry. But if you don't marry no one, you can't have *anyone* like you want to, man. That shit's out the window, huh? You got to wear the garment of righteousness, man." He tapped his temple. "Discernment, man, Surah 7. C'm'on, you know that."

"I know it, man, I do know it," Omar said, "but it's hard to find a righteous sister out there, hard to know I can

2

provide for anyone else. Have enough trouble providin' for me."

"You still up at that restaurant?," Hamaas asked.

"The Luau Hut? Yeah. Sometimes. Hard to get worked up to go up there every day though, man , sloppin' shit and what-all."

Hamaas waited for Sonny to fade out. *St. Thomas* jumped up next, but this was his shot at getting Omar on the righteous side.

"Hey listen, man," he said, "I hear you. Let me talk to Abdul, my son-in-law, you met him up at my place? He's got a jewelry shop down in Georgetown. Maybe he could fix you up with something."

"That'd be fine, but I don't know nothin' about jewelry."

"You got a driver's license?"

"Yeah."

"Okay," Hamaas said. "Maybe you could do some drivin' for him. He's got a van, makes --"

A hard knocking on the apartment door interrupted them.

"Who's there?" Omar said.

"Khadyia. Hamaas' wife. Is he there?"

Omar shot Hamaas a quizzical look. Hamaas pushed himself up out of the seat.

"I told her to come by when she finished her grocery shopping and I'd take her back home."

Omar popped up and opened the door to see a woman standing in the hall, probably about thirty-five from what he could see, big brown eyes shining out from beneath her black khimar, a brown jibab cloaking the rest of her.

"Salaam Alaikum. Is Hamaas Khaalis --", she started to ask, then saw Hamaas over Omar's shoulder. Hamaas saw sweat gleam on her forehead.

"Khadyia," he asked, "how far did you walk? The Giant's only a few blocks."

3

"No, it's not that. Oh, it's so, so – oh! Exasperating!"

Omar gestured for her to come in.

"Come," Hamaas said, and directed her to the chair. "Come sit."

She fell into it and covered her eyes with her hands, then shook her head.

"I was in the check-out line fifteen minutes! It took forever. I finally get to the counter, I unload the bags and I reach into my pocketbook and I don't feel my purse. I go through it, go through it again – not there. Nothing. I figure I must have left it at home."

"You sure nobody took it?," Hamaas asked.

"Not up there, at the Giant?," she said. "And I had the bag locked up tight. So, I can't find my purse, but the man behind me, a brother named Abdul, he sees me going through all this and he asks me what happened and I tell him and that I have no car and he very nicely says he'll drive back to the house for me and get the purse."

"Did you give him the house keys?"

"No," Khadyia said. "Hamaas, please. I told him there were people there who would let him in and give him the purse. I told him to ask for Amina or Bibi so they knew he was telling the truth."

"And?"

"And --," she slapped her hands on the arms of the chair -- "he never came back! I would have been here a half an hour ago but I was waiting and waiting and no Abdul. He never came back!"

"All right," Hamaas said, picking his brown leather cap off the corner of Omar's bed. "Come. I'll drive you back to the store. We'll buy what you need and go home."

She covered her eyes again and shook her head.

"No, please," she said, "I just want to go home now. I've had enough of that place for one day."

Hamaas and Omar exchanged glances. Hamaas reached down to help her up.

"Come, my pearl, we're going home. Omar, will I see you at salah tonight? Sunset's 5:13."

Omar looked at the clock next to the bed. 3:18.

"Hamaas, I can't," he said. "My shift starts at 4. I ain't even got space to lay out a mat there."

"You'll catch up in your own time," Hamaas said. "Peace be with you. And I will call Abdul Aziz and let you know what he says."

When they got in the car, Hamaas asked again, "Khady, do you want to go back to the store or home?"

Khadyia's stare gave him all the answer he needed. They rode 16th Street the ten minutes down from Omar's place. Hamaas made a right on Jonquil and turned left down the alley to the driveway behind his house. When he passed behind the synagogue next door, he was surprised to see four black men on foot, all in dark long coats, heading down his driveway in a hurry.

"Who are they?," Khadyia asked. "Do you know them, Hamaas?"

Hamaas sped up and drew abreast of the men now heading his way in a line along the side of the alley closest to the house. Their grinning faces whizzed by. As he turned into the driveway, one of them yelled back at him. "Don't mess with Elijah Muhammad!" Then they took off running.

Hamaas' throat constricted and he turned the car up the driveway fast. A car he didn't recognize was already there, blocking him from pulling into the garage, so he jolted his car to a stop behind it, leaped out, and ran to the right, up the steps and onto the walkway along the side of the house. He tried to place the key in the lock but his hand kept jumping. Khadyia knelt down to look under the shade covering the window to the left of the door.

5

"Hamaas, there's a man!," she yelled. Suddenly he felt the door pull away from him. He pulled back on the doorknob with all his might.

"He's trying to get out!," Khadyia called out from her knees.

"No! You're not! You're not!," Hamaas yelled and bent back, straining to keep the door closed. The man inside tugged it open, an inch then two. Hamaas couldn't see his face.

"No! No!," he heard himself say. The door lurched toward him, then away. Khadyia moaned. She pushed herself to her feet and ran back down the walkway and the steps, hiking her jibab up to keep from tripping.

"Khady, no!," Hamaas screamed, and hurtled down the steps after her. He missed a step and fell face first into the concrete at the bottom, his cap tumbling across the grass. He tasted blood in his mouth and heard a loud, hard smack behind him. He spun his head to see the front door bouncing back off the wall and a running black man in a hat disappear towards 16th Street. He scrambled back up the steps to give chase, then stopped and tumbled to all fours.

Khady! What if there were still more of them in there? He leaped to his feet and reeled back down the steps, then around the corner, and staggered across the driveway, banging into the garage door and pushing his way off onto the stone steps up to the back patio.

"Khady!," he screamed again, frantic at where his wife may be, who may be with her. He dashed up the steps until he saw the bushy brown hair of his daughter Amina spread across the stone deck up to his left, Khady's head buried in her chest.

"Ay!" he cried out and bounded ahead up the steps, then saw his daughter's blood drenching the deck, oozing towards him down the stones ahead. The shock knocked him off his feet back to the driveway,. He lay there on his back, screaming indecipherable sounds until the keening of

6

Khadyia brought the world back to him in all its horrific truth. He rolled and pushed himself to his feet and stared, disbelieving, at the sight of his wife pleading with their bleeding child.

"Amina! Mina! Open your eyes! Mina!," Khadyia cried. Mina gave no response.

He spun around, and around again, not knowing whether to tend to his daughter, run into the house to see if the others -- the children! -- were harmed, or to go after the men that did this to her. His body made the choice for him, lurching back to the car. He threw the door open, leaped into the driver's seat, roared back down the driveway, and sped up the alley.

They were gone, nowhere in sight. At Jonquil, he looked left, then right. He spied two men rounding the corner to the right on 16th, back in the direction of his house. He screeched right onto Jonquil. The light at the intersection with 16th was red and two cars sat ahead of him, waiting for it to change. He leaned on the horn, then swerved to the right and up onto the sidewalk. Blaring his way down the concrete, he lurched right, onto the sidewalk in front of the synagogue, and bumped over the curb onto the street. Another car honked from behind him but he paid it no mind. He leaned forward, still pumping the horn, scanning, searching for some sight of them somewhere.

He saw two black men dart across the lawn of the other synagogue across the street, towards Juniper, which was roaring up in front of him. A line of cars approached the intersection from the other direction, coming up 16th. The first car crept through the crossing, oblivious to his relentless honking, and the second one kept coming too, but screeched to a halt when Hamaas cut him off. Too late, he saw a car come up at him in the right lane, but he was not stopping and the oncoming car fishtailed into the left lane.

Hamaas saw no one ahead. He floored it across an alleyway that ran parallel to 16th, swiveling his head left and

7

right as he went across, then stomped on the brake when he saw a pack of men running down the alley to the right. He threw the car into reverse, spun the rear back, then floored it down across Juniper in pursuit.

He made up the distance quickly, blasting the horn all the way down. Ten yards from them, he saw the group duck away from a man at the front who turned and lifted a gun right at him. Hamaas ducked his right shoulder into the steering wheel, spun the wheel to his left, and flattened the brake, all in one motion. The windshield shattered. Glass sprayed everywhere but he kept his head down, hearing another shot and another one zip by. The car spun back up the alley, flattening a chain link fence on his right. He lifted his head up high enough to steal a peek at the rear view mirror and saw the men flying down the alley towards Iris Street.

He threw his head back and let out a low guttural roar that turned into a jagged high whine then a wordless scream. He slammed his head into the steering wheel, then again and again. His brain reeled, exploded. By the time he looked back up into the mirror, the alley was empty.

The words he heard that jackal yell back at him rose again in his fevered mind. Were they true? Did Elijah Muhammad send these animals? What other carnage did they wreak, all in the name of the God they profaned?

He raced back up the alley and swung left on Juniper, then barreled onto 16th, hammering the horn as if he hoped the noise would wipe away his fears and visions. A police car headed towards him down 16th. He made a left turn in the middle of the road to block its way and scrambled out of the car to flag it down. As the cruiser slammed to a stop, he ran to the driver's side window.

"My family's been attacked!," he screamed, pointing up the street. "My daughter is bleeding to death!"

"Slow down, sir," the policeman said. "Take a breath so I can understand what you're saying."

"I can't! I can't!," Hamaas shrieked. "Follow me, follow me! I beg you!"

He jumped back in the car, circled around the cruiser and tore back up 16th, waving at the cop to follow him. In his rear view mirror, he saw the car make a U-turn, lights flashing. He thanked Allah and made sure the cop stuck with him back up the driveway, then beckoned him to follow him up the steps to where Amina still lay, her head cradled in Khadyia's lap, Khadyia's hands clasping her right hand. She was still breathing, praise God! He stroked her forehead and cooed softly to her.

"Mina, Mina, please stay with us, please. If you hear me, squeeze your oummi's hand, please."

Her fingers did not move. He heard the cop talk into his walkie-talkie.

"Yeah, this is Levow," he said. "My twenty's a house at the corner of 16th and Juniper Northwest. We need rescue. Woman's been shot. She's on the landing at the back."

He laid a hand on Hamaas' shoulder.

"Sir, what's the address here?"

"7700 16th."

Levow repeated it into the handset.

"Don't know," he said. "I'm going in now." He listened for a few seconds. "No." Then, "Standing by. Roger."

He put the phone back in the holder on his belt, then walked past Hamaas and gestured at the storm door before him.

"This go into the main house?"

"Yes."

"Any other way in or out other than the garage doors or the front door?"

Hamaas stood up and approached him.

"No," he said, then leaned in to Levow and said as quietly as he could, "Other people are in there. My family."

Levow turned to Khadyia.

"Ma'am," he asked, "have you heard anyone? Seen anyone else?"

Khadyia shook her head no without taking her eyes off of Mina.

"Have you heard any noise coming from inside the house?" Levow asked.

Khadyia shook her head again.

"Please, Officer," Hamaas said, "may I go with you? There are children, babies in there, probably scared out of their minds."

Sirens wailed in the distance. Officer Levow drew his revolver from his holster.

"We're both going to wait for the backup," he said. "Give us a minute to walk through. If everything's cool, I'll bring you in."

Hamaas nodded. He leaned into the window next to the door, cupped his eyes, and peered in until Levow gently pushed him back. He saw the table next to the sofa was knocked to the ground and papers strewn about, but no one was in the dining room or the hallway to the living room. Maybe Bibi took the children out for a walk. Maybe the babies slept through whatever happened to Mina. Maybe.

The sirens grew nearer, then a police car and a rescue squad van pulled slowly down Juniper past the house and parked at the curb. Two medics jumped from the van, each with a big metal box in his hand, and ran up the alley and the driveway to where Amina lay. Two cops right behind them jogged up the stairs to Levow. The taller one's name tag read Hague; the other one's Jandorf. Levow nodded at them, then raised a hand to Hamaas.

"Wait right here," he said and they went into the house, revolvers in their hands.

10

Hamaas' mind began to reel again. He raised his hands to the top of his head and walked in small circles on the patio, his closed eyes shutting out everything swirling about him. 'Don't mess with Elijah Muhammad!' filled his head, over and over again. Was that it? His letters to the devil Muhammad and his followers, so-called Muslims? He wrote what was in his heart, what he knew to be true. He dictated the first one to Aly in one sitting. That was what, three weeks ago? And he instructed him not to sign either of their names, out an abundance of caution. But then, with the rage still burning in his soul, the fire in his head unceasing, he abandoned caution and signed his full name to the next letter, in large flowing letters. That one, he dictated to Aly a week or so later, maybe two weeks ago.

"God, what have I done?," he moaned and fell to his knees. He smacked his hands to his eyes and began to weep.

"Bismillahir rahmanir rahim," he cried, "In the name of God, the most gracious, the dispenser of Grace, oh please, my Lord and God, please, I beg of you, spare my babies!"

The fear, the guilt that overflowed him, pinned his head to the stone. He dreaded hearing Officer Levow tell him what he already knew in the marrow of his bones. He had worked for Elijah Muhammad for years. He knew what he and his deceivers, just like those he saw fleeing up the alley, were capable of. He prayed to Allah for his bountiful mercy, then turned his head to look across the stone to where Mina still lay. The rescue squad people kneeling at her side blocked his view of her but he could see Khadyia still stroking his daughter's hand, and murmuring a prayer for her survival. He pushed himself to his feet and looked into the open doorway to his house. He hear a sharp guttural noise from the window above him, then nothing. He could wait no longer.

He quietly entered the house through the space that served as his family room and the prayer center for the Hanafis who gathered there for the daily prayers and the

11

wisdom of his counsel. He drew back at the sight of the still glistening streaks and drops of blood on his carpet and floorboards. He heard coughing and talking from above him up the stairs. He moved quietly to the staircase and stepped on the carpeted section of each step to keep the cops from knowing he had disobeyed their orders as long as he could. When he could see the upstairs hall, he saw Officer Jandorf on his knees facing him, wiping his mouth with the back of his uniform jacket sleeve, a pool of vomit on the carpet in front of him. Jandorf raised his gaze to see Hamaas come into view and waved him away with the back of his hand.

"No, no, please, sir. Get back down there now, for your own good."

Hamaas knew he now had no choice. He ran up the rest of the steps and through the doorway just past Jandorf on the left. Officer Levow was on his knees by the bathtub, blocking his view.

Levow whipped his head around, his eyes brimming with tears, his face pallid and contorted.

"Sir, I told you to stay down there!"

But it was too late. Khady, Mina's beautiful baby girl, stared back up at him from the water with lifeless eyes. Her stepbrother Abdullah spread his little wings next to her, face down.

Hamaas sunk to his knees again. His head crashed onto Levow's shoulder, his eyes shut in anguish, trying to blind himself to what he had just seen. Levow patted his back slowly and gently.

"Sir," he said. "Sir. There's more, I'm afraid."

Hamaas opened his eyes and saw Tasibur, his nine-day old grandson, rolled on his side towards him, beads of water still dripping off his little tummy to the floor.

"I – I thought he was a doll," Levow said. "I'm sorry, I'm so sorry."

Three beautiful babies, none older than fourteen months, the lights of Hamaas' life, dead and gone forever.

He went weak and fell back onto Levow, the millions of thoughts crashing in his brain rendering him unable to speak, sit up, or do anything but shudder and breathe. How he wished he was with them, in the presence of Allah, the most gracious, the sustainer of all the worlds.

Levow was the first to move. He pushed himself back and held Hamaas by the shoulders, then rose and helped him to his feet. Hamaas kept his eyes averted from the children, hoping he could shut the sight from his memory forever, knowing he never would.

Jandorf had made it to his feet and met them at the door of the bathroom. He held Hamaas lightly by the elbow and brought him to the doorway of Rahman's bedroom at the end of the hall.

"Sir?," Jandorf said.

"Hamaas," Hamaas quietly said. "Hamaas Khaalis."

"Mr. Khaalis," Jandorf said. "I need to tell you. I'm sorry but there's a body in here, a man, and a lot of blood. If you can do it, we need you to identify him."

"A man? That's my son's room. Rahman. He's only ten, only ten!"

Jandorf put a hand to Hamaas' chest.

"This is not a ten year-old, Mr. Khaalis. This is a man, in his twenties, I'd guess."

My God, Hamaas thought, Daud, my other son, is 26. Can it be?

"Are you ready, sir?," Jandorf asked. "Do you think you can do it?"

"No," he said, "no, no," but he let Jandorf lead him in anyway. They entered the bedroom and saw a dresser with the drawers pulled out, clothes flung in every direction. Hamaas rounded the corner of the closet and turned to the bed. A man lay there facing him, vomit caked on the pillowcase and the gag in his mouth, his hands and feet tied. Dark red blood, still wet, drenched the blanket.

13

Hamaas exhaled and shook his head. "I don't know who that is."

"He doesn't live here?," Jandorf asked.

"No, and I've never seen him at prayer, or anywhere else. I don't know him." Hamaas remembered the strange car in the driveway. "Maybe he's the man who drove here to get my wife's purse from the Giant, I don't know."

"Okay, is she the lady outside?"

Hamaas nodded. "Khadyia." The memory of her stroking Amina brought the tears back in a cascade flowing over his cheeks and spilling to the floor.

"Okay, we'll ask her to take a look. I need you to come down the hall with me," Jandorf said. "There are more."

Hamaas fell back against the closet door and stared out the window across from them. The sky was light and peaceful, a pale gray silhouetting the bare branches of the large oak tree on the front lawn. Young Jewish children played on each side of 16th Street, waiting for their schools to start. Were his children even alive? Rahman, only their age, Daud, his son by Bibi? Where was she?

He let Jandorf pull him gently back up the hall to the bedroom closest to the steps, on the left. When they crossed the doorway, Hamaas saw Rahman's sneakers first, then the blood on his khaki pants.

He shrieked "My son! My son!" and spun around the corner and threw himself next to Rahman, then wrapped him in his embrace, rocking, weeping, cursing the infidels, praying to Allah that this nightmare was only a test of his faith, his humility before God, but his boy's blood sticking to his face and hair was too real to be only a nightmare.

He heard heavy footsteps run up the stairs just outside the bedroom door, then hushed quick conversation between two of the cops. He sensed their presence but couldn't release Rahman to turn their way.

"Mr. Khaalis." It was Levow's voice. "There's a woman downstairs," he said, "in the basement."

Hamaas howled to the moon and the stars and the sun. His body trembled.

"No, no, no!"

"She's alive," Levow said. "She's still breathing. We'll take care of your son if --"

Hamaas kissed Rahman over and over, wailing his distress in Arabic and English until he finally let Levow and Jandorf help him up. Levow led him down the stairs to the living room, then down the second set of stairs to the basement and back to the furnace room.

It was there he saw Officer Hague standing over two men from the rescue squad huddling over Bibi, his younger wife, even younger than Amina. She too was gagged and bound, head and foot. Blood surrounded her. Hamaas fell to his knees again, cradling his head, shaking it to try to deny the existence of all the horrors he had witnessed.

"She's still alive," Hague told him, but her breathing was the only sign of life. Her eyes were closed like she was sleeping the sound sleep she always did, and nothing else moved or even twitched. Pieces of skin and bone laid on the floor next to her.

From the big sink at the back wall, a rescue squad man came towards him gingerly, holding something wrapped in a wet white towel, a red stain spreading through it. Hamaas saw him look at Hague, who nodded to him to go to Hamaas. The rescue man knelt in front of him.

"Sir? I need to --" but Hamaas didn't hear the rest. The top of little Bibi's nappy hair peeked through the top of the towel at him.

"Bibi! Oh my little one, my Bibi!" he moaned, and fell on to his back.

Did the Prophet inflict this upon him in His name? Was he Job, forced to suffer to prove his faith? He recited the passage from Surah 21 aloud, his eyes closed, his body trembling.

"And we remember Job!," he cried out, "When he cried out to his Sustainer, 'affliction has befallen me: but Thou art the most merciful of the merciful!'"

He remembered the next verse as well, but he said it to himself, wavering, afraid to believe its truth. "Whereupon We responded upon him and removed all the affliction from which he suffered; and We gave him his family, doubling their number as an act of grace from Us, and as a reminder unto all who worship Us."

He strove to believe but in this moment of his darkness, he pleaded with Allah, don't give me what you gave Job, give me back what I had.

When he opened his eyes, Levow was kneeling at his side, rubbing his arm. He was as white as a marble statue.

"Mr. Khaalis. Can you hear me?"

"Yes, yes."

"Okay. I think you passed out. You didn't answer me the last time."

Maybe it all was a dream, Hamaas let himself think, until he turned his head and saw the blood surrounding Bibi still closer to him.

"There's one more."

Hamaas was beyond thinking of who still might be accounted for.

"Alive?" he asked.

"No," Levow said, gripping his arm tighter. "He's dead, too."

He? Hamaas thought. Daud.

"Daud? My son?"

"About twenty-five, thirty years old?"

Hamaas laid there, wide-eyed. "He's twenty-six, my son. Daud."

16

"I hate to do this," Levow said, his shoulders slumping, "so help me God, I hate it, but can you look at the body and tell me for sure?"

It was Daud. Shot through the head, slaughtered like the others, like sheep. Not for a sacrifice to God, but for what? To please Satan? Hamaas had no tears left to shed. He whimpered and rocked his oldest boy for what seemed to him like hours. Finally, he felt Levow's hand on his back, where it had probably been for a long time. The bedroom was nearly dark, the air thick and humid with blood and sweat.

Hamaas let Levow gently push him forward and back down the two flights of steps back to the first floor. At the bottom of the landing, he heard voices murmuring on the patio through the closed front door, then silence. He made himself walk to the window next to the door, where Khady had knelt outside, and pushed the curtain to the side. Hague's back was to him under the arch, and past him he watched his pupil Saleem walk away from him down the concrete walkway, a prayer mat rolled under his left arm. Hamaas glanced up at the sky and saw that the light had melted away into a slate gray, streaked only by narrow clouds and the red streaks of sunset, turning darker still.

He let the curtain fall back in place and pushed a deep breath through his lips. He lifted his hands to his eyes and left them there for a long moment, then dropped them and turned to his left. Levow moved back a step to let Hamaas cross in front of him and watched him enter a bathroom off the hallway to the dining room and close the door.

Hamaas stared at the red eyes looking back at him in the mirror, the drawn brown face framing them, the gray hair in tight curls that circled his ears and flecked the tight natural above. Without breaking his stare, he turned the spigots on and waited for the water to get warm, then dipped his head to wash his face and hands. He dried himself, and stroked his hair with a brush that he laid back on the edge of the sink.

He pushed the door open and crossed back in front of Levow to a closet at the near side of the doorway. He opened the door and reached up for a white cap that he fitted snugly on his head, then reached back in and came out with a rolled rug.

He walked into the living room to his left, turned to his right, and unrolled the rug in front of him at a slight angle towards the window across from him. It was red, fringed in brown, decorated with a mosque and a lamp.

He stood with his hands at his side, closed his eyes, and murmured "I offer Magrib, the sunset prayers, three rakats, seeking nearness to God, in obedience to him."

Levow heard Jandorf's steps on the stairway near the door. When he saw him, he pointed at Hamaas. Jandorf looked over, then back at Levow, who gestured at him to come to him, then they both moved back a few steps into the hallway where they could only hear him.

Hamaas lifted his hands beside his ears. "Allah hu akbar," he said, then lowered his arms.

"Bismillahir rahmanir rahim. In the name of God, the most gracious, the dispenser of grace. All praise is due to God alone, the Sustainer of all worlds, the most Gracious, Lord of the Day of Judgment! Thee alone do we worship, and unto thee do we turn for aid."

The tears ran down his cheeks again but he spoke the words of his faith clearly and firmly. He reddened as he saw the face again of the fraud he once served, the conjurer who sent those men he saw in the alley, the men who spat at him, "Don't mess with Elijah Muhammad."

Then he clenched his fists and lifted his head and shouted with all that was left of his being.

"Guide us the straight way, the way of those upon whom Thou has bestowed they blessings, not of those who have been condemned by thee, nor of those who go astray!"

Jandorf looked at Levow. Levow stared at the wall across from them, streams of tears flowing down his cheeks.

18

March 9, 1977

1

He shook his head and grinned like he did every time he saw it. It didn't matter if he caught it out of the corner of his eye while he strolled down Indiana Avenue, or picked it out from up in an airplane, or even, like now and a couple hundred times before, took it in from the back as he crossed C Street, the Municipal Center of the District of Columbia still made him crack a smile.

Did anyone else in this city of majestic monuments get such a buzz looking at the bland brown backside of this homely building? No, Jake Katz thought. So why does he? Was it just nostalgia, a warm and fuzzy memory of the time he spent there during the year and a half he was a D.C. cop? Was it disbelief that he actually was a cop, and a good one who solved a murder committed on the stage of the Howard Theatre the night Martin Luther King was shot? Was it because so many of his old cronies and friends would still rise with a cheer and a hand slap every time he poked his head through their doors? Or was it something else? Did he just miss being a cop more than he enjoyed being an Assistant U.S. Attorney? Or did he really just miss being younger than thirty again?

That was way too much introspection for Katz, especially on such a cheery sunny morning, so he loped up the short flight of back steps, threw a quick salute to the Sergeant at the door, and went straight back to the panel of elevators. He took a second to steal a look at himself in the full-length mirror to his right. Still in decent shape, he thought. He'd never be tall but he hoped he'd keep his thick brown hair, never mind those gray strands over the ear he couldn't see but knew were there. Maybe he needed a few gray hairs to convince some of those old farts in Felony that he really was their supervisor now. Senior Trial Attorney sounded like such a glittering grand title when he got it nine months ago. Now, the shine was definitely off.

21

He shifted his standard phony brown leather government briefcase to his left hand so he could hit 3 with his right, and went up alone, contemplating a crusty, gray-haired Jake Katz. Why did everything make him shake his head today?

At three, he snaked through humans of all colors, ages, sizes, and shapes who wanted something from their government, and made his way around the corner to the Chief of Detectives' office on the right. Two detectives, both white, chatted at the far end of the conference table and paid him no mind when he nodded to them. Katz pulled out a gray metal seat halfway down, picked the pronged manila folders out of his briefcase, and started looking through the one on top. Because no one knew when something was going down on the streets, these meetings were always held whenever the arresting officer or the detective had the time, so he'd learned quickly to know what he needed exactly when he needed to know it.

He did a quick skim of the folder, picked his head up to hear the fat one turn the conversation from the fox he laid last night to the piece of ass waiting to smoke him tonight, and decided to interrupt.

"Are you guys it?"

"I got no idea," the skinnier older guy said. "I didn't get the invite list."

"Okay," Katz said, "let's get going. One of you got George Scarborough?"

"I do," they both said.

"Who's Kelly?" Katz asked.

"That's me," the heavy one said.

"That's whose name I got in the file," Katz said.

"That's bullshit," the skinny one spit out.

"Who are you?"

"Garranzo. Believe me, I had the guy. You don't forget an asshole like that."

"Then how come you're not in the file?" Katz asked.

22

"It's your file," Garranzo said. "How the hell do I know? I nabbed him for bad checks last year, idiotic scheme with his boat and his limos. I remember, believe me."

"Except it was my case," Kelly said. "With the Feds."

"There were no fucking Feds," Garranzo said. "It was all local, in Superior."

"Get out of here!," Kelly yelled. "You slipped a gear. It was mine and it was Federal, just like the other one, where that a-hole Pratt gave him probation instead of stickin' his ass in stir like he should have."

"Didn't happen. And whatever happened, happened in Superior," Garranzo told him.

"Hold on!" Katz cut in. "Let's go over this one at a time and make sure we're talking about the same Scarborough. I got him down for three months' probation in December for giving some IRS guys some shit."

"That was me," Kelly said. "The Feds went to his supposed office, up on Bladensburg Road, to take one of his limos because he owed Sam some money. He went batshit and they cuffed him and took him in too."

Garranzo tried to cut in but Katz held up his hand. "Hold it, hold it a second! What was number two?"

"Number two," Kelly continued, "was he was playing some idiot scam, getting suckers to pony up in advance for cruises. Then he'd cancel them all at the last minute, and send them back checks that bounced higher than this fucking building. Jackass Pratt said 'I know I'm giving you a slap on the wrist' but he gave it to him anyway. What a douche bag."

"That's the same as mine," Garranzo said to Katz. "Except it's in Superior. Same guy, same con, different douche."

"I got nothing on that," Katz said, flipping the pages in his folder, "Nothing."

23

"That just proves it again. You guys are more effed up than we are," Kelly said.

Katz could only agree on this one. His office was Federal but, because of D.C.'s weird political status, they were the local prosecutors too. Some cases went the Fed route to the U.S. District Court; some went local, to D.C. Superior. Five-plus years in the office, he still couldn't tell you exactly why every time.

He slapped his folder shut.

"So what are we going to do about it?," he asked. "Who's handling the Superior case, from us?"

"Brady? I think that's his name," Garranzo said.

"I know him," Katz said. "I'll talk to him, see if we can load up the probation revocation on number one, send our man away for some time this time around."

He started to scribble a note on his yellow legal pad, but stopped when the Chief's secretary tapped lightly on the door frame.

"Excuse me," she said. "Are you Mr. Katz?"

"I am," Katz said.

"We just got a call from your office. Something's going on downtown, it seems."

"What's going on?," Katz asked.

"Some people took over the Binnay Brith Building?, I think it's called."

"What people?," Katz asked.

"They said you know the man," the secretary said.

"I know the man? Who is he?"

She put on her glasses and tried to read what she wrote on the pink note in her hand.

"Oh dear, I hope this makes sense to you. They said his name was something like Hamas Kalas?"

Katz stared in disbelief.

"I know who you mean," he finally said. "Or I thought I did."

24

2

Katz raced down the steps rather than wait for the elevator. He hadn't thought of Khaalis for almost three years now, after the second murder trial in the case. He was the only line Assistant US Attorney on both of them, backing up his boss Bob Shuker, and Bob's boss, John Evans, who ran Felony Trials. The usual drill was to give an AUSA a case only after it was ready for court, but on this one, they pulled him in the day after it happened and a day after that, he was talking to Khaalis, trying to make sense of something beyond senseless. He actually didn't do much of the talking, then or any other time he came to his house. Khaalis did, relentlessly booming and blustering on about the murders, then Elijah Muhammad, then the Black Muslims, then the Jews and the Yehudi conspiracy, then back through them all, over and over again, until he finally wore himself out and Katz grabbed the chance to talk about whatever he came to talk about.

Running back to the Federal Courthouse, the visions that Katz had buried deep, the blood scarring the walls and smearing the carpets, the pillows with blood on one side and powder burns on the other, the photos of dead babies – a young boy, two young men, and the two women who somehow lived, one a vegetable forever, the other the witness they had to have – spewed back up at him from somewhere deep inside and iced his blood all over again.

He got out of the elevator on the third floor just in time to see Marty McAdoo come out of the stairwell in front of him. He took her all of her lean, blonde, soft, and pretty self in, and tried – but failed – to erase the vision of her pleasing him just for the hell of it last night.

Marty was unpredictable, so loving one minute, so explosively angry the next. The anger was what she had in common with Katz' ex-, but she was a handful not just for Katz, but for anyone who got in her way. In the courtroom or in a plea bargain, she always pushed for the longest sentence the law would allow, and almost always got it. "Maximum Marty," they called her. And when it came to their careers, she was full enough of ambition for both of them.

"I want us to climb that ladder together," she'd tell him, but would she wait for him if he fell a rung behind? For now, the right answer was: Don't screw a good thing up by asking.

He called out, "Marty!"

She looked back and eyed him with mock consternation.

"You rode up?," she asked. He lifted his briefcase to hide the finger he lovingly gave her, then hurried to catch up.

"You in on it too?," she asked.

"Yeah," Katz said. "Hamaas Khaalis, the guy who's supposed to be doing this? His family was the one murdered at the Hanafi Center."

"Ah, got it," she said. He waved her into the doorway ahead of them and they went straight back to Earl Silbert's office, the Office of the United States Attorney.

Silbert had been Harold Titus' principal assistant when Titus ran the office, then replaced him as Acting USA when Titus stepped down, right at the beginning of '74. Behind his pie-plate dark-rimmed glasses and below his receding hairline, Katz always thought Silbert looked exactly like Woody Allen's twin brother, only serious, and even smarter.

Earl was a recidivating graduate from Harvard, undergrad and law school, and had earned his reputation for being a straight shooter, always demanding the facts and the precedent to support any indictment, any motion. But Katz always felt a little wince every time he saw him, because he remembered the Watergate case, when Earl's diligence didn't serve him well.

26

Silbert was in charge of the original investigation and he relied on the only facts he had to indict Liddy and Hunt and some other lowlives for the break-in -- but none of the higher-ups, so he got into a world class shitstorm. When Archibald Cox got appointed Special Prosecutor, it was a smack in Silbert's face, but he went about his business like he always did, never showing a moment of doubt or resentment. Maybe it was pride, maybe it was defiance, but no one in the office gave up on him either, and after two nominations – first by Nixon, then by Ford – and endless grillings by the Senate Judiciary Committee, they all felt vindicated when, after twenty long months, the Senate finally let him stop "Acting" and made him the bona fide USA.

Titus was the USA who hired Katz but it was Earl who made him a Deputy Chief of Felony, and it was Earl who was giving him a shot at moving up again, to Senior Deputy, now that Shuker was being promoted to the Chief's job after Evans moved on to the Criminal Division in Main Justice. There were a few others who were serious contenders for the job, and a lot more who thought they were, so he was knocked out when Earl held him back after the staff meeting last week to tell him the job was his if he wanted it.

Now it was Earl who brought him back to the here and now.

"Okay. We've got a real situation going on downtown," he said. "A bunch of Moslems has taken over the B'nai B'rith building up on Rhode Island near Scott Circle. Nobody's made any demands yet, so no one knows why they're doing this, but they're not letting anyone in or out, so everyone in the building is a hostage at this point."

"How many people are we talking about?," Shuker asked.

"We don't know," said the uniformed MPD officer sitting to Silbert's left. Katz recognized him as Bob Rabe, the Assistant Chief. He was a solid guy with a round face

27

crowned by a sandy squared-off brush cut. The Queens accent that coated every word out of his mouth was the most distinctive thing about him.

"But it's the middle of a Wednesday," he said. "You got to figure there are a couple of hundred people there."

A guy in a black suit next to Rabe nodded. Katz didn't recognize him.

"Is MPD up there?," Earl asked.

"Yeah," Rabe said. "Our people and the FBI and some other Federal types have it surrounded. Nothing's happened – yet. Traffic's been diverted from Scott Circle and Dupont so it's a bitch on the streets."

"And Hamaas Khaalis?," Silbert said. "He's in charge of this?"

"I don't know who's really in charge," Rabe said, "but he said he was when he called us."

"What'd he say?," Earl asked.

"The Chief was on with him," Rabe said. "He had trouble keeping up with what the guy was raving about, then he hung up. We don't know exactly what office he's in and we haven't been able to make contact with him again, but we're working on it."

"We know Khaalis," Earl said. "He's the guy whose family was murdered up on 16th about three, four years ago? A bunch of black Muslims from Philly."

He turned to Katz.

"Jake, you worked the case. What can you tell us about him? Why do you think 's he doing this?"

"It's got to have something to do with that," Katz said, "but you never can tell with him. He'd start talking about one thing, then he'd be on to something else, and then he'd be all over the place. I want to say he was paranoid but I don't know if he really was. I mean, they really were after him."

"What else do you know about him?," Earl asked.

28

"I'd have to check back through the files to give you the details, but I remember his original name was Ernest McGhee. He was born somewhere in the Midwest, Illinois, Indiana, one of them. He was in the Army for a while but they discharged him sometime during World War Two, then he was a drummer, a jazz drummer in New York City, and, somewhere along the line, he became a Muslim. He worked for the Black Muslims up there for a while, pretty high up, but he said he was just trying to get inside, stop them from being deceivers and infidels and all that. At some point, he came down here and got some money from Jabbar to start a center for the Hanafi Muslims and that's what he was doing until he wrote those letters to Elijah Muhammad and they came down and wiped out his family."

"Jabbar?," Marty asked. "The Jabbar?"

"Yep," Katz said. "The Kareem Abdul Jabbar. Khaalis was Jabbar's kind of spiritual guide when he became a Muslim. Khaalis told me he picked Kareem's wife, named his kid. Jabbar bought the house here for him with his own money."

Marty looked impressed. Silbert recited the note in his pad as he scribbled it down. "Ernest McGhee. We'll check for any priors."

Then he turned to the bearded gentleman in a charcoal gray suit seated next to Rabe.

"Dr. Gordon, you're the psychologist. Any way you think we should try to talk to this guy?"

"It's hard to know at this point. Without any --".

The sharp ring of Silbert's phone cut him off.

Silbert picked it up, listened for a second, then extended the receiver to Rabe.

"It's Chief Cullinane." Rabe stood up and took the phone.

"Sir?," he asked. He listened for a few seconds, then closed his eyes and winced. "Right, right, sir. I will let him know. Where are you? I'm going there now. Ten-four."

He handed the phone back to Silbert and turned to face the table.

"They just took over the Islamic Center, up on Mass, past Dupont. Cullinane's heading there now. He wants me to get to the B'nai B'rith asap."

He grabbed his hat and headed for the door.

"The Islamic Center? And the B'nai B'rith? What the hell?," Earl said.

"I don't know," Rabe said. "Maybe the fucking White House is next."

Silbert drummed his fingers on the table for a few seconds, then gave it a sharp rap.

"Can I send Katz up there with you?," he asked Rabe. "Maybe Khaalis will talk to him, open up a line of communication."

Katz thought he knew why he was there, and this wasn't it, but he felt the cop juices roar back through him for the first time in a long time. Under the table, Marty slipped a hand over to squeeze his thigh tight.

Rabe motioned to Katz to get going and Katz jumped to his feet. Back in MPD, there were no questions asked, but he asked one this time.

"Can I just stop in my office for a second? I need to pick up a file."

"I'm going," Rabe said. "Now."

Now Silbert jumped up too.

"I just need to brief him for one second. He'll meet you in the driveway."

Rabe kept on walking. Gordon scurried past Silbert to catch up. Katz and Earl quick-timed down the hallway towards Katz' office. When they were well out of earshot of the doorway, Earl said "You got an answer for me yet?"

He knew what Earl wanted to know: Had he heard yet about the DOJ job? He hadn't but even if he had, he'd wouldn't have told him he was ready to take it if they offered it to him. Deputy Chief jobs in the Criminal Division didn't come along every day. Everyone's goal at the USA's was to get into the Department or start defending all the scum they'd been trying to convict. But the lure of big bucks didn't really get Katz's juices flowing. For better or worse, he was a public service kind of guy. The MPD suited him just fine, and so did the USA's office, but the leap to DOJ was the jump he wanted to take, and once he heard the word, he was going to take it, so he told Earl the truth, but not the whole truth.

"No," he said. "I'm still waiting to hear from DOJ. I want to call them, every day, but --"

"I got it, I understand, but I need to know too," Earl said. "If you're not going to take it, I've got to move on, and you need to let me know sooner rather than later. I don't want to lose anyone else who's thinking of jumping if you're just going to turn me down."

Katz nodded. "How soon?" he asked.

"Like tomorrow," Earl said. "Assuming you're not a hostage. Then I might give you an extra day or two."

Katz never, ever heard Earl tell a joke, so he didn't know if that was his idea of funny.

"Are you joking?" he asked.

"Yes," Earl said. "I'm joking. But only about the two days. Now you better get going. Good luck up there."

Katz nodded and ran the rest of the way to his office. Any other day, hearing a joke come out of Silbert would have been reason enough to feel the earth lurch below him, but he didn't think that was why he was reeling today.

31

3

Katz jumped into the back of the squad car. Rabe was on his walkie-talkie in the front passenger seat, too distracted to give Katz any shit for making him wait the extra minute. The driver bolted out onto Pennsylvania before Katz could slam the door shut. The cop sitting next to him was too engrossed in Rabe's conversation to even notice he was there. Their siren was blaring and traffic made way for them. Katz waited for Rabe to click off.

"Anybody hurt up there? Or at the Islamic Center?," he asked.

"No idea," Rabe said. "We'll find out in a minute."

The cruiser tore through a string of red lights on Pennsylvania then whipped right on 15th St., heading for Rhode Island. Katz quickly flipped open his folder marked "Khaalis Interviews – 1" and tried to catch up on the four years of fading memories he scrawled on the yellow legal pad.

He found the first time he met Khaalis at his home. His first note, "trees?", reminded him that when he went there the first time, just two days after the murders, every tree on the property had been cut down. "Scared out of mind" was what he wrote when Khaalis told him it was because he knew the people coming back to kill him would hide behind them.

"Jew?" he read. "Jew v. Muslim." Underlined, then "etc., etc.". He didn't bother to take notes because nothing Khaalis said had anything to do with the murders, just about Katz being a Jew and Khaalis being a Muslim. He practically quoted the whole Qur'an to him. As much as he could remember about it swamped his brain all over again.

"Katz?" Khaalis said. "They sent me a Jew? Does the torment never end?"

"Mr. Khaalis," Katz said. "I'm not here to torment you. I'm here to help find who --"

Khaalis didn't let him finish.

"So-called Black Muslims – deceivers, liars, charlatans – come to kill me, kill my family, my sons, my daughters, and the government sends another infidel to 'help' me? Forgive me, my Hebrew friend, if I do not rejoice in your presence."

"Mr. Khaalis," Katz said, "I'm not here as a Jew. I'm here to prosecute the bastards who did this to you and I need your help to do that."

"Spare me the noble words of the petty bureaucrat. Tell me, Mr. Katz, do you follow the word of God?"

"Yes," Katz said, now ready to take him on. "God, not Mohammed.."

Khaalis smiled and shook his head as if to pity him.

"Did you ever hear the expression, Mr. Katz, that 'you don't know what you don't know'? That is you, my friend. You do not know enough to even argue with Khaalis. You went to law school, huh? You think that makes you intelligent, huh? You are not intelligent, Mr. Katz. You need to learn a few things, starting with the fact that I and supposedly you worship the same God, huh? But we call him Allah. A-l-l-a-h. Allah. He is the same God as your God. Muhammad – do I have to spell that too, huh? -- is his prophet, his messenger, who brought his revelation to the people. Do you think you can remember that, my intelligent little Jewish friend? Huh?"

Katz remembered every word of his reply.

"Mr. Khaalis, can the insults, huh?" he mimicked him. "This smart little Jew is on your side. Let me do my job and I'll get out of here as soon as I can. Huh?"

Khaalis leaped to his feet and pointed down at him, mottled brown and red with anger.

"Do not mock me!" he roared. "I mock you, Mr. Katz, you and your people, the 'chosen people' – Ha! Ha! Your people desecrated the word of God! You too are deceivers, deniers, iniquitous, you trespass the bounds of what is right! You are no better than the scum who came here and murdered my children, masked in the name of Allah! And this is who the supposed Department of Justice sends to help me?"

Katz slapped the folder shut and tried to come back to the present. The cop next to him was telling Rabe about some guy holding hostages in Ohio.

"This fuckin' nut says he wants all white people to leave the fucking earth within seven days. You believe that? Then he lets the girl go -- for a TV set! But he's going to hold the cop until the President talks to him! And guess what? This fucking Carter says he's going to give him a call! What an asshole! Maybe he'll give this fucker a call too, let us all go home."

"That's bad business," Rabe said. "You start bargaining with these guys, you're only inviting trouble, loads of it."

"Fuckin'-A," the cop answered.

The car was coming off Scott Circle onto Rhode Island. Crowds lined both sidewalks, straining to see the B'nai B'rith building up ahead on the right. It was on the fringes of the new downtown that'd grown up around K, L, and M Streets and there wasn't a lot to do or see up here, so it was a new block to Katz. Blue saw horses cordoned off all four lanes. A cop moved one to let them through. The police filling the street moved out of the way just enough to give them a path to pull up behind a line of squad cars, their lights flashing up and down the block. The three cops threw their doors open and Katz fell into step behind them towards a tall white officer standing next to another white cop with a bullhorn. The sea of uniforms around them was calm, calmer than Katz expected.

"What do we hear?" Rabe asked the officer.

"Fucker wants us to bring down the assholes he says killed his family. We got no idea who he's talking about."

34

Katz jumped in. "The assholes did kill his family. Up on 16th Street, about four years ago. Seven people. We got the ones who did it and they're all in prison."

The other cop shot Rabe a look.

"He's with the U.S. Attorneys," Rabe said. "He tried the case, knows this Khaalis or whatever his fucking name is." He turned to Katz. "That's right, you know him, right?"

"Yeah, I do," Katz said. "But --"

Rabe didn't wait for the rest. He turned back to the other cop.

"Do we have a phone line to him?" he asked.

"Yeah," the cop said. "We're down in the basement. He's holed up with some hostages – don't know how many – up on the eighth floor somewhere."

"Okay," Rabe said and turned back to Katz. "You – what's your name?"

"Katz. Jake Katz. I used to work for you. 1st precinct. Sixty-seven, sixty-eight."

He watched Rabe tried to picture him younger, in blue, probably thinner.

"I worked the Brenda Queen case, at the Howard Theatre, the day Martin Luther King was killed?"

Now Rabe's face lit up.

"Right! With that fat kid!"

Katz nodded. "Right. Krebs, Floyd Krebs. Saved --"

Rabe cut him off again.

"Let's stroll down memory lane later," he said. "You're coming with me."

A cop ran interference for them through the crowd on the street, then across the sidewalk and into the building. A heavy-set cop with black framed glasses holding an M-16 dropped it long enough to salute Rabe. Katz read his name tag. Captain Sotzing.

"We got a Command Center?" Rabe asked him.

"Not yet," Sotzing said.

"Then that's job one," Rabe said.

35

He led Katz and Sotzing down a set of stairs into the basement. A swarm of policemen, some carrying M-16's, some with rifles, all of them with helmets, filled the space in front of them. A group huddled over a brown folding table to the right where a sweating red-faced cop wearing an oversized set of black headphones was fiddling with a black box between two phones. When he saw Rabe, he jumped to his feet and threw him a salute. The rest of them quieted down like he'd snapped their off switch.

Rabe made his way to the table. Katz stayed as close as he could. The cop at the table's name pin read Bohlinger.

"Sir – sorry, sir," he said. "I was trying to find the guy upstairs."

Rabe saw wires on the floor behind him running into a thin open closet.

"So here's our Command Center," he said. "Well done, Bohlinger. Have you found him?"

"Yes," he said, and dialed up the volume knob. They heard a voice screaming from the box. Katz knew it was Khaalis'.

"Don't get too cute with me!," he boomed. "I went to college too, Max!"

"All right, sir," another voice said. "You say you want a movie to stop. 'Muhammad, Messenger of God', do I have that right?"

Katz recognized the other voice. Max Robinson, one of the anchors on channel 9's local evening news. He was the only black man Katz ever saw anchor a newscast.

"Right!," Khaalis said. "It's an abomination. We want the picture out of the country because it's a fairy tale, it's a joke. Anthony Quinn? He's Hamza, the uncle of Muhammad? I'm Muslim and I'll die for my faith. It's a joke. It's misrepresenting the Muslim faith!"

"And the five people who murdered your family," Robinson said, "you want them brought to you, is that right?"

36

"That's right," Khaalis said. "They were laughing in court, jesting and making fun. The Cassius Clay gang was laughing when we were bringing out the biers of our little babies and children."

"Do you think the government will do that?"

"That's up to the government. If they don't, the worst is to come."

"What does that mean?"

"They can sit along and watch my family all day long for the next two years. If it won't be from here, it will be somewhere else from where you least expect. It will be worse. I got no more time for this. You get them to bring them here and stop that movie!"

"And you are demanding seven hundred and fifty dollars, is that right?" Robinson asked.

"Yeah," Khaalis said. "That dog ass Judge Braman held me in contempt for charging the murderers who murdered my babies. You think I'm going to roll over and play dead? What do you think I am, some jokester? I take my faith serious."

"And who --", Max started to ask but Khaalis was calling to someone.

"Keep stackin', boys," he said, "keep stackin'. Move faster! Make him move faster, Latif, work him!"

His voice came back on the line, "I'm done, Max, I got to go."

They heard the line click dead.

"Where is he? Khaalis?" Rabe asked Bohlinger.

"Is that his name, the guy upstairs?" Bohlinger asked. Rabe turned to Katz. Katz nodded.

"He's up on the eighth floor somewhere," Bohlinger said. "We're not sure where."

"You hear any shots? Anything else?" Rabe asked.

"Some of the people who ran out of here said they heard shooting when they broke in," Bohlinger said, "and they're throwing all kinds of shit down the stairways, front and back."

"What kind of shit?" Rabe asked.

"Everything. Drywall, chairs, desks, bookcases, all kinds of crap," Bohlinger said.

Rabe turned to Sotzing with a quizzical look.

"It's piled up all down the stairwells," Sotzing said, "maybe down to the fourth or fifth floor? It's hard to tell. We sent a few guys up but they started taking fire, so I got 'em back down here to wait for you or Cullinane to tell us what you want to do."

Rabe nodded and pointed at a wire running from the black box into the crowd of cops behind Bohlinger. A splitter on the table fed one line into the phone and another into a tape recorder.

"And where's this go?" Rabe asked.

"Phone box," Bohlinger said. "We should be able to hear every call coming in or out of there now that we found the right line."

"All right," Rabe said. "Make sure I know whenever he's yakking."

He turned to face the crowd of cops behind him.

"Who's the senior man here?" he asked.

"That's probably me, sir." A tall gray-haired man with major's stripes raised his hand.

Rabe made his way to him and shook his hand. Katz followed him. His nametag read Block.

"Good to see you, Gary," Rabe said. "This is Mr. Katz. He's with the U.S. Attorney's. Knows our man upstairs from the murders he was talking about."

Block shook Katz' hand.

"Lucky you," he said.

"Anybody hurt?" Rabe asked.

"A couple of guys who were in the wrong place at the wrong time when these clowns came in," Block said.

He slipped a pad out of his chest pocket and flipped a few pages.

"One named Hymes, the other one's Kirkland. Hymes, Wesley Hymes, works in the print shop here. The guys came in through the loading dock, saw him and shot him in the left shoulder, cut three of his fingers pretty bad, with what he said was a machete."

"A machete?" Rabe asked. "What the hell's he doing with a machete?"

"Back when I went to see Khaalis up on 16th Street," Katz said, "he had guards outside and inside. They were always wearing machetes hanging off their belts. They were hanging on the wall too."

Rabe shook his head. Block read more of his notes.

"Kirkland was in the same place, construction worker. He got stabbed in the back, the side of his chest, and in his leg, the thigh."

"Are they still here?" Rabe asked.

"No," Block said. "They went in an ambulance a little while ago, to GW."

Rabe took that in. "Why's a construction worker here?" he asked.

"They're re-doing some offices up on the eighth floor," Block said, "right where the hostages are being held. From what we've been told, it's just concrete floors up there now – and drywall, so that might be the stuff they've been chucking down the stairs. That's where they are now, best we can tell."

"Okay," Rabe said. "We know about the movie and bringing him the guys who killed his family and the seven hundred and fifty dollars. Katz, do you know what he's talking about?"

"Yeah. I do," Katz said, and saw it play out before his eyes all over again.

Khaalis sat in the first row of the gallery every day, usually behind the prosecutors' table, so Katz couldn't see his reactions, but Marshall McKinney kept telling them he was going to blow. One morning a few weeks into the trial, McKinney came over to their table before Judge Braman came in and gestured at the defendants.

"They're baiting that poor bastard," he said, "grinning at him, smirking at him. He's seeing it all and he is pissed. You fellows got to do something about that."

Katz pulled Khaalis aside at the lunch break that day and told him to cool it, but he just blew him off. Late that afternoon, a dreary day of testimony establishing the chain of custody of a gun used in the crime, he snapped. He jumped up out of his seat right in front of the jury box, and pointed at the defendants, flush with anger.

"It's over!" he screamed. "It's over! You killed my babies!"

Braman banged his gavel again and again and yelled at him, "Mr. Khaalis, sit down and be quiet! You will sit down and be quiet!," but Khaalis was having none of it.

"You killed my babies and shot my women!" he screamed. McKinney and a couple of the other marshals grabbed him and wrestled him to the door, then out into the hallway, but Katz could hear him still screaming.

"They killed them!" he screamed over and over, fainter and fainter until the courtroom door fell shut and the marshals pulled him into an empty courtroom down the hall. All the defense counsel jumped to their feet and demanded a mistrial. Katz remembered being more concerned about that than he was about Khaalis' outburst, but now he remembered Braman holding him in contempt and fining him $750 for the insult to the court.

He laid it all out for them.

"Is that something you can do something about?" Rabe asked. "Pretty cheap price to pay for getting these people out of here."

"I'd have to talk to Earl," Katz said. "It's a start, I guess."

"He's back on the phone!" Bohlinger yelled out. "He's telling some guy at WMAL that if nobody starts taking him seriously, heads are going to start rolling down the stairwells."

Rabe pushed a thick index finger into Katz's tie.

"Earl can fucking wait. You're talking to Khaalis. Now."

4

"Get that news fucker off the phone!" Rabe yelled to Bohlinger. Bohlinger threw his headset onto the table and ran back to the closet. He unscrewed the connection carrying the line, yanked a wire free, and scurried back to the table. He held one of the fat earpieces to his ear and heard nothing.

"She's gone," he told Rabe, then went back to the closet to re-connect the wire.

"Keep that line clear," Rabe said and motioned Katz to follow him to the far corner of the floor, as far away as they could get from anyone else.

"Now listen to me closely. You need to hear what I'm saying, okay? We've got a Certified Nut First Class on our hands, God knows how many hostages, and we're not going to be able to give him everything he asks for. That's where we are now, right?"

Katz gave him a quick nod and tried to ignore the cold dampness coating him deep within.

"So, your job now is just to listen, okay? Sympathize, understand, tell him 'Uh-huh, uh-huh, I see, I see,' but do not argue with him. Let him have his way. Right now, the main thing we have to do is stay cool and let this thing play out. Each of these fucking things has its own rhythm, its own pace, okay? We just got to stay with it. You got me?"

"I got you."

Rabe punched him in the shoulder and led him back to the table.

"Now get Khaalis on the phone," he told Bohlinger.

"Okay," Bohlinger said, "one sec." He ran back to the closet, fiddled with the wires again, and came back to the table. Rabe turned to Katz.

"I'll get on first, tell him you're here, you're going to be our main guy talking to him." He picked up the headphones. "I'll be listening. If anything comes up, tell him you have to talk it over with the police and you'll get back to him. Just keep him calm."

"As calm as he gets, okay?" Katz said, his voice suddenly raspy. He cleared his throat. "It doesn't take much to set him off."

"You've got the relationship with him," Rabe said. "Nobody else here does. Just keep it under control the best way you know how. Piece of cake, right?"

He smiled and pulled the headset on.

"Dial that asshole up," he told Bohlinger.

Bohlinger dialed the conference room. Before he could dial the last one, Rabe reached for the phone and pointed to the folding chair Bohlinger had been sitting in.

"Have a seat, Mr. Katz," he said. Make yourself comfortable."

Katz circled the table but he was too wired to sit anywhere. Bohlinger dialed the last number. Rabe held up his hand for quiet but the room was already still, all eyes on him. Khaalis picked up on the first ring.

"Khaalis," they heard him growl over the box.

"Mr. Khaalis," Rabe said. "This is Assistant Chief Robert Rabe of the Metropolitan Police Department."

"Assistant Chief?" Khaalis said. "That's who they send to talk to me? An Assistant Chief? I don't want to talk to you! And I don't want to talk to the Chief of Police and I don't want to talk to the Mayor! I want to talk to the President! Do I need to start chopping heads and dropping them out of the window here to get his attention, huh?"

"No, Mr. Khaalis, you certainly don't," Rabe said. "You know, we're still trying to figure out everything that you're doing and exactly what you want."

"You got a radio?" Khaalis said angrily. "I've been telling everyone that calls what I want. Ain't no secret."

"Mr. Khaalis," Rabe said, "we're listening to the radio and watching the TV but we want to talk to you man to man to figure out if we can get you what you need and make sure that no innocent people are hurt."

"Who are these so-called innocent people, huh?" Khaalis shouted through the line. "These deviant unholy Jews up here with me? The so-called holy men at the Islamic Center who didn't lift a finger to help me, call me, come see me when I lost my family? Them, huh? I'm the innocent people here and I have lost everything and everyone that meant anything to me and nobody gave a damn! So don't tell me about innocent people! That ain't goin' nowhere!"

"Mr. Khaalis, I understand," Rabe said. "You have my sympathy. I know what you must have gone through, what you must still --"

"You can spare me your phony tears now, okay, Mr. Assistant Chief?" Khaalis said, "Where were you and your Chief and Mayor Washington four years ago? Where've you been every day since? Took this to get your attention, huh? Well, we all in it now. It's judgment day!"

"Mr. Khaalis," Rabe said, "I'll be speaking to the Chief and the Mayor as soon as we hang up, I promise you. I do have someone else here I'd like you to talk to."

"It better be President Carter or this call is over."

"Hold on, sir," Rabe said. "One moment please."

Rabe extended the phone to Katz. The voice in his head screamed at him to not take it, to turn and run back to his little phony walnut desk and start worrying again about bail revocation hearings and oppositions to requests for continuances and squaring up his briefs and getting home to Maximum Marty as soon as he could.

But he took it.

"Mr. Khaalis? Hamaas?" He cleared his throat. "This is Jake Katz. From the trial?"

A silence filled the room.

"Jake Katz? Jake Katz? The Jake Katz?" Hamaas finally roared back. "I ask for the President of the United States and they give me some, what, some functionary, some little infidel Yehudi who I'm supposed to respect because he put four men in prison instead of letting me kill them?"

"Hamaas, I asked to talk to you," Katz lied. "I want to help bring this to an end before anyone gets hurt, including you."

"Always so good with the jury with that bullshit, Mr. Katz," Khaalis said. "Well, I ain't no jury. I'm the judge and the executioner, huh? Would you be on the phone if these Jews weren't here, huh? Who'd they send if I took over Catholic University and wanted the Pope? Some altar boy? I want the President, not Jacob Hebrew Katz."

Katz held the phone against his chest and silently pleaded for help from Rabe. Rabe spun his hand and whispered "Keep him talking. Ask him what he wants, spell it out."

"Hamaas, please." Katz said. "You need to tell us what you want specifically so we can see what we can do to help you out."

"And then what?" Khaalis asked. "Promise me everything and give me nothing, like they did with that fool in Indiana?"

Katz' mind flashed to the news report he saw last month about some guy out there who'd held somebody hostage for a few days. The police told him they'd give him immunity if he let the guy go, but they arrested him as soon as he did.

"No, it's not like that," he said. "Just let me make sure we get it right."

"All right, fine," Khaalis said. "Get your yellow legal pad out, my little Jewboy. Number one. Bring those murderous bastards to me so I can do to them what they did to my family. And I'm talking about all of them, not just the four you did. I want the killers of my babies. John Griffin too! I want to see them right here. I want to see how tough they are."

45

The four Katz convicted were William Christian, John Clark, Theodore Moody, and James Price. Griffin was convicted too, but Braman granted him a mistrial after Amina identified someone else as little Bibi's killer when she testified at Ron Harvey's trial later that year. Katz tried him two more times, but the first was another mistrial because Amina refused to testify, and he walked the second time when she didn't show up at all. Harvey was convicted at his trial, but Katz wanted to make sure Khaalis knew what happened to Price.

"Just a second, Hamaas," he said, still scribbling. "You know about Price, right?"

"You're damn right I know," Khaalis said. "That heathen got what was coming to him. I'm just sorry they beat me out of the chance to do it myself."

Right from the outset, Price's lawyer had let Bob Shuker know he was willing to testify for the Government if they gave him immunity. They gave it to him and kept it under wraps, but the rest of the defendants must have known he was turning, because all their lawyers filed a motion to dismiss, saying Price was giving the Government confidential information he'd gotten in all their meetings about the case. The morning he was going to testify, Marshall McKinney told Katz that while they were driving him up from Quantico, a guy named Louis Farrakhan from the Nation of Islam was on WOOK, saying something like traitors need to be careful because when the government is tired of using you, they're going to dump you back in the laps of your people. Price must have heard it too because he told them he was done talking. He never did testify, but after Griffin was put in Holmesburg on a different charge about six months later, he and two other inmates literally carved up Price's ass and his balls with a knife and a screwdriver and strangled him with their shoelaces in his cell.

46

"So that leaves four of them living," Katz said, "but they're not coming back. They're locked away, forever. You know that, right?"

Khaalis ignored him.

"Number two," he went on. "I want the three so-called Muslims who gunned down Malcolm in New York City."

Rabe shook his head.

"Nothin' from you, my Jew friend?" Khaalis asked. "You goin' to make that happen?"

"I'm writing it down. You got more?"

"Yes, I got more. I got a truckload more. Number three, I want that movie stopped. 'Muhammad, Messenger of God'. Anthony Quinn? Anthony Goddamned Quinn? He's Zorba so he can be Hamza too? That's more than a disgrace, more than blasphemy. That's got to stop now! Everywhere! In all the shadow houses in Washington, New York, wherever those mongrels have put it on. No fooling on that one, Mr. Katz. I got to spell Muhammad again for you, huh?"

Katz let it ride this time and looked to Rabe. He looked doubtful but mouthed "Maybe" to him.

"We might be able to do something about that, I think," Katz said. "You're just going to have to give me a little time. We've got to figure out --"

"What time you got right now, Mr. Katz?"

Rabe showed him his watch.

"A little before one. 12:59, to --"

"I'm giving you an hour. If that movie's not stopped by two o'clock, I'm going to start using these Jews' heads for bowling balls. You got that?"

"Hamaas, Mr. Khaalis --"

"You're wasting their time, Katz! Get on it!" The phone slammed down.

"Do we even know where this thing is playing?" Katz asked Rabe.

47

"I'll find out," Rabe said. Let's see if we can build a little trust on this thing."

He pointed to Bohlinger.

"Call MPD," he said. "Get me Bobbie in my office."

Bohlinger reached to take the receiver from Katz' hand. When he pushed down the button to get a new line, the phone rang.

"Yeah?" he said, laying the receiver back on the cradle.

"This is Chief Cullinane," Katz heard over the speaker. "I want to talk to Chief Rabe."

Katz pictured him. Short, stocky, slick black hair. He had met him once or twice when he ran field ops, but he became Chief after Katz had left. The cops called him "Wonder Boy" because he was barely forty when he became Chief.

"Yeah, Chief," Rabe said. "What's up?"

"You aware of this crazy Mohammad movie this guy's ragging about?"

"Yeah," Rabe said. "I was just about to call Bobbie to tell me where the hell it's playing."

"Don't bother," Cullinane said. "The guy who runs the Islamic Center, Dr. Rauf, he says that this Khaalis called up there about forty-five minutes ago and told him, he's got to stop it or they're going to start shooting the people they're holding there every minute until he does."

"That's pretty much what he said here," Rabe said. "What's this Rauf doing about it?"

"As much as he can with a gun to his head," Cullinane said. "He's been on the phone ever since, calling ambassadors from Egypt, Iran, Pakistan, I don't know where else, trying to get them to do something."

"And?" Rabe said.

"And nothing. No one knows what the hell to do. The only good news is it seems to be playing only in New York and LA so we might have a – wait a minute."

48

They heard someone talking in the background but couldn't make it out. Cullinane said something back, then came back on the phone.

"Bob, I'll call you back. They got somebody in Vance's office wants to talk to me."

"Who's Vance?" Rabe asked.

"Cyrus Vance. Secretary of State? I'll call you right back."

The click was the last thing they heard. Rabe shook his head and looked at Katz.

"Is this some shit or what?" he said. "He might get Carter down here after all."

5

The phone rang again. Rabe was waiting for it and grabbed it.

"Rabe."

"Okay, here's the deal," Cullinane said. "Vance's office is making some calls to see if one of these Arab guys can get the thing stopped asap."

"Unreal."

"And Rauf's making some calls too. Apparently, Khaalis called his boys at the Islamic Center there to tell 'em it was okay."

"Where are you?" Rabe asked.

"HQ. I've been talking to Rauf on the phone when they let me, and to you and the Feebies trying to figure out what's going on."

"What's going on up at the Islamic place?"

"Best we know," Cullinane said, "three guys came in around noon, supposedly to pray. Then they pull out some rifles and machetes and take everyone hostage. Same demands, same bullshit you've been hearing. Rauf says they're keeping a gun on him and there's eleven hostages he knows of -- including his wife, who sounds like a ball of fire. Every time I talk to him, I can hear her in the background letting those guys have it."

"So what's the plan?" Rabe asked.

"I don't have one yet," Cullinane said. "How many people they holding where you are?"

"Hard to know," Rabe said. "There's a bunch of them up on the eighth floor where Khaalis and some other guys with guns are, but we don't know if anyone else's being held hostage anywhere."

"Is anyone outside who maybe give you some scoop about who else's out there, who's missing?"

"Don't know," Rabe said. "There's a lot of people out there. Some of them might've run out of here but most of 'em are probably just looky-loos. We'll find out."

"Can you do a sweep?"

"Yeah, I mean, yeah we have the personnel, but we don't know if Khaalis has guys on other floors, if he's booby-trapped the place, or what."

"Hold on," Cullinane said. "Rauf's on the other line. I'll call you right back."

Rabe gave the phone back to Bohlinger and pointed to Katz and Block to follow him into the stairwell.

"Gary," he said, "I want you to grab some guys up there and sweep the first floor. No shooting, okay, just a recon."

Block snapped him a quick salute and scrambled up the stairs. Rabe turned to Katz.

"I'm going to get some guys to go out on the street, see if we can find anyone can get us some kind of list of who works here. Then we can start calling their homes, see if they've heard from them, see who's unaccounted for, anything that might help us out. Got it?"

"Sounds like you've been through this once or twice," Katz said.

"Yeah, once or twice," Rabe said. "Now, here's what you're going to do. Get back on the phone with assface and keep him talking --"

Katz raised a hand to start listing his objections, but Rabe raised his own hand and kept right on going.

"You can do this. I heard you. Whatever he wants to talk about, that's what you talk about. If you can get him to take a breath, you try and find out if anyone's hurt. Ask him what we can do to get them some food, medicine, whatever. Otherwise, you just hear him out. I'll be back in five minutes."

He took off up the steps.

51

"Try not to get anyone killed," he yelled back, then disappeared.

Katz's throat dried up again. His toes were cold, heading for numb. Then he remembered what he remembered every time he got like this on the streets when he was a cop. He heard his football coach one more time, telling his assistant to find some playing time for that scrappy little Hebe.

The scrappy little Hebe put one foot in front of the other until he reached the table.

"Get Khaalis back on the line," he told Bohlinger. "Rabe's orders."

Bohlinger dialed him up and handed him the phone. He stood up and gestured to Katz to take his seat, which he did.

"Khaalis," the voice on the other end said.

"Katz," his own voice said. "I just want to tell you we're working on the movie. It's going to take a little time, just bear with us."

"Bear with us?" Khaalis said. "What do you think I've been doing for four years? And what good did it do me, huh? That time is over! No more time! Two o'clock is going to be the end of time for somebody here, everybody here!"

His voice grew less distinct, like he wasn't talking to Katz anymore, but the room. He heard Khaalis' voice echo back across the line.

"Do you hear me, huh? Do you hear what I'm telling your Mr. Katz? One of your chosen people? Two o'clock! No movie! If that movie rolls, so do your heads! One at a time! Bounce down eight floors all the way to the street! Is that how you want to go out? You better start praying to your God, praying your Jewboy Jake Katz does what he's told!"

His voice came back through the receiver strong and clear.

"You hear all that, Jacob Katz? Huh? You catch all that?"

"Hamaas, come on, come on now. I'm doing the best I can. We got half the free world working on stopping this thing by two o'clock. Please, don't make a bad situation worse."

"You're making the bad situation worse! You!" Khaalis screamed at him. "Do I have to start killing these people now to get your attention? Won't be a problem, believe me!"

Katz was at a loss. Bohlinger and the rest of them were staring at him. The room was icy still.

"Hold on, Hamaas. Hold on. I'm getting some information for you here," he said and pressed his hand over the receiver. He waited a beat, hoping to hear Rabe's feet coming down the stairs, giving him something, anything he could give to Khaalis, to pacify him, put him at ease. Nothing. He put the receiver closer to his mouth, his hand still over it.

"What's that? What's that?" he said. "Okay, okay." Then into the receiver, he said "Hamaas, they've talked to the producer. They got hold of him. He said he's going to call the theater and get them to stop it."

"What theater?" Khaalis asked. "Who's he calling?"

"New York," Katz said without hesitation. In for a dime, in for a dollar. "He's calling the theater in New York."

"And how about LA? Who's calling the theater out there?"

Katz didn't skip a beat.

"He is. As soon as he gets through with New York. It's almost two East Coast time, so he started with New York, then he'll get to LA. More time till it shows there, right? Got it?"

He locked eyes with Bohlinger who didn't appear to be breathing. The line was quiet.

53

"I got people in New York, you know," Khaalis said. "You better be telling me the truth, Katz."

"You're going to have to trust me, Hamaas. Just like I have to trust you. I can't see what's going on up there. None of us can. We're trusting you that everyone is okay and getting what they need, right? Tell me, what do they -- "

"That goddamned movie better be off, Katz!" Khaalis roared. "Or you're gonna hear heads bounce sky high. You can trust that!" The phone slammed down.

Katz handed the receiver back to Bohlinger, who reached for it but still didn't seem to be breathing. The sound of heavy steps rumbled down the stairway. Rabe appeared in the doorway and looked at Katz looking at him.

"You're off already?" he said. "What did I miss?"

"Let's stop that movie," Katz said.

6

Rabe pulled a chair up to the table and dialed Cullinane's office at the Municipal Building. He put the phone on speaker so Katz could hear, and asked to be put through.

Katz heard a tinny "Yeah, Bob" on the other end.

"Hey, Cully. This guy Katz here, the AUSA who knows this asshole from the trial when his family got killed, he just got off the phone with him. The guy was real worked up about this movie, threatened to kill these folks if it wasn't shut down. Where are we on that?"

Katz heard Cullinane talking to someone else, then he got louder, and muddier.

"Bob, you there?"

"Yeah."

"I got you on the speaker phone. Silbert's here and we're expecting to get a call from Rauf about what's happening with that. He's been on the phone with Vance and the ambassadors, trying to figure out how to kill it."

"What exactly are they trying to do?"

"Not sure, to tell you the truth," Cullinane said. "Rauf's seeing if they know who the producer is, maybe they can talk to him about killing it."

"Not much of a plan, is it?," Rabe said.

"Not much," Cullinane said. "We just might have to bullshit this guy for a while to buy some time, maybe tell him it's stopped and hope he can't call our bluff."

Katz thought maybe he was more of a pro than he gave himself credit for.

Rabe asked, "Did he tell you exactly where it's play--"

Cullinane cut him off.

"Hold on, hold on," then to someone in the background, "Any way I can patch these guys in?"

The line went dead for a few long seconds, then Rabe and Katz heard someone else on the line.

" – calling Mayor Beame to call the producer."

"I didn't catch that," Rabe said. "Who was that? Can you ask him to repeat?"

Cullinane said, "Dr. Rauf. He just called. Dr. Rauf, can you say that again? I have my Assistant Chief on the line. He's been talking with Mr. Khaalis at the B'nai B'rith - -"

"I said," Rauf said, "that the Consul General of Egypt, up in New York, has called Mayor Beame, and that Mayor Beame said he will call the producer of the movie and get it shut down before it's shown at two o'clock."

And I thought I was bullshitting him, Katz thought. This guy is something else, making it all up with a gun at his head.

Rabe leaned into the phone. Katz knew he was trying to measure his words carefully so nobody did anything stupider than what they'd already done.

"I hope that works, I really do," Rabe said. "Does the Mayor need any help with that, knowing who the producer is, say?"

Rauf's voice echoed back. "He says he will take care of it. He knows what he's doing. I have no doubt about it."

Rabe meshed his hands together low in front of him like he was holding a thousand-pound sack of brass balls.

"All right," Cullinane said. "Should we let Khaalis know that?"

"I already have," Dr. Rauf said. "His colleagues here were good enough to put me on with him just before we called you."

"And what did he say?" they heard Cullinane ask.

Katz imagined hearing heads bounce down the stairs above them. They waited for Rauf to answer, both of them holding their breath.

"He said 'Your life depends on it'."

They heard a click. Then they heard nothing. The air got colder.

"Chief?" Rabe asked. "You still there?"

"Yeah," Cullinane said. "Rauf's off. Shit. I don't know what to believe. It's a damn sure thing Khaalis won't either and God knows what the hell he'll do."

Katz' mind was whirring with a million possibilities but he didn't know where to begin, what to say, what to do.

Rabe said "Can't we just find out where this thing's playing, get the FBI or the NYPD to go there and shut it down?"

"They went there about ten minutes ago," Cullinane said. "The only people at the theater were the ticket guy and the snack lady. They're waiting for the projection guy to get there. He's the guy with the keys to the projection room."

Rabe said what Katz was thinking.

"Now ain't that some shit, Cully? People are going to die in Washington, DC because some two-bit guy working a crumb-bum job in a New York movie house can't get his ass to work on time. What a fucking world."

"Hold on," Cullinane said. "It's Rauf again. I'll put him through."

He's still alive, Katz thought. That's something.

"The movie has been stopped," he heard Rauf say. "Mayor Beame's office just called. The police at the theater met the man who is responsible for distributing the movie. He was actually there to see the premiere, a Mr. Yablans, I think he said."

Katz bit his tongue to keep from saying "Are you fucking serious?" out loud. Rabe looked up and mouthed "Thank you, God."

"And Mr. Yablans spoke to the producer," Rauf said, "a Mr. Moustapha Akkad, a Muslim, from Syria, and he received his personal assurance that the movie was stopped everywhere it was playing and it will not play again, not in

57

New York, not in Los Angeles, not anywhere. I have just informed Mr. Khaa --."

The line went dead again. They heard a couple of clicks, then Cullinane.

"Bob, you there?"

"Yeah," Rabe said. "We're here."

"How do you like that? What are the chances? Wow!"

"Unreal," Rabe said. "Thank God -- or Praise Allah? Who knows? Who cares? Good to know miracles still happen!"

"So," Cullinane said, "you need to follow up with Khaalis, make sure he knows the movie's off and he's not going off half-cocked."

"10-4 to that," Rabe said.

"Then what?" Cullinane said. "What do you think?"

"I think I'm going to put Mr. Katz on," Rabe said, "so he can ask Mr. Silbert for the seven hundred and fifty bucks we need to take that off the table too."

He pointed at Katz.

"Your turn," he said. "Let's see if we can get home for dinner tonight."

7

Before Bohlinger could dial the phone, they heard footsteps slowly coming down the stairwell from the first floor. The first thing Katz saw were two pairs of spit-shined boots moving in tandem, with a pair of ladies' black shoes with blocky high heels coming into view between them. Katz waited to see two cops leading an older woman down the steps. One of them held her by each arm and waited for her to come down to them, then took the next step, until they finally came fully into view.

Katz did a double-take when he followed his gaze up from the boots on the left to the face of Tom Wallace. When they finally got her safely off the bottom step, he looked up to see Katz grinning at him and broke into an even wider grin.

"Katz!" he yelled. "What are you doin' here?"

"Thought it'd be a good day to drop by," Katz shrugged, "renew my membership."

He double-timed to Wallace and they gave each other a soul shake. The other cop walked the lady to Rabe.

"It is good to see you, my man," Wallace said. "How long's it been?"

Katz reflected back on the time they spent together on the Howard Theatre case, just about five years ago. Wallace was a detective then, Katz just a rookie patrolman, and Wallace wanted no part of a fresh little white kid trying to horn into his case. Katz returned the disfavor, but after Wallace rescued him from a beating at the D.C. Coliseum, they bonded and worked the case together to the finish. Katz had talked to him a few times since, most memorably after Wallace got knocked back to patrolman for spending some unauthorized time in Memphis pursuing a lead on the case, but he never laid eyes on him again until now. He saw some gray curls in Wallace's sideburns but he looked a little smaller than he remembered too.

"Jeez, too long, man," he said. "You look good! Did you lose a little weight? Or just shrink some?"

"Weight, man," Wallace said. "Lost twenty-two pounds in the last year. BP was up, hypertension, you know. You look good too, man. Big grown-up lawyer."

Katz felt a tap on the back. He turned to see Rabe staring at him, the lady at his side.

"If I may interrupt," he said, "Mrs. Greenspon is a secretary here. She was out on the street when we asked if anyone had a list of people who worked here, and she very nicely raised her hand and said she could get one for us, if we could get her into her office on the first floor. Block said it was clear, so I'm going to walk her up there and get a few people started on tracking down who's where."

"Okay," Katz said.

You," he pointed at him, "need to talk to Silbert pronto so you can get the seven fifty, then get your friend back on the phone to work out how we're going to get it to him, capisce?"

"Capisce. I got it," Katz said.

"And you," he pointed to Wallace, "come with me."

They headed to the stairs. Wallace turned to Katz and murmured "Yes, boss" before following Rabe up in something less than a hurry.

"I'll catch you later, Katz," he yelled back, and disappeared up the steps.

Someone had thrown a few more folding chairs around the table, and two more phones sat on top, each with a wire running to the same closet as the first one. Bohlinger pointed to a chair, then dialed up the number Katz gave him, and handed him the receiver.

Earl picked up his personal line on the first ring.

"Silbert."

"Earl, this is Jake."

"Hey!" Silbert said. "Congratulations on shutting that movie down. I just have one question, well, two. Did they really shut it down and, more importantly, does Khaalis believe they shut it down?"

"The guy at the Islamic Center, Rauf, told me and Khaalis the cops up there found the distributor sitting in the theatre, believe it or not, and he called the producer to shut it down everywhere, so unless the guy's an unbelievably good bullshitter, I think he got it stopped. As for Khaalis buying it, I don't know. I'm going to call him as soon as you can get me the seven hundred and fifty dollars he had to pay when Braman held him in contempt."

"What seven hundred and fifty dollars?" Silbert asked.

Katz refreshed his recollection.

Earl said "Holy cow, I'll give him the seven fifty myself if it gets this thing over with. Let me talk to somebody in Finance about getting a check cut to him asap. What's the plan then? You go with him to the bank?"

Another joke. The pressure must really be getting to him, Katz thought.

"No," he said, "there is no plan yet, but I'm sure Rabe'll figure one out as soon as we get the money."

"He's good at this, by the way," Earl said. "Really has the smarts -- and the patience. I worked with him on that thing at Alonzo's in Georgetown, when was it, last November?"

"I don't remember it," Katz said.

"Yeah," Silbert said. "Three guys took the place over. They shot a cop and held hostages for three or four hours. Rabe called them from the Indiana Building, then got to a book store across the street from the place and kept talking to them, on a pay phone, no less. Meanwhile, one of the guys got cold feet and ran out the back of the store with some of the hostages, and the brains of the operation's still up front on the phone with Rabe, no clue it happened. Rabe kept working with him, but never told him everyone else'd already scrammed, because he still had a few people up front

61

with him and Rabe didn't want him to panic and do something stupid. An hour or so later, he talks the guy into giving up. Nobody hurt. Incredible. He doesn't take any chances, unless he absolutely has no other choice. Just do what he says and you'll be fine."

"Well, that's what I'm doing," Katz said. "He said to call you about the money, so here I am."

"Okay, give me a couple of minutes and I'll get right back to you. What's your number there?"

Katz got it from Bohlinger, gave it to Silbert, and hung up.

Rabe came back down the steps and headed straight to Katz.

"You talk to your boss?"

"Yeah," Katz said, "we just hung up. He's going to figure out how to get a check cut and get it over here as fast as he can."

"All right, let's get our man on the phone and let him know that."

Bohlinger held up a receiver for Katz and started to dial the eighth floor when the phone on his right started ringing.

"Get it," Rabe said.

Katz took the receiver and Bohlinger took the call.

"What?" he said, then said it again, louder and more incredulous.

"What?" Rabe said. "What is it?"

Bohlinger clapped a hand over the receiver.

"They've taken over the District Building!"

8

"What?" Katz said.

"Who took it over?" Rabe said. "These guys?"

Bohlinger listened intently, then repeated everything he heard.

"They're on the fifth floor, in the Council offices. People have been shot."

The whole room came to a standstill except for Rabe.

"Oh, for Christ's sake!" he spat out. "How many people?"

"How many?" Bohlinger asked.

He held up three fingers. Rabe grabbed the phone. "This is Rabe. Who was shot?"

Katz strained to hear the voice on the other end. It was garbled and he couldn't pick out a thing.

Rabe kept listening, then asked, "Can they get them out of there?" After another few seconds, he muttered "Yeah, yeah. Shit! Let me know as soon as you know."

He threw the receiver in the general direction of the cradle, sending it bouncing over the edge of the table. Bohlinger grabbed the cord before the phone smacked the concrete.

"He said at least three guys were shot. One of them was Barry, the guy on the Council? The other ones he doesn't know who they are."

"Holy shit!" a cop behind Katz said. "Are they dead?"

"Don't know," Rabe said. "No one can get near them yet. They're working on it."

Katz was as stunned as they were. Barry was Marion Barry, a member of the City Council and a big activist in D.C. for years. He remembered seeing him speak once at GW, with another community guy named Catfish Mayfield. They started jawing at each other on the stage, arguing about who should get credit for what, then started throwing punches, falling off the stage and rolling on the ground before people broke it up. He could still picture Barry with blood and dirt all over his dashiki.

"Get me Cully," Rabe barked to Bohlinger. "You," he pointed to Katz, "get Khaalis on the other line and find out what's going on downtown."

"I'll get him," Bohlinger said, then pointed at his headphones. "But he's going have to wait until Khaalis is off."

"With who?" Rabe asked.

"Some news guy, I have no idea who it is."

"We've got to get these clowns to stop calling, or we'll never get him out of here," Rabe said, "or the Islamic place or the District Building or any other fucking place he plans on taking over."

He pointed to Bohlinger. "Any more of these press assholes calls, you cut them off asap. You got it?"

Bohlinger snapped him a salute. Rabe turned to Katz and pointed again.

"You tell him people have been shot, that changes everything! Ask him if he's got any more fucking surprises for us."

"And the money and the movies. I got it."

Rabe looked at his watch. 2:35. "I'm going to let them know up on the street," he said. "I'll be right back. Shit!"

He headed up the stairs.

"He's off!" Bohlinger said, and dialed the conference room. Katz slipped the headphones on just in time to hear Khaalis pick up, his anger throbbing through the line.

"Now who?" he said. "This better be the police or the President or these Jews are going to start meeting their maker."

"Hamaas," Jake said. "This is Jake Katz. What's going on down at the District Building? We're hearing three people --"

64

"That's a shame, isn't it? Such a shame that the bureaucrats of this city who couldn't protect me and my family, didn't protect me, can't protect me, now they got shot and you're all concerned about them?"

"Hamaas, you know I was concerned about your family. I spent a year and a half of my life getting the people who murdered them behind bars --"

"Not good enough, Jake Katz, not good enough!" Khaalis thundered. "They're still breathing the air, bragging about all their phony works for Allah, going on and on, and where's my family, huh? In the ground! I want those murderous devils down there with them!"

"Hamaas," Katz pleaded, "we need to stop this before more people get killed. The people that got shot at the District Building have families too, people who will lose loved ones just like you. We can't have any more of that."

"Your compassion and your sympathy truly move me, Mr. Katz. Is this all part of the police plan, huh? Put someone on who was paid to care about poor Mr. Khaalis? You didn't really care, Mr. Katz. Let's be real here, huh? It was your job to care. It was why you got a pay check. It's why you're telling me how much you care now, okay? You're getting paid to care. Don't think I'll ever think it's anything else."

Katz shook it off and kept pressing him.

"Hamaas, is this it or are your men going to show up somewhere else? Come on, we're talking, we shut down the movie, right? We're moving --"

"Oh, we're doing a lot of moving. Where's my money, huh? You moving that?"

"We are. I'm getting a check --"

"I don't want no government check. What's Khaalis going to do with that, huh? You're going to hand deliver it to me in cash. I want my seven hundred and fifty dollars back in green bill money, you got that? If I don't get that money delivered, by you, in fifteen damn minutes, you better have the fire department out there with nets catching all these bodies raining down on them. I'm starting the clock now."

"Hamaas, where else are you going? Just --"

"One," he heard. "Two. Three. Why you still there, Katz? Why aren't you getting my money?" he shouted.

The slam rang in Katz' ears.

"Call Earl," he told Bohlinger. Bohlinger dialed and handed him the phone.

"Silbert," he heard.

"Earl, Katz again. Hamaas wants cash, no check. In fifteen minutes. Can you get it to me?"

"Shit! I'll get it to you if I have to take up a collection, but fifteen minutes? Do what you have to do to stall him."

Katz handed the phone and the headphones back to Bohlinger and ran his hands through his hair. Bohlinger threw the headphones on, and listened to Khaalis pick up his phone again. Katz heard it through the speaker.

"Mr. Khaalis? Is this Mr. Hamaas Khaalis?"

"Who is this?"

"Linda Thomas, with WBBM-TV in Chicago.

"You're gone," Bohlinger said. He pushed his chair back and headed for the phone closet.

"No!" Katz said. "Let him talk! We need to buy some time!"

"Rabe told me to keep these news fuckers from hogging the line," Bohlinger yelled back to him.

"I heard him!" Katz said. "I know what he said, but we need to buy some time! If he's on the phone, that might distract him, give us a few more minutes. Let him talk to whoever he wants till we get the money. Then you can cut him off."

"Look, I don't work for you," Bohlinger said. "I work for Rabe, and he said to get rid of these fuckers, so I'm getting rid of them."

He headed back to the switches.

"Can we speak to you now?" Katz heard Linda Thomas say. "This will be going out live over the television."

Katz ran to Bohlinger, grabbed him by the shoulders, and spun him around. He grabbed handfuls of his police blouse in each hand.

"You're not cutting him off!" he screamed, and pulled him to the ground, pushing his face into the concrete. He spun onto Bohlinger's back.

"Get the fuck off of me!" Bohlinger said. He flapped his right arm back at Katz and tried to spin over, but Katz kept his head pressed to the ground. He could feel arms groping at him, trying to pry him off but he wasn't going anywhere.

"I want those that walked into my house. I want them!" Khaalis boomed over the speaker. "Are you listening? It has not even begun!"

The next voice Katz heard was Rabe's.

"What in the name of fuck is going on? Cut it out, for Christ's sake!"

The others backed off but Katz kept Bohlinger pinned beneath him.

"He's not letting me cut the phone off," Bohlinger screamed. "It's a fucking reporter!."

"We need to keep him talking," Katz gasped, "give Silbert time to get the cash here, before this fucking guy kills more people!"

Khaalis' voice filled the room. "We've been nice so far. We have some more wild men out there, in the name of Allah, for their faith – wild in the way of faith, because they believe it to the death."

"Get the fuck up!" Rabe said. "Now!"

Katz pushed himself to his feet and tucked his shirt in as he watched Bohlinger get to his knees, then push himself up, red-faced and sweating, his shirt in a clump, up on one side and over his belt on the other. Katz backed up to block the phone lines, his eyes never leaving Bohlinger's. Khaalis' bellowing was the only sound.

"You just tell Cassius Clay and Wallace X and Herbert that they got to report here to Washington DC, because people's lives depend on it. I want them to come here. They're not big people, they're roaches and rats and gangsters. I want them here. I want the killers here!"

"We're all very worried about it, sir," Linda Thomas said.

Rabe eyed Bohlinger, then Katz.

"Is Silbert coming?" he asked.

"Yes," Katz said, still breathing hard. "With the money, cash, as soon as he can. Khaalis gave him fifteen minutes or he'd start throwing people out the window. I figured he'd stay on this a while, buy us at least some time. Anyone else called, even better, more the merrier, just for now, that's all, just now."

He took a deep breath. Rabe kept looking at him. Katz played what he hoped was his trump card.

"He's killing people downtown, Chief," he said. "He's doing what he said he'd do."

"Do you realize when my family was wiped out, no one said one word?" Khaalis went on. "Not one. Not even a preacher. Not even a minister? Not even a spiritual adviser? Not even a City Council member. So, I'm very glad you're worried now. Huh? When they wiped out my family, I didn't hear about your sympathy and emotions. I got a letter the other day from my brother telling me how the brother was swaggering around in jail, the killer of Malcolm, walking around with guards protecting him. Well, tell him it's over. Tell him it's payday."

Rabe turned to Bohlinger.

"Let him talk," he said.

Katz said a quiet "Thank you".

They all stood still, hearing only Khaalis and the reporter.

68

"But why is today payday?" she asked.

"Why? Why? Payday always comes. Don't you know you have a payday coming? We all have to report."

"You're not going to hurt anyone, are you?" she asked. The news must not have reached Chicago yet, Katz thought.

"I'm a soldier. What do soldiers do? They protect and they defend. And I have a wife and children that were taken out for nothing by killers."

"But these people you have had nothing to do with it."

"All right," Khaalis said, "but I'm a soldier. So, the same way when this army marches into countries, right? There're people that don't have a lot of things to do nothing with it. Right? Come on, now. Back up now. Stop all this piety. Let's tell the truth. Stop it all! How many civilians do have anything to do with it when war comes? Don't they pay the higher price? Come on now. We're at war!"

The reporter started to ask another question, but they heard a phone slam and they knew the call was over. Katz looked at his watch. 2:53. Eighteen minutes after Khaalis slammed the phone down on him. Where was Earl, he thought?

He looked at Rabe. He had no idea what he was thinking.

He stole a look at Bohlinger. He knew what he was thinking.

9

Katz saw Earl first, a black leather attaché case swinging from his left hand in rhythm to his steps down the stairs. Katz glanced at his watch. 2:58. No calls from upstairs, no sounds of shots, no heads bouncing down the stairs. Maybe the cavalry arrived in time after all.

Earl shook hands with Katz, then handed Rabe the case.

"Sorry it took so long," Earl said. "It's a nightmare out there, even in a cruiser. We took the sidewalk pretty much the whole way from Thomas Circle."

"Is it cash?" Rabe asked.

"All fifties. We took down the serial numbers too. Just in case."

Rabe nodded and slipped the strap over Katz' shoulder. Katz teetered but it wasn't because of the bag.

"Okay, I'm going to call him," Rabe told him, "tell him we have the money, and that you're going to bring it up right now."

Rabe raised his hand and answered what Katz was just about to ask him.

"Because," he said, "he knows you and he trusts you, at least more than anyone else here."

Katz couldn't figure out a thing to say to that but he couldn't bring himself to nod his agreement either. Rabe put his hand firmly on Katz' chest.

"I'm not going to send you up alone, okay?, but I can't send anyone up there with a gun or anything else one of those guys might think is a weapon, so I'm going to ask him to let me send up one of the rescue squad guys with you, just to see if anyone needs any medical help, attention, anything at all."

Katz managed a grateful nod this time. Rabe walked him and Silbert back to Bohlinger who stared at Katz the

70

whole way over. Katz eyed him back. Silbert didn't notice but Rabe did.

"Get over it!" he barked at Bohlinger, then turned to Katz. "Both of you! We're all on the same team! Any questions?"

Bohlinger had none. Katz didn't either.

"Now call that jackass up," Rabe told Bohlinger.

Bohlinger handed him the receiver and dialed the phone. Katz and Silbert listened in over the speaker. The phone rang once, then twice. No answer. Khaalis had never let it ring that long before. Katz took a quick look at Rabe, who gave no clue if he thought anything was amiss. One more ring ratcheted up Katz' anxiety to the breaking point. He was actually relieved to hear Khaalis finally pick up.

"This is Khaalis," he said. He sounded raspy and tired.

"This is Rabe. I have your money."

"You're late."

"But I have your money now. All in cash, just like you asked for it. We want to bring it up to you."

Khaalis spit out a harsh laugh.

"Oh, I'm sure you do. So, what is it, Mr. Assistant Chief? A bag rigged with tear gas? A bunch of cops in the elevator? These Yehudis will be dead before the door opens."

"I'm giving the bag to Mr. Katz," Rabe said, "who will give it to you. The only other person coming up will be a rescue squad man, just to check on everyone's health, make sure they're all getting along as well as they can. No cops, no guns, no anything except Katz and the corpsman."

Nothing on the other end. Rabe fixed his eyes on Katz, tapping his temple with his index   finger. Katz held up crossed fingers, though he wasn't sure what he really hoped for.

"All right," Khaalis finally said. "You have them come up in the same elevator. If another elevator comes up with anyone on it, I'll shoot them on the spot and take every one of these infidels to meet their God with them. No one else, just the two of them – and no bags, no jackets, no hats, no nothing except Katz and one medical man, who better have his picture on an ID with him. You got it, Mister Assistant?"

"I got it all," Rabe said. "That's all you're going to see. Nobody else gets hurt, that's all we want."

"Send them up, now. We'll be waiting. One trick, anything, you've got a lot of Hebrew blood on your hands. Got it? Huh?"

"I --," Rabe got out, but swallowed the rest at the sound of the click. He pulled out his walkie-talkie.

"Base to first, come in," he said. In a second, he said, "I need a corpsman or a medic down here pronto to pay a visit to Mr. Khaalis upstairs to see if anyone needs any medical attention. No guns, no bags, no surprises, just someone with an ID who can go up there with our Mr. Katz and not faint on the spot."

He listened for a minute, then said "Okay, sounds good. Make sure he's sharp enough to be able to tell us something about what he saw when he gets back down here, all right?" Another pause, then "Have him meet us at the elevators, down here. Right. Out."

Rabe tucked the walkie-talkie back into its holster. He drummed his fingers waiting for the corpsman to come down the steps, then reached into his pocket for the note pad and scrawled something on it.

In a few seconds, a red-haired reed of a guy in a dark blue medic's outfit skipped down the stairs and weaved his way through the crowd of cops to Rabe and Katz. He tried to smile, but couldn't quite pull it off.

"Collins," he got out, "Corporal Collins, Corporal Mitchell Collins."

Rabe lifted the nametag hanging around his neck, eyed it closely, then let it go. He made the introductions and

72

Collins shook hands with both of them. Katz couldn't be sure if the sweat on his palm was Collins' or his own. Rabe nodded towards the rear elevators and they headed down the hall side by side. No one said anything until they got there. When Katz turned to Rabe, he saw a sea of faces peering back at him over his shoulder, every one of them giving him their own personal version of "Better you than me." He focused in on Rabe as keenly as he ever focused in on anyone before. The cold memory of jumping into the riots off the back of a deuce-and-a-half chilled his veins for the first time in a long time. Rabe reached up to pat his shoulder and moved his gaze between them intently.

"You can do this, both of you. We're doing something nice for him, something he wants, right? You've only got to do three things, okay? Give him that bag of money, take inventory of what you see, and give him this, that's it."

Katz looked at a phone number on the note paper Rabe put in his hand.

"That's our number here. Anything comes up, you ask him to call us before he does anything. Any questions, anything he's got on his mind, we need him to stay in touch with us, okay?"

Katz nodded. The look on his face must have reminded Rabe of one more thing.

"Oh yeah, and get your asses back down here in one piece."

He pushed the UP button between the elevators. Katz heard the car on the right slowly rumble down to them.

"What if there's trouble up there?" Collins drawled with some kind of nervous twang. "What if they hold on to us for ransom or somethin'?"

"Won't happen," Rabe said, with way too much conviction for Katz. "They don't need more hostages. They need him" – he jerked a thumb at Katz – "to keep being a go-between and they need you to make sure nobody up there's

73

going to die or get hurt and keep them in jail longer they already have to be, okay?"

The elevator doors opened. Collins nodded and headed inside. Rabe looked at Katz with an expression that said "Pretty good bullshit, huh?" and Katz might have laughed, if he wasn't inside the elevator too. Rabe pressed "8" and held the doors open.

"I'll call up there in a minute just to make sure everything's cool, all right?" He eyed them in turn and gave a sharp nod.

"All right," he said and let the doors close.

Katz heard a muffled "See you in a few," and felt the elevator start to climb. The light above the door took forever to display the next floor. He suppressed the notion to hit 5, then 6, then 7. Only when the car bounced to a gentle stop on 8 did he and Collins look at each other. Katz nodded to him and the doors split open.

Two dark-skinned men stood right before them, each with a shotgun pointed into the car. The one to their right lifted the barrel of his weapon straight at Katz' head, and the one on the left pointed his at Collins'.

"Off, off, let's go, quick, quick," the one on the right barked.

Katz tried to register more than the mouth of the gun gaping at him. Each man hid his eyes behind sunglasses. The man on the right was taller and wore a hat, a shiny black brimmed cap. Neither of them was Khaalis.

Katz and Collins stepped out side by side. Collins raised his hands and Katz lifted his too. He heard the doors slide shut behind them.

"Is that the money?" the man on the right said, pointing his shotgun at the bag hanging at Katz' waist.

"It is," Katz said.

"Take it off -- slowly," the gunman said, "then open it and turn it upside down."

Katz did as he was told. A packet of fifty-dollar bills fell to the floor.

"Shake it," the man said. Katz did, and nothing else came out.

"Now drop it and back up."

Both of them took a step back. Collins' heel hit the elevator door. The man across from him pulled back the grip below his barrel and pushed it forward. Katz heard a shell lock into place.

"Easy," the other man said. "Easy."

He took a step forward and picked up the money, then slipped off a rubber band and counted the bills. Katz kept count along with him and said a silent thanks when he reached fifteen.

The man with the money said to the other one, "You wait here. Either of them moves, you blow them up."

He turned to his left, and strode across the elevator lobby. The floor was bare concrete but his soft shoes made no sound as he walked. He edged around some scaffolding and opened a closed door to his left, then closed it again. Katz didn't see anything but darkness in wherever he went in. He took a quick look at Collins. Sweat shone off his face, tiny rivulets making their way down his smooth cheeks.

Katz turned back to face the man aiming the shotgun at him. He allowed himself to dream how he might be able to hit him low, drive his head up through his arms, knock the gun loose, grab it, and kill him. "Then what?," he thought and the fantasy ended.

The other man appeared back in the doorway and pulled the door shut behind him. He cleared the scaffolding and called out, "Which one of you guys is Katz?" Katz waved his right hand.

"And you're the medic?" the man asked Collins.

"Yep," Collins said.

"Katz, you first. Then the medic, when I say so. Come on, man, don't make me wait."

The man with the shotgun gestured it towards the scaffolding. Katz shot Collins a quick glance and headed across the hall. The gunman at the door pushed it open and nodded at Katz to go in first. He felt the barrel of the shotgun nudge him in as he cleared the doorway.

The lights were off. Bright glares of sunlight sliced through ragged openings between streaks of brown and white paint smeared all across the windows. Brown paper and cardboard blocked any light from coming in some of the panels. A haze of cigarette smoke clouded whatever light there was and made Katz' eyes water. He raised his hand to squeeze them shut, then squinted, trying to adjust to the dimness of the room and take it in as quickly as he could. He figured it to be about forty to fifty feet long and maybe twenty, twenty-five feet across. There were no chairs or tables and no carpeting, only men and women, maybe a hundred of them or more, sprawled all across the concrete floor and along the wall across from him and to his right. It looked like only men were to the left, women to the right. Drop cloths spread out against the right wall covered what looked to be a lot of equipment, probably the workers' gear. The room was totally silent.

He turned his head to the left and saw Khaalis, sitting in a folding chair next to him, a black turban on his head, both feet on the floor, hands in his lap, a long cigarette in his right hand. His red eyes looked up at Katz, a tight smile on his lips. He was older than Katz remembered him, more seams in the face, more gray in the hair, but his body seemed thicker, fuller. He radiated power even sitting down.

"Mr. Katz," Hamaas said.

"Hamaas," Katz replied. Neither of them made a move to shake hands.

"I'd offer you a seat," Khaalis said, waving the hand with the cigarette in front of him, "but it seems our hosts really weren't ready for guests."

"That's okay. Did you get the money?"

76

Khaalis nodded.

"I should have charged you interest," he said. "You got off light."

Katz couldn't be sure that was a joke, so he changed the topic.

"There's a medic outside. He's just here to help anyone who needs help."

"Does that include me, Mr. Katz? Is he going to help me too? I need more help than any of these people, unless, of course, you don't bring me the swine I asked you to deliver to me. Then these people are going to need all the help their Jehovah can give them."

Short intakes of breath and snatches of English and Yiddish swirled around Katz.

"Yes," he said, "he's here to see if anybody needs helps, including you and your men."

But he's a medic, not a shrink, he kept to himself.

He could see better now. Many of the people on the floor, maybe all of the men, had their hands bound behind them. Most of the women sat against the walls. Their hands seemed free. Another man, with a rifle in his hands and the hasp of some kind of sword or knife hanging from a sheath at his belt, glared at him from the back of the room.

"No one's been hurt, as you can see," Khaalis said. "Everyone is fine. Now. You and your police and the mayor and the President will decide how fine they stay, okay?"

"Okay, but we didn't have a chance at the District Build --"

Khaalis leapt to his feet and rushed at him, his face crimson, muscles and veins stretched tight all the way up his neck. He was only about 5'10" but Katz felt dwarfed by his presence.

"Those people were shot in self-defense!" he screamed.

Now Katz heard a louder ripple, cries of fear jumping up in the dark all around him. He tried to resist the impulse to challenge Khaalis, but the impulse to resist the bully was stronger, always stronger.

"Against who, Hamaas?" he said. "Councilman Barry?"

"No!" Khaalis roared. "The policemen who were coming at them! That's who! Two policemen were creeping along the floor, their guns drawn, and they protected themselves! Don't put their lives on me, Mr. Katz! Their blood is on your hands. Your hands!"

The same pain that Katz saw etch his face four years ago was there again now. Khaalis waved his cigarette in Katz' face, ashes dancing in the shards of light, then disappearing into the darkness.

"I have a radio and a telephone and I know about it," Khaalis boomed, "and you and your police have a thousand people all over the city and no one bothered to tell you about it? You are a deceiver, a lying deceiver, and I will not let you mock me as a murderer!"

A man Katz hadn't seen before stepped quickly to them, a machete held high in his hand, looking at Khaalis for a sign to take one more stride across the room, swoop it down, and kill the infidel. Khaalis kept his gaze on Katz.

"Should Khaalis let him kill you, Mr. Katz? Send you to your God, your Yahweh?" Gasps filled the room again. "Would I have let these Jews live this long if I wanted to kill them, or your Mr. Barry? Would they be here now, alive and breathing? Would you?"

Katz could not part his lips to speak. He tried to shake his head, but didn't feel it move. He could only stare back at Khaalis, and prayed to God, as he never prayed before, that he would spare his life.

After an eon, Khaalis turned his head to the man with the machete and nodded at him to move back.

After another eon, he did.

Heat swelled back through Katz' body. Khaalis ground his cigarette into the concrete and turned slowly back to face him.

"Mr. Katz," he said as emotionlessly as Katz had ever heard him, "there are people I did come here to kill. Five people." He counted them on the fingers of his left hand. "William Christian. John Clark. Theodore Moody. John Griffin. Ron Harvey. Not Mr. Barry, not those policemen. I am here to avenge the death of my little Bibi, my Tasibur, my Khady, Abdullah, Rahman, Daud. Do you even remember their names, Mr. Katz? My Amina, my babies' mother Bibi, who will suffer from their wickedness every day of their lives?"

"I remember them, Hamaas, every one, and Abdul Nur too. I put those bastards away for the rest of their lives, Hamaas. You remember that, I know."

"Not enough, Mr. Katz, not enough! They have answered to your so-called justice system but they need to answer to Allah! Surah 5:45. Do you remember what it says? Do you remember anything I told you?"

Katz barely knew what the Old Testament said after years of Hebrew school, but he remembered enough of Hamaas' harangues from four years ago to know what was coming now.

"Hamaas, please, I --," he said, but Khaalis wouldn't be stopped.

"You don't know, or I wouldn't need to tell you again. The Qur'an demands just what your Torah commands, even says the Torah demands it. Surah 5:45, huh, huh? Pay attention this time, Mr. Katz. 'And the Torah ordained therein for them: Life for life, eye for eye, nose for nose, ear for ear, tooth for tooth, and wounds equal for equal.'"

Katz felt the floodwaters rush over him again.

"And," Khaalis went on, "I will tell you – as I told you before – that the Qur'an is more beneficent than your Torah. Khaalis does not want to take the lives of their women or their children because they slaughtered mine. Khaalis wants only them. You bring them to me, Mr. Katz, and all these people go home the same minute, huh? No one else needs to die. Only them."

"Hamaas," Katz said, "I promise that I will tell them you have promised no bloodshed if those bastards are brought to you, I will. I know why you're doing this. But for now, please, will you let the medic here come in and talk to these people, make sure no one else has to suffer? Please."

Khaalis stared at Katz in silence. Rabe had sent him up here, believing that because he and Khaalis knew each other, Khaalis would trust him. But he was wrong. Katz knew the anguish and the sorrow that engulfed Khaalis four years ago, dominated his every thought, drove his every action. But now, he couldn't even begin to understand what drove him to believe that holding these people hostage in these buildings would somehow bring him justice.

Khaalis turned slowly to the gunman who led Katz in.

"Bring the medic in," he said.

The gunman ducked back out the door. Khaalis turned back to Katz.

"Allah is merciful," he said, "but he is only merciful to those who show mercy to others. I have shown my mercy. Now you show me justice."

10

The gunman came back through the door, Collins and another gunman right behind him. Even in the dark, Katz could see all the color had fled Collins' face.

Khaalis turned to the room and held his hands up, as if they needed a cue to give him their full attention.

"Okay," he said. "Listen up, Jews. This man is here to make sure I have kept you healthy and hearty for the past --" he turned his left hand and looked intently at the watch face on the inside of his wrist, "four hours and thirteen minutes. If you have any complaints that I have mistreated you, if you are not feeling well, this is your chance to speak up."

He scanned the room from side to side. No one moved. Katz felt their distrust as clearly as he'd heard their fear.

"No one?" Hamaas said. "You are all happy Jews?"

No one raised a hand. No one made a sound. Khaalis turned to Katz.

"You see, Mr. Katz? All of your Jews are happy and healthy."

Katz surveyed the room. He wondered how many of them had survived Hitler, come to America to re-create some form of the life they had to abandon, and make the best new home they could for themselves, new children, new grandchildren – only to find themselves at the whim of yet another madman who hated them just for being Jewish. Born and raised here, barely 30 years old, he tried to find one thing to say that would put them at ease, let them grasp this straw of freedom, let them know this time might be different.

He found it.

"I'm Jake Katz," he said, looking directly into as many eyes as he could while he let it sink in that he was a *lantzman*, another Jew, here at their side, not their captor's, trying to make them trust him that this time would be different.

"I'm here because Mr. Khaalis does not want any of you to suffer. That's the truth," he said, "the *emes*."

He stifled the thought of how his mother would be so proud to see him now. His father, dead and gone even longer, would have taken them all on and pitched them through the window, but he knew Sam would have found the humor in his son the lawyer trying to talk his way out of this one.

"He's allowed us to bring a medic in here in case any of you need medical attention," he went on. "There's no reason anyone here needs to suffer. Isn't that right, Mr. Khaalis?"

Khaalis shook his head at him, impressed at whatever the Moslems would call his *chutzpah*, if nothing else. He turned back to face the group.

"Mr. Katz is always so good with the words," he said. "So come now, Jews, you've heard it from the lips of one of your very own Hebrews. Who now wants the medic to see them?"

Katz saw hands raise before him. He counted seven before he heard a phone ring down the hall. Was it Rabe? Would he send the SWAT guys up if no one answered? Or would he keep his cool and try again? He bet on coolness. Hamaas spoke again, this time to Collins.

"Okay, Mr. Medic. You have five minutes. Go, go now."

Collins crossed quickly to a heavy woman in a light blouse and gray skirt lying just to their left. Khaalis watched him kneel over her, heard him ask her what was wrong, then turned to the guard in the shiny black cap.

"You keep an eye on him. Five minutes. I'm going to have a talk with Mr. Katz."

He nodded to a gunman in sunglasses, another one Katz hadn't seen before, then pointed to the door. The three of them left the room and walked down the bare hallway to an office on the other side. The phone was still ringing but clipped off just as they came to the doorway.

Another man, short, with a goatee, stepped out of the office and pointed a shotgun at him. Katz wondered how many more of them there were, and where else they might be. He struggled to keep count of the ones he'd seen.

"They'll call back, whoever they are," Khaalis said, and turned to the gunmen.

"Both of you wait here. Let me know when it's five minutes."

He pointed to Katz to enter the office. Khaalis fell into a black cushioned swivel chair behind a gray metal desk just to the left and motioned Katz to take a seat in the brown folding chair on the other side. A telephone and a transistor radio sat on the desk. The radio played the familiar refrain Katz'd heard ever since he came to Washington.

"Eddie Leonard Sandwich Shops, you should try 'em. For the very best in sandwiches, just buy 'em. No matter where you are, you'll find that you're not far from an Eddie Leonard Sandwich --"

Khaalis clicked it off.

The room was as unfinished as the larger room across the hall. Some drywall was left in the wall behind Khaalis, empty frames where they ripped it out and pitched it down the stairways. A second desk sat in the middle of the room, a set of specs across it, held down by a level in one corner and a tape measure in another. Katz could see Khaalis was unarmed. He glanced at the doorway. The gunman trained his shotgun at him.

The phone rang again. Rabe again, Katz prayed.

Khaalis reached for the phone and picked up the receiver.

"Khaalis," he said, then "Yes, brother Nuh. Are you okay? Was anyone in there shot?"

83

Katz felt a small emptiness in his core. Khaalis listened for a minute.

"Okay, I am glad you are --". Brother Nuh must have cut him off. Khaalis listened a little longer.

Yes, I know," he said in a minute. "I am getting no rest from them either but we must talk to them, let them know why we are here. Is Muzikir there with you? Tell him to get a paper and pencil, then put him on."

In a moment, he spoke again.

"Abdul, listen, I am going to dictate a statement to you that you are going to read every time one of those press people call you so that you will say only the right things and get off the phone quick in case I need to talk to you, all right? So, take this down and you show it to Abdul Nuh too, in case he picks up the phone, huh? Okay, so you say this. We are Hanafi Moslems to the death. And if the police have any ideas about storming this room, it will put all of our lives in immediate danger, as well as the over one hundred hostages at B'nai B'rith and the Islamic Center. This is all for Islam. It's not a personal grudge. It's just that justice should be done. That's it."

He listened for a moment, looking at Katz, then said, "Who? Mr. Grip? Okay, then you have him call them and tell them. And you stand over him with the sword, huh, to make sure he says just what I just said to you -- only what I said to you, then he hangs up, huh? That's it. Okay. Do you see or hear anyone else up there?"

Another pause, then "Who is laughing there?" Another glance at Katz, then "Tell him to stop playing with it. Put it back on the wall. Do as I say now, remember."

He hung up the phone and rubbed his face with both hands.

"They are like children," he said. "Playing with a machete they saw on a wall."

He shook his head. Katz sensed maybe he was having a flicker of doubt, that this may be a good time to

84

remind him of the connection they managed to make four years ago.

"Hamaas, do you remember my story about Rahsaan Roland Kirk?"

Khaalis stopped rubbing his face and placed his hands on his thighs. He looked baffled.

"What is this?" he said. "What story did you tell me about Rahsaan Roland Kirk?"

Maybe their connection wasn't what Katz remembered. Maybe Hamaas needed to be reminded. Katz allowed it wouldn't be the top thing on his mind at the moment, so he plunged on.

"Yeah. I was at the Newport Jazz Festival, 1969? It was the year it started to shift to being a giant rock concert, about a month before Woodstock. So there were all these rock 'n' roll guys playing, but then Rahsaan Roland Kirk came out, blind, playing three horns all at the same time, different melodies coming out of each one? Then he starts yelling 'How come the Beatles are on Ed Sullivan? How come I'm not on Ed Sullivan? Fuck the Beatles!', and the crowd went crazy, we gave him a standing ovation. It was unbelievable. You remember that, right?"

Khaalis stared at him. His face turned from quizzical to dumbfounded. He lifted his arms, as if to the heavens, and screamed at Katz.

"Why in God's name would you tell me your little story now, Katz, huh? I have no idea what you're talking about! I do not remember your cute little, what is it, an anecdote? Do you think that I somehow embraced you, warmed to you, trusted you because of this simple, little – thing you tell me? Are we now blood brothers because you saw a man with a Muslim name play a manzello, a stritch, and a clarinet – I tell you the horns he plays so you can remember them the next time you tell your spectacular story – is that what you think? Is that your little fairy tale?"

Katz wanted to take it all back. He'd been living with a delusion for four years and he picked the worst possible time to share it with the worst possible person. There was a bond then, he felt it, he knew it, but it was obvious now he didn't have a clue why.

The brassy ring of the phone rescued him from digging his hole any deeper. This time, his prayers were answered, twice over. It was Rabe.

"Yes, Mr. Rabe," Khaalis said. "I have your man Katz here. He tells delightful stories, did you know that? Perhaps he will share his splendid tales with you if you ask him. I was very lucky. I didn't have to even ask. Ask him to tell you the one with the Muslim and the three horns, and ask him to name the horns. I am so hopeful he will remember."

Katz waited until he finished to look at him. Hamaas looked almost jolly. Maybe it wasn't so bad. Maybe he cheered him up, got him to give a little more than he would have. Then Khaalis' face darkened. Maybe not.

"I have given him five minutes," he told Rabe. He swiveled his head to see the short gunman pointing at his watch. "And his five minutes are up. He will be coming down, with your friend Mr. Katz and all of his wonderful stories."

Katz could hear Rabe on the other end. He couldn't make out what he was saying but he figured it out listening to Khaalis.

"No, Mr. Assistant, there is no quid pro quo. There is only what Khaalis wants. And what he wants is that you bring him that Cassius Clay gang and Mr. Wallace Muhammad. Khaalis wants those innovators! He will show them the true meaning of Islam, not their so-called religion."

Who was Wallace Muhammad?, Katz wanted to know. He knew who Elijah Muhammad was from the 1973 murders, and he knew there was a Herbie Muhammad who worked for Muhammad Ali, but he had no idea how Wallace

Muhammad fit in, only that he sounded like one more impossible demand. Khaalis was impatient, waiting for Rabe to finish whatever he was saying.

"He's fine," he said. "He is fine and the medic is fine and the Jews are all fine. Yes, he's right here. Do you not believe me, Mr. Rabe? Hold on, I will put him on the speaker phone."

Khaalis scanned the phone for a second, pushed a red button, and put the receiver back on the cradle.

"Are you there, Mr. Assistant?" he said.

"I'm here," Katz heard Rabe crackle through. "Katz, are you there?"

"I'm here. All is well."

"Good. Did you give him our phone number?"

Katz had forgot all about that. He stood up, slid a hand into his pocket, and laid the paper on the desk in front of Khaalis.

"Yep," he said. "He's got it."

Khaalis looked at the number and flicked the paper back across the desk.

"What does the medic say?"

"The medic is still with the Hebrews," Khaalis answered. "I am going now to send him back to you."

"We want anyone who needs help to come down here with him," Rabe said.

"All these Jews need help, from their God," Khaalis said. "You have not met my demands."

"Mr. Khaalis," Rabe said, "we are meeting your demands. The movie has stopped. You have your seven hundred and fifty dollars back, right? We're moving on what we can move on now. You see that, I know you do."

"You have not given me what I seek the most, those five wolves in your custody. I want them and the rest of that gang to answer to me!"

"Mr. Khaalis," Rabe said. "We have men working on all of that. We're doing everything we can as fast as we can do it. All I'm saying now is just what you said to me before. You don't want any more dead people on your hands, right? Let's take the risk out of that, okay? If we get the people who can't handle this down here and get them the help they need, we'll all be ahead of the game, won't we? Can you see your way clear to doing that?"

Khaalis rubbed his eyes with both hands.

"Khaalis will let you know!" he said.

He lifted the receiver and smacked it back down onto the phone. He took a deep breath. His eyes gazed far past Katz, then lowered to meet his.

"Let's go," he said.

The two gunmen fell in behind them and they crossed the hall back to the conference room. The guards followed Khaalis and Katz into the room, then closed the door and flanked it, their guns across their chests. Collins was standing inside the doorway waiting for them, his face wet with sweat, his weight shifting from foot to foot. He seemed to almost swoon seeing Katz again.

"So?" Khaalis said to him. "Do we have any sick children of Israel here, pleading for mercy on death's doorstep?"

"There's a couple of them bruised and bleeding pretty bad," Collins said. He pointed to one man lying on his side, his right eye black and swollen, blood caked on his right cheek and down his neck. The blood coating the front of his shirt still looked wet.

Khaalis waved his hand at him.

"That is nothing," he said. "A down payment. That's all, Mister Medic?"

"No," Collins rasped. He cleared his throat. "Two of them said they've got high blood pressure, so I took their pressure and they're both way up there, one sixty over ninety and one eighty over eighty. They don't have their medication and I think they need it. Mr. Khaalis. Sir."

"Who are they?" Khaalis said. "Let me see them."

88

Collins turned and pointed to the woman Katz had seen him go to first, sitting at an angle against the wall.

"She's the one sixty," he said, and turned to point past Khaalis at a white-haired man lying on the cement, his white shirtsleeves rolled up and a dark tie lying across his chest, touching the floor.

"He's the one eighty," Collins said. "Sir, we really ought to get them downstairs to get them some help," then added, "with your permission, I mean."

Khaalis mulled it over for a few seconds, then said to Katz, "You and Mr. Medic here will leave, now. I will consider what to do with my sick Hebraic friends."

Katz started to say something, then didn't. It would be better for all of them if Khaalis thought he was in command of the situation, making the right decision on his own, rather than resisting whatever Katz or Rabe tried to talk him into.

"That would be appreciated, Hamaas," he said. "Thank you."

Khaalis nodded to the door and the man with the machete walked over and pulled it open.

"You two," Khaalis said to him and the gunman who let them into the room, "go with them to the elevator. When it comes up, if anyone is on there – anyone! – you call out and we will start the slaughter of these Jews! All of them! No questions asked! You understand me?"

"Yes, khalifa," they both said.

"And you will fight for Islam to the finish and slaughter them all out there, do you understand that?"

"Yes, khalifa," they said in unison. Khaalis turned to Katz.

"And you, Mr. Katz, do you understand that as well?"

"I do," he said.

"Do you wish to call Mr. Rabe and tell him what I have said too, huh?, just in case the two of you decided you would send some men up here when we called for the elevator to send you down? Isn't that your plan? Come now, Mr. Katz, you are in the house of your Hebrews. Tell me the truth, eh?"

"You're giving us too much credit, Hamaas," Katz said. "There is no plan. There will be no men on that elevator. No one wants a bloodbath." He hoped that was true.

"It is all up to you, Mr. Katz," Khaalis said, "you and your Mr. Rabe and your Chief and all the rest. You can go now."

The man with the machete pushed Collins out the door and Katz followed, the gunman just behind him. At the elevators, the gunman pushed the button, took two steps back, and lifted his eyes to see which elevator would come. When the down arrow lit above the door to the left, he knelt in front of it, raised the stock of his shotgun to his shoulder, and peered down the barrel.

From the corner of his eye. Katz saw a machete glint above him. He heard the man holding it say, "If there's a cop on it, he's dead and you're dead."

The car quietly pulled to a stop behind the door. Katz tensed himself. The door slid back silently and slowly to the right. There was no one in the car.

The man with the machete pushed each of them through the door. Collins thumbed the B button furiously and Katz turned to take a quick look back before the door shut, just in time to see the man with the machete thrust it at Collins and yell "Hah!" right before the door closed. Their laughter faded out as the car descended, Collins poking the button all the way down.

"Jesus Christ," he said. "Get us the hell down there!"

When the car lurched to a stop, he said, "Jesus Christ, my Lord and Savior, get me the hell off of this!"

When the door finally slid back, he said "Oh Jesus fucking Christ, thank God!," bolted out of the car, and smacked right into Rabe.

Katz was amused, but Rabe wasn't. The dark shields on the dozens of helmets behind him made it hard to tell what they were thinking.

"Where are the fucking hostages?" Rabe said it to the medic but looked to Katz for the answer. Katz stepped off the elevator and heard the door slide closed behind him.

"He's thinking about it," he said.

"How long's he going to think about it?"

"I don't know. He just said 'I will consider it'."

Rabe pulled his hand down over his face. It was the first time Katz had seen him show anything resembling frustration. It didn't last long.

"Okay," Rabe said, "if – when, he lets the sick ones go here, we're going to ask him to let them go at the District Building and the Islamic Center too."

"Sounds good to me," Katz said. "Did I miss anything while I was up there?"

"Yeah," Rabe said. "There's one guy dead at the District Building, and another three wounded."

"Oh, Jesus!" Katz said. "Is Barry dead?"

"He's one of the wounded ones. Another guy, a reporter for some radio station is the dead one."

"What happened?" Katz asked.

"A guy with the reporter said they were just getting off the elevator and walked right into the guns going off. Our guys heard the shooting and went up there, but they backed off after they took some fire. Barry got hit somehow, I don't know, We got him out a window and over to GW. A security guard was hit too, and one of the hostages, a law student. They're trying to get him out of there."

Katz couldn't help but remember Khaalis in his face, screaming that his men shot only in self-defense.

"Who was shooting who?" he asked. "Why was anyone shooting?"

"I got no idea," Rabe said. "Why are they there? What's the District Building got to do with anything?"

Katz had no idea either.

"Anyhow," Rabe said, "they got them barricaded in there, up on the fifth floor. Tucker's office, the City Council President?"

"How'd they do that?" Katz asked.

"Not 'they'," Rabe allowed himself a smile and shook his head. "He."

"Who's 'he'?"

"You remember Hook Traylor?"

Katz did remember him. He was unforgettable. A huge white guy, probably six-six, two hundred and fifty pounds, played football at Alabama or somewhere. A *bulvan*, his mother would have said. A mean son of a bitch, everyone else said.

"I do," Katz said. "Who wouldn't?"

"He did it," Rabe said, "all by himself. Dragged a bunch of tables, desks, chairs, anything he could get his hands on, piled them up across there, sealed the bastards in."

"How'd he pull that off?" Katz asked. "Why didn't they shoot him?"

"Probably scared shitless, that's why. They told me he was screaming at 'em the whole time, 'You motherfuckers! You touch one hair on anybody's head, you're answering to me!' All kinds of shit." Rabe laughed. "He's one miserable mean fucker, but he's our mean fucker. You gotta love him."

"Wow!" was all Katz could manage.

"Oh, and I sent some of the guys here up to five."

"Why?" Katz asked.

"We got a call from someone who said her father called her, told her he was holed up there with some other people. He got off quick so we didn't know how many or where they are. They just came back down, with eight of them. They were hiding behind desks, bookshelves, all over. The medics are checking them out."

"How'd the cops get up there?" Katz asked.

Rabe pointed down the hallway to his left.

"Stairways," he said. "They had to pick their way over a lot of the crap those guys threw down but it was the only way. No way we're sending anyone up in an elevator if we don't know where your buddy has all his buddies."

Katz flashed back to the man with the machete at the elevator. He knew Rabe would do the right thing, but then he thought a little more about what he just said. Was he just a distraction? Did he risk his life up there just to provide the cops a little cover? He wanted to believe Rabe was just taking advantage of an opportunity, but still. He let it pass, but filed it away.

"And they just gave me an update on who's still unaccounted for." Rabe pulled a small pad from his chest pocket. "Fifty-one so far, and they've still got a shitload to call."

"There were a lot more than that up there," Katz said. "I'm figuring at least a hundred, maybe more."

He saw Rabe pick his head up, then turned to see the arrow above the elevator he just got off start to spin to 1. He watched it swing slowly to 8, then stop. No one made a noise. The arrow stayed at 8. Katz looked back at Rabe. Rabe nodded up at the arrow. Katz turned to see it, pointing at 7 and dialing back down.

"You two," Rabe said. His index fingers pointed at Katz and Collins. "Get out of the way."

Katz was sorry he ever questioned Rabe's motives. They wasted no time.

By the time the arrow reached 2, all Katz could see was a sea of black backpacks, blue helmets, and brown rifles pointed at the elevator. The arrow pointed at B and after a long second, the door peeled back. A red-faced white-haired man in an untucked white shirt held a crying older woman in his arms, her face buried in his chest, tears running down her cheeks. By the time the man looked out the door, the rifles were down and the front line of cops was pulling them out.

A cop just in front of Katz yelled, "I'll get the stretchers!" and ran to the stairwell.

Rabe extended a hand to the man, who grabbed it with his free left hand and shook it hard.

"Welcome back," Rabe said. "Are you all right?"

The woman clung to the man, her chest heaving, her face flush, eyes closed.

"I'm okay, a little woozy," the man said. Katz heard the trace of a Yiddish accent. A glimpse of his mother flashed back through his head. "She's not."

Rabe put his arm around the woman's back and gently separated them.

"Ma'am. We've got you now," he told her. "You're okay. You're going to be fine."

A corpsman walked her slowly out of the crowd to where a cop was unfolding a chair. The corpsman helped her get to it and she plopped down with a small grunt, then patted him a thank-you on the wrist. Rabe turned back to the white-haired man.

"You're both going to the hospital as soon as they come back with the stretchers. Can you give me a quick idea of what's going on up there?"

"Sure," the man said and took a deep breath. "I was on the fifth floor, in my office, doing something, I don't even remember, oh, I was taking some papers to the copy machine, when the door bursts open and these three hoodlums, Arabs, whatever, all of a sudden they're in there and shooting, like with shotguns, I don't know, but I ducked down and crawled behind a desk. They were like animals hunting for prey, that's all I could think of, and they found me right away and I thought I was gone. I saw them, one of them, give a *zetz* to my friend Edward, knock him cold, then they dragged him out into the hallway and pushed me and everyone else out too, piled us all up on the floor on top of each other. This is it, I'm thinking. But then they brought us up to the eighth floor, on the elevator."

94

"How many of you are up there?"

"A lot. I didn't count. Maybe eighty, ninety, a hundred? I don't know."

"What did Khaalis say, the leader?"

"The leader? He's a *meshuginah*, a nut, *forshtayst*? He kept telling us he's going to cut our heads off and throw them out the window if he doesn't get what he wants. Over and over, he's going on about the Jews, the Yehudis, the Protocols of Zion, what the Koran says. Then he starts again with the heads coming off, and the blood up to his ankles, and it just goes on and on. Every time I hear the phone go off down the hall, I thank God because that's the only time we get some peace. He's a crazy man who hates the Jews, is that something new?"

Medics ran around the corner, trailing two gurneys behind them. They helped the woman onto one and pushed her back down the hall.

"Okay," Rabe said. "I want you to get fixed up. Anybody else up there need help?"

"Probably, but they're too afraid to say so. A couple of the men with me on the fifth floor got *knacked* on the head with guns, you know, handguns, by those animals. I saw them both bleeding," he pointed across his forehead, "while they were painting. They could use some help."

"Painting? What were they painting?" Rabe asked.

"The windows. Brown paint, white paint, all over, so nobody can see in. He put all the young men to work, some painting, some carrying furniture, throwing it down the steps. Like I said, a *meshuginah*."

The medics were at his shoulder. Rabe patted him on the arm.

"Thanks. You're going to be fine."

The medics helped him lie down on the gurney and pushed it around the corner. Before Katz could turn back to Rabe, he saw Marty flying around the corner in her stocking feet, high heeled shoes in one hand, a pocketbook and a manila folder in the other. She pulled to a stop right in front of him and Rabe. Rabe took her in, up and down.

"Who are you?" he asked. Jake answered so Marty had a second to catch her breath.

"She's with me, at the USA. Marty McAdoo. Chief Rabe. What's that?," he said, pointing at the file.

"Just the beginning," she said.

11

Marty handed him the file.

"This just came in from the Maryland USA," she said, "hot off the telecopier, so to speak."

Silbert had been very excited that they were getting this super new machine that would let them get information from the FBI and U.S. Attorneys' offices all around the country without waiting for it to come through the mail. It was almost the size of a bathtub and had a revolving drum that somehow copied a piece of paper and sent it over a regular phone line. It sounded great – until they actually started using it. Katz remembered watching Silbert wait for the first document to come through, a witness statement from the FBI in Philadelphia. It took six minutes just for the cover sheet. Earl had seen enough.

"I could walk it from Philly faster than this," he said, and walked out of the room.

"What is it?" Katz asked.

"The U.S. Attorney up in Baltimore called Earl to tell him they had a case against Khaalis a few years ago," Marty said. "They nolle prossed but he thought we might want to see it anyhow, along with a whole slew of doctors' reports on his mental condition."

Katz did a quick flip through the folder, then turned to Rabe.

"Do you need me right now?" he asked him. "I just want to do a quick read, see if there's anything might help with this."

"No," Rabe said, "go find a seat. Let me know what you find."

They found an open classroom and sat at desks next to each other.

"That is some weird shit," Marty said.

"You read it?" he asked.

"On the way over. Go ahead, read it, then we'll talk."

Katz opened the folder and started reading out loud.

"Indicted, October 29, 1968." He did the quick mental calculation: about eight and a half years ago, before his family was wiped out.

"Four counts." He knew the statutes listed like he knew his own name. "Extortion, using interstate facility, bank robbery. Wow, what did our boy do?"

"Keep reading," Marty told him.

"'On June 9, 1967,'" Katz read out loud, "'the manager of a Maryland National Bank in Bethesda got a phone call from an unknown person instructing him to put $25,000 in a package in a phone booth at 8th and G Northwest within an hour.' Blah, blah, blah. 'The caller said he had two men at home with his wife, but the manager was single' – Oh, Jesus! Brilliant! – 'and his mother, who he lives with, received no calls or visitors.'"

Katz turned and stared at Marty.

"Criminal genius at work, I know," she said. "But wait. Read on."

Katz read on.

"'The manager, observed by the FBI, placed a dummy package in the booth and left; within a minute later, Khaalis picked up the package and was arrested by FBI.' Charged with four counts, blah, blah. Okay. Huh. They recommend dismissal of the indictment. Why?"

He ran a finger along the page to make sure he got it right.

"'Although we believe the defendant is unquestionably guilty of the crimes charged, we feel the Government's case is extremely weak. It would be extremely hard to disprove Khaalis' statement that he merely went to the phone booth to make a call and that he was curious to find out what was in the package.' Okay, I get that," he conceded, and read on.

"'The other evidence is questionable. We can probably prove he was in his D.C. office before the call and not in it after making it. The manager tentatively identified his voice but that could be a denial of due process under Palmer v Peyton and Stovall. In addition, the FBI tried to interview his wife'" – which one?, Katz thought – "'but she said her husband told her not to talk to anyone unless they had fifty thousand dollars and if you have fifty thousand dollars, you will know what I am talking about. It is highly questionable whether this would be admissible evidence. The defendant has considerable psychiatric history with the VA, with Dr. Fitzpatrick saying he does not pose a danger to the community.' No prior criminal record, blah, blah, blah."

He turned to Marty and recited the last notation.

"'No prosecution is recommended.'"

"Could've been in the pen today if they tried him," Marty said, "and everyone here could be going about their business, doing their little jobs, rather than this," she searched for the right words, then found them, "total fuckup."

Katz shook his head to disagree. "Even if they nailed him, those counts? He'd be back on the street already."

"But maybe he wouldn't ever have written those letters," she said. "And maybe his family would be alive today."

"Those are good maybes," Katz agreed, but it was too much to think about, especially now, so he changed the subject.

"You said there were medical records?"

"Yeah, well, mostly from psychiatrists."

"What did they say?" Katz asked.

"No idea," she said. "They're still crawling in over that thing. Earl handed me this and told me to get it to you right away, so that's what I did."

Katz nodded. Marty smiled at him.

"Oh, and one more thing," she said.

She dipped into her pocketbook and pulled out a handful of pink "While You Were Out" slips. She held them up next to her head.

"I also stopped by the front desk to see if you got any calls while you were running around out here."

"Oh, yeah?" he smiled. "That's so nice of you. Anything interesting?"

"Not to me so much, but you just might be interested in the one on top," she said, and handed him the pack.

He took it and read it to himself. Mike Davidson. Criminal Division, DOJ. A phone number and a note: "Home number 338-4333. Call anytime get chance."

"That is interesting," Katz said.

"Interesting?" Marty said. "That's more than interesting. That's a job offer."

"You don't know that," he said.

"What does it say?" Marty said "'Call me at home? Any time?' That's a job offer, sweetie."

She stood up and held her arms open to him. He stood up and they hugged each other tight.

"We don't know that's what's up yet," he cautioned her.

She slid a hand down between them and along the front of his pants.

"Something's up," she smiled. "Lonely Boy."

He smacked her hand away and regretted one more time telling her that she was only the second woman he'd laid since Lisa walked out on him in '68. That was last year, the first time they ever had sex, and she'd called his dick 'Lonely Boy' ever since. He pushed them apart. She took a quick glance down.

"Still up and at 'em, sorry," she smiled, and squeezed back into him. "Want me to take care of him now? Take some of the stress off?"

He pushed her back.

"Later," he said. "Take a walk. I'll meet you outside in a minute."

She smiled down at him again and sashayed more than walked back to the door. She blew him a kiss, then

100

disappeared back down the hall. He readjusted himself, pulled a pencil from his inside suit pocket, and smacked Lonely Boy with it, hard. In a moment, he was back at ease.

He left the room and went looking for Rabe. He found him on the phone.

"Okay, good to know," he said. "Keep me posted."

He hung up and looked up to see Katz.

"That was the District Building," he said. "They just let a guy go. Heart condition. Must have got the word from the big mahaf here. What was in the folder?"

"The Feds in Baltimore had him on a bank robbery charge about eight, nine years ago, but they didn't prosecute. Too many holes."

"Well, that's a shame, isn't it?" Rabe said.

"They're also getting a raft of medical reports on him, mostly shrink stuff."

"Okay. When you get them, let me know. I'll have Doc Gordon take a look, see if he sees anything we can use."

The phone down the table rang. Bohlinger picked it up.

"Command Center," he said, then "Yes sir, doctor. He's right here. Hold on." He extended the phone to Rabe.

"Dr. Rauf, at the Islamic Center."

"Put it on speaker," Rabe said. In a second, Bohlinger nodded at him.

"Dr. Rauf. This is Rabe. Everything all right?"

"Mr. Khaalis just called here," they heard. "He told one of his men here, Brother Abdul Rahim, who is sitting right here with me, that if anyone needed medical help, we should let them go but only if a medic looked at them and said so."

"Does anyone need help?" Rabe asked.

"I think so," Rauf said. "We have one woman here who has been having chest pains. I think we should have him take a look at her."

"Okay. We can send a medic up there, right away."

"Also, we're all getting a bit hungry here. Buthayna -- my wife -- went upstairs to our apartment around lunch time and brought down whatever was in there. It wasn't much though so people are pretty hungry. Can you get us some food, soon?"

Rabe glanced at his watch. Two minutes to four.

"Yes, we can arrange that. I'll talk to Mr. Khaalis about how exactly we're going to do it, but we'll work it out. Nobody wants anyone to go hungry."

"And it's got to be halal," Rauf said. "Permissible for Muslims to eat."

"I'm sure Mr. Khaalis can help us out there too," Rabe said.

Katz heard the phone muffled, and strained to hear what Rauf and someone else were saying. Rabe looked at him and shook his head. Then Rauf's voice came back through the line.

"You talk to Mr. Khaalis and have him call us."

The phone went dead.

Rabe handed the phone back to Bohlinger.

"Get me Khaalis. Put him on the speaker."

Bohlinger did as he was told.

"Khaalis," came back quickly over the line. He must have been down the hall already.

"Mr. Khaalis, this is Rabe. Mr. Rauf just called us from the Islamic Center. He said they got the okay from you to send someone up there to check out a woman who's having chest pains. Do I have that right?"

"Not someone, Mr. Rabe," Khaalis said. "Just a medic, just like here."

"Exactly, right. I want to send the same man you saw already, Corporal Collins."

Rabe stared at Katz.

"And Mr. Katz, just to report back to me on anything else we might need to know, make sure we get it straight."

102

Katz' heart sunk a little. He didn't know how welcome a Jew would be at the Islamic Center in the best of circumstances, never mind now.

"Of course, Mr. Assistant Rabe," Khaalis said. "Let him see and tell you what I have been telling you is *al-haqq*, the truth, huh?, that Khalifa Khaalis is not some bloodthirsty savage, but a soldier in the war against infidels and innovators."

"Okay, also, they --"

"Oh," Khaalis interrupted, "and perhaps while Mr. Katz is there, he could regale all of them with his account of seeing Mr. Kirk, just like he did here. Please ask him to do that as a special favor to me."

Rabe mouthed "what the fuck?" to Katz. Katz rubbed his forehead.

"I will ask him," Rabe told Khaalis. "Also, they told me they're hungry there. They need some food, halal food, and I told them you could tell us where to get some."

The phone was quiet, then Khaalis spoke.

"I will call Abdul Aziz, my son-in-law. He's in Georgetown. You have Mr. Katz and the medic pick him up at the address I give you and he will take you to the halal grocer, then he will go with you to the Islamic Center to deliver them the food, and then he will come here to deliver us the same food. Do you understand?"

"I understand," Rabe said. "Give me his phone number and I'll call him to work out the details."

"No, I will call him, then he will call you to tell you what we have arranged."

"How about the people at the District Building?" Rabe asked. "I'm sure they could use something too."

"After the food comes here, we will arrange how to deal with them. This is enough for now. Take down this address. It is his jewelry store."

Rabe wrote down an address on Wisconsin Avenue.

103

"No funny police business, Mr. Rabe. I need not tell you the consequences again, do I, huh?"

"I know the consequences, Mr. Khaalis, I assure you. They're on their way."

The phone clicked off. Rabe stood up and pointed at Katz.

"I'm going to get you an escort. Then you're going to tell me what this Kirk guy's got to do with all this shit."

12

Katz fell into step with Rabe's jog up the stairs, Collins in cadence right next to him. When they hit the sidewalk, Katz was stunned to remember that this was still the same sweet and sunny day he'd enjoyed just a little more than six hours ago, racing back to the courthouse. It seemed like six weeks ago but it was less time than he normally spent cramped up in his little office at the USA's. The breeze tickled his hair. He closed his eyes and let it cuddle him, tease him into regretting what he'd missed all day. Then he opened them and reality smacked him back to the present.

Every inch of the sidewalk that wasn't teeming with cops was teeming with reporters. People crowded the pavement behind blue saw horses across Rhode Island, down the Avenue as far as he could see on the left and up and around the corner to Scott Circle to his right.

Katz spotted the guy on the Daily News' crime beat. He was the first to get to Rabe.

"Mr. Deputy," he asked. "Can you tell us what's going on in there? How many hostages are there? How many have been hurt? Anyone killed?"

Now they came from all sides. Rabe pushed back microphones from WMAL radio and WTOP TV and forced his way through them all, Katz and Collins following him like he was Fuzzy Thurston. Katz couldn't hear anything but fragments of Rabe over a Babel of voices.

"Nothing to say here. You call the press office. Now move, please. Move please."

A cop pulled back the saw horses at the edge of the sidewalk. Rabe pushed the two of them through and into the back seat of an idling squad car pointed down Rhode Island towards M. He circled around to the driver's side and handed the cop at the wheel the note with the address of the jewelry shop.

"I think I know that place," the cop said. "It's in a little mall like around P or Q"

"Okay," Rabe said. "Get them down there. A guy should be waiting for them, Abdul Aziz. I have no clue what he looks like, but this guy probably does," he said pointing back to Katz.

"He's this Khaalis' son-in-law," Rabe continued, "so don't do anything he's going tell the old man about. He should be in the shop or waiting outside. You're going take the three of them up to some grocery store this guy knows to pick up some food these characters will eat, then you're going to drop some of it off at the Islamic Center. I'll get some guys to go to the Safeway and bring back something for here, so you don't have to take all day at the store."

Katz rolled down the back window and looked at Rabe.

"Just one thing," he said. "A lot of these people probably keep kosher, so I'd pass on Slim Jims and any other stuff with pork in it. They won't eat it."

"Okay, I'll let them know," Rabe said. He bent down and looked past Katz at Collins.

"You're going to do the same drill there you did here, okay? If someone's sick, heart, blood, a cold, doesn't matter. You let Katz know and he'll call me."

Collins managed a short nod. Rabe turned to Katz.

"You call me when you get there and I'll call Khaalis, let him know what's what. When you're done, you come back here, you fill me in, I fill you in, and we go from there. Any questions," he said more than asked.

Katz and Collins looked at each other, then back to Rabe. A line Katz recalled from his days growing up with soul music on Philly radio popped into his head again.

"Ain't nothin' to it but to do it," he said.

Rabe nodded, stood up, and tapped the roof of the cruiser. The driver threw on the lights and revved up the siren. Two cars in front of him and one behind did too, and they surged off towards M.

Once they hit M, traffic was everywhere, but it still amazed Katz how fast it got of the way when a cop let them know he had somewhere to go in a hurry. Cars squeezed right and left. Some lurched up on the concrete dividers that separated the lanes. The sirens drowned out the honks ahead.

The driver spun in and out of lanes and up onto the sidewalk once till he cleared 22nd St. He bolted towards 23rd, barely missing a fat blue Pacer that waddled out of the way just in time. He tapped the brakes once to veer around a D.C. Transit bus camped in the intersection, then floored it. Katz glimpsed the Call Carl sign at 24th zip by faster than he ever saw it zip by before. The driver took a peek at Pennsylvania just before it merged with M at 28th and floored it up to Wisconsin. He had the light this time and zipped right and up past P. He jerked to a quick stop in front of a small strip of shops running back from the sidewalk. Their escorts pulled over too, sirens off but lights still flashing. Katz saw the driver in the car in front of him poke his finger to the right.

A slim light brown-skinned man, probably an inch or two shorter than Katz, walked leisurely towards them across the parking lot. He wore a white rain hat, black sunglasses, a brown corduroy sports jacket, and chocolate brown pants. His hands were in his pants pockets. He paused for a second, bent down to see who was in each car, then headed Katz' way, a tight smile on his face.

Katz asked Collins to roll down the window, then crouched down and called out.

"Mr. Aziz. Jake Katz."

"I remember you," Aziz said. Katz remembered him too. He was Amina's husband and helped get her to testify and identify the murderers at the first two trials. After she mistook Clark for Griffin at Griffin's second trial, he stopped trying, and she stopped testifying. He didn't know what to expect from him now.

The cop driving the car threw open his door and stood up to face Aziz. Katz couldn't see his face but he did see his right hand come to rest on his pistol.

"Let's see your hands please, sir."

Aziz kept smiling and raised his empty hands. The cop circled the front of the car and walked quickly to him. The cops in the other cars were on the sidewalk now too, but held their ground, hands on their revolvers.

The cop ducked his hands into Aziz' coat pockets, then his inside pockets. He patted his front pants pockets, then circled around him and tapped his rear pockets. He knelt and ran a hand down each pants leg from the crotch to the cuff, then stood up and nodded to Katz. The bemused expression on Aziz' face stayed the same. The cop pointed to the front passenger door, then followed Aziz to it. When he was in, the cop closed the door.

"Salaam alaikum, Mr. Katz. How have you been?"

Katz remembered the last time the name Abdul-Aziz crossed his mind. A guy in the NBA named Don Smith decided last year to change his name to Abdul-Aziz, and M. L. Carr, a black guy playing for the Pistons, made a joke about it. "Now that I'm in Detroit," he said, "I'd like to change my name from M. L. Carr to Abdul-Automobile." Katz laughed at the time, but he wasn't laughing now. His memory of this Abdul-Aziz was a little fogged by time, but he asked him about one person he'd never forget – his wife.

"I'm fine," Katz said. "How's Amina?"

"She's all right, man. She's doing fine," Aziz said.

"Really? No lie?" Katz asked.

"Really, man, I'm telling you."

That was as incredible now as it was then. Not only did John Clark shoot her three times in the head at point-blank range and she live to tell about it, but one of the medics told him that when they were wheeling her into emergency,

the guns. Katz pitched a fit, because he knew if they raided the place, Khaalis would snap. He'd never trust the government again, never let Amina testify, take justice into his own hands. He never dreamed Khaalis would wind up doing that anyhow, but then, he was desperate to stop it. He called Aziz at the jewelry store and asked him to register the guns asap, make the case go away. He had no idea Khaalis even knew about it, much less gave him an ounce of credit for it.

"I do remember it now," Katz said. "You registered the guns."

"Because you told me to," Aziz said. "And I told Hamaas."

"I'd forgotten all about that."

"Well, he didn't," Aziz said, "and I sure didn't. I had a lot to lose. My business, who knows? I'm glad I got the chance to thank you again."

"Not necessary." Katz meant it, because he hadn't been the least bit concerned about what it meant to Aziz, only what it meant to the case.

"It's not in the Khalifa to thank you," Aziz said, "but I thank you on his behalf."

Katz stared out the window, as if lost in the memory, not willing to say "You're welcome," and take the credit he didn't deserve. The cop bailed him out.

"Okay, ace, gimme it again," he said to Aziz. Katz saw they were almost at the end of Piney Branch.

"Take a right on Arkansas, then take that up to Georgia and make a left. It's about a mile or so up there, on the left."

In two minutes, they were there. Katz saw the people on the street take in the four police cars stopping at the halal grocery, lights still flashing, cops getting out of each one with a medic, a black man, and a white man in the suit, and try to figure out why they were there. An older black woman walking by leaned in to a younger lady next to her and muttered something, but everyone else, black and white, kept on their way. No one knew what was going on, and no one wanted to know.

"Okay," the driver asked Katz, "What's the drill?"

Katz turned to Aziz.

"Do you know if they have a kitchen at the Islamic Center?" he asked. "Should we get them something they can cook for dinner?"

Aziz shook his head. "No. The only kitchen is up in Dr. Rauf's apartment. They're not cooking anything."

Katz tried to think what Rabe would do. If they brought them too much food, that might only make it easier for them to stretch things out, put more people at risk, but if they brought too little, that might put more people at risk too, especially the older ones. He remembered what Rabe said about each of these things having their own pace. He'd play it one meal at a time.

"Okay," he said. "Rauf said there were eleven hostages up there, plus at least a couple of guys holding them, so why don't you get enough for twelve, fifteen people? Get them some vegetables, chips, you know, whatever they'll eat, something to drink, at least tide them over through dinner."

"Okay," Aziz said. "You got the money for this? I got like six bucks on me."

Katz hadn't given money a thought. He pulled out his wallet and counted. Thirty-four dollars. He looked at the door to see if they took American Express, the credit card he kept just for emergencies. They didn't. He took a quick look up and down the block to see if there was a Riggs Bank. There wasn't. He bent down to ask Collins what he had on him. He was leaning back in the back seat, eyes closed, mouth wide open. He looked at the driver, who gave him the blankest look he'd ever got. He handed the cash to Aziz.

"Get what you can for forty bucks," he told him. Aziz headed for the store.

"I'm going with him," the driver said, "keep an eye on the money."

He pointed to one of the other cops to follow him in. The other two kept leaning against the side of the cruiser behind him and watched them go.

Katz checked his watch. 4:27. A Belmont TV store next to the grocery had three sets playing in the window, two portables and a console. Each of them was on a different channel. One had The Gong Show on, but the other two were showing local news. He couldn't catch any sound but he saw Carl Rowan talking to Max Robinson on channel 9. Katz couldn't remember ever seeing two Negroes talking to each other on a news show.

He walked to the glass door of the grocery and shielded his eyes to peer in. The cop who drove them was talking to the guy at the register. The cashier turned to look down the row of customers and waved Aziz up front. He squeezed his cart in ahead of an elderly black woman who didn't appreciate it one bit, then emptied a few armfuls of vegetables and fruit, two loaves of bread, and some bags of raisins and nuts up onto the counter.

In a minute, Aziz came through the door, his arms around three brown paper bags. The cops followed him out, empty-handed. Katz took a bag of celery and carrots from Aziz and walked with him around to the passenger side. They looked through the back window at Collins, now snoring, and drooling. Katz opened the door and threw the bag in his lap. Collins' eyes shot open and he almost smacked his head on the ceiling.

"Shit, man!" he screamed, then looked around to see where he was. "I thought you were that A-rab with the sword!"

13

Traffic was going nowhere on California. The urgent whine of their sirens only added to the frustration of every stop and start. All the way to Massachusetts, the roadway was packed with a slow shamble of cars and pedestrians looking to get a peek at the Islamic Center.

The driver grabbed his bullhorn and bellowed out the window, "Get out the way! Police! Get out of the way!," but everyone ignored him. Katz remembered how he drew courage from everyone else ignoring the cops during all the marches he walked in when GW was basically the home team for the anti-war movement.

The driver cranked the siren up to no visible effect. He banged the wheel, then muttered to no one, "Fucking hippies!"

Katz thought this might be a good time to ask Aziz a question that had been bugging him since the siege began. He tapped him on the shoulder.

"Abdul, just so I know. Why the Islamic Center? What's his beef with them?"

Aziz sighed and waved his hand at the traffic ahead.

"Not even this will last long enough to give you the whole story. I will try to break it down to give you an answer that makes sense, at least sense to Hamaas. Do you know the name Wallace Muhammad?"

"I know it now, but I don't know who he is."

"Okay, so do you know that he is the son of Elijah Muhammad?"

Katz shook his head no. Aziz smiled his tight smile.

"So this is what you need to know," he said. "Wallace Muhammad's father was Elijah Muhammad, the head of the pack of jackals that killed the family, the NOI, the so-called Nation of Islam. You know that Elijah Muhammad pretended to be a true believer, a servant of Allah, but he was not, far from it. It was discovered that not only had he killed Hamaas' family but that he and his henchmen were responsible for the murders of many, many other people. In addition, he had fathered children out of wedlock, and behaved for all purposes like the most sinful of sinners, never mind the holy leader of a faith. Do you follow me so far?"

"Sure," Katz said. "I know all about Elijah from the trial."

The patrol cars pushed ahead. Katz saw flashing lights way up ahead at what he figured was Massachusetts. The driver kept throttling up the siren. Collins seemed to be trying to follow Aziz, like he wanted him to make some sense of the day for him too.

"So now you know that Wallace Muhammad was his son," Aziz said.

"So, like father, like son?" Katz asked.

"Actually, no," Aziz said. "Wallace was also a victim of Elijah, his own father. I could go on for days to tell you how, but just know that his father committed such perfidy against him, even when he was a child. He let Wallace spend a year in prison for being a draft dodger because he wouldn't let him do a plea bargain with the government, but that's not the worst of it by far. By the time he got out, Wallace had become a traditional Sunni and he called his father out for his many affronts to Islam, but all that earned him was Elijah keeping him in poverty, making him pluck chickens, haul garbage, anything he could to keep him away from anyone he might teach or influence, even his mother. Only when Elijah was on his death bed did the old sinner for some reason – maybe, finally, a respect for Allah! – decide to do the right thing, He named Wallace the new head of the NOI. So, maybe two years ago, right away after Elijah died, they made Wallace the new Supreme Minister."

"So Hamaas must've been happy about that, right?"

"Yes, and no. He was happy to see Elijah dead and gone but sorry he didn't get to do it himself."

"That sounds familiar," Katz said.

"Yes," Aziz agreed, "but also, he saw Elijah's death as an opportunity for him – Hamaas – to be the new leader of Islam in the United States. That was his dream, his vision, and he thought he was making progress, making new important friends – until he hears, and he reads that Wallace Muhammad is coming back from the middle East with sixteen million dollars – sixteen million dollars! – from the Sheikh of Sharjah, one of the Emirates, the United Arab Emirates, and he is declaring that he, Wallace, is the sole trustee for all Muslim organizations in the United States!"

"Really?" Katz asked. "How did that happen?"

Collins leaned in to hear over the siren.

"Seems that right after Wallace became the Imam," Aziz said, "that is what he calls himself now, the Imam – he met in Chicago with Sadat, the Egyptian President? Then he starts sucking up from one to the other, cultivating them all until" – Aziz clapped his hands and spread his arms – "it all pays off for him. He gets this sixteen million dollars that he, Wallace Muhammad – not Hamaas Khaalis – will be using to buy a mosque and build a new school and Allah knows what else. You see now? Do you see? Betrayed! By all sides!"

Katz' head was reeling. So many names, so many reasons, too much to make any sense of, except to Hamaas, for whom it all must have made perfect sense. It reminded Katz of a bible story he remembered from his days at Hebrew school, a parable, a way of keeping the Jews in dread fear of their Lord.

"You know the story of Job?" Katz asked. "That's what this sounds like."

"Yes, I know the story very well," Aziz said. "In the Qur'an, Surah 21. 'And we remember Job! When he cried out to his Sustainer, "affliction has befallen me: but Thou art the most merciful of the merciful!" But Hamaas has suffered more than Allah allowed even Job to suffer, Mr. Katz. The Surah says that 'We responded upon him and removed all the

116

affliction from which he suffered; and We gave him his family, doubling their number as an act of grace from Us, and as a reminder unto all who worship Us,' but that has not happened. He has no greater family. He has received no grace. He continues to befall calamity upon calamity with no respite from the Creator. Do you not see that?"

Collins cleared his throat. Katz and Aziz turned to look at him.

"'And God said to Job,'" Collins recited with his slow drawl, "'Gird thy loins now like a man. And He said, cast abroad the rage of thy wrath, and behold everyone that is proud and abase him. Look on everyone that is proud and bring him low and tread down the wicked in their place. Hide them in the dust together and bind their faces in secret. Then will I also confess unto thee that thine own right hand can save thee.' That's Job, Forty fourteen right there."

He fell back in his seat, suddenly red, and turned to look out the window. Katz saw the driver's eyes stare back at Collins in the rear view mirror. Aziz nodded silently in agreement.

Massachusetts was just ahead, the Islamic Center about a hundred yards up the road to the right. Aziz turned to Katz.

"So now we bring the tale full circle," he said. "You asked me why the Islamic Center? Now you know most of the why, but the final why is that this man, this holy learned man Dr. Rauf here, he has made his bed with Wallace Muhammad. Is it because he so respects him as a leader and a messenger for his faith? No, it is because he is weaseling himself into Wallace's good graces so that he can, as they say, get a taste of that sixteen million dollars. He stands to gain a great deal more from making nice-nice to Mr. Muhammad than to Hamaas. If that money had been given to Hamaas, I assure you that Dr. Rauf would have been praying at the Hanafi house five times a day for these many months, laughing at his jokes, patting him on his back, oh so jolly. But he is not. He is silent as a clam, never to be heard from. So you see, it is torment from all sides, without cease. He is Job, no question, and beyond Job. He is Hamaas, alone among all in his suffering."

14

On Mass Av, the cops were herding the crowd off the street and onto the sidewalk so the cruisers buzzed the two hundred yards up to the Center in a hurry, then waited for a helmeted rifleman to pull back a sawhorse and let them through. Katz's driver pulled up to a cutout in the curb, rolled to a stop, and threw it in park. Katz stepped out and took a look at the Islamic Center across the lights swirling over the roof of the car.

He remembered driving or jogging past the place dozens of times over the years, but he never spent a second of time looking at it. He took his time now. In the dusk, past the cops milling on the sidewalk, he surveyed a two-story white sandstone building probably fifty yards long, with five arches in the middle and wrought iron fences connecting the pillars holding up them up. A small Spanish kind of roof overhung an arch at each end of the building. A white tower rose behind the building. High up, Katz saw a deck and a stone spire leading up to some kind of urn and a metal ring at the very top, framed against the darkening sky.

A husky middle-aged police officer in a blue helmet came down off the curb and shook hands with the driver.

"Commander Hanson, second district," he said. "You here with the grub?"

"Yeah," the driver said, "and these guys."

Collins and Aziz were out of the car now too. Collins saluted. Aziz held up a hand. Katz introduced himself and Collins, then pointed to Aziz.

"He's Khaalis' son-in-law, the guy at the B'nai B'rith? We're going to go up with him to deliver the food and see if anyone needs a doctor or anything we can get them. Khaalis said they'd let us in, so here we are."

Hanson nodded.

"I heard all about it from Chief Rabe," he said, then smiled. "You're sure you want to do this?"

Katz saw Collins shake his head a slow no.

"No," he laughed, "but we're going to anyhow. Anything we should know?"

"Well," Hanson said, "best we can figure, they're holed up in two rooms over here." He pointed to the arch at the end on the right. "We think some of them are in the secretary's office, and some are back in the Director's office all the way at the end."

"How many are there?" Katz asked.

"According to the people who ran the hell out of there when these guys came in, ten, maybe twelve. Not everyone's accounted for yet. They've got the director, Mr. Rauf, and his wife whose name I couldn't pronounce if you paid me --"

"Buthayna," Abdul Aziz said.

"If you say so," Hanson said. "And there are four, five, six people who work here as far as we can tell, and some kids from a tour group. Some got out but three of them are still in there, including the teacher who brought them."

"Muslims?" Katz asked.

"I don't think so," Hanson said. "They're a bunch of college kids and one of the guys who's still in there is a reverend. Picked a good day to drop by, didn't they?"

They heard a siren coming down Massachusetts and looked up. In a few seconds they saw a white Bethesda-Chevy Chase rescue squad truck cut across the empty avenue and pull alongside them. The driver leaned out the open window.

"We got the floodlights?" he said to Hanson.

"Okay, we'll get out of your way," Hanson said. "Turn around and fix 'em on the arch all the way down on the right. That's where we want to keep an eye out."

The driver started a U-turn into the street. Hanson waved them all up onto the sidewalk. Katz watched the truck for a second, then spotted a cop with a rifle crouching behind a tree on the other side. He looked up the street and saw a second one behind another tree.

120

"So," he asked Hanson, "how do you want us to do this?"

"Well, the way I'm thinking," Hanson said, "I should let Rabe know you're here and let him let your pal's father-in-law know, and get our signals straight with him. If that goes okay, I expect he'll call these fellas here and tell them whatever he told Rabe. Once we get all that squared away, then we'll go about getting the food up there however they say."

"Sounds like a plan," Katz said.

"Okay," Hanson said, "let me go make the call. In the meantime, you all might want to move down the street a ways, make yourselves less visible, if you catch my drift."

He took a few strides to a patrol car, took a seat on the passenger side, and reached for the phone in the console.

Collins led them double time down to the corner at Belmont. Katz marveled at all the looky-loos here too. Why?, he asked himself. Just to say 'I was there'? Take a picture, he thought, it'll last longer.

At the corner, he looked back towards the archway closest to him, the one just outside where Hanson said the hostages were. He saw two wide wooden doors on the patio, at ninety degree angles to each other. He knelt down to look past a tree blocking his view. Just past the patio, he saw another arch, flush with the side of the building, framing three long windows that he was sure were closed, keeping the world from seeing whatever those people were enduring inside.

He heard someone behind him yell out "Hey, hey, shush! It's him!"

Across the street, behind the sawhorses, he saw a tall black guy with black shades, a bushy brown fro, and a huge black plastic box with a silver metal grid hanging from a strap around his neck. It had a tape deck door and two round speakers behind the grid. It was like a portable stereo system, something he'd never seen before.

121

The guy rolled up a knob on the side and the sound rose enough for Katz to hear someone ask "Are you making any progress in your negotiations?" The next voice he recognized as Khaalis'.

"That's up to the Government," he said. "The Government can play if it wants to, and it's going to find out. You can see one side of the moon, right? The other you don't, right? That answers that."

"How about the other demands, about the --"

"Well, that's up to the Government," Khaalis cut in. "You see, they got a lot to cry over tomorrow, too, haven't they, if they've been playing games?"

"Have you set any deadlines?" the interviewer asked.

"No, we're not going to set deadlines. This way, they're going to find out that I'm not joking. They can play if they want to, and this way they can find out that I'm not joking. No, uh-uh, I'm not like that. I know that they don't hold fast to their promises. You know, like the man in Indiana?"

Katz winced as he remembered his own call with Khaalis this morning.

"No, they don't hold fast to their promises," he went on, "and then they brag about it. See, all they did was make it worse. You understand? We know that already, when we walked in here."

"Well, then, what are you waiting for?"

Katz couldn't believe it. Was this idiot daring him to do something? Rabe was right. They had to shut these guys down. He held his breath and waited for Hamaas' answer.

"Don't you worry about it," he finally said. "I know what I'm doing."

Katz exhaled. A guy between him and the guy with the radio yelled, "Yeah, right."

"You're the leader," the interviewer persisted.

"Allah let me be the leader," Khaalis said. "Even wild horses have a leader, so there's nothing wrong with that.

Don't call us no Black Muslims like one of you fools did earlier."

"No, I won't do that," the reporter said. Thank God for small favors, Katz thought.

"Because if you do, I'll beat the hell out of somebody over here," Khaalis roared. "You'll cause somebody to get a head beating. You're not listening, see? The Zionist press wants to keep twisting things and we're not gonna have it that way. They try to tell the people Cassius and Wallace are Moslems. We going to stop this foolishness. Everybody's going to know."

"We're not referring to you," the newsman said, suddenly contrite. "We haven't been referring to you as black Muslims."

Maybe someone just got him the word from Rabe to cool it, but Khaalis was still rolling. Katz pictured him, eyes flaring, teeth bared.

"Don't put that stigma on us," he screamed. "We don't call people by those South African terms."

A phone slammed down.

"That tape was made just about fifteen minutes ago," he heard an announcer say. "We'll keep you updated here on WMA --"

Katz felt a tap on the shoulder and turned to see Hanson.

"Let's go," he said. "Rabe said the big cheese okayed it."

"Great," Katz said. "Let's go before he changes his mind."

They hightailed it up the block. He heard Collins breathing heavy, just behind him. At the patrol car, Aziz opened the passenger side door and grabbed one of the bags of food on the floor. Collins started to grab the one on the back seat, but Katz said "No, let's save them for the B'nai B'rith. Just in case."

"Follow me," Hanson said. They walked single file across the stone courtyard, then to the right along the sidewalk just in front of the Center. The sound of their shoes on the concrete was the only sound. Katz turned to look back to the street. He saw two police snipers lying next to each other, their rifles focused on the patio below the arch ahead of them. The crowd across the corner at Belmont was still and silent.

They stopped just before the arch.

"What's your name again?" Hanson asked Aziz.

He told him, and Katz reminded Hanson of his name and Collins' before he could ask. Hanson nodded and stepped up two steps to the door to the left. He rapped his knuckles on it two times.

"Gentlemen," he said loudly, "this is Commander Hanson. I have the people here with the food, Mr. Aziz and Mr. Katz and Mr. Collins. Can you hear me?"

He stepped back from the door. Katz heard someone talk excitedly behind it and someone else answer him. Then the door popped open, maybe two inches. He couldn't see a face, but heard a man's voice with no trace of an accent.

"Leave the food outside the door," he said. "Knock on the door when it's there, then back away, off the patio."

Hanson nodded to Aziz and walked back to join Katz and Collins on the sidewalk. Aziz walked up the steps and laid the bag on the patio. He tapped on the door and backed down to the rest of them.

They waited for the door to open. When it did, wider this time, they saw an older light-skinned brown man in a gold and green striped shirt, dark brown slacks, and tan walking shoes standing stiffly at the doorway, his hands bound in front of him with a tie. They heard the voice they just heard shout out from behind him.

"No tricks! He will get the bag and bring it in here. Anyone moves, this man will be shot!"

No one moved.

They heard the voice again, this time lower, grunting something into the ear of the man in the doorway. The man edged forward a step, and bent down to look inside the bag. Katz saw a brown hand below a black jacket sleeve pressing a revolver to the man's temple.

The man at the door said something he couldn't make out. The voice muttered something back. The man picked up a box of raisins, then a bag of chips. He stirred his hand around in the bag and said something softly. The voice grunted something again, then the man put the items back in the bag, picked it up, and held it to his chest. As he backed into the doorway, he looked at them and seemed to lock eyes with Aziz. Just before the door slapped back shut, they heard the voice yell out, "You just wait now! No moving!"

Katz threw Aziz a questioning look. Aziz mouthed "Rauf," then turned back to face the door. Collins had wrapped himself in a tight hug.

Katz lifted his wrist high enough to see his watch. 5:33. He waited for the minute hand to sweep past the twelve, then looked at Hanson.

Hanson called out, "Gentlemen, we're still here."

In another minute, Katz heard a scrabble of heated conversation behind the door, then saw it crack open again.

"Just the Jew and the medic come in. You others, leave," the voice behind the door said.

"The big boss clear all that?" Hanson asked.

"Yes, now scram!" the voice said. "Leave! Now!"

Katz saw only darkness through the crack, then just the door as it slammed shut again.

Abdul Aziz patted him on the shoulder.

"Bitowfeek," he said. "Good luck."

Katz watched him amble back down the walkway, his hands in his pockets. Part of him wished he was going with him but a bigger part wanted to stay and see it through, whatever it turned out to be.

Hanson slapped Katz on the shoulder and gave Collins a thumbs up, then followed Aziz, a bit quicker.

Katz looked at Collins. "You ready?" he said, but didn't wait for the answer. He walked up onto the patio and rapped the door twice.

"This is Katz," he said loudly. "Just me and the medic out here now."

The door popped open enough for Katz to see Rauf and another man's head just behind him covered by a dark blue wool cap. The muzzle of the revolver peeked out from behind the door, still tight to Rauf's temple.

"Open it two more inches," the man behind Rauf said. Rauf opened the door another two inches. The man's eyes darted right and left, then right again before they fixed back on Katz.

"Come on in now," he said, "one behind the other, slow. And keep your hands up. No bullshit or Mr. Rauf here and everyone else is dead. You understand me?"

"I understand you," Katz said. "He does too," he said, nodding back at Collins.

Rauf stood very still in front of him, his eyes weary and resigned. A hand on his shoulder pulled him back and Katz slipped through the door sideways, followed by Collins. The room was in shadows, then darker still when the door slammed shut behind them. The four of them were the only people in the room. A quick glance told Katz they were in a small storeroom of some sort. Metal shelves lined the wall just across from him. He could make out stacks of brown cardboard cartons on the floor at his right. Through a crack in the doorway behind Rauf and the man with the gun, Katz could see people sitting on chairs and lying on a wood tile floor.

"In," the gunman said to him, "You first."

Katz went in first. As soon as he cleared the doorway, the gunman yelled at him again.

"Stop now! Lift your hands!"

126

Katz did as he was told. A younger dark-skinned man in a field jacket and blue jeans crossed the room towards him, his double-barreled shotgun pointing directly at Katz' chest. He pointed the shotgun up while he ran a hand inside Katz's suit pockets and patted down his pants. The fantasy of fighting back flickered in him and died again.

He used the time to do a quick count. Five people were in the room, including the one groping him. Three women sat in chairs, one man lay on his back, his hands bound with rope. He looked to be a Latino, maybe still in his teens.

The only sound came from a clock radio on a desk behind the two women to his right.

"Do you watch Charlie's Angels or Policewoman?" an announcer intoned. "If so, you'll love the beauty of this zippy 280Z Datsun. See it today at VOB Datsun, Rockville."

The man with the shotgun stepped back and trained the barrels at his head. Katz felt someone bump into him from behind. He looked back to see Collins with his hands in the air, Rauf and the first gunman just behind him.

"Move, keep moving!" the gunman said.

Katz lifted his hands higher and stepped forward calmly, his eyes intent on the eyes of the gunman holding the shotgun right in front of him. He stopped a foot short of the gun.

"We're just here to see if anyone needs a doctor," he said.

"Yeah, sure," the man said. "And tell the fucking fuzz exactly what's going on here, right?"

He wiggled the shotgun up and down, his finger on the trigger.

"Rahim," the gunman behind him said, "enough! The Khalifa has said what he wants from them. Let them see what they are here to see, and then they will leave."

"Is this everyone?" Katz asked.

127

"There are more in the other room," the voice behind him said. "You'll look at these here first."

Katz brought his hands down slowly and turned to Collins.

"Go ahead," he said.

Collins stepped to the woman on his left. She was a solid, stout woman, about forty, Katz guessed, with dark nappy natural hair rising high from her head and a deep scowl etched into her face. She sat upright with her arms crossed over a dark brown top and her legs crossed under a flowing green skirt, and glared at the man behind him. Collins bent down to her.

"Ma'am, if I could," he said, "I'd like to take your blood pressure and ask you a few --"

"You don't need to ask me a thing," she snapped, "and you don't need to take my blood pressure. I am perfectly fine, perfectly calm! The only thing I need is to get these terrorists out of my house."

"Quiet! Now!" Rahim said. "We've heard enough out of you!"

"This is my house and I will talk as I like," she stung back. "If you don't want to hear me, then you can go, any time you want, and the sooner the better."

"Buthayna, please," Dr. Rauf said, "again, I beg of you, let's not make a bad situation much worse, eh?" He looked at Katz and gave him an apologetic shrug. "She is my wife."

"Yes," she said to Katz, "and I live here with my husband, and I am a faithful wife and a faithful servant of Allah, and I cannot abide one more moment of these insolent infidels soiling my house and the name of Islam. And if my dear husband does not think I am patient or sweet enough to suit his tastes, so be it. This time I will speak my piece."

"Buthayna, my flower," Rauf said. "You have spoken your piece, time and time again, and I have asked you again and again to be silent."

Buthayna kept her eyes fixed on Katz. Rauf went on.

"The allies of these men have killed people, at the District Building, you know that," he said. "I do not wish you to expose yourself – or anyone else here – to this risk."

Then he spoke to her in what sounded to Katz like Arabic, and raised his eyebrows when he finished. Buthayna glared through Katz. Tears filled her eyes before she could get herself under enough control to speak. She lowered her hands into her lap and turned to Rauf.

"Yes, dear husband," she said. "I know the Hadith. I know that the woman who obeys her husband when he gives a command, and does not go against his wishes by doing anything of which he disapproves, is best. I know this and I will strive to honor it. I trust you will forgive me."

She wiped her eyes with the back of her hand, then turned sharply to Collins and dismissed him with a wave of the same hand.

"I am fine," she said. "You help the others."

Collins looked at Katz. Katz nodded to the two women across the room. Collins moved across the room and knelt in front of the first one. He reached into his bag for the pressure cuff. The woman, middle-aged with short dark hair, laid her hand on his arm, and spoke to the gunman behind Katz in the language he couldn't understand. He had no idea what she said but it sounded like she was asking something, very nicely. The guard in the field jacket barked something back at her.

She watched Collins fix the cuff to her arm and begin to pump it up.

She said to him, "I asked him if I could give you the name of my son, so you can call him and tell him I am fine. He said it is up to the Khalifa, the man at the other building. Can you talk to him, ask him if I could please do that? He will be worried sick. Can you please do that?"

Collins looked up at Katz. Katz turned to Rahim. "Is it okay if I tell her son she's okay?"

Rahim looked to the first gunman he'd seen, the older one in the blue wool cap.

"Rahman, is it okay --"

"It's not okay," Rahman man said, "unless the Khalifa says it's okay."

"Can I ask him if it's okay?" Katz asked.

"I'll ask him," Rahman said. "After you go."

"Can I just get her name?" Katz asked. "Can I get everyone's name, just to --".

Rahman sliced the air with his hand.

"No names! You're here to see they're healthy, then you're leaving. I'll speak to the Khalifa about what he wants, not you, not her."

There was silence for a moment, until the woman next to the woman with Collins raised her hand. She was white, her hair thick and black, streaked with gray, maybe sixty or so.

"Can you pass around the food?" she asked Rahim, then turned to Rahman. "We could use some food."

"No food, no talking, no nothin', until they're gone," he said. "Keep your fucking mouths shut, all of you!"

Katz heard an intake of breath from Buthayna, like she wanted to say something, but she held herself back. She laid her hands on her skirt and gripped her thighs, then slapped them with both hands, stood up, walked to her husband, glowered into his eyes, and snatched the grocery bag from his grasp. The gunmen and everyone else watched her stride across the room and hand it to the woman who asked for the food.

"You take what you need," Buthayna said to her gently, "then," she looked intently at her husband, "I will pass it around."

The woman took a quick look from Rahim to Rahman, then peered into the bag. She pushed a few items around, then fished out a bag of almonds and a full bunch of celery. She cracked off a stalk and opened the bag to shake out a handful of nuts.

"Enough for you?" Buthayna said.

"Yes," she said. "Thank you."

Buthayna extended the bag to the woman with Collins.

Collins said, "Just one minute."

He pumped the cuff up, then let it deflate.

"Okay," he said to the woman. "You're fine. One twenty-seven over eighty."

"Thank you," she said and looked into the bag.

Katz shifted his gaze to Rauf, then to Rahman.

"That's it," Rahman said. "He's fine. Into the other room. Go! Go!"

Katz led them past Rahim through a doorway to an outer office. A slim young girl, maybe eighteen, sat behind a desk where Rauf's secretary must have ordinarily sat. Five men lay on the floor, an older white man with a gray beard closest to them, a heavyset man with dark brown mottled skin who looked like he might have been in his fifties, and three younger men who looked like they were from somewhere in the Middle East. The older men's hands were bound by ties, the others' by ropes. Another man in a white T-shirt with a silver revolver in his hand and a machete in a sash around the waist of his blue jeans stood at the far wall. He looked a lot like Rahim, only younger, maybe twenty or so.

Rauf came into the room ahead of Rahman.

"Two of these people are our guests." He gestured at the young girl and the white man. "The rest work here." He pointed at the heavy man. "This is my Deputy Director, Mr. Abdul Rahman Osman --"

"Silence!" Rahman shouted at him. "No names, no introductions! This ain't no party here!"

The girl at the desk asked him, "Can they let my father know I'm all right?"

131

"No!" he said. "No calls, no names, no phone numbers. They are here only so the cops know we ain't laid a finger on you. Don't push me!"

Collins tended to Osman first. Buthayna's voice rose from the other room.

"Please, spare me your great and deep knowledge," Katz heard. "I know more Islam in my little pinkie than you know in your whole empty head!"

"You will be silent, now!" he heard Abdul Rahim say, then a sharp bang.

Katz looked at Rauf. His eyes were full of fear.

"Rahim?," Rahman called back over his shoulder. "Is everything okay?"

It was Mrs. Rauf who answered.

"He beat his little gun into the ground," she said. "He had a little tantrum."

"Quiet, you!" they heard Rahim cry out in exasperation.

Rahman squinted in frustration, then looked to the gunman at the front of the room.

"I'll deal with this," he said. "Al-Qawee, keep your eyes on them."

He spun back into the other room and slammed the door. All Katz could make out was excited muttering in Arabic. He caught eyes with Rauf, who closed his eyes and shook his head. Katz tried to think of how he could use the moment to his advantage. Al Qawee was focused on the door to the other room, trying to hear Buthayna and Rahim.

Katz turned his back to the gunman and stepped towards Rauf.

"Can you chat up Al Qawee up there for a minute?," Katz asked. "I want to try to talk to a few of these people."

Rauf nodded, then paused a second to decipher the din next door. He shook his head.

"She will be the death of us all," he sighed, "literally."

132

He edged past Katz and walked to Al Qawee with his hands held high.

"Sir, can I ask you a small favor?" he said. "These binds are about to fall off and I'm having a devil of a time keeping them on. Can you re-tie them for me?"

Katz watched Al-Qawee try to figure out why one of his prisoners wanted to be tied up tighter. Rauf tried to clear it up for him.

"I want to make sure you don't think I'm trying to escape," he said with a little laugh.

Al-Qawee tucked his revolver into his sash. When he reached for the tie, Katz moved to the side until Rauf's head blocked Al-Qawee's view of him, then knelt down to talk to the bearded man.

"Hi," he whispered. "Tell me your name, quick."

"I'm Bob Tesdell," he whispered back. "I'm a reverend."

Rauf started humming something loud and tuneless.

"I run the World Association for Travel," Tesdell said. "We brought a bunch of kids here from Boston University and Temple, to tour the mosque, then these guys burst in and herded us all in here. I don't have any idea why or what they want us for."

"No one does," Katz said. "Are all these people with you?"

"No. Most of them took off and got away, thank God."

Katz heard Rauf say, "That pinches just a little. Can you loosen it just a bit?"

"Are you all okay?" Katz asked.

"Yes," Tesdell said, "but they keep threatening to cut people's heads off when they get agitated. And we've heard them next door. They're very upset with someone."

Katz patted him on the shoulder, stood up, and cleared his throat loudly.

Rauf tested his new restraint.

"Thank you," he said. "Much better. Shokran."

"Now get back there," Al-Qawee said. "Back off."

Rauf turned and gave Katz a look that asked "Okay?" Katz nodded a silent okay back at him.

The other room was quiet. Rahman pushed the door open and threw it shut behind him. He glared at Rauf.

"When the first head is cut," he hissed, "hers will be first. Right after I personally cut out her tongue."

Rauf only nodded. Katz wondered if the same thought might have crossed his mind a few times.

Rahman spun to Katz.

"Are we done here?"

Katz looked at Collins pumping up the cuff on Tesdell.

"Give me just one more minute," Collins said. In a few seconds, he pulled the cuff down Tesdell's arm.

"He's okay," he said. "I think they're all okay."

"Anyone hurt that you know of?" Katz asked Rahman. "Anyone, any way, bumped into a wall, maybe, fall down, anything?"

"No one," he replied. "Nothing. Everyone's fine, everything is cool. Now you can get your asses out of here and tell them that, okay? Let's go."

Katz nodded to him and back at Tesdell, then let Rahman push him, Rauf, and Collins back into the other room. Everyone was just where they left them, including Buthayna. She was even glaring the same glare he saw before, except this time it was trained on Rahim. Katz didn't know who to feel more sorry for.

In another few shoves in the back, he and Collins were back on the patio. The sky was black. Katz' watch told him it was 6:21. He'd only been in there forty-five minutes, but it felt like a century.

15

The ride back to Georgetown was a lot quicker. Katz got out with Abdul-Aziz and shook his hand.

"Many thanks, man," he said. "We needed you."

"It was nothing," Aziz said.

"If this thing goes on," Katz said, "I might have to ask you to do this again. Can you handle that?"

"I can handle it," Aziz said. "I'll wait to hear from you. Ma' a salaama."

Abdul-Aziz clasped his hands together behind him and walked his slow walk back to the jewelry store.

Katz climbed into the front seat and the cruiser shot forward. He rolled down the window, closed his eyes, and let his head sink into the head rest, happy to let the rushing air and the screams of the siren flood his senses all the way back to the B'nai B'rith.

When the car pulled to a stop, Katz got out and counted up eight floors. All he saw was dark. The crowd on the sidewalk was gone. Except for a few idlers across the street stopping to look up and point, the only people out now were cops and reporters, and most of them weren't doing anything more than killing time. An arc of light burst open around one of the TV reporters updating everyone at home.

Katz and Collins headed for the front door. Halfway there, it swung open and Rabe came through, a man in a hurry.

"Hey!" Katz said. "You getting some air?"

"Hey yourself," Rabe said. "I'm going across the street. Collins, is that your name? Head downstairs. We may have some business for you. Katz, take a walk with me."

Katz spun around and fell in step with Rabe. A few reporters raced up but Rabe waved them off and kept walking.

Katz saw they were heading for the Holiday Inn across the street. Almost every room was lit up, a front row seat to the best show in town.

"What'd you find out at the Islamic Center?" Rabe asked him.

"There're three gunmen," Katz said. "They're holding eleven people in two rooms. Collins said they're all okay. One guy told me he was heading up a tour when the guys burst in. Most of the kids – students – got away, but a few didn't. They're college students, BU and Temple."

Katz held the door to the Holiday Inn open for Rabe, and followed him in.

"Elevator?" Rabe asked a cop with night goggles perched on top of his helmet. He pointed his rifle down the hallway.

"Straight back, then right."

Rabe nodded. They followed him back.

"How'd you find all that out?" he asked over his shoulder.

"Rauf kept one of the gunmen busy while I talked to him."

"Good job, Mr. Katz," Rabe called back. "Any time you want to come back on the force, you let me know."

"This is enough for me, thanks."

Rabe turned the corner and pressed the Up button next to the elevator.

"Anything else?" he asked.

"No," Katz said, "except Rauf's wife, Buthayna or something like that. She's a handful. Cussing out the guys holding them, no let up. She's something, man."

Rabe snorted a laugh. "Maybe they'll give up just to be rid of her."

An elevator opened on the wall behind them. Rabe got in first and pressed 8, the top floor. The doors closed and the car started its climb.

"What about Khaalis?" Katz asked. "What do you hear from him?"

Rabe rolled his eyes.

"Just hung up with him," he said. "Fun and games at the District Building."

"What happened?"

"Let's see. The good news is we got three cops back safe and sound. They went up to the fifth floor – on one of those long ladders off a fire truck? – and they went in the other side from where the hostages are. They rounded up like twenty-five, thirty people who were holed up all over the floor and got them back there in one place, got them some food. They're fine, at least as fine as they can be. The other good news is they did hustle the Mayor out of there. He's going down to the Command Center they've set up at HQ."

"Okay," Katz said. "What's the bad news?"

"The bad news," Rabe said, "is that the fucking numbnuts at TOP showed the cops on the ladder live as it was going on, and Khaalis saw it on the TV and gave me a call to let me know that everyone was going to die in two minutes if anyone came in the building. We told those TV guys, the newspapers, all of 'em, 'Don't say anything, don't write anything about anyone else up there' and they pull that shit. Unbefuckinglievable."

He drew both hands down across his face, then fixed his eyes on Katz.

"It was everything I could do to convince him they were only bringing up the food for his guys and the hostages. Those assholes could've got 'em all killed. Cully's reading 'em all the riot act right now. One more fuckup, they're going to have to wait and see what happens like everyone else. Bunch of assholes! No other way to put it."

The elevator jolted to a stop and the doors split open. A handful of cops in full riot gear turned to check them out. The tallest one saluted Rabe and waved them down the hall.

Another cop stood in front of the last door on the right. He pushed it open and let them in. The room was dark, but Katz could make out another five cops, including the one sitting at a desk facing the window, squinting through a telescope pointed across the street at the B'nai B'rith. Rabe waited for him to lean back and take a look up at him.

"Hey, Chief," the cop said. "How you doin'?"

"I'm doing good. What do you see?"

"Take a look," he said, and got up.

Rabe took his seat and squinted into the lens. He adjusted a knob at the side of the scope and leaned in.

"Holy shit!" he said. He pushed the white tube a little to the left, then said it again.

The cop who got up turned to Katz.

"We can make out shotguns, pistols, at least fifty or sixty ammo boxes, explosive shit like shooting stars, an automatic bow and arrow, and that's not even half of it. Probably got more stuff up there than Herman's and Irving's put together."

Katz was stunned.

"I was up there," he said, "I didn't see any of it."

"They probably covered it up," the cop shrugged, "make sure you didn't."

It smacked him like a bat across the forehead.

"They were under the drop cloths," Katz said. They weren't covering the workmen's gear. They were covering an arsenal.

"Probably," the cop said. "There's a bunch of 'em over there."

"Oh, Jesus Christ!" Katz said. He laid a hand on Rabe's shoulder. "I am so sorry. I should've seen that. I just --"

Rabe turned back and looked up at him.

"Don't beat yourself up about it, Mr. Katz. Wouldn't have changed a thing. They'd still be in there and we'd still be out here."

He stood up and motioned to Katz to take a look.

"Let's just be thankful Khaalis' boys weren't too slick with the paint."

Katz peered into the telescope. Over to the left, through streaks of glass the paint didn't quite cover, he saw the arsenal, right where he had seen the drop cloths. He cursed himself again, quietly this time. Now something else hit him. He turned to Rabe.

"Why didn't the people he let go tell us? Why didn't they say something?"

"Who knows?" Rabe said. "Maybe they were a little shell-shocked. Maybe we should've asked. Forget about it. Now we know."

Katz stood up and the cop took his seat back.

"What else've you seen?" Rabe asked.

"It looks like there are seven guys in there," he said, "six of them with rifles or shotguns, it's hard to tell, plus the leader who's doing all the talking but he's not carrying anything as far as we can see. He's coming and going somewhere all the time."

Katz saw him glance at the clock on his desk. It was just about 7.

Rabe turned to Katz.

"Is that how many guys you saw? Seven?"

Katz replayed the movie in his head, but the scenes jumbled and overlapped. He counted the two guys with shotguns at the elevator, the guy with the machete, the two guys who took him across the way, and Khaalis, but there was one more he couldn't place. Rahman, Rahim, and Al-Qawee's faces spilled across his brain, but they were at the Islamic Center. There were too many of them to keep straight. Then he remembered the one with Collins. That made seven, but after not seeing the guns, he didn't trust himself anymore, so he hedged his bet.

"I can remember seven," he said. "If there was anyone else, I didn't see them."

"I'll take that as a yes," Rabe said and turned back to the cop.

"Anything else?"

"Not much you probably don't already know. They're not doing much of anything in there now, eating, talking, sleeping. that's it."

Rabe slapped the cop on the back and turned to the group around him.

"You guys are doin' a hell of a job," he said. "Stick with it, and everyone'll go home, the sooner the better. Anyone got any questions?"

Everyone shook their heads.

"Bright ideas? Happy thoughts? Unhappy thoughts?"

Nothing again.

"Okay," Rabe said. "Keep me posted."

He snapped a salute and went out the door. Katz caught up to him at the elevator.

"I have a question," he said. "When I saw you on the street, you told Collins you might have some business for him at the B'nai B'rith. What's going on?"

The elevator opened and Rabe got in first. He poked 1 and turned to Katz.

"We're getting some people out," he said. "Now."

16

Rabe and Katz came out the doors side by side, even quicker than they went in. Rabe laid it all out for him.

"We figure there are at least twenty-five people in there spread out all over floors below eight. From the folks we called from the payroll list the lady gave us, and a bunch of people who called in saying they heard from their husbands, wives, whoever, we know there are people hiding on at least three, four, and five. If they're any higher, we can't get to 'em anyhow with all the shit on the stairwells."

"Does Khaalis --?"

Before Katz could finish the question, the swarm of reporters was on them again. Rabe didn't even bother to wave them off this time. He just barreled through and Katz stayed close on his shoulder. He ran ahead to hold the door for Rabe, then hurried back up to finish his question.

"Does Khaalis have men anywhere on the other floors?"

"No one said they saw any of them," Rabe said. "They were scared shitless to move, make any sound. Took some of them hours to get the nerve to pick up the phone."

They skipped down the stairs in time to each other.

"That's why I went over across the way," he went on, "make sure all of his guys were accounted for."

He swiveled his head to Katz.

"You said they were. Seven, right? You're as sure as you can be."

It was more a question than a statement. Katz knew people's lives depended on the answer, so he replayed his trip to eight one more time. He was sure, at least of who he saw.

"I'm sure about the seven I remember," he said, "but like I said --"

Rabe stopped in the middle of the staircase and placed his index finger on Katz' chest.

"I heard what you said. You said you saw seven up there. That's all I need to know, Mr. Katz. No one's sure if there's anyone anywhere else, okay? We're just guessing, okay, but it's probably a good guess. Why?"

He counted on his fingers.

"One. The guys back there said they saw seven. Two. You did too. Three. Nobody hiding up there says they've seen anyone. Four. We haven't heard our man talk to anyone anywhere else in the building. And five, we haven't seen anyone going in or out of any other floors on either of the stairwells. So maybe that means no one else is anywhere. But maybe it doesn't."

He spread his hands wide like he was trying to explain it to a child.

"So, we have a choice, okay? Do we do our best to get whoever's hiding up there down now? Or do we wait and hope his Khalifaship doesn't find them first? Sometimes, you have to make a call, and my call is we get 'em, now."

Katz had always thought he was cool under pressure, on the football field, at the Howard, upstairs with Khaalis, but Rabe was showing him what real cool was, risking his career on a gamble that might mean people died, maybe a lot of them. Their families, those reporters outside, the public tuning in and out on TV, they'd all demand his scalp, call him a cowboy, a dope.

But if they all came down safe, he'd get no credit from any of them. He'd be invisible. He did what he was paid to do, period. Maybe so, Katz thought, but to him and the cops waiting for him down below, this guy had the balls to make the choice to do what had to be done. Katz was as ready as they were to follow him into hell and back.

They took the rest of the steps and walked to the cops waiting across the floor. There must have been twenty or thirty of them, every one in a dark blue flak jacket and a light blue helmet with a gleaming black visor tilted up over it, rifles and semi-machine guns pointed up in the air or down at the floor. Most of them were white but a lot of them, a lot more than when Katz was a man in blue, were black.

"All right," Rabe said, "listen up." There wasn't a lot of noise before he spoke. Now there was none.

"Count off by two's from the left, until I tell you to stop."

They counted off. Katz counted four pairs before Rabe spoke again.

"That's it," he said. "Hold it right there. The rest of you stand down. You men, let's take it down the hall."

He led the eight of them back and just around the corner to the stairwell. Katz trailed behind and hung back by the corner. The stress of the day was catching up to him. His pits and his chest were drenched in sweat. He was pretty much running on empty, but he knew the guys across from Rabe were just getting started, maxed out on adrenaline, ready to take on whatever he told them laid dead ahead.

"Here's the drill," Rabe said quietly. "Two guys to each floor. You two," he pointed to the guys closest to the doorway. "You're going up to five."

He pointed at the rest of them in turn and gave them four, three, and two.

"Wherever you go, you're going to be quiet as mice, okay?," he said. "Everybody got cards, say who you are? Check, now."

Katz watched them all dig into pockets and wallets. Most of them held a bunch of cards up. One guy held just his hands up.

"I'm out," he said.

Rabe dug into his wallet and pulled out a short stack of his own cards.

"Take some of these," he told him. "It doesn't matter who it says you are, just that it says MPD."

Rabe tucked his wallet back in his pocket.

"Okay," he said, "now listen up. Once you get where you're going, you got three things to do."

143

Katz waited for it. Rabe didn't let him down. He held up his index finger.

"One," he said, "you're going to split up and cover your floor, the whole floor. Every inch, look under every desk, inside every closet. I don't care if it's a B'nai B'rith office or someone else's, they might be anywhere."

He turned to the left and looked at the guys heading for the third floor.

"Somebody called from an insurance office up on three. There's at least four ladies up there, under desks somewhere. You're going to find them."

They nodded. He turned back to the group.

"There are at least twenty-five people somewhere up there between two and five. We've talked to some of them, so we know there are at least the four up on three and there are some on four and at least one woman's up on five, but they could be anywhere, and we don't know exactly how many of them there are. So, you come to a door that's closed, I don't care if it's a closet, a ladies room, whatever it is, you knock on it, tap, tap, tap, and you ask if anyone's there, quiet, but loud enough for someone to hear. Anybody's behind there, they don't know if you're a bad guy or a good guy so if you hear anything, a cough, somebody breathing, you slip one of those cards under there and you let them know you're a good guy. Okay?"

Katz watched the silent nods all around. He had their attention.

"That's number one." He held up his middle finger next to his index finger.

"Two, you are going to move as quiet as you can possibly move. We just got a good look at El Capitano and his boys up on eight. They're all accounted for, but we can't be one hundred percent sure if he's posted anyone anywhere else, so you see anyone with a gun or a sword or anything that looks like he doesn't belong there, you pull back, okay?,

144

you retreat. We don't want to set him off up there, we all capisce?"

Nods all around again.

"And three," he held up his ring finger, a gold band at the bottom. "You bring anyone you find back to this stairwell, and back down here. If the other one's closer, don't take it. Take this one. It's clear below six and it's the farthest one from where they are upstairs. No elevators, no noise, no shooting, no nothing except those three things, all right? Look everywhere, don't make a sound or confront anyone, and get everyone down here in the same condition they went up. That's it. Any questions?"

"What if we have to defend ourselves?" a stocky black guy at the left asked. "What if they start shooting at us?"

"You back off and you clear out," Rabe said. "No OK Corral, okay? No one fires on anyone. We got a hundred some people trapped upstairs with a lunatic who says he's going to kill 'em all if things go bad. We're not going to give him an excuse. I hear any gunfire up there, you better be come back with a hole in you or you don't come back. You got it?"

The cop gave the smallest of nods.

"Everyone got it?"

Rabe scanned them all until he got some sign of yes from all eight of them.

"All right, men," he said. "I know you can do this. Bring 'em back down."

He walked to the stairwell, silently turned the knob, pushed the door open, and waved them forward. As each pair approached, he whispered their floor, and held them back until they couldn't hear the group above. Only when they had all climbed the stairs out of his sight did he close the door, quietly.

He held up his crossed fingers. Katz did the same and walked with him back around the corner. Bohlinger was double-timing their way.

"What's up?" Rabe called to him.

"Cullinane's on the phone," he said. "Needs to talk to you pronto."

They followed him back to the desk. Bohlinger gave Rabe the receiver and put the phone on speaker.

"Yeah, Chief," he said, "this is Rabe."

"Bob, I'm at the Command Center we set up here. I've got an Ambassador here. Hold on a sec."

They heard him talk to someone, then come back on.

"He's the Ambassador from Iran," he said. "I'm not even going to try his first name, but he's Ambassador Zahedi. He wants to help end this thing."

"Okay." Rabe said. "What's he got in mind?"

"He wants to talk to Khaalis, directly, Muslim to Muslim, tell him what he's doing doesn't square with the Koran."

"He's there now?" Rabe asked.

"Yeah," Cullinane said.

"Can he hear me?"

"No."

"Okay," Rabe said. "between you and me, it's a little late for that, isn't it? Khaalis has been telling everyone that everything he's doing is absolutely square with the Koran. I don't think getting into a religious debate with this Ambassador's going to all of a sudden make him say 'Hey, I got it all wrong. Sorry, bye'."

"Uh huh," Cullinane said. "That's a good point, Bob. He's right here now and I'd really like you to see if you could make that happen."

Rabe and Katz caught eyes.

"So, we got no choice, is that what you're telling me?" Rabe asked.

"There you go, Bob," Cullinane said. "Thanks!"

Rabe drew his hand down his face again.

"Okay, okay," he said. "But he's going to have to wait."

"How long?" Cullinane asked.

"Until the guys I just sent up to get the folks on the other floors come down in one piece."

"Ah, I see," they heard.

"Tell him it's for his own good," Rabe said. "If he calls him now, and Khaalis hears anything going on below, he's going to think we set him up to divert his attention, and he won't trust him – or any of us – again."

"That's a good point too, Bob," Cullinane said. "I will definitely tell him that."

"And you can tell him the second they're all down here, I will call you and then he can call and give it his best shot, okay?"

"Okay, Bob. Let me know the second you know. Bye."

Rabe handed Bohlinger the receiver.

"Cully's got the worst of it," he said to Katz. "All I got to deal with is a nutso jackoff with a bunch of hostages. He's got to deal with politicians."

"So what do we do now?" Katz asked.

"We wait," Rabe said and started walking down the hall towards the stairwell.

Katz walked with him, but let him think about whatever he was thinking about. At the end of the hall, Rabe waited a second and stood still. He looked at the stairway door to wherever and whatever he had just sent his men. After a few seconds, he turned around and walked back up the hall, lost in thought. Katz kept him company. Almost all the way back, Rabe turned to him.

"The guy who died, at the District Building?"

"Yeah?" Katz said.

Rabe shook his head.

"He was just a kid, black guy, a reporter, with the Afro-American, the negro newspaper?"

Katz froze in this tracks. His only black friend at GW was a reporter for the Afro-American. John Benton then, Johnny B when he tried to help Katz figure out who killed Brenda Queen at the Howard the night Dr. King died. He made himself ask the question he didn't want Rabe to answer.

"What was his name?" he said. "Do you have the name?"

Rabe eyed him curiously, then fished the pad out of his shirt pocket. Katz aged a thousand years waiting for him to find the page.

"Williams. Maurice Williams," Rabe said finally. "You know him?"

Katz reached out and braced himself against the wall.

"No," he said. "I don't. I'm sorry to hear that."

"Twenty-two," Rabe said. "His whole life in front of him, then gone. And for what? Why?" He shook his head. "Got off the elevator with another guy just when they started firing. Killed him, clipped Barry, the other guy walks away. What can you say? Wrong place at the wrong time."

Katz pictured Johnny B laying there dead. His head was swimming.

"Hey," Rabe barked at him.

"What?" Katz asked.

"I almost forgot. I got something for you. Come on."

They walked to the table where Bohlinger sat. Rabe picked up a manila folder at the other end and held it out for Katz.

"That girl who works with you? She left this for you. The rest of the stuff from Baltimore about his nibs upstairs."

Katz grabbed the folder and flipped it open. It was about two inches thick.

"I just riffled through it," Rabe said. "Lot of medical mumbo-jumbo."

"What's it say?" Katz asked.

"Same thing, fifty ways," Rabe said. "He's nuts."

17

Katz shuffled down the hall a few steps, took a seat on the tiles with a grunt, and leaned against the wall. He found the strength to push his soggy shirt sleeve up enough to see his watch. 7:37. He closed his eyes and took a deep breath, then another.

He woke with a start to see the papers in the folder Marty left for him spilling across his lap and down the floor to his right. He got himself to his knees and slid them back into the folder, then fell back against the wall with a louder groan than he expected.

He glanced over to the table. Rabe sat with his back to him, but Bohlinger was staring at him, slowly shaking his head. Katz started to give him the finger but decided to save his strength. His sleeve was stuck to his arm right where he left it. The watch said 7:45. He hoped an eight-minute nap would be enough to keep him going long enough for wherever this thing was headed.

He flipped the stack over and tried to concentrate on what he read. The first papers were part of the bank extortion case the Maryland USA. decided to nolle prosse, in 1970. He skimmed through a long letter from a doctor who had talked to Khaalis. Katz tried to look for anything that might have anything to do with today.

Khaalis told the doctor that he'd been locked up in mental hospitals because of "a nervous condition that I had at that time" that he said was brought on by "being a Negro in the United States." The doctor said Khaalis "presents himself as one who is sane but put upon, even to the point of persecution. What insight he does have has been distorted in the service of the illness, so that in order to relieve his symptoms, he increases the abnormal mental content. This is very typical of the paranoiac course until a sudden explosive outbreak occurs."

Katz sat up straight and started to read every word.

"Because of the marked compartmentalizing of the mental functions, this patient is able to do any number of activities or hold any number of abnormal ideas without overtly being disturbed by contradictions. For an example, he is quite capable at any time of criminal activity and at the same time, protesting his passionate attachment to truth and justice. He may have any number of abnormal ideas, carefully hidden, and even though those do not at all coincide with reality, he can be unaware of the discrepancy and undisturbed by it. The course of such paranoia is very unpredictable. I believe this patient is a potential danger to himself and others."

"At some time," the doctor wrote, "this patient will no longer be able to blame his illness on this nation, the law, the police or various branches of government, on racial injustice and intolerance, on the immediate circumstances which he now finds himself in. At some time, somewhere he will be forced to confront the real nature of his illness. It is at this time that we may expect an explosive reaction, most likely an immediate one. The fact is that no matter what hardships the patient has endured, whether any at all or a great deal, they have nothing to do with his mental illness, which is that of a paranoid state or possibly paranoid schizophrenia."

Katz tried to take that all in. The guy had hit it right on the head that Khaalis might go off anytime, anywhere, but he wasn't too sure his hardships had nothing to do with his craziness.

He tried to put himself in Khaalis' shoes. What if he hadn't been blessed with the parents he had, with a community that at least tolerated Jews, and with a dream that his parents drummed into him incessantly that, in America, he could grow up and be anyone he wanted to be?

What if that dream was a lie? What if he was stifled at every turn, kept out of schools, out of jobs, out of the life he dreamed just because of the religion he was born into – or

151

the color of his skin? At least Jews could hide their religion, change their names, do what they needed to do to escape the hatred. What could Khaalis do to hide the skin color he was born into? What would Katz do if he were Khaalis?

For a second, he felt the chill of the despair and the futility that Khaalis felt for his entire life. Even for that one second, he had no doubt it could drive him crazy enough to do anything, even what Khaalis was doing now.

In September, 1970 another doctor gave his opinion on whether Khaalis could understand the proceedings against him, if they did bring him to trial. "Speech is pressured, forceful, intense, colorful, and continually involved with his religion, which is Muslim," he wrote. "There is looseness of association with continued hinting of some special power."

Khaalis thought the FBI was jerking him around by addressing their letters to Ernest McGhee, not Hamaas Khaalis. He told the doctor he knew his folder was on desk of President Nixon, who knew everything about his case. He said he had called President Kennedy collect and asked to see him immediately because he was in danger; he was dead two weeks later. People are forcing him to be quiet but he would never do anything to harm anybody. He often speaks of himself in the third person.

The doctor felt that he could understand the proceedings, but "his interpretation of them becomes delusional because they're out to get him because of 'Hamaas' great powers and knowledge.' Though he is delusional and grandiose, he does not appear at present so disorganized or dangerous to himself or others that he requires commitment to a mental hospital." His diagnosis: "Schizophrenia, paranoid type."

The next papers all seemed to be from the '60s. He read what Khaalis told a psychiatrist in early 1963.

"I find it very impossible to live a myth because of skin power in this country, and as a citizen of this country it is unjust and absolutely wrong. This is the main complaint that I have and that affects my outlook objectively and subjectively, and I say that the root of this commences from the time I volunteered for the services and was denied entrance in the Marine Corps because they did not take what they called Negroes in the Marines. I volunteered for the Navy, and was told I could go as a mess boy. For my country, think of that, complaints that lie not only with me, but half of this country. How can you tell a man just by the skin, I want to know? And this because of my service connected disability which has caused erratic employment and hardship for my family, and an attitude that has affected my entire way of life in this country, which is my country."

He told the doctor the government had deceived him even earlier. "While at Purdue University I was denied to enter the ROTC because I was a Negro. The government wants me and my family to live in a myth. America is a myth. It does not exist."

The shrink asked him about his treatment in the Army. Khaalis said "In the Army I was like a lion in a cage. On one occasion I had to ride in the box car with chickens because Negroes were not allowed to ride in coaches with the white men. I belonged to Islam because there are no colored lines, all men are equal, and teach that all men came from Adam."

The last sentence of the report said "He has no plans for the future because 'America is a volcano swept under the rug and some day it will explode." His diagnosis was "Schizophrenic reaction, in partial remission, competent."

In 1965, he was examined again, by the Veterans Administration. This doctor said he was "alert, friendly and in good contact. His big complaint is that 'he is disgusted with America – social injustice'." His diagnosis: "Schizophrenic reaction chronic, undifferentiated type. Incapacity moderate to marked. Competent."

153

The next papers were from the '40s and '50s. In late 1952, Khaalis told a doctor that his condition was not psychiatric but the fault of society. "He said he hated white people," the doctor wrote, "but also expressed contempt for many Negroes. He said the Negro employees at the VA seemed happy and content, and he felt that they were traitors and he had no desire to be like them." The doctor noted that he did speak warmly of his wife, Khadyia. "If it were not for her he did not know what he would do." This doctor too diagnosed him as "schizophrenic reaction, paranoid type."

In August 1949, Khaalis told a VA doctor that he resents all social discrimination and what he called the "caste system". The doctor wrote "his ideas of personal and racial persecution are extreme and he becomes upset at what he reads in the newspapers."

The last sheaf of papers dealt with his discharge from the Army, in 1944. He scanned the page for the reason why and was not surprised to read "Psychosis - dementia praecox – paranoid." He flipped the page to a doctor's report of his session with Khaalis in June of that year.

The report went on about his nightmares, his laughing for no reason, the voices he heard, his feeling that he was a lone wolf. The doctor recommended that he be sent to a VA facility.

Katz was just about to close the file when he saw that Khaalis made his statement under something called "narcosynthesis". He scanned the page for some explanation of what that was, but found only a footnote that said "The drug used in this treatment was in 10 cc of distilled water injected intravenously." The drug was not identified.

Katz thought back to the time his old college roommate Andy Scheingold offered him some "unbelievable shit" that was supposedly on a sugar cube sitting on a piece of aluminum foil in his hand. Katz turned him down, but about ten minutes later he found Schein sprawled across the red couch they had bought from Goodwill, telling him how

154

"it all fits, man, it all fits." When it was all still fitting about two hours later, Katz started to get worried and asked him what was on the cube.

"LSD, man," he told him. "I'm trippin'."

He remembered running to the Encyclopedia Britannica in his bedroom to look it up. He didn't remember much of what he read, but he did remember his surprise to read that, way before the government banned it, the Army actually used it during World War Two for some kind of therapeutic purpose. Was that the narcosynthesis Khaalis underwent? Was that a bad trip that still screwed him up today?

That was the last paper in the folder. Katz closed it, leaned his back against the wall, and closed his eyes. There was no chance he'd fall asleep now. His mind was dealing with a thousand questions.

Which came first, the discrimination that consumed Khaalis, or the paranoia? Maybe it wasn't paranoia at all. Like Rabe said this morning, it's not paranoia if they're really after you.

Whatever caused or didn't cause the other one, what was it like to live with both of them as a fixture in his life, day after day, year after year?

What did they give Khaalis in the Army, and did it make a bad situation even worse? Was the government somehow responsible for today, giving him a drug they now say is dangerous enough to ban?

When Khaalis came home to find his family murdered, what did that do to his already fragile mental condition?

Could any of the answers to those questions tell him, or anyone, why this was happening? And at this point, did it even matter?

Katz struggled to his feet.

We're here, he thought, and the only question that needs answering now is how do we get these people out of here alive.

He turned at the sound of a door opening at the bottom of the stairwell. A cop in riot gear came through first, then two ladies, crying and clinging to each other.

Hostages were coming down.

18

Rabe and Bohlinger ran past him. The short black cop who asked Rabe about shooting someone was holding the stairwell door open. The first two women squeezed through together, holding each other's hand. Rabe came to them and wrapped them in his arms. They cried into his chest. In a few seconds, a third and a fourth woman appeared, then one of the cops.

"That's everyone that was up on three," he told Rabe.

"Outstanding," Rabe said. "No sign of the bad guys?"

"None," the cop said.

"Well done," Rabe said.

He squeezed the women tighter. The one in his left arm, tall with long, matted black hair, looked at him, her dark eyes tired and glossy, but wide with wonder.

"You're like a dream," she told him, "after a nightmare."

"Thank you, thank you, thank you," the other one said, her head still pressed to Rabe's chest, her face hidden by a sweaty nest of dark brown hair.

Rabe kept his arms tight around them and rocked them a little. When they caught eyes, Katz gave him a thumbs up. Rabe held them a little longer, then moved his hands up to their shoulders.

"Ladies," he asked, "can you tell me just a little about what happened to you up there?"

The lady with the brown hair pushed back the strands stuck to her forehead.

"It was a nightmare, like she said. An absolute nightmare."

"What happened in the beginning?," Rabe asked. "Take me back."

"About eleven this morning – what time is it now?," she asked.

"A little after eight," Rabe said.

"Oh, my God," she said. "So we were up there, what, nine hours?"

She shook her head in amazement.

"Okay," she said, "so I was at my desk, in the accounting department, and right about eleven, I hear all this glass breaking out front. I run out of my office to see what's going on, and there's a man out there with a gun – a long gun! – and he's yelling, 'Get out, get out, everybody get out!,' so I got out. I ran to the insurance office next door where these other ladies were. After a few hours, forever, I really don't remember when, we heard a phone ring and we were all too scared to pick it up, but it went on and on, so finally, I picked it up and it was you, one of you, a policeman. He told us what was going on and told us to sit tight – on the floor, away from any windows – so that's what we did."

"And did you hear anyone, see anyone after that?," Rabe asked.

"No," she said, and turned to look at the other woman, her head down, still clinging to Rabe's arm.

"Elizabeth, are you all right?"

Elizabeth lifted her head and managed a weak smile.

"Yes, thank God," she said, then faced Rabe. "I called my husband. We all called our houses, just once, to let everyone know we were okay, but that was it. The rest of the time we just talked to each other, whispering that this was like a movie or a TV show or something. We started to talk about what might happen sometimes. But not too much. We were scared, in shock, you know? I just told the three other women, if you know how to pray, pray."

"Okay, do you feel all right?" Rabe asked. "Both of you."

The black-haired lady shrugged.

"I am just so happy to be down here, that's all I know. Can I call my husband? He's going to be a wreck."

Rabe pointed at the cops still standing by the stairwell.

"These gentlemen are going to take you over to the Gramercy Inn just up the block. There's phones and coffee, cookies. You can call your families and let them know you're out of harm's way. We're going to get your names and phone numbers so we can contact you after we're through with all this. There are also some medics up there who're going to check you over. If they say you're okay, you're free to go. If you're not, we'll take you to GW and let them look you over. Okay?"

"God bless you," Elizabeth said, then turned to the two cops who brought them down. "All of you."

Rabe walked the four women over to the cops, then walked with all of them to an exit door down the hall. The black cop pushed it open. Katz watched Rabe hug each lady before she left, then wait to wave them goodbye. He pulled the door closed, then hustled back up the hallway towards Katz. Katz marveled at him.

"Where do you get the energy?" he said. "I can barely stand up."

"Clean living," Rabe said, moving past him. "You got enough left to talk with me to this Khan?"

"Talking I can do."

Rabe kept moving and Katz followed, around the corner and all the way up to Bohlinger.

"Those were the guys from three," Rabe told him. "They brought down four women. I want you to grab a detail of guys and go back there and wait for the rest of them to come down. Send all of 'em out the back door over to the Gramercy. You don't have to take down anyone's names, they'll do that over there. Just keep score of how many they bring down so we can tally 'em up later. You got it?"

"I got it," Bohlinger said and threw him a salute. He picked up his yellow pad and scurried down the hall.

"Take a seat," Rabe told Katz. "I'll call Cully."

159

He didn't need to ask him twice. Katz plopped onto a brown metal chair, stifling most of the grunt this time.

Rabe dialed the phone. In a second, he said, "Cully?", then put him on the speaker phone and took a seat across the table from Katz.

"Bob, you hear me?" they heard.

"We hear you, chief," Rabe said. "I got Mr. Katz here, the lawyer from the USA's? It's just me and him."

"Okay, that's good," Cullinane said. "His boss is here with me and the mayor. Did you get anyone out?"

"Yeah," Rabe said and brought him up to speed.

"All right," Cullinane said. "Sounds good. Just so you know, a bunch of the relatives, friends, what have you, might be at the Methodist church, over on 16th Street, the Foundry? You might want to send someone over there to bring them up to speed too at some point, let them know who's out."

"Roger," Rabe said. "Will do. So, the Ambassador, Mr. Zahedi, is he still there?"

"Yes. Let me put you on the speaker so he can join in."

Katz heard a couple of clicks, then nothing, then Cullinane again.

"Bob, can you hear us?" he said. The shrill echo of his voice made it almost unintelligible. Katz put his hands up over his ears and winced at Rabe.

"Hey, Cully," Rabe said, "try it again. You sound like you're trapped in a mine or something."

They heard the line go dead a few more times, then click back to life.

"How's this?" Cullinane said. He was just a little tinny this time, and a little clearer.

"Good enough," Rabe said. "So what's the plan?"

"That's what we're trying to figure out. Mr. Zahedi's still here with me, and now we also have Mr. Ghorbal here. He's the Ambassador from Egypt."

160

"Call me Ashraf," Katz heard someone say in a clipped, formal tone.

"And," another voice said, "I am Ardeshir Zahedi, the Ambassador from Iran you talked to before? I would be pleased as well if you would call me by my first name, but I will answer to Mr. Zahedi too, whichever you prefer."

"Thank you, Mr. Zahedi," Rabe said. "We really appreciate both of you trying to help us out."

"And also," Zahedi said, "I should mention Mr. Khan, the Ambassador from Pakistan. He too is willing to help and should be here shortly."

"Well, that's great," Rabe said. "So how do you all see this playing out?"

"We want to kick that around with you, Bob," Cullinane said. "See what you think before we decide on anything."

"Well, let me ask you this," Rabe said. "Do any of you know Mr. Khaalis? Mr. Katz here does, from the murders. He prosecuted the guys who killed his family and so he has a relationship with him from that."

"That's right," Katz cut in. "But it's not always a good relationship."

He heard chuckles on the other end.

"Not to worry, Mr. Katz," Ghorbal said, "each of us knows him well, as does Yaqub, Mr. Khan."

"How do you know him?" Rabe asked.

"From the Hanafi Center and the murders, of course," Zahedi said, "but also from the Islamic Center. Each of us is a member of the Board of Directors there, where we have come to know him, probably more than we would like."

"He is not the easiest person to get along with, we are well aware," Ghorbal chimed in.

Rabe shot Katz a curious look. Katz thought back to what Abdul-Aziz told him about Khaalis not getting the $16 million that Rauf got from the Muslims in the Middle East. He rubbed his thumb against his fingers.

161

"Money," he mouthed. Rabe nodded he got it.

"So what are you gentlemen thinking?" he asked.

"Well, the main thing," Zahedi said, "is that you permit us to talk to him on the phone, and counsel him as to what the Qur'an and the Hadith – the commentaries of the scholars – say about this situation he has created."

"No offense," Rabe said, "and I'm sorry I'm so ignorant about this, but he's been telling everybody that everything he's done is square with the Koran. I don't want him to start lobbing heads down the stairs because you fellas stir him up by telling him he's got it all wrong. You see my point?"

"We see your point, Mr. Rabe, trust me," Zahedi said. "His interpretation of what our faith tells him to do in these horrible circumstances – I am referring now to the slaughter of his family – is not an unreasonable one. Our Qur'an is much like your Bible. You can select a passage somewhere that will justify any position you want to take. But, there are also other passages that may better convey the spirit of the book, of the faith, you see? So we would like to educate him a little about some of those words, have him reflect, consider that the Qur'an gives him the guidance to bring this matter to an end, with no further killing. That is our desire, and yours too, no?"

Rabe put his hand over the speaker.

"What do you think?" he asked Katz. "Anything I should be asking him?"

Katz recalled Khaalis mocking him as so good with the words. This guy was better, and a Muslim, to boot. He looked at Rabe and shook his head.

"Can't think of a thing, except when can he start?"

"It sounds good to us, Mr. Zahedi," Rabe told him. "Cully, how do you want to go about gettin' 'em started?"

"How do you want to start?" they heard Cullinane ask them.

"Can we talk to him now?" Ghorbal said.

162

Rabe looked at his watch. Katz looked at it too. It was almost 8:30.

"I'd like to wait just a little bit," Rabe said, "until everyone we sent up to the other floors comes down okay. I can't give you an exact time, but once they come back, I'll call over to the Holiday Inn and make sure everything's cool upstairs. As soon as I get the word from them, I'll call you. That work?"

In a few seconds, Cullinane said "That works. Get back to us as soon as you can."

Rabe clicked off the speaker.

Katz heard a door swing open down the hall behind him. He turned and saw Rabe rush past him. In a second he saw why and summoned up the energy to catch up to him.

It was like the Exodus, he thought, but with a police escort this time. A parade of men and women, most of them old, but some of them maybe as young as twenty, streamed through the door. Katz watched as each of them tiptoed to the bottom of the steps, then hustled through the door as fast as they could. They hugged each other, burst into tears, and cried their thanks to God in English, Hebrew, and Yiddish.

His mother could have been one of them. Katz winced at the memory of her passing, then broke into sobs himself when one of the ladies leaped at him and clung to him for dear life. He hugged her back even tighter, closing his eyes and feeling his mother in his arms one more time.

Finally, he kissed her on the top of her head and let her go. He wiped the tears from his eyes and stole a look at Rabe. He was misty too, hugging one after another of them as they made their way past him on the way to the door. Katz was grateful for the cover and let his own tears flow.

He held the arm of a wispy gray-haired woman and walked her slowly back to a cop at the door. One after another, they came by him, patting his hand or his cheek in thanks or stopping to hug him and be hugged one more time

163

before reaching for a policeman's hand to help them take the last step out of hell.

Rabe parked himself by the door and counted the cops on the walkway and in the hall out loud. When he got to eight, he turned to Katz.

"Everyone accounted for," he said. "Job well done."

When they were all out of sight, Katz couldn't tell if he'd been there five minutes or five hours. He stole a look at his watch. 8:49. This Exodus hadn't even taken twenty minutes.

Katz followed Rabe back to the table. Rabe found the number for the Holiday Inn scribbled on Bohlinger's pad, and dialed it up. After one ring, Katz heard a muffled voice on the other end.

"Yeah" Rabe said. "How do things look across the way?"

He looked at Katz while he listened, then said, "Okay. I got off the phone with Cullinane a little bit ago. He's got some Ambassadors, Muslims, that want to try to talk some sense to our boy, now. I told him I'd call him back after we cleared the other floors and I talked to you."

Rabe paused, then said, "Yeah, as many as we could find. Thirty, forty, I don't know, I lost count. So, Khaalis, is he up?"

He listened again and nodded to Katz. Katz covered a yawn with his hand and tried to focus.

"Do you see a problem if they call now?" Rabe asked. "Any reason to think that'd unhinge him any more than he already is?"

He nodded no. Katz gave him another thumbs up.

"Okay, I'll let them know," Rabe said. "If you see anything going on while he's across the hall, let me know and I'll cut them off in a heartbeat. 10-4."

He put down the phone and looked at Katz.

"All right," he told him. "He says he's up and chitter-chatting with his boys and the hostages every once in a while.

He doesn't see a problem, so I'm going to let Cullinane give them a shot. You see anything I'm missing here?"

"No," Katz said, then yawned again. "I just hope they can do what they say."

Rabe stared at him.

"You look like hell," he said. "You need to go home and get some sleep."

"If you can handle it, I can handle it," Katz said.

"No, you can't," Rabe said. "I got a cot here where I can catch a few z's anytime I want, and I ain't sharin' it with you, trust me on that one. Go home."

His bed, with Marty in it, flashed through Katz's brain. He was tired and he was tempted, but he wanted to stay and see it through.

"Let me stay for a while," he said. "If I fade, you'll be the first to know, I promise."

"Okay, but unless these guys can sprinkle some pixie dust over this thing tonight, I'm going to need you to be fresh for tomorrow, so you need to sack out some, okay?"

He wasn't looking for an answer so Katz didn't bother giving him one.

Rabe dialed the phone and put it back on speaker. They didn't hear a ring before Cullinane picked it up.

"Bob?" he said.

"Yeah," Rabe said. "Okay, you and your pals can give it a try. A whole raft of them came down a few minutes ago, maybe thirty or forty. They'll get a count over at the Gramercy, names, everything."

"That's great, Bob!" Cullinane said. "Nice to have some good news finally. How about Khaalis? What do you hear?"

"He's awake," Rabe said, "and things seem to be cool, so if you want to put the Ambassadors on with him, go ahead."

"All right, we'll call him up. Same number, right?"

"Here's the one we've been using." Rabe read it to him.

"Okay, same one we've got," Cullinane said. "Anything else before we dial him up?"

"Just keep him calm as you can," Rabe said. "We'll be listening in."

"Roger," Cullinane said and the line went dead.

Rabe stood up and stretched. Katz saw Bohlinger coming towards them down the hall but ignored him. When he got to the table, Rabe asked him a question.

"What religion are you?"

"Me?," Bohlinger said. "I'm a Protestant, Lutheran. Why?"

"Between you, me, Katz, and the guys calling Khaalis, we've got it covered," Rabe said. "Say a prayer like you mean it."

19

Katz heard the phone ring, then ring again and again. He counted fifteen before he heard someone pick up.

"Yes?" the voice said.

"Mr. Khaalis?" he heard Cullinane ask.

"Who is this? Who wishes to speak to him?" It was Khaalis, but his voice was raspy and tired.

"This is Chief Cullinane."

"Ah," Khaalis said. "The big boss. But where is Mr. Deputy Chief Rabe? Where is Mr. Katz the Hebrew lawyer? Has Khaalis tired them out? Have they gone home to sleep in their comfortable little beds?"

"No, Mr. Khaalis," Cullinane said. "They're actually on the line, listening in --"

"Of course they are," Khaalis interrupted. "That is what you do. You listen to my phones. Khaalis has not made a phone call for years without you or Mr. Hoover or Mr. Carter or one of your agents listening to me."

Rabe looked at Katz and twirled his finger around his temple.

"Do you think I did not know this?" Khaalis went on. "How did you ever become Chief, Mr. Cullinane? By being so honest or so stupid?"

Cullinane ignored the insult.

"Bob," he said, "are you on? Can you hear us?"

"We can hear you," Rabe said. "Do you want us on mute so we don't muck up the line?"

"Mute is good," Khaalis said. "Mute is perfect. Khaalis has heard enough from Mr. Deputy Rabe begging him to be a good boy and Mr. Katz boring him with his little fantasies. I beg you to be mute. Enjoy the privilege of listening to Khaalis."

Rabe pushed the mute button.

"I'd rather have a hemorrhoid," he said. Katz laughed out loud.

"Mr. Khaalis," Cullinane said. "I have three gentlemen with me here who would like to talk to you, the ambassadors from Egypt, Iran, and Pakistan. They say they know you and --"

"They do not know me!" Khaalis roared, now in full and firm voice. "But I know them. They are the thieving fakirs who stole my money. Dr. Rauf is only their puppet. They pull his strings!"

Another voice came over the line.

"Mr. Cullinane, please, may I?" he said.

"Please," Cullinane said. "Be my guest."

"Mr. Khaalis, Hamaas, this is Ardeshir Zahedi, the Ambassador from Iran?"

"I know who you are," Khaalis said with a sneer that Katz could picture. "You are the false worshipper who sleeps with the Jewess Elizabeth Taylor. Do I have the right Ambassador Zahedi, or is there another one?"

"What the hell's he talking about?" Rabe asked Katz.

Katz had lost track of who Elizabeth Taylor was sleeping with. He knew Eddie Fisher, he knew Richard Burton, but he never heard of her and Zahedi. He just shrugged.

A faint chuckle came over the line.

"Hamaas," Zahedi said, "if I may call you that, sir. Yes, I am a good friend to Miss Taylor but --"

"You may not call me that!" Khaalis roared. "You are an infidel who makes love to a harlot Hebrew. You may call me only Khalifa Khaalis."

"Well, this is going great," Rabe said.

The silence on the phone seemed to last for minutes until Katz heard a different voice.

"Khalifa Khaalis. This is Ashraf Ghorbal, the Ambassador from Egypt. Before you say anything, please allow me to speak just for a minute. I do know you, and you know me. We have talked to each other at the Islamic Center several times, I am sure you remember. I am here – all of us

168

are here – to listen to you, and to hope that you may listen to us as well. We are not agents of the United States, or the police, or anyone who has caused you any harm. We are just coming to you as brothers in Islam, to discuss with you what the Qur'an and the Hadith say about what you are doing. Can we do that, Khalifa?"

"Are you through now?" Khaalis asked. "Do you permit me to speak now?"

"Please," Ghorbal said.

"Yes," Khaalis said, "I do remember talking to you at the Islamic Center, listening to your pious words, your smooth soothing talk. But I don't remember hearing from you – or from any of you! – after my family was wiped out. Where were you then? Where have you been since? Did this finally get your attention?"

"Khalifa, if I may," Ghorbal said, "I did pass on my deepest condolences to you and your family, when we met several years ago, and the thought of their loss is always with me when we meet. How could it not be?"

"Words," Khaalis replied, "mere words. Tell me, Mr. Ambassador, did you think of me when you and your cronies gave Dr. Rauf his sixteen million dollars? Where were you then, huh?"

"That's the money you meant from the last call?" Rabe asked Katz. Katz nodded.

No one answered so Khaalis stormed on.

"Where were you, huh? I am the true servant of Allah in this country, not Mr. Rauf and his money-hungry charlatan friends! I have been the oppressed all my life! I saw the light and turned away from the darkness. Elijah Poole tried to gun me down just like he did Malcolm, but he couldn't find me, so what did he do, huh? He gunned down my children, my babies! So where were you then, huh? Your soft little words supposed to heal all that? How about some recognition of who am *I* am, what *I* mean to people, what *I* came from? Doesn't that deserve a little more than

169

your so-called kind words? I'm the one who knows the seven ways to destroy the world and the seven ways to save it, not you, not any of them, me! So where's mine, huh? A pile of dead bodies, gone and forgotten forever, is that mine, huh? Just that?"

Katz and Rabe sat dead quiet. Katz stared at the wall across from him. He had heard, read a cry like that somewhere before. Job? Somewhere else in the Bible? Then it came to him. College, his American Drama class, sophomore year. Willy Loman. Death of a Salesman. "Attention must be paid!"

But that was fiction. This was real life.

Another man's voice cracked the stillness.

"Hamaas," he said, "I was not in this country when you suffered your tragedy, but I have also met you and expressed my profound grief at your loss. Yaqub Khan, from Pakistan, do you remember me?"

"Yes, General Khan, I do remember you, and you I respect. You are a true fighter for Allah, a warrior on the battlefield. You know my cause is just, my heart pure. You must!"

"I have no doubts, Hamaas, none at all," Khan said. "But, you know, I am no longer a soldier."

"I did not know that," Khaalis said.

"Yes," Khan said, "I am no longer a General. I resigned my post. Did you hear this?"

"I did not."

Katz had never heard Khaalis say anything so short. He waited for more, and Khan must have too, because he paused before continuing.

"Let me explain it to you then," he said, "as briefly and clearly as I can. You know that before Bangladesh was liberated by the Indians in 1971, it was East Pakistan. In our elections the year before that, one of the parties won almost all the votes in East Pakistan and another party won in the West. The head of the party that won the East, which is

170

almost all Bengalis, was supposed to be the Prime Minister, but the head of the West Pakistan party refused to accept his role as the leader of an opposition party and got our President to postpone the National Assembly, our Congress, if you will, from meeting. The head of the Bengalis then stirred up an unrest that the government wanted to put down, quickly and without mercy. You understand so far?"

"I understand," Khaalis said.

"So the President directed me to lead the assault against them," Khan went on, "an unarmed populace that was only seeking the country to do the will of the voters. I could not in good conscience do so, so I resigned."

"I am sorry to hear that, Mr. Ambassador," Khaalis said.

"I was sorry too," Khan said, "but I did not believe that my faith, our faith, permitted me to kill innocents. So, now we are back to you, yes?"

"Back to me?" Khaalis said, the shock obvious in his voice. "How are we back to me? There are no innocents here! These Jews are deceivers, blasphemers! You puppet masters at the Islamic Center stole from me what was rightly mine! Those politicians won't let me do justice to the wolves who slaughtered my family!"

"Khalifa --," Khan tried to interrupt, but it was too late.

"Exactly who are the innocents here, I ask you – except me?" Khaalis spat at him. "I'm the righteous Muslim brother who has tried to live his life according to the holy law, who has taught our brothers and sisters how to observe the faith! When does Khaalis get his justice, huh, answer me that?"

The sound of the phone smacking down on its cradle told them he wasn't waiting for the answer.

"Bob, give us a call," Cullinane sighed, and hung up.

Rabe hung up, then dialed him back.

"Not too good a start, huh?" Cullinane said.

"No," Rabe agreed. "Not good."

"What do you think? Should we let him cool down a little, try him again in a little bit?"

Rabe glanced at his watch.

"You know, it's just about 9:30," he said. "I don't know if it's going to do anyone any good if we talk to him again tonight. He's tired and fed up, we're tired and fed up. We've got him under surveillance from across the street. I think we ought to give everyone a rest, get some sleep. Maybe the world will look a little different to him tomorrow. That's what I think, anyhow."

"Hold on a minute," Cullinane said. Katz heard him ask the Ambassadors what they thought. It was a short conversation.

"Okay," Cullinane said. "We're all in agreement. We'll stand down and give it another shot tomorrow morning – but if you see anything over there before then, you'll let me know asap, okay?"

"10-4," Rabe said. "If everything's cool, we'll talk what, 0700?"

"I'll be here," Cullinane sighed again. "Have a good night's sleep, Bob. You earned it. Good job there."

"You too, Chief. I'll talk to you then."

Rabe put down the phone and looked at Katz.

"You look worse than I feel. Go home."

Katz put up no fight this time.

"I'm going. 0700 right here?"

"Yeah," Rabe said. "I'll have someone pick you up. Where do you live?"

Katz gave him his address on East Capitol.

"Look for a black and white outside about five of," Rabe said. "I'll let you sleep in."

He smiled and stretched out a hand. Katz shook it.

"I can't say it's been a pleasure," he said, "but it's been great working with you, watching you. They'd have to invent you if you weren't around, honestly."

172

"You done good too, Mr. Katz," Rabe said and picked up his walkie-talkie. "I'll get you a ride home. Look for him up on the street. Get some rest and we'll go at it again tomorrow."

Katz slogged up the steps and saw a cop by a cruiser at the curb wave him over. He got in the passenger seat, let his head fall back, closed his eyes, and saw the million sights of the day swirl through his head. Then he saw nothing.

20

Katz came to when he heard a horn beep.

"What?" he said, then tried to figure out who he was saying it to. A cop in the driver's seat of a car turned to him.

"1524 East Capitol?"

"Yeah?" Katz said.

"That's where you live?,"

"Yeah," Katz remembered.

"Then you're home," the cop said.

Katz looked out the window to his right, then turned to the left. That was indeed where he lived. He had no idea how he got here. He bent his head up and saw the time on the dashboard. 21:37. It all came back to him.

He grabbed his briefcase, got out, and shut the door. The cruiser darted up to 16th St., hooked a quick right, and disappeared. He looked at the town house at 1524, then down to the door to the walk-in basement where he and Marty lived in sin, his mother would have called it. Shacked up, they called it. She still had her place in Southwest, but this was becoming their place, a little bit more every day.

He went down the half set of stairs. Behind the door, the hallway light was on. He reached into his pocket for the keys, but before he could pull them out, the door flew open.

"You're home! Oh, my poor baby!"

Marty hugged him hard at the doorstep, then clung to him as he trudged down the hall and veered into the living room to the left. He saw the sofa, and sprawled all over it.

"I'll be fine," he said. "Just let me die here."

He felt Marty tugging his suit coat off. He did his best to help her without moving, or opening his eyes. When it came off, he groaned his thanks. He felt her sit next to him and rub his back.

"Was as it as bad as it looks?" she asked.

"No," he said. "Worse."

After a minute, he made himself roll over. She helped him lift his legs and laid them across her lap. He heard the TV set for the first time and turned his head to look at it. A TV reporter was talking from Mass Avenue in front of the Islamic Center. The TV cut to footage of a thin young woman being led by two police officers across a stone courtyard. A man ran up from the sidewalk to hug her. The camera got in closer and Katz recognized her.

"Hey!" he said. "I know her! She was one of the hostages. I saw her in the outer office, sitting behind the desk."

The TV reporter said, "That happened just a few minutes ago. The name of the released woman is Mushk Ara. That was her father she was being reunited with after more than fourteen hours in captivity. Mr. Ara works for the Bangladesh Embassy. Here's what he had to say."

On their black and white set, they saw the face of a middle-aged, dark-skinned man, his hair cut close to his scalp, hugging his daughter tightly.

"I thank God for her release," he said into the microphone, tears coating his eyes. "She just started working here last week, and this had to happen. It is only by the grace of God that they let her go."

"Do you know why they decided to release her?" a man's voice asked.

"I called them, I kept calling them," Mr. Ara said. "I told them, she is a young girl, she is from Bangladesh, she has nothing to do with these local events. No, no, no, they told me every time. And then, just a few minutes ago, they called *me*, at my house, and they told me 'You can take your daughter,' so I called the police and now she is free. I am most grateful, most grateful."

He hugged his daughter even tighter.

"Gee," Marty said, "what a prince of a guy that Khaalis is. You guys have him all wrong."

175

"You're right," he said. "Call Rabe, tell him I'm not coming in tomorrow."

She asked him for the latest, and he told her. When he got to the part about the cops going up the stairs to get whoever wasn't on eight, he saw her steal a look at her watch.

"What?" he asked. "Enough already?"

"No, it's not that," she said. "I want to hear all about it, but I need to tell you something, a couple of things actually."

"What?" he asked.

"You got a call a couple of hours ago."

"From who?"

She reached for the message pad next to the phone on the white Parsons table at the other end of the sofa.

"Mike Davidson," she read. "Ring a bell?"

Katz barely remembered his own name.

"I give," he said. "Who's Mike Davidson?"

"The guy from the Criminal Division?" she said. "United States Department of Justice? He called you at the office this afternoon?"

Katz peeled away all the other memories of the day and focused in on that one.

"Right," he said. "I remember now."

"Well," Marty said, "he called back. Here, tonight."

He sat up and grabbed the note from her hand.

"So what did he say?" he asked.

Marty's face seemed to redden a bit. If he didn't know better, he'd swear she was embarrassed, but Marty didn't embarrass, ever, about anything.

"Okay," she said, "well, he didn't want to leave a message. At first."

"At first," Katz said.

"Yeah," she said, "at first. But then he did."

Marty could be very persuasive, Katz thought, but he didn't know she could do it over the phone.

176

"Okay," he said. "Out with it. Let's go."

"I told him he could leave me the message, because I was your wife."

When Katz recovered the power of speech, he got to his feet as quickly as he could manage.

"You told him you were my wife," he said. "Let me put it another way. You lied to a Federal attorney – in the Criminal Division, no less – that you were my wife?"

Marty seemed to resent his tone. She crossed her arms across her chest.

"Calm down, Jake!" she snapped. "It's a good thing I did because if I didn't, neither one of us would know something now that we've both been wanting to know, real bad."

He took a deep breath.

"Okay, I'm sorry," he said. "Tell me."

Marty crossed her legs and made him wait another few seconds. When she felt he'd waited long enough, she told him.

"I told him I was your wife," she said," and that I was worried sick about you because you were at the B'nai B'rith Building trying to get the hostages out. He went crazy, asking me what you were doing, saying how brave you must be, how cool that was, etcetera, etcetera. And then he said he was happy to give me some news that would brighten up your day."

And then she stopped. Just to torture him.

"Marty, please," Katz pleaded, "Enough. I'm begging you."

A smile filled her face.

"They're offering you the job! Deputy Chief of Fraud!"

Then they were in an embrace, half-dancing, half-hopping across the floor together. He made happy noises he never knew he could make. Her kisses covered his face. In a minute, his body reminded him how tired he was. They collapsed together back on the sofa.

"Oh, wow! Oh, wow! Oh, wow!" Katz said. "I am freaking out!"

She hugged him tight around the waist and buried her face in his neck.

"I will call him back first thing in the morning!" he said. Then remembered his last conversation with Rabe.

"Oh, Christ!" he said. "Except they're picking me up at seven and God knows when I'm going to have any time after that."

Marty lifted her head.

"So call him now," she said.

"Now?" Katz said. "It's almost ten o'clock. How can I call him now?"

"Read the note," she said.

The note was on the floor. He picked it up.

'Call any time,' it read.

"I can't call him now," he said. "He's probably sleeping."

"Call him!" Marty said. "'Call any time' means call any time. Believe me, he'll want to hear from the conquering hero, tell everyone all about it tomorrow. He'll be the king of the water cooler. Call him!"

"Hold on," Katz said and pried himself loose from Marty's grip. "Let's just talk this through a minute, okay?"

"Okay," Marty said. "We'll talk it through. Go ahead."

Katz stood up. He felt like a toxic mixture of sweat and adrenaline. He didn't trust himself to think clearly this late at night, especially this night, but he did trust Marty. She was every bit as good as him at parsing through a tough case, and probably better when it came to a job decision. One time, in the heat of an argument, he called her a sour cherry. He apologized but he was right. She wasn't always sweet, but she was always sharp.

178

"Okay," he said. "Earl told me this morning he needs to know whether I'm going to take the Deputy Felony job, like asap."

"Okay," Marty said.

"That's such a great job," Katz said. "I'd give my right arm to get that. You would. Anybody would."

"Of course. We've talked about that," Marty said. "You're absolutely right – in normal circumstances. But these are not normal circumstances. You're in a once in a lifetime situation here. The U.S. Department of Justice, the biggest law firm in the country, is offering you a great job, and they're dying to get you – you! Jake Katz! – the man who's going to be on the front pages of the Post and the Star and the Daily News tomorrow. Tomorrow! This is your time, Jake. You need to take that job, honey."

"Okay, but Deputy of Felony in D.C.?," Katz said. "That's – "

Marty cut him off.

"*A* Deputy, Jake, not *the* Deputy. Earl's got two already, and you'd be number three. Who knows how many he's going to wind up creating, just to keep people like you from flying the coop, or going over to the other side, like Ernie Fucking Hutchison?"

Ernie Fucking Hutchison was a buddy of theirs who came to the USA's the same time they did, but took off last year to get the big bucks at a white collar defense firm on K St. Marty never forgave him. The Fucking was permanent as far as she was concerned.

"All right, all right," Katz said, "but, if I may, your honor, let's think about what I'd be doing here, with Earl. He got the first crack on Watergate, right? Anyone commits fraud here, I'm the one prosecuting them – Congressmen, Cabinet officials, anyone. This is Washington, DC. We're the home team for fraud."

"And who will you be prosecuting down the street at DOJ?" she challenged him. "The same guys, but

179

everywhere! And let's face it, ever since Earl and Watergate, they're going to take all the juicy cases popping here too for a good long while."

Katz' head was spinning again, big wide orbits in every direction, all at once.

"Jake, listen," Marty continued. "It's your call. You're the one who's going to have to live with whatever choice you make. I understand that, believe me. But just call him back tonight, so you don't lose the shot at DOJ. He's going to be over the moon hearing from you tonight, I promise you."

Katz was tired of arguing about it, tired of thinking about it. He picked up the phone.

"Read me his number," he said.

Marty read it and Katz dialed it. With every ring, he felt more sure this was a bad idea, but he hung on. In for a dime, in for a dollar again. Then someone picked up.

"Hello?" he said.

"Mike Davidson?" Katz asked.

"Yeah?" Davidson said.

"Hey, I'm sorry to call you so late," Katz said, "but this is Jake Katz. My --".

Before he could figure out if he should come clean on Marty, Davidson made it easy for him.

"Hey, hi!" he said. "Your wife told me where you'd been all day. Oh, man, I'm so glad you called. How was it? How are you?"

"I'm great. I mean, I'm tired, but I'm fine," Katz said.

"Yeah, wow!" Davidson said. "It's still going on, right?"

Katz heard the theme from the Rockford Files in the background. Davidson must have figured he heard it too.

"I was following it on TV all day," he said, "I swear, but I just turned it off. I love Quincy, M.E., what can I say?"

"It is still going on," Katz said. "They just sent me home to get some sleep. I would've waited till tomorrow to call you, but they're getting me at seven and who knows what's going to happen after that, so I just --"

"No, no, Jake, I'm so glad you did," Davidson said. "I want to top your day off with some good news."

"I'm ready for some good news," Jake said.

Marty raised her fists and made a nervous little happy face.

"I'd like to offer you the job we talked about," Davidson said. "Deputy Chief of Fraud."

"Jeez," Katz said. "Thank you. I don't know what to say."

"Say yes, of course," Davidson laughed. "I'm sorry it took me so long to get back to you, but they finally did the right thing. Once I let them know that the Jake Katz at the B'nai B'rith was the Jake Katz we interviewed, that made up their minds right away."

"I am so flattered, believe me," Katz said.

"Between you and me, it was the political guys who'd been holding it up," Davidson said, "but they're the same guys who popped it loose today. So, hey, no blood, no foul, right?"

"No, I get it. No problem. But I need to tell you what else is going on on my end now."

Marty rolled her eyes and flopped back on the couch. Katz held up a hand. She mouthed "okay" but crossed her arms across her chest again just to let him know it wasn't so okay. Katz laid it all out for Davidson.

"So, I understand it's a great place to be," he said. "I've got a great choice. I just have to make the one that's right for me."

"I got it, Jake," Davidson said. "You're a hot property. I know that and I won't even lay the guilt on you about how hard it was to get you through the Deputy and Thornburgh today, okay? Friday's his last day so if he didn't take care of it this week, God knows when it would have happened, but never mind that."

Katz laughed.

"But," Davidson went on, "this is where you need to be, in my humble opinion. D.C. is a great office, no question. You get all the local stuff as well as the Federal. I know a lot of that can be fun, but a lot of it can be a drag too. I know I'm not telling you anything you don't know."

Katz remembered his conversation this morning with the D.C. cops about whose bad check case was whose. It felt like a thousand years ago now, but he had one of those discussions almost every day.

"I hear you," he said.

"We're strictly Fed," Davidson said, "but, we're also national. You might get a lot of what we do too, but it's our call about who gets what. You want the biggest cases? Senators, Representatives, contractors? They're all going to funnel through here first."

And that funnel was going to get smaller, Katz knew, without Davidson having to say it. Marty already did. Earl was in the doghouse, for no fault of his own, and who knew how long that was going to last.

He knew he had to look at the big picture.

He knew he'd never be in this position again.

He knew what Marty wanted.

He knew he had no better answer.

"Okay," he said. "You convinced me. I'll take it."

Davidson said "Terrific!" but Katz didn't hear it because Marty's tackle knocked the phone out of his hand onto the floor. She pinned herself to him and was not letting go. Katz finally pulled the receiver up to his ear by the cord.

"Sorry about that," he said. "We're a little excited here."

Davidson laughed.

"No problem. Glad to make two people so happy. You've got to be beat, so like they said about Vietnam, I'm gonna declare victory and go home. I'll get the paperwork started as soon as I get in tomorrow morning. Welcome aboard, Jake! You're going to love it and we're going to love having you. I'll let you know as soon as I know."

"I can't wait," Katz said.

He threw the phone down on the couch and swung Marty around until he couldn't. She took his face in her hands and gave him a deep, long kiss.

"I am so happy for you, Jake!" she said. "This deserves a special celebration."

She pushed him into the bedroom, slipped off her clothes, stripped off his and led him into the shower. She washed him all over, then went to her knees and reminded him again why he called her Maximum Marty.

March 10, 1977

21

He slapped at the radio alarm button but couldn't find it, so he was forced to face the enemy. He squinted one eye at the yellow plastic box on the Parsons table next to the bed.

6:15.

He closed his eye, but that didn't do anything to shut out "Disco Inferno". He'd set it to KISS because that's where Marty wanted it. He wanted the R'n'B on WOL, but that was just one more decision he lost on a one-to-one vote.

He clawed at the box to find the volume knob and flicked the sound off. He rolled onto his back and smacked his right wrist against Marty's exposed left breast. He quickly pulled it back, then heard her laugh.

"Last night wasn't enough?" she asked.

She rolled to him and tickled her fingers down his chest, then his stomach. Lonely Boy rose in anticipation of company.

Katz smiled, popped his eyes open, and gently relocated her hand to her own stomach. He rolled over to kiss the honey blond strands of hair falling over those lovely green eyes.

"There's nothing he'd rather do," he said, "and nobody he'd rather do it with, but he's gotta go with the rest of me. Sorry."

He took a good look at Marty up close, and parted her hair to lightly kiss her lips.

"I'll bring him back as soon as I can, I promise."

She smiled and kissed him back.

"I know you will," she whispered. "Bring all of you back."

She lifted her head to take a look at the clock, then pushed him with her feet.

"Till then, get going!'" she said. "Go, go, go! You've got a half hour! Up and at 'em."

He offered no resistance and let her kick him to the edge of the bed. He rubbed his face and took another look at the clock. 6:19. He got going.

At quarter to seven, he was ready. He turned the TV on and flicked the dial to see if anyone was reporting anything new about the takeovers, but all the tape was from yesterday and so was the information. He'd been wrestling with an idea ever since he stepped into the shower, so he went to the phone and gave Rabe a call.

Bohlinger picked up.

"B'nai B'rith command center," he said.

"Hey," Katz said, "is Rabe around?"

"Who wants him?" Bohlinger said. Katz didn't know if he was jerking him around or really that stupid, so he took the high road and chalked it up to stupidity.

"Katz," he said.

"Hold on a minute," Bohlinger said.

Five minutes later, Katz knew he was being jerked around. Rabe finally got on the phone.

"You ready?" he said. "I just sent a car for you."

"I'm ready," Katz said. "But I've been thinking about something that should be in my files, maybe another way to get through to Khaalis. Do I have time to stop by my office on the way back?"

"Yeah, fine," Rabe said. "The guys across the street say nothing's happening – yet – so go ahead. I'll see you when you get here."

At five to seven, he was on the sidewalk in front of the house. There was something he wanted to check in his files. That was true, but it wasn't the whole truth. He also wanted to leave a note for Earl, tell him he'd told DOJ yes. There might not be a good time to do it anytime soon, so he wanted to take care of it asap, for everyone's sake.

A cruiser headed his way from 15th Street. When it got to him, the driver rolled down his window.

"You call for a cab, Mr. Katz?"

186

Tom Wallace beamed a smile at him broader than Katz had ever seen him beam before.

"Officer Wallace!" he said. "Yes, I did."

Katz got in the passenger side. They shook hands and slid into a soul shake. Katz told him about his call with Rabe, and Wallace headed for the U.S. Courthouse.

"So," Katz said, "you're still on the street?"

Wallace gave him a look.

"Washington v. Davis, man. Supremes did me no favors."

Katz remembered the Supreme Court's decision the year before, holding that even though D.C.'s police test was discriminatory, it wasn't unconstitutional because MPD didn't mean to discriminate.

"So this is it for you?" he asked him. "No way to get back to Detective?"

"It just may be, man," Wallace said. "I don't know. The Department's making a lot of noise about new training, new tests, just because we scared the shit out of 'em with the lawsuit, but I'll believe it when I see it."

"You going to take it again?"

"Hell, yes! I'm a pro at it by now," he laughed. "Didn't I tell you about the study groups Tilmon O'Bryant started, back when you were on the force?"

"Yeah, I remember that," Katz said. Wallace told him that O'Bryant and some other older black cops basically told the young black recruits they had to play the game if they wanted to get ahead, and set up study groups to help them pass the detective tests.

"Well, I'm teaching 'em now," Wallace said. "I passed it, once, so I got some street cred with the young 'uns."

"You passed it then," Katz said, "you can pass it again."

"Maybe," Wallace said. "We'll see. Right now, I'm just happy to be back on the street and out from behind that crappy desk."

Katz pictured the tight box of a room they screwed Wallace into when they jerked him out of Detectives for the Memphis foulup. No door, no window, just a gray metal desk and a splintered wood file cabinet. He smelled the mentholated smoke that filled it every time he dropped by one more time.

Wallace spun the cruiser into the driveway off Constitution and brought it to a stop right in front of the doors to the courthouse.

"I'll be back in a few minutes," Katz said. "I need to pick up some files and leave a note for my boss."

"Makes no never mind to me," Wallace said, flicking off the ignition. "I'm paid by the hour."

Katz took the elevator up and headed for Earl's office to leave him the note. He saw the men's room door swing open up ahead. Earl came out.

"You're here early," Katz called up to him.

"You too," Earl said. "Come on and give me the latest."

He followed Earl across the hall and back to his office. Earl circled his desk and pointed Katz to one of the chairs on the other side.

"So, bring me up to speed," he said.

Katz got to the point, not about Khaalis, but about himself.

"I was going to leave you a note, but you're here, so I can tell you personally. I got the job offer from DOJ."

It took Earl a second to compute.

"Ah," he said. "And?"

"And I accepted. Last night."

Earl stood up and offered his hand, ever the class act.

"Well, congratulations," he said. "Well deserved. Good for you, Jake!"

188

They shook hands and sat back down.

"I know it's going to sound lame," Katz said, "but it was a hard decision. I love this place, I love working for you."

"I appreciate it," Silbert said. "You've been great to work with. We'll miss you. When's it going to happen?"

"Don't know yet," Katz said. "But they want to get Thornburgh to sign off on it before he leaves, which is tomorrow, so soon, I guess."

"Okay, that sounds great," Earl said. "I'm going to offer the Deputy job to Riordan then, let him stop sweating about it." He smiled. "And bugging me about it."

"That's great for him," Katz said. "He deserves it. I hate to go, Earl, truly, but --"

Silbert held up his hand.

"Say no more," he said. "It's our loss. Let me know when it's official and I'll have Florence set up a farewell party. Let me guess. A.V.'s, right?"

A.V. Ristorante was Katz' favorite Italian joint. But then, it was probably Earl's too. It was pretty much everybody's.

"Sounds good," Katz said.

"All right," Earl said. "So. Khaalis?"

"Not much since around ten last night. He hung up on the ambassadors, you probably heard."

"I did," Earl nodded. "Not good."

"Rabe told me to go home after that. I just checked in with him, and all's quiet."

"That's what I heard too, from Cullinane. Only thing else I know is that your new employer wants to get involved now."

"Thornburgh?" Katz asked.

"Not directly," Silbert said. "Pete Flaherty? Ever hear of him?"

"No," Katz said. "Who is he?"

"He was the Mayor of Pittsburgh, but Carter just nominated him to be Deputy AG."

"So he's not in yet?"

Silbert shook his head.

"He still has to be confirmed," he said. "But that's just a formality, right?"

He grinned, and Katz picked up on it right away. Sure, a formality, one that only took Earl almost two years. It was the only time he ever heard him refer to it, even obliquely.

"Yeah, right," Katz said. "Piece of cake. Nothing like throwing him to the wolves before he even gets started."

"Welcome to D.C.," Earl agreed. "Anyhow, that's all I know that's new."

"I did come by for another reason," Katz said. "It came to me this morning, thinking about the fuckup with the ambassadors. I remembered there was something in my files about the people Khaalis really trusted, his Muslim teacher back in the forties and fifties, and the guy who wrote those letters to Elijah Muhammad with him. Maybe they'd have a better shot at talking him into getting this over with."

"Do we know where they are?" Earl asked.

Katz shook his head.

"I don't even know who they are, and I don't know if their names are even in the files, but I thought I ought to take a look."

Earl shrugged.

"It's like Shuker used to say," he said.

"What?" Katz said. "He used to say a lot of things."

"'Even a blind pig finds an acorn once in a while'," Earl said. "Sure. Give it a shot."

Katz stood up and extended his hand again. Silbert stood up and shook it. There was nothing more to say, so Katz headed for his office.

He crouched in front of his file cabinet and slid out the bottom drawer. He'd sent most everything from his

Khaalis files to Records, but even before then, he'd started keeping copies of a few things from big cases just as a little reminder of the cool things he got to do every once in a while. He hoped he'd held on to what he was looking for.

He pulled a brown manila folder from the back of the drawer and started to leaf through it. He pulled out a sheaf of legal-sized paper with his notes scrawled all over the top sheet. The heading read 'Khaalis 1/19/73' in blue ink.

It was his first interview with him, early in the afternoon the day after the murders. Katz could still picture it. He sat on an ottoman. Khaalis slumped on a low brown couch made of something coarse and woven, the shades on the window behind him pulled low but still letting enough sun glare in to make it tough for Katz to see his face. Joe O'Brien, the Inspector who worked the case with him from start to finish – or at least what Katz thought was the finish – was the only other person in the room, sitting in a hard-backed rocker to his left. Katz felt his back tighten up again from the strain he got bending over his pad on the coffee table in front of Khaalis.

He looked over what he'd written. He didn't think much about it at the time, but he never heard Khaalis sound so reflective, so small and quiet, as he did that day. Katz had asked him if he had any idea who might have done it. Khaalis' eyes watered and he told him he did. Katz' notes said 'Don't mess with Elijah Muhammad'. He asked him to explain what he meant and Khaalis told him the whole story.

He'd been a Muslim since the day he picked up the Koran in 1947. A few years later, he met a teacher, the woman whose name Katz tried to remember in the shower that morning but couldn't. He'd just scribbled it down as 'Grzy?'. He couldn't spell it then and he couldn't remember it now. He scrolled through his notes looking for the other name he hoped he'd written down right.

Khaalis told him that before he met the woman, he studied Islam at Columbia, taking some graduate courses to get a Masters in Middle East Studies. He used to go to his professor's house but wound up dropping out because he was getting more from the woman than the professor. He leafed forward, then found the spot he was hoping to find.

Hamaas had sent two letters to Elijah Muhammad. The first one went out at the end of December, about three weeks before the murders. He mailed it to all 57 temples of the NOI. The letter criticized their doctrine. He quoted a lot of Islamic scripture. He took on Elijah Muhammad personally, telling them he was fooling and deceiving them, robbing them of their money, and dooming them to hell. He tried to read his writing.

"Leader teaching 'new Islam' no Prpht o/Allah can bear witness to/invntd own books. Threw EM's words back at him: if cvlzed person doesn't perform his duty, shld be punished severely.'

He found the name he was looking for.

"Told Aly ? hit them again. Aly Hashim – co-wrote letters, taught HK's kids Arabic & Hebrew at house."

Katz punched the air and spelled the name out carefully on his pad. He started to close the folder, but he had to read what he knew came next one more time.

Neither of them signed the first letter, but they both signed the second one. Aly took dictation from Khaalis, added the right religious references, made copies of the letters, and mailed them. Katz read his notes.

"Letters strident, personal attack v EM -- lying deceiver/sinister/diabolical, masters o/deceit; eaters o/dead brothers flesh/EM 'grieved, blackened, laden w/sin'."

When Katz wrote those words, he thought he had the key clue, the marker showing him the path he needed to follow. He had no idea the path would lead him right back here.

22

Katz jogged back to the car and got in. Thelma Houston was swooping through "Don't Leave Me This Way."

"You a disco fan now, Officer Wallace?" Katz said.

"Shit, man," Wallace said, "that is some righteous good old fashioned soul."

Katz had heard it on KISS too many times to buy that, but he let it go.

Wallace popped the car into gear and threw on the sirens and the flashers. He shot the cruiser onto Constitution and stayed right when it merged with Pennsylvania. Katz drifted back to that night at the D.C. Coliseum when Wallace picked him up off the floor and literally saved him from his own stupidity after he jumped on a black guy who'd brained him with a folding chair. It was a debt he could never repay.

Wallace must have drifted back too.

"You ever get that song I told you about when I was down in Memphis?," he asked.

Katz could hear Wallace mumble it over the phone again, drunk, depressed, his career down the toilet because he went down there to try to solve the Howard case, but didn't ask anybody if he could go because he figured all they'd do was tell him no anyway.

"Staples Singers, right?" Katz said.

"Yep," he said.

"'Got To Be Some Changes Made'."

"There you go."

"I did get it. Great song, " Katz said.

It was a great song. He bought the album, but the first time he heard the Staples sing it, it was Wallace's voice he heard and he never put it on again.

Wallace zipped the car zipped right, up 15th, then hung a left back onto Pennsylvania. They watched the White House shoot by on the left.

"Hey," Wallace said, "whatever happened to your fat friend? What was his name?"

"Scheingold," Katz said. Schein had gone to the Coliseum with Katz, and Wallace's partner wound up pulling him out of the pile on the floor. Wallace had laid eyes on him for only a few minutes, but he must have left a lasting impression. Schein had a way of doing that.

Wallace made a fast hard right onto 17th.

"We don't see each other too much anymore," Katz said. "Might have something to do with me being on the law enforcement side of things."

"Ah," Wallace said. "He smoking the weed, or something more? Either way, wouldn't surprise me a bit."

He laughed again and shook his head.

"I really don't know," Katz said, "and I really don't want to know."

He had a bad feeling about all things Schein these days, so he changed the topic

"Hey, do me a favor," he said, "put on TOP, let's hear if they got anything new."

Wallace pushed a button on the console. They heard a man ask, "How are you being treated?"

"We're being treated very well," another man said. "We've asked for cigarettes, they've gotten them. We've asked for a newspaper, they've gotten it. We've asked for fruit for breakfast, they're getting it. They've allowed us to have our hands tied in front of us instead of in back, which is a lot more comfortable. We're allowed to stand or sit or lie down, whichever is more comfortable. We're allowed to have coffee or tea."

The first man said "This is Steve Thompson. We're speaking with Alan Grip, the spokesman for Council President Sterling Tucker. Mr. Grip is one of the hostages still being held by gunmen at the District –"

Grip cut him off.

"I'd like to read you a message they've asked me to read you," he said.

"Of course," Thompson said.

Wallace pulled the car to a stop at the corner with Rhode Island while a cop pulled a saw horse out of their way.

"We are Hanafi Moslems to the death," Grip said. "And if the police have any ideas about storming this room, it will put all our lives in immediate danger, as well as the over one hundred hostages at the B'nai B'rith. This is all for Islam. It's not a personal grudge. It's just that justice should be done. That's it."

"Okay," Thompson said. "Can you tell us a little about the conditions there?"

"Everyone is fine. The women are sitting in chairs. The men are on the floor, sitting against the wall. We're all calm and well cared for."

Wallace edged the cruiser through the opening the cops made and put it in park in front of the Holiday Inn. A few people were behind the barricades up on the sidewalk, but not nearly as many as yesterday. Katz looked left to the B'nai B'rith building. Cops in flak jackets and ball caps milled around, chatting and smiling like they did every day.

"Okay, that's good to hear," Thompson said. "Does anyone have any other messages for us?"

"No. Goodbye," Grip said, and the line went dead.

Katz and Wallace looked at each other.

"You locked those people up, right?" Wallace said, "The ones who killed his family."

"He wants us to hand them over to him," Katz said.

Wallace thought that over for a few seconds.

"Hard to say what I'd do," he said, "someone took my family out, you know?"

Katz didn't have a family anymore, just an ex-wife, but he knew what Big Sam would've done to anyone who laid a hand on his son, his *zuninkeh*, his *shayna boychik*. He also knew he'd never do it to anyone else.

Too much philosophizing too early in the morning again. He punched Wallace's shoulder and got out of the car.

"Stay in touch, man," he said.

"Go do some justice, man," he heard Wallace yell back at him over his shoulder, "whatever the hell that is!"

Katz made his way through the cops and down the stairs to the table where Bohlinger sat and Rabe stood with his back to him, talking on the phone.

"They just let another one go," Rabe said. "A woman, with chest pains. We took her over to GW."

Katz moved over to watch Rabe listening intently. His face looked tired. His eyes were red but still more with fire than strain, Katz thought.

"The Red Cross," Rabe said. "They're bringing in some coffee and doughnuts from the Hilton, and some medicine. Aspirin, some prescriptions they said they needed."

Another pause, then "10-4" and he hung up.

Katz watched Bohlinger flick his finger around in a little circle. Rabe turned around to see him.

"Well, Mr. Katz," he said. "Good to have you back."

"What've I missed?" Katz asked.

"You just heard me?" Rabe asked. Katz nodded he did. "Then that's about it. The Red Cross people should be here any minute. You find anything interesting in your files?"

"Yeah," Katz said. "The name of the guy who wrote the letters with him, to Elijah Muhammad? It's Aly Hashim. It may be worth trying to find him, see if he's willing to talk to Khaalis, maybe tell him the religion says something different than he thinks it says. Maybe it's too much of a longshot, I don't know. It's your call, obviously."

Rabe didn't hesitate.

"A longshot's better than no shot, which is what we got now. I'll get a detective on it, as soon as I can find one. They're a little tied up now."

196

A thought came to Katz. He tried to hit another longshot.

"I got one for you," he said. "A detective."

Rabe gave him a sideways look.

"How do you have a detective for me?" he asked.

"Well, he's not a detective now," Katz said, "but he used to be, when I was a cop. Tom Wallace. The guy who picked me up this morning."

"Okay, I know who you're talking about. Remind me why he isn't a detective now."

"Remember the Howard case I told you I worked?" Katz said. "He was the detective on it."

"All right, okay, I remember," Rabe said, "he was the guy who decided to take a vacation down south somewhere without approval."

"Right, sort of," Katz said. "He didn't ask for anyone's approval, but he went to Memphis on a lead on the case, not a vacation."

"'Anyone' means me," Rabe said. "I approve travel. Why didn't he just give me the paperwork like he was supposed to?"

Katz suddenly wished he hadn't started down this path at all. No good deed goes unpunished, he thought, same as always. He didn't want to get into telling Rabe that Wallace was the same guy who accidentally shot his partner after they were hit by a drunk driver years before, that he had a role in Washington v. Davis, and, most especially, now that Katz knew Rabe was the guy Wallace didn't trust to approve his paperwork, that he thought MPD was racist.

"It's a long story," he finally said. "He thought he had a good reason at the time. It was all about the case. I can guarantee you that."

Rabe looked at him like he already had a thousand more questions all lined up to ask him, but Katz knew he had a thousand more important things to do too. Finally, Rabe

took a deep breath and asked him the only question Katz
hoped he'd ask.

"Where is he now?"

"Probably right up front," Katz said. "He dropped me
off at the curb five minutes ago."

Rabe turned to Bohlinger.

"Take a walk up there and bring me back a guy
named Wallace."

Bohlinger headed for the stairs. Rabe pulled his pad
and his pen from his breast pocket.

"Give me the name again, Aly who?" he said to Katz.

Katz spelled it out for him and waited for Rabe to
finish writing it down.

"I appreciate it," he said. "It was a very long story."

"I got no time for long stories today," Rabe said.
"And neither do you."

"Why's that?" Katz asked.

"As soon as the Red Cross shows up?" Rabe said.
"You're going up there with them."

23

"Why am I going back up there?" Katz asked.

"Same reasons as before," Rabe said. "Make sure everyone's okay, let him know we're doing everything we can, etcetera, etcetera. I want to know what you see, and what you think."

Rabe's confidence in him kicked his own to the sky. He nodded he got it.

"By the way, you hear the interview with Alan Grip?" Katz asked. "From the District Building?"

"No," Rabe said. "What'd he say?"

Katz told him.

"Khaalis dictated that to him," he said. "I heard him, yesterday."

Rabe cocked his head.

"But we didn't," he said. "On the phone. I didn't hear him dictate anything to anyone."

Rabe mulled it over some more, then winced.

"That means he's got another phone line up there that we're not hooked into. Or maybe more than one. Shit in my hat!"

He pointed at Katz.

"Put that at the top of your list," Rabe said. "If he's talking to people and we're not hearing it, that's a problem, a big problem. You go up there and you look and you listen too. Goddamn it!"

Katz nodded, then saw Rabe look past him and try to calm himself down. He turned to see a squadron of Red Cross ladies advancing upon them, all in white with red crosses on the chests of their frocks and their caps. None of them looked more than five feet tall, except the one in front who must have been six feet tall, with flaming red hair and skin whiter than her frock. She pushed a brown metal cart with some urgency and stopped it just short of them.

"Do you know where we can find Deputy Rabe?" she asked Rabe.

"You found him," Rabe said. "That's me."

"Good morning, sir," she said. "I'm Tibie Monheim, Registered Nurse. These ladies are with me. We're here to bring some food and medicine upstairs."

"Right," Rabe said. "We've been expecting you --"

Tibie's alabaster skin turned bright red.

"Well, I'm very sorry, sir. These things take a little time to organize."

Katz grimaced. This was all they needed, a prima donna to set Khaalis off. But Rabe handled it like he handled everything else thrown at him.

"I appreciate that," he said with a smile, "I was just trying to tell you how happy I was to see you. No offense intended."

Tibie glowered at him.

"This has already been a very stressful morning for us, Mr. Rabe," she said. "No sense in adding to it now, is there?"

Katz sensed somehow that she wasn't used to anyone else being in charge. He looked to see if Collins was around. He wasn't. Rabe tried his best again.

"My apologies," he told Tibie. "We're all under a little pressure here. Forgive me."

Before she could figure out a way to bristle at that, he turned to Katz.

"Let me introduce you to Jake Katz, from the U.S. Attorney's office," he said. "He'll be going up with you. He knows Mr. Khaalis, the man who's holding everyone hostage up there. He's our eyes and ears who's going to let us know what's what when he comes back."

Tibie flicked her eyes to Katz, then back to Rabe.

"So I just want to get our signals straight, all right?" Rabe went on. "There's only two things I want you and your nurses to do, okay?" His fingers unfurled again.

"Number one, you pass out the food and the medicine just like Mr. Khaalis tells you to. Number two, you see anyone looks like they need help, you tell Mr. Katz, and he'll talk to Mr. Khaalis about it. That's it. That's all I want you to do, all right?"

Katz watched Tibie's skin color lighten. Only her cheeks were crimson now. She unclenched her hands from the handle of the cart and stood up straight.

"That's perfectly fine," she said. "I only have two things on my list, too. One for us and one for you."

Rabe looked at her blankly.

"First," she said, "we'll do exactly what you and Mr. Khaalis and Mr. Katz want us to do, just like you asked. We're nurses. We know our job. We will do it and do it well, I assure you."

"I have no doubt," Rabe said. "What's my job?"

"Get us back down here safe and sound," she said.

Rabe's eyes weakened for a moment, like he knew for the first time what he was putting her through, everyone through, through no fault of his own. He cleared his throat.

"Miss Monheim, was it?" he said. "That's my job. I'll do it well too. You have my word."

Tibie looked satisfied, more at getting the last boot in than with anything Rabe said, Katz thought.

"Well, all right, then," she said. "Where do we go and when do we go there?"

"I'm going to call Mr. Khaalis right now to work that out," Rabe said. "Just stand by."

Katz watched Rabe slip a look at the cart. He saw a stack of Krispy Kreme boxes and three coffeepots on the top shelf. Four fat black leather bags with handles sat on the bottom shelf.

"What's in the bags?" Rabe asked.

Tibie tried to call it up by memory.

"Pressure cuffs, thermometers, bandaids, gauze, Vaseline, aspirin, oh, some of the prescriptions they asked for. Do you want to take a look?," she asked Rabe, suddenly sweet.

"No," he said, "as long as there's nothing in there Khaalis might think was a weapon."

She thought about that.

"Tongue depressor? Stethoscope? That's about it."

"Okay," Rabe said. "I'll give him a call and let him know you're coming. In the meantime, why don't you open up each of those bags as wide as you can, just so he doesn't get any wrong ideas when you get up there."

Tibie nodded. A few of the nurses knelt down to tend to the bags. Rabe waved Katz to come with him.

When they got to the table, Katz asked him a question.

"Why are you letting them bring the stuff up, instead of just having the medics do it?"

Rabe stuck three fingers out.

"First and foremost," he said, "I want our joyboy up there to think we're only interested in making nice to him, not pulling any funny business. Who's nicer than a carload full of nurses? Second, we might need Nurse Ratched again, and there's no point in pissing her off. She was just scared. Plus, you see any medics lining up to volunteer?"

"No," Katz said. "I was looking for Collins, but I didn't see him."

Rabe laughed.

"Just like cops, right? Never around when you need 'em. That's okay, he did his part, they'll do theirs. It won't be --"

The phone in front of Bohlinger interrupted him with a harsh ring. Bohlinger picked it up and said hello. Then his face blanched and he held it up for Rabe.

"It's Khaalis," he said.

"Put it on speaker," he told Bohlinger. Bohlinger hit the button and put the phone back on the cradle.

202

"Thank you, very much," he said. "I am appreciative, forever."

"Can you give us an idea of what's going on up there?" Rabe asked him. "Just a little, whatever you can tell us. Don't push yourself."

Siegel licked his lips and squinted his eyes closed. When he opened them again, he turned to Rabe.

"I was on the seventh floor yesterday, seems like a million years ago. I hear some noises I don't usually hear, people running, shouting. I go to the door and I see my secretary running up the hall to me, crying. She says there are mad men in the building, *schwarzes* – you should pardon the expression – crazy men, shooting. I pull her into my office and a few other people run in, Mr. Kirkland, the maintenance man, I can't remember the rest. I lock the door. In a minute, there's banging on the door, and they knock it down, two men with guns. One of them has a big knife, more than a knife, like a machete, and he slices poor Mr. Kirkland in the back and the leg. He goes down, bleeding all over."

"Right, we know who he is," Rabe said. "We got him over to the hospital yesterday."

"Ah," Siegel said, "he should only be well."

Katz heard footsteps coming down the hall. He looked up to see the cop Rabe sent leading Tibie and her nurses around the corner, then did a double take when he saw Abdul-Aziz round the corner behind them, his arms full of grocery bags.

"Then what do you remember?" he heard Rabe ask.

"They took us down to the sixth floor," Siegel said, "by the stairs, guns at our backs, and made us lie there a while in front of the elevators, more and more people coming, lying on top of each other. All I could think of was Auschwitz, what else could I think? Then they herd us into the elevators and take us up to eight, to the new conference room."

Tibie knelt down next to Katz.

"Can we check him now?" she asked Rabe. "He's going to have to be still if we take his pressure."

"One minute," Rabe told her, and turned back to Siegel.

"Okay," Rabe said. "How about today? What's it like up there now?"

Siegel shook his head.

"He's crazy, going on and on about the Black Muslims one minute and the Jews the next. Oh, he says that smoking is good for thinking and that the Jews are against smoking because we don't want his people to think. What kind of person thinks this? And once he gets going, he doesn't stop. On and on, *vay iz mir*, like a top that won't stop."

"Why did he let you go?" Rabe asked.

"Last night," Siegel said, "I told one of his men I was having chest pains. He comes over, the Khalifa he calls himself, a real *shtarker* you know, like a muscle man, and his men come over and they untie me and they pick me up and they stand me facing up against the wall with my feet spread out, and he leans over my shoulder and he says, like booming, in my ear, 'You're not going to die on me, are you? If you're going to die, you ought to die like a man', then he picks up a sword – a sword, a real sword! – and he holds it over my head. This is it, is all I'm thinking. I start saying the *shema*, and then! – he walks away, leaves me there, how I didn't have a heart attack then and there I'll never know. I go back down on the floor and they tie me up again, hands and feet. Then sometime in the night, he's a different person. He comes over to me, unties my hands and tells me it's okay to lie on my stomach with my hands in front of me. Then this morning, they untie my feet and they take me to the elevators with the guns and the swords. But before they pushed the elevator button, they made me praise Allah. I did – I'll atone on Yom Kippur – and they said if any of you

206

were on there, they would kill me. But, thank God, you weren't, and by a miracle, here I am."

He was red and sweatier now from living through it one more time.

Rabe patted him on the shoulder.

"All right," he said. "That's enough for now. Miss Monheim here will give you a good checkover, then we'll send you over to the hospital. I'm glad you're back down. God bless you."

"He already has," Siegel said.

Rabe and Katz stood up. Katz walked him over to Abdul-Aziz.

"Abdul, this is Chief Rabe."

Aziz put down his bags and shook Rabe's hand.

"Chief, this is Abdul Aziz who went with me yesterday to deliver the food to the Islamic Center. He's Khaalis' son-in-law."

"Pleased to meet you," Rabe said.

"Likewise," Aziz said, "though maybe under different circumstances."

Rabe gestured to the bags.

"We're going to have to go through those before they go up," he said.

"Of course," Aziz said.

He laid them on the floor. Rabe pointed to two of the riflemen.

"Take a look through there, will you?"

They pulled the bags to the wall and lifted out oranges, bananas, and chocolate bars. One of them pulled out a tin of Peppermint Sucrets, eyeballed it, then held it up for Rabe to see. He turned to Aziz.

"Khadyia threw them in there," he shrugged. "His wife, my sister. Hamaas asked for them."

Rabe and Katz exchanged glances.

"They're fine," Rabe told the cop. They emptied the rest of the bags. All the rest was produce and crackers.

"Okay, that's all fine," Rabe said and turned back to Aziz.

"Don't take this the wrong way, Mr. Aziz," he said. "but I'm going to have someone else bring all this up to him. I don't want to risk you giving him messages or false hopes or anything. I just can't let you go up there, okay?"

"It's okay," Aziz said, glancing at his watch. "I have a business to run,"

Katz saw it said 9:25.

"Mr. Katz will take it up there?" Aziz asked Rabe.

"Him and a few nurses," Rabe said.

"Then it will be perfectly okay."

Aziz turned to Katz.

"I told Hamaas last night that I told you the real story of why he trusted you. He carried on a bit, as ever, but he still trusts you and he will have no problem with your going up there, believe me."

"That's good to know," Katz said, "I think."

Aziz bowed and made his way back around the corner. Katz turned to Rabe, who was beet red and not happy.

"That's the last time I want to hear about what he's doing up there that I don't know about," Rabe said.

He jabbed a thick finger into Katz' chest.

"Get those fucking phone numbers," he said.

208

24

Katz let Tibie in the elevator first, then the nurse with the cart, then the rest of them. Rabe held the door until everyone was on. When Katz turned back to face him, Rabe gave him a thumbs up, then let the doors slide shut.

Katz felt compelled to reassure them about what he wasn't too sure of himself.

"It'll be fine," he said. "I've been up there and lived to tell the tale."

Tibie had nothing to say for a change. They all stared at the numbers slowly changing over the doors. The car stopped at 8 with a little jolt. Katz steeled himself. There was no sound.

The doors parted in front of him. One of the same two guys who saw him and Collins off yesterday was waiting for him again, with another man, the one Katz thought he saw at the back of the conference but he still wasn't sure. The one he remembered was the one with the machete. He still had it, but it was hanging off his waist. Now his arms held a shotgun pointed straight at Katz' head. A few feet to his left, the other man's M-16 pointed straight at his chest.

"Ah," the man with the shotgun said, "the Jew comes back to join the sheep for slaughter."

"Off, off, off!" the other one shouted.

Katz raised his arms, stepped forward, and blocked the doorway.

"These are the nurses Mr. Khaalis said could come up," he said. "They've got food and the medicines he talked about with Chief Rabe."

The elevator started buzzing, loudly.

"Off, off, all of you!" the man with the M-16 shouted, and swung it toward the nurses.

Katz heard the gasps behind him. He knew he was the one person who had to stay cool here, no matter what happened. From nowhere, his mind's eye brought Rabe's face into focus. He'd watched him long enough, seen him catch everything flying at him from every direction. He knew what he had to do.

He had to be Rabe.

"Okay," he said calmly, "they're coming off. Everything's cool."

He extended his hand to Tibie.

"Ladies," he said.

He watched Tibie nervously survey who and what lay in front of her. He reached for her elbow and escorted her off, then reached for the nurse with the cart. The others stepped out in turn.

Katz came off last. The elevator buzz snapped off and the doors slid shut behind him.

He pointed to the cart.

"The food's on top," he said to the man with the shotgun. "The medicine's in the bags on the bottom. We opened them up so you could see there's no surprises."

The man kept the shotgun trained on him, and twisted his head to the other man.

"Abdul Adam," he said to a tall man with large black frame glasses. "Check them out."

Abdul Adam slung the rifle over his shoulder and knelt down to go through the bags. He pawed through each of them, then stood up and swung the weapon back into his hands.

"They're clean," he said. "Just medicine, doctor stuff."

"Okay," the other said. "Let's go."

He gestured to Tibie to fall behind him, then led them all to the closed door of the conference room and opened it. Katz followed the nurses, the muzzle of Abdul Adam's rifle nudging him forward. The man with the shotgun opened the door and waved the weapon at the nurses to go on through.

A cloud of cigarette smoke drifted out at Katz. Another nudge from Abdul Adam sent him through the doorway into the darkness again. He pinched his eyes shut to help him adjust, then opened them to see Khaalis standing across from him, a shadow almost obscured by the smoke and the light zigzagging in between the paint streaks on the window behind him.

Katz raised his hand to shelter his eyes and make him out better. Khaalis sucked a deep drag from his cigarette and exhaled almost all of it in a long plume coming right at him.

"I am in the middle of a lesson, Mr. Katz," he said, "but I am happy to start over for you and your nurses, so that you too can learn from the Khalifa's wisdom."

Khaalis extended his arms to the room.

"So that all of you can learn, truly understand what I am telling you about the history of your people and your great eminent founding fathers."

Katz did a quick sweep of the room. All the women were on the floor. The tarpaulins that he misread before were under some of them now. Some of them stared back at him numb and listless, their heads flat against the tarps or the concrete or plastic rug savers like the kind he had under his chair at the USA's. Most of the men sat against the walls all around the room, their hands behind them or tied together in front.

"So, again," Khaalis boomed, "here is your history lesson, my Hebrew friends, you so-called chosen people who are blind and deaf of heart to your God. Take heed and learn from Khaalis. I told you, George Washington, the father of your country, didn't want you in it! And do you know why? He said you were pestilence! Vermin! Why doesn't that show up in the history books? You know why! You own the book companies, so all they say is that George Washington chopped down a cherry tree! That's not even a good fairy tale. Is that the best story you could make up?"

Khaalis scanned the room again, like he expected someone to actually answer him. His voice was deeper, clearer, more emphatic now, energized by his new audience, Katz guessed.

"What about Ben Franklin, you say?" he rolled on. "What about wise old Ben Franklin who discovered electricity and whored around Europe? Surely, he was more enlightened than Mr. President Washington? You know what he said? He said the Jews would destroy American within two hundred years, huh? We're there, right now! And you're still up to your old tricks!"

He made a small circle, taking in everyone in the room. He stopped to stare at Katz and lifted his arms.

"Do you not see this, Mr. Katz? All of your so-called truths? They're lies! Six million Jews were killed in Europe – that's a lie because there weren't even six million Jews *in* Europe! All lies, all myths, all to create this little pestilent nation of Jews in the middle of Islam. Your Prime Minister of Israel! So-called Israel. I call him the Prime Minister of Palestine! You know why? Because Israel means servant of Allah, that's why!"

Katz was sickened by his wilful ignorance, and angrier still at the fear he was sending through these people, some of whom had to be the children, sisters, and brothers of people murdered in the Holocaust he mocked, all of whom did nothing more than show up to do their jobs on a Wednesday in March. But he gave Khaalis nothing that would let the bastard know he was getting to him. He stared back.

Khaalis turned to his left, then to his right. Some of the women had buried themselves under the tarpaulins to try and shut him out. Men stared at the floor or held their eyes shut. Katz was revolted after two minutes. They'd had to endure him for almost twenty-four hours.

"The Jew is not the seed of Abraham," Khaalis said, wagging his finger back and forth. "No. They get mixed up between Israel and Judah. The Germans wiped out a village of a couple hundred old men and women and children right after World War Two and they're still crying that they have been burnt up in ovens. Am I the first one – "

A man at the wall closest to him stood up, barely kept his balance, and weaved past him.

"Oh ho, now!" Khaalis said. "Where are you going this time? Sit back down!"

But the man kept moving, taking one uncertain step after the other. He listed in Katz' direction, then lurched to his left, tripping over a woman, then regained his equilibrium, but just barely. Another woman scrambled to her feet in front of him.

"Mr. Blotnick," she said, "please, sit down. Sit down with me."

"Yes, Mr. Blotnick," Khaalis said. "Do what Mrs. Neal tells you. Sit down. Now."

But Blotnick kept walking, in his own way. He was an older man, heavy, probably in his sixties. His hands were bound behind him with a tie. His white shirt strained at his stomach and hung down over his brown pants. His feet were shoeless. When he stumbled in Katz' direction, Katz saw a man in distress, eyes glassy and unseeing, his mouth frozen in a twisted half-frown. He fell to his knees but showed no reaction. He pushed himself up and walked back towards where he started, his legs wide and his feet splayed.

Katz turned to Tibie. She looked back at him, wide-eyed. He mouthed "What's wrong with him?" If she had an answer, it stuck in her throat.

Blotnick reeled right at a gunman. The man pushed him away and Blotnick fell to the ground. He tried to get up. The gunman levelled his rifle straight at him. Another gunman, short and stocky, in a gray shirt and pants, grabbed his arm.

"Razzaq, no!" he yelled at the rifleman. "Show him some mercy!"

213

Razzaq held his weapon steady and looked to Khaalis. Khaalis watched Blotnick get back to his feet, then teeter away.

"Put him in a chair and tie him there!" he directed Abdul Adam. "Make him sit!"

Abdul Adam handed his M-16 to the gunman next to him and crossed the room to Blotnick. He grabbed him by the shoulders and held him tightly as they weaved together to an empty dark folding chair at the far end of the room to Katz' left. He watched Abdul Adam pull Blotnick's arms back behind him and methodically tie them to the back of the chair. Blotnick rocked his head back to try to look at him. After a minute, Abdul Adam stood up and nodded to Khaalis.

"That should hold him," he said.

Khaalis looked at Blotnick slumped in the chair, his head down, slowly bobbing, then he turned to Katz.

"You know that I know you have your sharpshooters staring in at us here all the time, don't you? You don't think Khaalis is that stupid, do you?"

Katz said nothing.

"Maybe you do, Mr. Katz, maybe you do. I'll tell you a little secret anyhow. I'm going to hang Mr. Blotnick and some of these other old Jews by their feet from the ceiling to give them a little target practice. Want to help us, Mr. Katz? You're too short to hang them up there but maybe we could sit them on your shoulders while we tied the knots, huh? Want to give us a hand?"

Katz played out another fantasy in his head, choking Khaalis and smashing his head apart on the concrete.

But he said, "Hamaas, please. Show these people some mercy, like your man said. These are people, with children and husbands and wives and grandchildren."

Just like you were, he didn't say, but he knew Khaalis would make the connection himself. Or he hoped he would.

214

Khaalis snorted and flicked a long ash onto the floor. He took another look at Blotnick, who looked back with a wet vacant stare. He turned back to Katz.

"You're coming with me," he said. "You and Mrs. Neal."

Khaalis turned to the woman who had pleaded with Blotnick to sit down, and gestured to her to get up. She was a pretty redhead who looked to be in her mid-forties.

"Come," Khaalis said to her. "We have some calls to make."

She slipped on her shoes and got to her feet. Khaalis wiggled his finger at Katz and pointed him to the door. Katz waited for Mrs. Neal to join him, then watched Razzaq push the door open. The three of them went into the hallway and waited for Khaalis. Katz tried not to notice Razzaq's weapon pointing at his heart.

He extended a hand to Mrs. Neal.

"Jake Katz," he said.

She took his hand and squeezed it.

"Betty Neal," she said, "but you can call me BJ. Everybody does."

"How are you holding up?" he asked.

She pulled a cigarette from the soft pack of Marlboros she clutched in her other hand, then pried a matchbook from inside the cellophane wrapper. He watched her light it and pull down a long draw. No smoke escaped.

"I'm his secretary," she said, rolling her eyes.

"What do you mean?" Katz asked.

"Yesterday, he was getting crazy – crazier, I should say – with all the phone calls, so he asked for somebody to help him out. No one said anything so I raised my hand. Why? I really couldn't tell you. He asks me if I'm a troublemaker or something. I didn't say anything because I didn't really know what he said. Then he asks me my name, and I tell him, then he asks if I'm Jewish and I say no, and he tells me to come with him."

"So what do you do for him?" Katz asked.

Before she could answer, Khaalis came through the doorway with Abdul Adam.

"Quiet," Razzaq said, "you be quiet now for the khalifa."

Khaalis laid a hand on his shoulder.

"Razzaq," he said, "You come with us, keep your weapon trained on Mr. Katz at all times. No harm is to come to Mrs. Neal, you understand? She is a mother of small children."

He lifted his head to her.

"How many children did you tell me?"

"Four," she said and took another deep pull from the cigarette.

"Four children," Khaalis smiled, "that is beautiful."

He pointed to her, his own cigarette between his fingers, and turned to Abdul Adam.

"You tell the others what I said too, huh? When we come back, no matter what transpires, no harm is to befall her, by the khalifa's command."

Abdul Adam nodded and went back into the room and closed the door. Razzaq peered down his sights at Katz. Khaalis took the scene in and turned to face Katz.

"But you and the rest of the Yehudis?" he grinned. "That remains to be seen."

Katz was sick of being bullied. He struggled to keep his tongue.

Khaalis barked a laugh and ground his cigarette out on the concrete.

"Come with Khaalis," he said and walked towards the office down the other side of the hallway.

Katz waited for BJ to follow Khaalis, then fell in behind. He didn't need the reminder, but the nose of Razzaq's muzzle behind him let him know he was coming too.

It sounded like two phones were ringing across the way. Khaalis let BJ run in front of him. She tripped out of one of her low-heeled shoes, cursed it, slipped out of the other one, and carried them into the room. By the time Katz entered, she was back in her shoes and talking on a phone on a desk in the middle of the room. He strained to recall the first time he was there. He looked at the desk closest to the door. He remembered that phone, but not the one BJ was on.

Khaalis motioned to Razzaq to stay out and closed the door halfway.

Mrs. Neal put her hand over the receiver and pointed it at Khaalis.

"It's Channel Seven," she said. "WMAL."

He walked over to take the phone. She came back to stand next to Katz.

"This is he," Khaalis said. He listened for a moment, then reached for a pack of Benson and Hedges on the desk. He fished one out, pulled a lighter out of his pocket, and lit it. He pulled it out of his mouth before he even inhaled, agitated at whatever he heard.

"I don't care," he said. "I don't care about any of that. Let me tell you something. The D.C. cops have sat in the rabbi's office at the Hebrews' synagogue across the street from me every day since. Now what do you think they're doing there, trying to protect me or to spy on me? Protect my family or spy – "

He must have been interrupted. He didn't tolerate it long.

"No, listen to me now!" he screamed. "Don't be so naïve. What do you *think* they were doing? You think I don't know? They told me one of my most trusted friends was a rat who was double-dealing me from inside. Why would they do that? No, I don't want you to answer, I'm telling you!"

Katz and BJ exchanged glances, then Katz noticed a second line light up on the phone. He waited until Khaalis

217

turned his back to them, then backed away from BJ far enough to stay out of Abdul Razzaq's line of sight through the doorway and keep both her and Khaalis in his field of vision. He waved at her. When she looked over, he held up two fingers and nodded to the phone Khaalis was on.

"Two phones?" he mouthed.

BJ nodded yes.

"How many lines?" he whispered.

"Seven," she mouthed. She pointed at the phone on the front desk and held up three fingers.

Khaalis spun back around, exasperated. BJ froze. He looked right at her.

"They can sit along and watch my family all day long for the next two years!" he cried.

BJ stretched and yawned.

"If it won't be from there," Khaalis screamed, "it will be from somewhere else where you least expect it. It will be worse."

He spun away from them.

BJ pointed to the other phone quickly. "Four there," she mouthed.

He rolled his eyes. Two phones. Seven lines. No wonder they didn't know everything Khaalis was saying, or when, or who he was saying it to.

He looked at her and scratched the palm of his left hand with the index finger of his right.

"I need those numbers," he mouthed. She nodded.

Khaalis turned back to them, weary of hearing whatever Channel Seven had to say to him.

"Listen, listen to me," he said. He closed his eyes tight and raised his hand to cover them. "No more groveling, no more pleading, no more reasoning, okay? We came here to fight to the death. And there'll be a lot of good people who won't come out, either – you know that, right? We are committed to retribution. Our law allows that. There is no justice without the sword."

218

He listened for another few seconds, then muttered a grunt of disgust, shook his head, and dropped the receiver back on the cradle. He stood still for a moment, his back to them again, his shoulders slumped. Katz saw him reach both hands to his face.

The phone next to BJ rang. She looked to Khaalis. It rang again before he turned to her. His eyes were bloodshot, his face more gray than brown. He pointed to the phone.

"Find out who it is," he said.

She reached for the phone and listened for a minute.

"Hold on," she said. "Let me get a piece of paper."

She reached across the table for a small spiral note pad and picked up a pencil.

"Okay," she said. "Give that to me again."

She listened and wrote, then listened some more. In a few seconds, she sighed and shook her head, then hung up the phone. She ripped the sheet she'd been writing on off the pad and crumpled it up.

"They hung up," she said.

"Who was it?" Khaalis asked.

"Another joker," she said, "maybe the same one as before."

She turned to Katz.

"Some asshole called before," she said, "first thing this morning. Came on all serious, says the cops are coming up the stairs for us. Mr. Khaalis called Rabe. He told him nothing was going on, it was a prank call. This time, it was the same thing, only he said he was a doctor."

"Doctor who?" Khaalis asked. "What doctor?"

"I don't want to tell you," she said.

"You tell me," he said.

It took her a few seconds to make up her mind, then she sighed and told him.

"He said he was Doctor Neebin."

Khaalis looked at her quizzically. She blushed.

"Doctor Lou Neebin," she said.

219

Katz got it but Khaalis still looked at her with the same puzzled face.

"Lou Neebin?" she said. "Loony bin?"

Now Khaalis got it.

"Funny man," he snorted. "We'll see who laughs last."

The phone by BJ started ringing again. She looked at Khaalis. He flicked his finger at it. She picked up the phone and listened, then held it to her chest.

"Associated Press," she told Khaalis.

He walked over to her and took it.

"Khaalis," he said. He listened for a few seconds.

"No, no, no," he said. "Didn't I tell you all this already? Earlier this morning?"

He listened for a few more seconds and shook his head.

"Then you need to talk to each other and not waste the Khalifa's time. I told him Cassius Clay is as guilty as Elijah Poole. He was in on the murder of my family, just like Elijah and just like his son, the leader of the so-called World Community of Islam. He's not the leader of my community! I have nothing to do with him!"

Katz heard a knock on the door. Abdul Razzaq's head poked in. Khaalis looked at him while he listened on the phone.

"The nurses," he said. "They're through."

"We will be there in one minute," Khaalis said, then bellowed into the receiver.

"No! No! No!" he roared. "You cannot be so stupid. Khaalis does not have the time or the patience to tell you the difference! Would you ask the Pope why he is not King of the Jews? Then why would you ask me that? They do not speak for me, or Islam. None of them! This call is over!"

He threw the receiver at the cradle and missed badly. The hum of a dead line followed its smack against the concrete. BJ reached down, picked it up, and placed it back on the cradle.

"Let's go," Khaalis said. "Enough of these imbeciles!"

He led them back across the hall. Just outside the conference room, BJ stepped out of one of her shoes again and tripped. She put a hand on Katz' chest to keep her balance while she put it back on.

"Thank you," she said and patted him on his suit pocket. She turned and he followed her into the room.

Everyone had their doughnut and coffee. It looked like no one had moved, except Tibie, who was tending to Blotnick. The rest of the nurses were back close to the door, putting their equipment back into the bags.

Tibie picked her way back through the women to the door.

"So, Miss Nurse, have you found any Yehudis in extremis?" Khaalis asked her.

"Three of them are way up over normal," she said. "They're under a lot of stress."

"We're all under a lot of stress," Khaalis said.

"I'm especially worried about Mr. Blotnick," she said.

They all looked over to him. He sagged in his chair, asleep.

"He looks just fine now," Khaalis said.

Tibie shook her head.

"Because I gave him his pill," she said. "In a few hours, you're going to have to give him another one."

Khaalis answered that with a sharp laugh.

"Am I now a pharmacist, Miss Nurse?" he said. "These are not my patients! They are my hostages!"

"Hamaas," Katz said. "Please. Show them some humanity."

Khaalis held up a palm.

"Enough from you, Mr. Katz. Enough false piety from the infidel Jew," he said and turned to Tibie. "And enough from you. Your visit is over."

He turned to the room. He spoke to them in dead earnest.

"Listen, Jews. Listen to me well. This is the last time on this earth that you will see Mr. Katz or the nurses or anyone besides the khalifa and his soldiers, do you understand? Besides us, the next thing you see will be your maker, your so-called Jehovah, huh? We're are all in it together from now on, from this second on. Just us, every one of us. No one else goes home to mommy or daddy or anyone else. No one!"

He turned to Katz, barely a yard away, and shouted at him, his face distorted by the rage exploding through every pore. Katz felt his spittle fleck his face.

"You tell your Mr. Rabe and your ambassadors that we are through with visitors! You tell Mister Police Chief Cullinane and Mister Mayor Washington and Mister Carter that we are through with all of them! Unless they wish to come up here themselves and trade places with one of them, huh? Then we'll talk to them, and only then!"

He seethed a moment more, for once out of words.

Katz listened for Rabe's voice to guide him. He heard nothing, so he tried his own.

"Hamaas," he said, "please. Let's work together to bring this to an end, not keep it going."

Khaalis waved the back of his hand at him.

"Take him away," he said. "Take them all away."

Abdul Adam and Abdul Razzaq pushed them out the door and across the hall to the elevators. Adam thumbed the button over and over.

Katz turned back towards the conference room. Razzaq knelt in the middle of the hall and squinted up through his sights at his forehead. Khaalis slowly walked out of the room. He stopped just behind the gunmen.

222

"Do you remember my words before, Mr. Katz?" he asked him, quietly, suddenly serene. "Do you remember what I told you the Koran demanded of me?"

The elevator bell rang. Katz heard the nurses scurry aboard behind him, the wheels of the cart rolling across the floor. He kept his eyes on Khaalis, knowing what he would hear, hoping he wouldn't.

"Surah five, verse forty-five, huh?" He thrust out his jaw. "'Life for life. Eye for eye. Nose for nose. Ear for ear. Tooth for tooth, and wounds equal for equal.' You remember now? You tell them that's the last word you heard from Khaalis!"

Katz heard the elevator door buzz again as he watched him turn and disappear into the darkness of the conference room. The door slammed shut.

He turned to see the nurses huddling in the back of the car and Adam in the doorway cradling his rifle in his arms.

He edged past him onto the car and turned back to see Razzaq still training his weapon at his head.

Abdul Adam stepped back. The buzzing stopped. The doors slid shut. The car began its drop. Gravity loosened its pull on them all, but Katz felt the weight of the world on his shoulders more than ever before.

Then he remembered something and reached into the chest pocket of his suit. He fished out a crumpled piece of spiral note paper.

The elevator braked to a stop but Katz didn't feel it. He suddenly felt lighter than air.

223

25

Katz held the door open for the nurses with one hand and uncrumpled the note with the other. He read the seven numbers that BJ had written and blessed her.

Footsteps raced towards them from the hallway around the corner to his left. Katz looked up to see Rabe and Bohlinger double-timing into sight, trailed by what looked a regiment of SWAT team guys carrying a truckload of weapons.

Before Rabe could say anything, Katz held up the paper and grinned.

"I got the fucking numbers," he said.

Rabe took it from his hand.

"Seven?" he said. "He's got seven goddamned numbers and we're on one of them? Jesus Christ!?"

He looked back at the paper, shaking his head.

"How the hell did you get these?" he asked. "He write 'em out for you?"

"No," Katz said, "BJ, Betty Neal did, one of the hostages."

That much he knew. He tried to put the rest together.

"Did Khaalis get a crank call before I got here this morning?" he asked Rabe.

"Yeah," Rabe said. "Some guy told him the cops were on their way up to get him. He called down here to tell us he'd blow everyone to kingdom come if we were. I managed to convince him we weren't. What's that got to do with this?"

"This BJ's acting as his secretary," Katz said. "She took a call for him while I was up there, and I'm not real sure if this is true or she just made it up, but she said it was another cuckoo. She hung up on him – or whoever it was – and crumpled up this paper she was writing notes on."

He stopped and saw all the pieces fit in place.

"Come back to me now, Katz," he heard Rabe say. "You've gone somewhere."

"She's brilliant!" Katz laughed. "She wasn't writing notes on whatever the person on the phone was saying. She was writing down these numbers! Then when we went back across the hall to the conference room, she pretended to trip so she had a chance to lean on me while she put on her shoes. That's when she stuffed the paper in my pocket!"

He looked at Rabe with awe. Rabe stuck out his lower lip, impressed.

"Pretty damn amazing to cook that up and pull it off on the spot," he said. "If we had her down here, she could probably figure out how to end this thing in five minutes."

"Yeah, well," Katz said, "that's a whole other thing. It doesn't sound like anybody's coming down any time soon."

"Why's that?" Rabe asked.

"Things were definitely tenser up there than yesterday," Katz told him. "Khaalis basically threw us out and told them we were the last outsiders they were ever going to see. He said no one's getting out from now on."

"He says a lot of stuff," Rabe said.

"Yeah, but the whole vibe up there was really weird," Katz said. "He went on and on about the Jews and George Washington and the holocaust, and this one guy, Blotnick, got up and started careening around, falling down. They tied him up and the nurses gave him his pills so he was fine when we left, but the whole thing's a powder keg. I just got the feeling he could blow any time for any reason, even more than before."

"Okay," Rabe said, "all the more reason why we need to monitor these TV guys and these dumbass creeps calling in all the time."

He held up the crumpled paper.

"I can tap these, right? We've got an emergency here."

225

Rabe knew the law as well as Katz did. Ordinarily, Earl needed to get a judge's permission before he could get a wiretap, but, in an emergency, he could just do it and get the judge's okay sometime in the next two days.

"If this isn't an emergency," Katz said, "what is? Go to it."

Rabe handed Bohlinger the paper.

"Find those lines," he told him. "I'll get another table and more headsets down there and the heads to put 'em on."

Rabe and Katz headed back up the hallway. Bohlinger didn't move. Rabe stopped and turned back to him.

"Is there a problem?" he asked.

"Yeah, maybe," Bohlinger said. "Yesterday, you said you wanted to cut all these outside guys off, and we didn't."

He threw a quick glance to Katz, who still had the bruises to show for their discussion.

"And here we are a day later," Bohlinger said, "and they still haven't stopped."

"What's your point?" Rabe asked.

"Should I just pull all these lines?," Bohlinger said, "Cut him off now?"

Rabe thought about that for about half a second.

"We're not going to do that and here's why," he said.

He stuck his index finger out one more time.

"First off, if he's as freaked out as Katz says he is, I don't want to take a chance setting him off by cutting every line. He doesn't get to talk to his wife or Mr. Aziz or whoever, who knows what he'll do?"

He stuck out his middle finger.

"Second, there's not enough TVs and radios in the world to let us know what he's saying to every newshound he's talking to."

He stuck out his ring finger.

226

"Third, *we* need a line, and if we ever get him to talk to the ambassadors, we'll need another one. So let's just hold tight for a while. We can always cut off anyone we need to, okay?"

Katz marveled at how Rabe could figure everything out and lay it out so clearly in the time it would take anyone else to just put three fingers out.

They went back up the hall and Bohlinger caught up to them. As they came around the corner, Katz saw Wallace coming down the stairs. They met him at the table.

"So," Rabe said, "what's up?"

"I got his number," Wallace said.

He slid his MPD card across the table face down, a phone number on the back.

"Aly what's-his-name?" Rabe asked.

"Aly Hashim," Wallace said, "yeah."

"You call him?" Rabe said.

"I did," Wallace said.

"And?" Rabe said.

"I told him I just wanted to confirm who he was because some higher-ups at MPD wanted to talk to him."

"How'd you find him?" Katz asked.

Wallace looked at him like he couldn't be serious.

"I still have my contacts, man," he said. "I didn't lose those."

If Rabe took it as a shot, he didn't show it.

"So what'd he say?" he asked.

"He said he used to work for Khaalis, but he doesn't anymore. And he thinks it'd do us more harm than good if he got involved."

If Katz didn't know Wallace, he might have thought he made the whole thing up, make it look like he pulled it off, with a convenient excuse about why Hashim wouldn't talk. But he did know him. The squint of disbelief in Rabe's eyes reminded Katz he didn't.

Rabe picked up the card and held it up.

"This his number?"

"Yep," Wallace said.

Rabe picked up the receiver and dialed. When the phone started ringing, he put it on speaker. A man's voice answered.

"Hello?" he said.

"Hello," Rabe said. "Is this Mr. Aly Hashim?"

"Who's asking, may I ask?," the voice said.

Nobody trusted anybody, Katz thought.

"This is Deputy Robert Rabe from the Metropolitan Police Department. Did you get a call from a police officer telling you we were trying to get a hold of you?"

"I did. Hold on." He paused a second. "Name of Thomas Wallace?"

Katz looked to Wallace. Wallace kept on his game face.

"Did he tell you why?" Rabe said.

"He didn't have to," Hashim said. "I assume it's about Hamaas."

"That's correct," Rabe said. "I have you on speaker, Mr. Hashim. I have Mr. Wallace here, and Jake Katz from the U.S. Attorney's office."

"Yes, sure, Mr. Katz from the murder case. Hello," Hashim said. "So. What do you want to know?"

"Before I get to that," Rabe said, "can you just tell me what you think about what he's doing here? If you think he's doing the right thing by Islam, then we don't need to talk."

Katz heard Hashim snort a laugh.

"I think it's a misguided conception of what the religion says," Hashim said. "Let me be clearer: It's an abomination of Islam."

"Okay," Rabe said. "So the deal is pretty simple. We're looking for someone to help us end this thing as soon as we can. Mr. Katz said that you helped Mr. Khaalis write the letters that led to his family being murdered. Is that right?"

228

"Sadly," he said, "it is."

"And do you think you could help us out here, talk some sense to him?"

"Sadly again," he said, "I don't."

"Why is that?" Katz asked. "He counted on you to write the letters with him. I'd think he'd respect your judgment."

"Maybe once upon a time, Mr. Katz," Hashim said, "but not now. I'm afraid we had a falling out soon after the murders."

"What happened?" Katz asked.

Hashim sighed.

"Hamaas was my teacher, and I absorbed his every word. I tried to be a good and faithful student to him, and a good and faithful servant of Allah. Being both was a challenge in the best of times, but after the murders, he became more and more withdrawn, more and more erratic. My heart went out to him, of course, and I tried to be patient, but sometimes he would explode at me with such anger, accuse me of putting him up to send the letters – which was not the truth. Then other times, he would treat me like his dearest brother. I began to tire of it – and I began to question whether he was teaching true Islam."

"When was the last time you saw him?" Katz asked.

"I couldn't really tell you," Hashim said. "I haven't been back to the house since probably late '73, the year of the murders. I have seen him at Friday prayers maybe once or twice at the Islamic Center, but he is always guarded, probably by the same men with him now. He never even looks in my direction."

"Is there anyone else you think could talk to him?" Rabe said.

"No one," Hashim said. "He listens to no one, nothing but his own aching heart."

"All right," Rabe said, eager to end the conversation. "Anything else you want to tell us?"

229

"No," Hashim said. "Just that you should know that he truly believes what the Qur'an says, that the earth is only a way station, a place where you prove yourself by resisting temptation, by overcoming nonbelievers, by struggling all the time to be good, and if you succeed, you will be rewarded with paradise after you die. I believe that too, but to him, because I did not do everything his way, the ritual cleansing, the prayers, everything, I became an infidel."

Katz grimaced.

"That's a big club, " he said.

"Mr. Katz," Hashim said, "I am not an infidel. Islam permits some shades of gray, the hadith, the scholars tell us so. Like the Jews and the Christians. All of you have your different denominations and practices, your own ways of following the word of God. Anyway, whatever I was, I left. I had given him my time, my money for his *zakat*, his stipend, so he did not need to be worried about trivial earthly needs like food and clothing, but I was done with doing all that for him, so I left."

Rabe looked to Katz and Wallace to see if they had anything else to ask. They didn't.

"Well, Mr. Hashim," Rabe said. "I'm sorry you won't be able to help us."

"I wish I could tell you someone who could," Hashim said, "but by now, he probably feels that everyone has betrayed him. He is alone against the world. He has made his bed, now he must lie in it. Isn't that the saying?"

"Yeah, "Katz said, "but why do the hostages?"

"Allah will decide their fate," Hashim said. "Goodbye, and good luck."

They heard him hang up.

Rabe took another look at Katz, then Wallace.

"Now what?" he said.

"I'll call Earl," Katz said. "Get those taps in place."

"What else?" Rabe said. "Anybody?"

All he heard was silence.

He turned to Bohlinger.

"Call Cully," he said. "The ambassadors are all we got."

26

Katz took a seat at the end of the table and called Earl. His secretary put him right through.

"Hey, Jake," Silbert said. "How's it going there?"

"Not good," Katz said. "I just came back from upstairs. Khaalis is crazier than usual and he threw me and some nurses out. He told the hostages we'd be the last people they'd ever see. He's going off the deep end if he hasn't already."

"What's Rabe say?" Earl asked.

"We need the ambassadors to try again," Katz said. "That's it. That's all we got. What's going on at the other places?"

"Did you hear Grip this morning on the radio?"

"Yeah," Katz said. "Did he say something else?"

"No, that was the only real news," Silbert said. "Besides that, Khaalis' guys just made a couple of calls about getting some food, coffee, cigarettes. Same with the Islamic Center. They're like us, I guess, waiting to see what happens at the B'nai B'rith. You talk to Cullinane?"

"Rabe's calling him now," Katz said.

"Cully just said he was going to call him. Seems like Hamilton Jordan called him to check on how things were going."

"Who is Hamilton Jordan?" Katz asked.

"He's President Carter's chief of staff," Earl said. "He told Cully he wants this Flaherty to sit in on any negotiations."

"Let's hope there are some," Katz said.

"Oh, and check this out," Earl said. "Jordan told him the British Prime Minister was in town and he wanted to check if they could go ahead with the usual ten-gun salute."

"Are you serious?," Katz said. "What did Cullinane tell him?"

"'Fuck no!'" Earl laughed. Katz laughed too for the first time all day.

"Here's the reason I'm calling," he said. "We need to put in a wiretap application for all the lines Khaalis is using up there. Turns out we were on one but he's on seven."

"Oh, Christ!" Silbert said. "How'd you find out?"

Katz filled him in.

"No problem," Silbert said, "this is an emergency. We're doing the papers for all the ones we hooked up yesterday at all three places. I'll find some more tape recorders for you too. Let me get Marty on, so she can take down all the details."

"Good deal," Katz said.

"Oh, by the way," Earl said, "before I get off, Riordan took the job. Just so you know."

"That's great," Katz said, "good for you. I'll call him when I get a chance and congratulate him. He'll be great."

"Yeah," Earl said. "Hold on. I'll get you Marty. Stay in touch."

Katz picked up the phone and his folding chair and carried them as far down the hall as the cord would let him. Marty's excited voice burst through the line.

"Hey, honey," she said. "How you holding up?"

The 'honey' threw him.

"I assume you're not with Earl," Katz said, "or anyone else."

"Nope," she laughed. "All by myself, just pining away for you. How are you?"

"I'm fine," Katz said, "but I'm ready for this to be over and done with. Did Earl tell you we need more wiretaps?"

"Yeah," Marty said. "He tell you Riordan took the job?"

"He did," Katz said. "I'll give him a call later."

"Better make it a lot later," Marty laughed. "A bunch of them just took him to A.V.'s to congratulate him."

233

Katz looked at his watch for the first time all morning, only to discover it was almost the afternoon. 11:57 to be exact.

"They couldn't wait till after work?" Katz said.

"Oh, it'll still be going after work." Marty said. "You already forget who you're dealing with here?"

Katz heard someone whistle behind him, then call his name. He turned around to see Rabe on the phone and Bohlinger waving him to come back.

"I gotta go," Katz said. "Duty calls. Take these numbers down." He read them off, then said "He's on every one of 'em and we need to hear what he's saying to anyone, for obvious reasons. Do your thing and make it sing."

He tucked the phone under his ear and carried the chair back to the table.

"Will do," Marty said. "Go and come back to me in one piece. I love you."

"Me you too," Katz said. "I'll see you later."

"I'll be there," Marty said.

He hung up.

Bohlinger pushed the speaker button on Rabe's phone. Cullinane's voice rang out.

" – too many of these out of towners tying up the line. The locals have been working with us, but we've heard him talking to New York, Chicago, Australia, for God's sake!"

"And it turns out we haven't been hearing 'em all," Rabe said. "Katz just came back from up there with seven goddamn numbers he's using. That's six more than we knew about."

"Oh, Jesus!" Cullinane said. "That's horrible."

"I made the call we should keep listening for a while before we cut anything off," Rabe said. "You okay with that?"

"Yeah," Cullinane said. "Just make sure nobody cranks him up too much. It's only going to make things tougher on all of us."

"I will, believe me," Rabe said. "We'll pull 'em if we have to."

"All right," Cullinane said. "Sounds good. So, Mr. Khan and Mr. Ghorbal are here with me again. Let me put them on speaker."

Katz heard the babble level pick up on the other end.

"Mr. Zahedi's not here yet," Cullinane said.

"That might not be so much of a loss after last night," a voice said.

"That was Mr. Khan," Cullinane laughed. "Not me."

"You may be better off without me, too," another voice said. Katz placed him as Ghorbal, the Egyptian.

"Sorry," Cullinane said, "too late for that. Anyhow, you've had a chance to sleep on it overnight, so what do you think? How do we get him to call it quits and get everyone back home?"

The silence was overwhelming.

Finally, Katz heard Khan's voice.

"Mr. Zahedi put it right last night, I think. We must remind him of what the faith says, what Islam requires," he said. "And I do recall what Mr. Rabe said, and it is true, Hamaas has many peculiar ideas. But the fundamental truths of the religion are not in dispute. This is what we must counsel him about."

"You're the expert, not me," Rabe said. "I just think that's a tall order."

"Is there any other route we could go?" Cullinane asked. "Any close relations, friends, other religious leaders he might listen to? We just got a report that someone named Wallace Muhammad is coming here this afternoon, wants to talk to him. Does anyone --"

Before Katz could shout out his "No!" he heard stereo shouts on the other end.

"Whoa!" Cullinane said. "That's a bad idea, I take it?"

"It is a bad idea," Ghorbal said. "with all respect. There's a lot of – how do you say it? – history there. Suffice it to say, that would only inflame the situation."

"There's money involved," Khan said, "and power, and, of course, Wallace Muhammad is Elijah Muhammad's son, so the murders too. Wallace suffered at his father's hands at well, but Hamaas does not factor that in. Truly, it is best to leave him out of this anymore than he is already in it."

"I got it," Cullinane said. "I'll tell them thanks, but no thanks. So back to square one."

"The talks must start where Mr. Zahedi and Mr. Khan say," Ghorbal said. "I agree. I also think Mr. Khan should be the one to talk on our behalf, at least to start. Hamaas respects him, as he should."

Katz heard a bitter laugh.

"I am not so sure of that," Khan said. "Do you remember who he hung up on last night?"

"That's a merit badge, Mr. Khan," Rabe said. "He's hung up on me more times than I can count, but he does get back on, trust me."

"All right," Khan said. "I will give it a try. How do we start?"

"Cully, I guess you ought to call him from there," Rabe said. "And we'll listen in from here."

"Okay," Cullinane said. "Should I tell him you're on?"

"Might as well," Rabe said. "He's going to think we are anyway, even if you tell him we're not."

"All right," Cully said. "You said he's got seven lines. Any of them better than the other?"

Rabe looked at Katz.

"No," Katz said. "The phones are pretty much next to each other, so it all depends on whether he's across the way or already talking to somebody. I'll give you the numbers, and you can just pick any one."

"All right," Cullinane said, and took down the numbers.

"Everybody ready?" he asked. "Bob, hang up and we'll be right back. I hope."

Rabe killed the call. In a minute, a red light flashed on one of the lines. When it did, Bohlinger pressed the button again and hit speaker.

"Hello?" a woman's voice answered.

"BJ," Katz mouthed to Rabe. He recognized the voice, but it was a lot more tired than he remembered it just an hour or so ago.

"Who is this?" Cullinane asked.

"Betty Neal," she said. "Who's this?"

"This is Chief Cullinane of the Metropolitan Police Department. I'm trying to reach Mr. Khaalis."

"He's on another line," she said. "Hold on."

The wait was interminable. He's screwing with us, Katz mouthed to Rabe after a solid two minutes had passed on his watch. Rabe pulled on an imaginary dick in the air.

A minute later, Khaalis' voice came on, raspier and more tired than Katz had ever heard it, even in the wake of the murders.

"Mr. Chief?" he said.

"This is Chief Cullinane, Mr. Khaalis. I have Mr. Khan and Mr. Ghorbal on with me too."

"Ah," Khaalis said, "but where is Mr. Zahedi? Still whoremongering with his Jew goddess at this hour?"

"He is en route, Mr. Khaalis," Cullinane said. "He should be with us at any moment."

"I am tired of all this, Mr. Chief," Khaalis said. "I am tired of talking. Where are the jackals who killed my children, my grandchildren, huh? This should have all been over by now. All the Yehudis back in their homes, all the people downtown and up at the mosque spared all this endless chatter, all the fears and anxiety you have put them through needlessly."

237

Katz heard the energy spike in his voice, the venom too.

"Where are the wolves I asked you to bring me yesterday?" Khaalis cried. "Khaalis will spare you the great burden and expense of keeping them in your prisons for the rest of their miserable lives! Everyone can go home, and I will enter the eternal hereafter, fulfilled and thankful. But now here we are, right back where we were, what, twelve hours ago, thirteen, all because you have not moved a muscle to deliver them to me. Is there anything else to say, huh? Anything else to talk about?"

He finally stopped and the line went quiet until Katz heard Khan speak.

"Mr. Khaalis," he said. "This is Mr. Khan again. Mr. Ghorbal and I want to talk to you, but we want to speak to you, just man to man, Muslim to Muslim. Can we do that?"

"How is that going to happen, Mr. Ambassador?" Khaalis said. "The police are on the line, aren't they? Mr. Rabe and Mr. Katz, they must be there too. Hello to you! Who else? Mr. Hoover? Mr. Carter? Who is going to miss the opportunity to hear Khaalis, especially now, huh? This is moving day, Mr. Khan, one way or the other. You are bringing those animals to me or I am giving the orders to have everyone enter the Kingdom of Heaven with me today!"

"Mr. Khaalis," Khan said. "You said last night that you respected me. I am honored to have your respect, sir, truly. But we must back up our words with action, both of us. I promise you, as a brother in the faith, that only Mr. Ghorbal and myself will be on the line with you – if you promise us that you will listen to what we have to say. Listen, eh? Hear what we have to say and reflect upon it. And I promise you that we will listen to you and discuss the situation – and by this, I mean your whole situation, your family, the wolves who slaughtered them, the enmity between you and Mr. Rauf, everything, okay? Not just the situation today but yesterday, all the yesterdays, all right? I

238

ask this of you as a man of faith, our faith. Do this for us now and let us begin to try and trust each other."

Katz was moved by his words. He held his breath and prayed that Khaalis was too.

"I will speak with you," Khaalis said. "Give me one minute."

Katz heard him say something muffled to someone. He heard a woman's voice, then a door close.

"I am alone now," Khaalis said. "Now you say goodbye to your friends and we will talk."

"One moment, Mr. Khaalis," Khan said.

Cullinane came back on the phone.

"Mr. Khaalis," he said. "This is Chief Cullinane again. I'm getting off the phone and I'm asking Mr. Rabe to hang up now too. I'm giving the phone to Mr. Khan, and Mr. Ghorbal is getting on another line, okay? We'll let you talk. When they hang up, they'll fill us in and we'll go from there, all right?"

Khaalis made them wait again.

"Let me talk to them," he said.

"Here you go," Cullinane said. "Bob, we'll call you in a bit."

"10-4," Rabe said and hung up.

"He didn't say anything about the tap," Bohlinger said.

"He ordered us to get off so give yourself a breather," Rabe said.

Bohlinger stood up and stretched.

"But before you go," Rabe said, "turn on that tape recorder."

27

Bohlinger turned on the recorder, then disappeared towards the men's room down the hall. Katz stretched his back and arched it from side to side. Rabe drummed his fingers on the table, then looked past Katz.

"Uh, oh," he said. "Here comes trouble."

Katz turned to see a strapping guy in a dark suit, dark brown hair, maybe in his late forties, skipping down the steps. Two even more strapping guys were just behind him, black suits, white shirts, dark ties. They didn't skip. Last down was Earl.

"You know him?" Katz said.

"I got no fucking idea who he is," Rabe said, "but I know the guys with him. They're Feebies."

Feebies meant FBI to the DC cops and MPD was never happy to see them at any crime scene. As bad as the USA's Office had it trying to figure out which case went to what court when, MPD had it much worse. There were only two real courts in the District – the Federal Court and D.C. Superior – but there were way more police forces, maybe dozens. The Secret Service, the Capitol Police, the Executive Protective Service, Embassy Police, private outfits, all of them got in the way some time but the FBI got in MPD's way more than any of them. Being the Federal Bureau gave them the trump card and they played it every way they could. Katz braced himself for how they'd try to lay it down this time.

The guy at the head of the pack headed for Rabe as soon as he saw him. He kept a grim look on his face, suitable for the occasion. He stuck out his hand.

"Hi. I'm Pete Flaherty. The Justice Department sent me here to see if we could be of any help."

Rabe shook his hand and introduced him to Katz. Earl edged by the agents and joined the party.

"Chief, I thought you could give us an up-to-the-minute report on what was going on," he said. "Can you give us the sixty-second special?"

Rabe brought them all up to speed on Katz' visit, the phone lines, and Khaalis' latest threats.

"So right now," he said, "he's on the phone with two of the Ambassadors, from Pakistan and Egypt. Another one's supposed to be coming, the guy from Iran."

"Is Cullinane on with them?" Earl asked.

"Nope," Rabe said. "Nobody's on but them. That was the deal we made with him. Just trying to establish a little trust, go from there."

"Can we listen in?" Flaherty said.

"Probably not a good idea," Rabe said. "His eminence hears any click on the line, there's no telling what he'll do. He's a little, uh, erratic."

"Paranoid schizophrenic is another way to put it," Katz said.

"Jake knows him better than any of us," Silbert told Flaherty. "He got to know him prosecuting the murderers of his family back in '73."

"Right," Flaherty said. "They filled me in on the background a little."

He turned to Katz.

"You put five guys behind bars for life, and that's not good enough for him?"

"No, sir," Katz said. "He wants a death sentence he can deliver personally. Today."

Flaherty shot him an are-you-kidding-me look.

"He's got to know that's not going to happen," he said.

"He's not hearing us when we tell him that," Rabe said. "That's why we've got these guys talking to him. Maybe he'll listen to them."

"And if he doesn't?" Flaherty asked.

241

He turned to the last page before any of them, Katz thought. No one knew what was on it yet. Rabe told Flaherty what he told Katz when this thing started a million hours ago.

"Mr. Flaherty," he said, "all these things take as long as they take. We think we're heading in the right direction. No one's been shot since the takeovers, and he's let some people go, and he's talking, so we just want to keep it going that way. It's going to end when it ends. We need to just keep working it, working it, working it."

He held up his hands to show that was the end of the story.

Flaherty nodded, then turned to Earl.

"Come with me for a moment," he said, and pulled Earl a few yards back up the hall toward the steps. The Feebies joined them.

Katz walked over to stand with Rabe. The hall was filled with cops, some just milling and chatting, a few heading up and down the stairs, all of them waiting for whatever was next. Earl was doing the talking with Flaherty. That was a good thing. He turned back to Rabe, who was giving the agents a hard stare.

"What do you think of him?" Katz asked.

Rabe shrugged.

"He's a pol. I don't trust him. End of story."

Katz had nothing to say about that so he just nodded. Rabe moved his head to shift his stare to Flaherty.

"You know," he finally said. "D.C. really gets it in the ear. All these guys come from somewhere else. We can't even vote here – except for Mayor now, which doesn't count for squat – but we get all the shit for the bad guys everyone else sends here. We got no choice but to let 'em come, then we get the rap for all the bullshit they do. How fair is that?"

242

"It's not," Katz said. "Maybe that's why they send them all here. Get them out of there and make them our problem."

"I hadn't thought of that," Rabe said. "I think you're on to something."

Silbert and Flaherty walked back toward them. The agents stayed where they were, shoulder to shoulder.

"Okay, listen," Flaherty said, "I'm not real sure why they sent me here. When I was the Mayor of Pittsburgh, the last thing I wanted was someone who didn't have a clue about anything look over my shoulder and tell me everything I was doing wrong, especially if he was a Fed. I'm not doing that."

"I appreciate that, sir," Rabe said.

Flaherty nodded towards Silbert.

"I told him, whatever you want me to do to help you end this thing, I'll do it. You name it."

"I don't know what that is yet," Rabe said, "but I'll let you know when I do."

Flaherty shook his head.

"Ever since the Attorney General told me to come over here, I've been trying to think if I had anything to share with you that might help you out, but I'm coming up short. The closest thing I ever had to deal with was when a lady, a white lady, shot a black kid to death in Manchester, one of our neighborhoods. I got out of my office, got in the car, and went up there to calm things down. They did, but that was a walk in the woods compared to this."

He looked at Rabe.

"Earl tells me you've dealt with this kind of thing before. I'm going to let you deal with this one too."

Rabe nodded his thanks.

"If and when you get this guy to sit down and talk, then maybe I can help," Flaherty said. "I've had more than my share of union negotiations. You've never negotiated till you've sat face-to-face with Pittsburgh teamsters, I'll tell you that."

He reached his hand out to shake Rabe's. Before Rabe could put out his own, Katz heard Bohlinger call out.

"They're off!" he said.

28

Rabe and Katz hurried back to the table, Silbert and Flaherty right behind.

"How do you know?" Rabe said.

Bohlinger held the phone out to him.

"Chief Cullinane," he said.

"Speaker," Rabe said.

They surrounded the phone.

"Cully, what's up?" Rabe said. "We got Mr. Silbert and Mr. Flaherty from DOJ here with us too."

The agents joined them, but Rabe didn't bother to mention it.

"They're off," Cullinane said.

"And?" Rabe said.

"And, I think Khaalis agreed to talk with them."

"What do you mean, you think?," Rabe said. "What did Khan say?"

"Just that," Cullinane said, "then he went off to do his prayers."

"What?," Rabe said.

"He said he was late for his noon prayer, so he was going to take care of that, then get back to me."

Katz glanced at his watch. 12:35.

"So how long's that going to take?" Rabe asked.

"Bob," Cullinane said. "I'm a Catholic. I got no idea."

Rabe shot a look at Silbert, then Flaherty, then Katz. He remembered having to wait for Khaalis more than once.

"Usually ten, fifteen minutes," he said. "If he's got his prayer rug with him."

"He's got it, he said," Cullinane said. "In his car. So whenever he comes back, I'll call you. Hopefully before one."

"In the meantime," Rabe said, "we'll listen to the tape."

Cullinane laughed.

"I should have figured," he said. "Good. If you hear before I do, you can tell me."

"Ten-four," Rabe said.

Bohlinger pushed the speaker button off, then pressed the rewind button on the tape recorder. In a minute, he pushed play.

"Mr. Khaalis," Katz heard, "thank you for talking to me."

"So," Khaalis said, "you wish me to drop my weapons, hug the Yehudis, and leave, is that it? Does Khaalis have it right?"

Khan chuckled.

"I wish to talk to you, Mr. Khaalis, that's all. We can just talk, no?"

Khaalis sighed.

"I am tired of talking, so tired," Khaalis said.

"Then allow me to talk a while," Khan said. "You can talk when you like, or you can just listen, how is that? May I call you Hamaas?"

"Please. And you are Yaqub, is that right?"

"It is," Khan said.

"So you talk, Yaqub," Khaalis said, "show Hamaas the error of his ways."

"We will get to you and I and all the rest in due course," Khan said, "but for the moment, let me ask you, do you know the poet Rumi?"

"Of course," Khaalis said.

Katz didn't. He looked to the rest of them. Nothing. Khan filled them in.

"He wrote such beautiful poetry, eh? All about getting back to God in our daily lives, even then, the 1200s. Even then, they felt cut off. Can you imagine how he would feel today, with automobiles and skyscrapers and televisions all cutting us off from nature so much more than he could ever imagine?"

246

Khaalis didn't answer.

"It is that unity with God that we miss more and more every day, is it not?"

The tape continued silently. Bohlinger rolled up the volume knob. Khaalis' voice boomed from the speaker and he rolled it back down.

"The only one I really remember is the love poem I used to say to Khadyia when I was courting her," Khaalis said.

"Ah," Khan said. "Which is that?"

The tape was silent.

Then Khaalis said, "The minute I heard my first love story, I started looking for you, not knowing how blind that was. Lovers don't finally meet somewhere. They're in each other all along."

"That is one to remember," Khan said.

"I'm not one for poetry," Rabe said. "Fast forward."

Bohlinger pushed a button and looked to Rabe for the signal when to stop. Rabe nodded at him. It was Khan again, still with the poems.

"— are many verses of his like that. The quality of mercy, you see, is a quality of God, he believed. Here is another. 'If you wish mercy, show mercy to the weak.'"

"I do not wish mercy," Khaalis said, "I don't expect mercy. I am well aware of what I have done, what I must do. If they bring them to me, I will slaughter them like they slaughtered my family, then give myself to them to do what they will in their so-called justice system."

"I understand, Hamaas," Khan said, "but consider these words of the poet too. 'Everyone can distinguish mercy from wrath, whether he is wise or innocent or corrupt --'"

Rabe looked at Silbert, then Flaherty.

"Can I?" he asked, then swirled his finger at Bohlinger without waiting for an answer. Rabe waited longer than before, then held up his palm. Bohlinger hit Play. They heard only the hiss of a blank tape.

"Roll it back," Rabe said. Bohlinger reversed it for a few seconds, then let it play. Katz heard Khan again.

" – you take your time, then we'll talk again, all of us, eh? Mr. Zahedi, too. He's not such a bad fellow. Between you and me, I have my differences with him, his lifestyle, as they say. But again, that's between him and Allah, no? He is a wise man, very sharp, and he can help us here. So we will talk again?"

Khaalis made a grunting noise.

"I will call you back," he said.

The hiss returned. Bohlinger shut the machine off.

"So what do you make of that?," Flaherty asked Rabe.

"I don't know," Rabe said. "He said he'll call back. Talking's better than not talking."

"But when?" Silbert asked. "And who's 'you'? Is that just Khan, or all of them, or who?"

The phone rang. Bohlinger picked it up, then put it back on speaker.

"Rabe here," he said.

"Cullinane. Khan just got back. He says Khaalis said he'd call him back, but he doesn't know when, so I don't know where that leaves us."

"Right," Rabe said. "We just heard them. Very up in the air."

"So what do you think?" Cullinane asked.

Rabe dwelled on that a minute then said, "Either talking to these guys is going to work or it's not. What do you think about bringing them over here, and then telling Khaalis they're here to talk to him, face to face?"

"Do we want to risk that, Bob?" Cullinane said. "He's got an arsenal up there. One of these guys gets hurt, we've got a big-time international incident on our hands."

"Yeah," Rabe said, "but on the other hand, if they're here, our chances are better that he won't do anything crazy to anyone. He respects these guys, at least Khan, from what I heard. They might be a good insurance policy, if nothing else."

"Let me talk to Khan about it, get his take," Cullinane said. "I'll get back to you."

They both hung up.

"I wish I could be sure they're as tight as you think, Chief," Earl said.

"They recited love poems to each other," Rabe said. "How much tighter can they get?"

29

Earl walked Flaherty and the Feebies up the steps. Just as they disappeared, a line lit up again. Bohlinger threw on the headphones and clicked on the recorder.

Katz and Rabe watched him listen.

"Another news guy," Bohlinger said. "Pat Mitchell. Channel Five."

"This has got to stop," Rabe said. "We need to keep these open now."

"Want me to pull it?" Bohlinger said, a little too eagerly to Katz's ear.

"No. Call them, get the news director, " Rabe said.

Bohlinger flipped off the headphones, pulled over another phone, and dialed 411. Katz picked up the phones and cupped one of the fat black cushions to his ear.

"I have nothing more to say," he heard Khaalis say. "I've been talking and talking to everyone, all of you, telling you the truth --"

Bohlinger scribbled down a number, dialed it, and handed the phone to Rabe.

"You sound tired," Mitchell said.

"I am tired," Khaalis said. "I've been talking incessantly because someone has to tell the world what is happening here in America."

"And what do you think is happening in America now, Mr. Khaalis?," Mitchell asked.

"Do I really need to explain that to you?" Khaalis said. "After what I've done, after everything I've said since we started? Is it so incomprehensible to you still?"

Katz looked to Rabe doing a slow burn on the other phone.

"They put me on hold," he said, then someone came on.

"Are you the station manager?" Rabe said.

He waited for a second.

"Well, this is Deputy Chief Rabe of the Metropolitan Police Department. You've got one of your people talking to Mr. Khaalis right now at the B'nai B'rith Building and you've got to get him off, now. He's tying up a line we need."

He waited for a split second.

"And that's it for the calls, from anyone. He talks to anyone from now on, it's us, period. Got it? Good."

He hung up with a bang and pointed to Katz.

"You let me know when His Excellency's off."

Khaalis was in full gear now.

" – know what I want. It's no big secret, is it? I --"

And then he was gone.

"He's off," Katz said and snapped his fingers. "Like that. They cut him off in mid-sentence."

"Good," Rabe said. He looked back to Bohlinger. "Let me know when you hear Cullinane on there."

An elevator bell rang around the corner and Rabe took off in a hurry. Katz ran to catch up. A cop ran around the corner towards them, then stopped and waved them back.

"We need a gurney!" he yelled. "Get a gurney!"

He ran back around the corner. Rabe yelled back to Bohlinger.

"Get a gurney!" he shouted. "And a medic!"

Bohlinger ran to the stairway. Rabe ran to the elevators, Katz just behind.

When they rounded the corner, Katz saw two cops leading a heavy sweaty man off the elevator.

It was Blotnick.

They heard the gurney roll down the hall behind them and turned to see it careen around the corner towards them, a medic pulling it, another medic pushing it, then Bohlinger. Katz and Rabe watched the medics walk Blotnick to the bed and lay him down on it.

"That's the guy I told you was acting crazy up there this morning," Katz told Rabe.

251

They watched one of the medics strap him down gently. The other put a pressure clamp on his arm and watched the dial in his hand. Blotnick breathed very lightly, his eyes closed.

Katz walked around the other side of the gurney from the medics and laid a hand on Blotnick's arm. The old man's eyes fluttered, then closed again.

"We've got to get him to the hospital," the medic taking his pressure said. "Stat."

"Go! Go!" Rabe said, and backed out of the way. Katz backed up too, but stopped when he saw a small white envelope scotch taped to Blotnick's shirt pocket.

"Hey, wait!" he said and pointed. "What's that?"

The medic across from him peeled the tape off Blotnick's shirt quickly and slid the contents of the envelope into his hand. Three pills fell into his palm.

"That must be his medicine," Katz said to him. "They gave him some when I was up there, a few hours ago."

"Okay, thanks," the medic said. "We'll let the docs know."

He slipped the pills back into the envelope and they pushed the gurney back around the corner. Katz, Rabe, and Bohlinger followed them.

"Maybe all that mercy love talk actually worked," Rabe said.

Before he could answer, they heard a phone ring up ahead. Bohlinger scurried ahead of them to answer it. When they got to the table, he turned and held the phone up.

"Cullinane," he mouthed, and put him on speaker. Rabe jogged to the table.

"Cully," he said, "what do you hear?"

"Khan's back," he said. "I talked to him and they're up for it, all of them. Zahedi just got here."

"All right," Rabe said. "He just sent down another hostage. He wasn't doing real well, so we sent him to GW. So what's the plan?"

"I think we ought to put Khan back on with Khaalis and let him know they're coming, so there's no surprises. Sound right to you?"

"Absolutely," Rabe said. "He needs to trust them, trust us, every step of the way."

"Okay," Cullinane said. "We'll make the call."

"If he okays it, we should probably talk to him too," Rabe said, "set some ground rules. No guns, no machetes, no cronies, and we probably don't want him down here where he can actually see everything we're listening him to with. We'll set some tables up on the ground floor and clear the lobby and the street. How's that sound?"

"Good," Cullinane said. "You might as well just listen in to him and Khan, then speak up when they're done. He'll think you're on anyhow, so what the hell?"

"10-4," Rabe said. "Dial him up whenever you're ready."

"Okay," Cullinane said, "we'll make the call. It doesn't matter which line, right?"

"Pick any one," Rabe said. "We'll be on when he picks up."

"Stand by," Cullinane said. "God bless us, every one."

The line clicked off.

In a few seconds, a line lit up on a phone down the table. Bohlinger reached over and put it on speaker. They waited for Khaalis to pick up. The voice they heard was BJ's.

"Hello?" she said.

"This is Chief Cullinane," they heard. "May I speak to Mr. Khaalis?"

The next voice was Khaalis'.

"Why are you calling, Mr. Chief," he asked. "I said I would call you back, did I not? Or do you have the murderers in hand now? Allah be praised, tell me that is why you're calling."

253

"Mr. Khaalis, I have Mr. Khan here," Cullinane said. "Mr. Ghorbal and Mr. Zahedi are here with us too, and Deputy Rabe and Mr. Katz are on where you are."

"Those are not the names I want to hear from you," Khaalis said. "I am still waiting to hear you say that you have John Clark and William Christian and Ron Harvey and Theodore Moody and John Griffin with you right here in this building, right now. Where are they, huh?"

"Hamaas, this is Yaqub," Katz heard Khan say. "Here is what we propose. Please listen to me. All of the people on the phone right now wish to come to where you are and sit down and talk with you."

"There has been too much talking," Khaalis said. "There is no point in any more. Heads must roll, if not those animals' heads, then the Yehudis', and Dr. Rauf, and the District people. What else is there to talk about?"

"Hamaas," Khan said, "we started talking about mercy earlier. Let us continue that discussion."

"Hamaas," Katz cut in, "you showed your mercy by releasing Mr. Blotnick a few minutes ago and sending his pills down with him. We all saw your kindness. Let's build on that."

"It was a mercy indeed, Mr. Katz," Khaalis said, "for us. That old Jew was a torment."

Rabe leaned into the phone.

"Mr. Khaalis," Rabe said. "Let's just give it a chance. It will just be us, no tricks, no surprises. You don't lose anything by talking, right? Let's just take a shot are seeing what we can work out."

Katz held his breath. Rabe was motionless. They'd played their last card. They waited for Khaalis to play his.

"No guns," Khaalis said.

Katz exhaled.

"No guns," Rabe jumped in, "us or you. Agreed."

"And no snipers," Khaalis said, "no sharpshooters, down there or up here, no one even at the windows or on the street. "

"Done," Rabe said. "We'll set up a table on the ground floor, at the back of the lobby away from all that."

"And no one goes up the stairs or the elevators while we talk," Khaalis said. "The Yehudis will drown in their own blood before they make it to the second floor."

"Agreed," Cullinane said.

Khaalis was silent.

"It'll take us about fifteen minutes to get over there," Cullinane said. "Bob, when can we start?"

"Give us a half hour to set it up and clear everyone out," Rabe said.

Katz pushed up his sleeve to look at his watch. 2:25.

"Let's make it three o'clock then," Cullinane said, "That sound good to you, Mr. Khaalis?"

They waited for an answer.

They heard a click.

30

Rabe ran up the steps, Katz and Bohlinger trailing in his wake again.

The lobby was filled with cops. It looked like a hundred, but sounded like a thousand. Their chatter echoed off the ceiling and the walls.

Rabe stuck two fingers in his mouth and sliced a sharp whistle through the din that cut it dead. They all turned to see his sweaty red face glaring back.

Rabe walked over to an officer by the door holding a bullhorn. He turned his back to Katz to talk to a knot of cops behind him. They moved back against the wall.

Earl and Flaherty came up to Katz and Bohlinger.

"Something up?" Earl said.

"Khaalis is willing to talk to us, and the ambassadors," Katz said. "We think."

"You think?" Flaherty said. "What --"

Before he could finish, Rabe turned back to face them and the crowd of uniforms surrounding them. He lifted the bullhorn and snapped it on.

"Now listen up," he said. "We're going to have some visitors here in the next thirty minutes, so we need to get every man jack out of the lobby asap, and everybody out from in front of the building too. That goes for cops, reporters, anyone in here or out there who's not me or him or him or him," he said, pointing at Katz and Silbert and Flaherty.

He had their undivided attention.

"And that goes for across the street too," Rabe said. "Push 'em up the block, down the block, I don't care, but get 'em away from the building. We're going to set up right back there," he pointed to the back of the lobby, "and I don't want anyone looking in, listening in, taking pictures, nothing. Set the barriers up at the perimeters of the building, both sides. Any questions?"

He got none.

"Then let's move!" he said and snapped off the bullhorn.

The cops moved, out onto the street and down the sidewalks in both directions.

Rabe laid the bullhorn on the floor and turned to the handful of men behind him.

"You're going to set us up," he said. "We need two long tables and nine chairs."

He looked around and pointed to the gift shop.

"Try there first," he said, "or anywhere else you can get into up here."

They all saluted and took off. Earl and Flaherty crossed the floor to him, Katz and Bohlinger just behind.

"So what's the drill?" Earl asked.

"We think we're sitting down with Khaalis up here," Rabe said, "as soon as the Chief and the Ambassadors get here, in a half hour or so."

Flaherty finished the question he started to ask Katz.

"What do you mean, 'we think'?" he asked.

"You're never sure about anything with him until it happens," Rabe said. "We set some ground rules, and we're getting everyone here, betting on the come. That's all I can tell you."

He turned to Bohlinger.

"You need to get back down there and stay with the phones in case anything happens while we're up here," he said. "You get me on the walkie-talkie if you need me."

Bohlinger nodded but didn't look too happy about it. He headed back down the stairs.

Rabe turned back to the rest of them, then looked over their shoulders. Katz turned to see two of the cops setting up a table at the end of the hall. The others were setting metal folding chairs against the wall. Rabe headed their way, the others in tow.

257

"So there's going to be the four of us," Earl said to him, "plus the Chief, plus the three ambassadors, and Khaalis. That's the nine chairs?"

"Right," said Rabe.

"How do you think we should set them up?" Earl asked. "Someone going to be at the head?"

Rabe thought about that for a second.

"Let's just put five on one side and four on the other," he said. "Put Khaalis in the middle facing the ambassadors. The rest of us can just fill in around them. What do you think?"

Flaherty laughed.

"It took eighteen months for us and the North Vietnamese to agree on the shape of the table," he said. "You could have got us out of there in five minutes."

"I'll take that as a yes," Rabe said. "Anyone else?"

Nobody had a better idea.

The cops brought another table out of an office. Rabe told them where to put the chairs. When they were done, he called them together in front of him.

"I want you guys to go down to the basement, three of you at each elevator shaft, front and back, okay? A guy named Bohlinger is down there listening in on the phones. You see or hear anything funny from the elevators, the stairs, wherever, you call in to Base, let him know, he'll let me know, all right?"

They picked their weapons off the wall and took off down the steps.

Rabe looked at his watch. 2:55, Katz saw. He looked out the glass doors. The sidewalk and the street were empty. Ten minutes after Rabe gave the order, everything was done.

Rabe unclipped his walkie-talkie from his belt.

"Base to Holiday," he said. "This is Rabe. Who's this?" He nodded. "What's going on up there?"

Katz turned to Earl and Flaherty. He pointed across the street and up.

"The sharpshooters," he said, "eighth floor."

"All right," Rabe said, "good. So, here's what's going on over here. Cullinane and a bunch of ambassadors are coming over in a few minutes to talk to his nutship about getting this thing over with. He's coming down when they get here and no one's going to have any guns, us or him, okay? We're going to be on the first floor, back off the street, out of everyone's sight, including yours. He knows you're up there, so you need to be back off the windows, out of sight too."

He paused a second, then forced a smile.

"Right," he repeated for their benefit, "God forbid we should scare him. I know, but the point is to get this thing over with, without anyone else getting killed."

He listened again.

"Okay," he said. "You see anything funny going on up there while he's down here, you let me know pronto. 10-4."

He put the walkie-talkie back in its clip and drummed his fingers on his belt. After a minute, he looked at Katz, then the others.

"You see anything I'm missing?" he asked.

Katz was flattered to be included but the next time he thought of something Rabe didn't would be the first time.

"No," he said quickly. Silbert and Flaherty shook their heads too.

"Then let's take a seat," Rabe said. They followed his lead and grabbed a chair.

Rabe looked at his watch. Katz looked at his. Three on the dot.

"Nothing to do but wait," Rabe said. "They should be here any minute."

Any minute stretched into five minutes, then ten, then Katz stopped checking his watch because he didn't want to know. Silbert and Flaherty made small talk for a while, then gave up trying to kill the time.

Now Katz worried they were missing something. He looked at his watch, then caught eyes with Rabe.

"It's about a quarter after," he said.

"Yeah?" Rabe said.

"It's almost an hour since we talked to Khaalis," Katz said. "What do you think?"

Rabe looked at his own watch.

"I think they're late," he said.

"No," Katz said. "I mean you think we ought to call him now, tell him we're just waiting for them to show up?"

"This isn't a date, Mr. Katz," Rabe said. "We don't have to let him know we're running late."

Katz started to answer but he knew Rabe knew best so he stifled it.

When they still hadn't arrived five minutes later, Rabe got up and headed for the steps to the basement.

"I'll be right back," he said. "I'm calling Cullinane."

The rest of them nodded and waited. Too edgy to sit still any more, Katz walked back through the lobby to look out the window, see if he could spot a police car coming up Rhode Island or 17th. Nothing.

He went back to the table and took his seat. He looked at Earl, who looked back with a tight grin and held up his hands as if to say "What's there to say?" Flaherty stared out at the street, lost in thought somewhere, maybe Pittsburgh, Katz thought.

In a few minutes, they heard steps coming back up the stairs. Rabe's head popped into view.

"I called the command center," he said. "They said they left about ten minutes ago but they had to stop at the Iran Embassy first."

"Why?" Earl asked.

"I have no idea," Rabe said. "Neither did they."

"Where is it?" Earl asked.

Katz knew the answer to that one. On his more ambitious days, he ran past it.

"It's up Mass Avenue," he said, "a little past the Islamic Center."

Rabe answered the question Katz didn't ask.

"Bohlinger said he got no calls from upstairs," Rabe said, "so I think we ought to keep waiting till they get here, let a sleeping khalifa lie."

"Okay," Katz said. If he didn't know better, he'd think Rabe was doubting himself, but he did, so he didn't.

Fifteen minutes later, they heard sirens off to their right grow louder. When they saw two MPD cars pull past, they got up and headed for the door. They went through onto the sidewalk and watched them hang ueys and roll to a stop in front of the building.

A stocky black man got out of the first car with a taller man with an open face and straight black hair combed back from his high forehead. He recognized the stocky man as Walter Washington, the Mayor, but he didn't know he was that short. He figured the other man was one of the ambassadors but he had no idea which one.

Cullinane got out of the second car with a short, balding, light-skinned Arab-looking man with a full face framed by large black glasses, and a taller man with a large angular nose, also with a receding hairline and glasses, but more olive-skinned.

Rabe led them over and they exchanged handshakes all around. The tall man was Zahedi, the short one Ghorbal, the other one Khan.

"The command center said you were making a stop," Rabe said to Cullinane.

"Right," Cullinane said, "Mr. Zahedi stopped by his embassy to get a copy of the Koran."

Zahedi held up a thick black book with both hands.

"For counseling Mr. Khaalis," he said. "To help make our points."

Rabe turned to Washington.

"Mr. Mayor," he said, "are you going to be sitting in with us?"

"No," Washington said, "the Chief thinks I ought to go back to the Command Center, keep in touch from there in case you need anything. I just wanted to come by to thank you all, for everything you've done to keep him calm, keep these people safe."

He offered his hand and Rabe took it.

"Thanks," he said, "but we still have a long way to go."

"I asked the Chief if we should be thinking about some kind of Plan B, a backup plan, if these talks go nowhere," Washington said. "He said we should wait to talk to you."

Rabe winced a little and shook his head.

"If we need a Plan B," he said, "it's going to be bad, whatever it is. We can talk about coming in through the roof, throwing in some gas, if you want, but it's going to be ugly, whatever we do."

"Let's give this a good shot," Cullinane said to Washington, "before we get too serious about doing anything else. He hears noise on the roof or us coming up the stairs, there's no telling what he'll do."

Rabe nodded his agreement, and so did Washington.

"I'm leaving it to the pros," he said. "I'll head back and wait to hear from you. Good luck, and thanks again."

He threw them a salute and headed back to the car. Cullinane led them into the lobby.

"So what do you hear from him?" Cullinane asked once they were back inside.

"Nothing," Rabe said. "I haven't talked to him since he hung up on us."

Cullinane started to say something but decided not to.

"So, should we perhaps take a few minutes," Khan interrupted, "and talk about how we might --"

Rabe interrupted back.

"You know what?" he said. "I'm getting a little nervous about not talking to him for so long."

Katz let out a breath. Rabe looked at his watch.

"It's just about an hour and a half since he hung up on us," he said. "I'm going to call him and let him know you're here and ready to talk."

He turned to Khan.

"He's taken his time on pretty much everything up till now, so we should have plenty of time to figure out how we're going to play it before he comes down."

Khan held up his hands to show no argument on his part.

"I think that's the way to go," Cullinane said. "Plus we'll get an idea what's on his mind now. Okay with everyone?"

Katz scanned their faces.

"What did the Mayor say?" Flaherty said. "I leave it to the pros."

"All right," Rabe said, "take a seat at the table over there. I'm going down to the basement to give him a call."

He turned to Katz.

"Come on down with me," he said, "you're a pro now."

31

The basement hallway was empty except for Bohlinger. Rabe led Katz to the table.

"Those other guys post down here?," Rabe asked.

"Yeah," Bohlinger said, pointing to the two banks of elevators, "three went back there, three up there."

"All right, good," Rabe said. "Dial him up, the hand job, upstairs."

Bohlinger called and put the phone on speaker.

"Khaalis," they heard, scratchy and tired.

"Mr. Khaalis," Rabe said. "This is Deputy Rabe, with Mr. Katz."

"Deputy Rabe," Khaalis said, "has it been half an hour already? I thought you had forgotten us, moved on to more important matters. I was about to remind you we're still here."

Katz flashed on the room, and the gunmen.

"Mr. Khaalis," Rabe said, "I apologize for the delay. It took us a little longer than we wanted for the ambassadors to get here, but they're here now."

"And who else is down there now?" Khaalis said. "A SWAT team? A few sharpshooters to pick off Khaalis who comes down there because he is too stupid to know he is being lied to by the police, huh?"

"No one's lying to you, Mr. Khaa--," Rabe tried to say.

"You are lying, Mr. Rabe!" Khaalis screamed hoarsely. "You told me they would be here in thirty minutes and now it's two hours later. You lied and you have been scheming with your Chief and your Mayor all the while. Khaalis is not a fool, Mr. Deputy, he hears the radio! He knows they left the police building an hour ago! Don't play me cheap, Mr. Rabe! Khaalis still holds the trump cards!"

"Mr. Khaalis," Rabe implored him, "we know that. I assure you they just got here. They stopped by the Iranian embassy to pick up a Koran before they got here. I should have called you earlier to tell you, but I didn't. It was a mistake, that's all, not a lie."

"And you're making another mistake," Khaalis said, "lying to Khaalis again. How can I trust you and come downstairs?"

"Hamaas," Katz said. "This is Jake Katz. I've never lied to you, you know that, and Chief Rabe has never lied to you. The street is clear, the lobby is clear, there's no one down there but Chief Cullinane and my boss and a bigwig from the Justice Department and the three ambassadors. All we're missing is you."

Khaalis spat out a harsh laugh.

"How about Rahsaan Roland Kirk, Mr. Katz?" he said, "Did you invite Mr. Kirk to play some melodies for us so I can remember your idiot stories while we talk?"

"Mr. Khaalis," Rabe said, "everything is just as Mr. Katz told you, and I told you. You hold those folks hostage up there, you control the situation, we all know it. Nothing will happen to you when you come down here. None of us is going to do anything to put anyone up there or anywhere else at risk. Just come down and hear what we have to say."

"You told me that two hours ago," Khaalis said, "when you said you would call me in thirty minutes."

"And I'm telling you that again now," Rabe said. "The only difference is that everyone is here now, ready to talk."

The phone fell silent. Katz pictured Khaalis rubbing his face.

"We need more coffee up here," Khaalis finally said. "And more doughnuts."

"We'll get you those right away," Rabe said, "and we'll have some at the table down here too, okay?"

Khaalis made them wait again, a good long minute this time.

"I will come down, Mr. Deputy," he said.

"All right, that's good to hear," Rabe said. "When?"

"In thirty minutes," Khaalis said. "Just like you promised me."

The next sound was a dial tone. Rabe and Katz looked at each other.

"What's that mean?" Katz said.

"What does anything he say mean?" Rabe said. "Who the hell knows?"

He turned to Bohlinger.

"Get them some coffee again," he said, "and some fucking doughnuts. When they get here, I'll call him again."

Rabe and Katz climbed the steps back up to the first floor. Rabe filled them in on the call.

"All right," Cullinane said, "so what I get out of that is he's still coming down, he's just jerking us around over when. So let's make some good use of the time, figure out exactly what we want to say to him, whenever he gets here."

"I have been giving this some thought," Ghorbal said, "like we all have. There is much in the Qur'an to remind him of. For instance, in Ar-Ra'd," he turned to Cullinane, "I'm sorry, the thunder, Surah thirteen, it is written that they to whom evil is done must repay it with good – not more evil. When you are wronged, you repel the evil by forgiving it and doing good to those who did it. The way to repel evil is with good, is the point. That would be a good starting point, I think."

"I'm no religious scholar," Cullinane said, "but that doesn't seem to square with all this eye for an eye, tooth for a tooth stuff he's been spouting."

"That is why I say we must remind him," Ghorbal said. "He may have forgotten these precepts, or maybe he never knew them at all."

Zahedi was turning the pages of his Qur'an.

"Mr. Cullinane," he said, "there is much of what Mr. Ghorbal says in the Book. I am looking for the chapter that tells us that when we are moved to anger, we must readily

266

forgive, and that if we try to pay back evil, that is an evil too. Ah, here."

He pointed at a passage on the page in a typescript Katz had never seen before. He read it in English.

"'If one is patient in adversity and forgives,'" he said, "this, behold, is indeed something to set one's heart upon.'"

"All of this is true," Khan said, "but I fear we are going down the wrong path if we try to tell him that everything he says, every reason he has taken this action, is wrong. From what I understand not only today and yesterday, but in our previous dealings as well, Hamaas can be very proud and stubborn."

"His way is the only way," Zahedi said.

"Precisely," Khan said, "I think we gain no advantage by telling him he is wrong in his understanding of a religion he has given himself to for some thirty years, and held himself out to be a scholar in, no less."

"Do you have another tack in mind?" Ghorbal asked.

"I do," Khan said, "but I am not too certain about this one either, I confess. These are verses from the fifth surah, the repast, which I know Hamaas knows only because so much of his enmity against the Jews seems to come from it."

"I've heard him," Katz said, "more than once. I know it by heart. 'The Jews are blind and deaf of heart to their God.' We're the infidels."

Khan nodded.

"He is correct in that that quotation comes from the Qur'an, Mr. Katz," he said, "but the same surah, the same chapter, also says that the truly devout Jew who adheres to the teaching of his Torah need not fear the wrath of God. The Qur'an is a very embracing book, and the religion is a very embracing religion to those who truly follow God's word."

"I'm not arguing with you, Mr. Khan, believe me," Katz said, "but there are a hundred people upstairs who might take some exception to that."

267

"I understand, truly, perfectly well," Khan said, "and I do not propose that we try to convince Hamaas of the error of his ways regarding the Jews. That would be futile and, in fact, pointless, because he has taken Christians and his fellow Muslims as his captives too, not only Jews. But I do propose that we rely on the same chapter, a very powerful chapter that occurred during the Prophet's Farewell Pilgrimage, to make a different point."

Ghorbal said, "You are referring to the second verse of the surah?"

"I am," Khan said. He recited it from memory.

"'Let not the hatred of some people in shutting you out of the Sacred Mosque lead you into transgression and hostility on your part; help one another in righteousness and piety, but judge not one another in sin and rancor."

"Doesn't that say the same thing I said?" Ghorbal said.

"Yes, Ashraf, it does," Khan said, "but I think there's something more in it that Hamaas might respond to. It does not quite call for him to repay evil with good, it only calls on him to not follow the evildoers, and to forebear from judging them."

"That's asking a lot, isn't it?" Katz said, "not to judge the people who murdered his children? Even a completely rational person would have trouble following that, never mind him."

"I agree with you, Mr. Katz," Khan said. "He will never forgive the murderers. And I concede that to you. If we must convince him of that, our cause is lost. He will not, even if we can convince him that is Allah's command. But I am hoping we can cause him to reflect on one of his other grievances."

He pointed to Ghorbal and Zahedi next to him.

"With us."

"You've lost me," Rabe said. "Give it to me in words of one syllable or less."

268

"Let me see if I follow you, Yaqub," Zahedi said. "He thinks we are the people shutting him out of the Sacred Mosque because we sit on the Board of the Islamic Center, and the Center got the money he somehow thought was his."

"Precisely," Khan said. "It is perhaps not at the core of his grievance. The murders truly are, and must be. But this is a sore that has festered within him for the past year or so, and maybe, as they say, it was the straw that broke the camel's back."

"So," Ghorbal said, "if we here, the three of us, all express our understanding and even our sorrow at what transpired with the money, then perhaps he might feel understood."

"And that's enough for him to give up the ghost?" Cullinane said.

"That I cannot say," Khan said, "but I do believe it's worth a try. If we, as his brothers, can persuade him we understand his grievance, what he feels he lost, and sympathize with his plight, it might at least push us towards the way out."

Cullinane looked to the rest of them.

"Bob? Earl? Mr. Flaherty? Mr. Katz?" he asked. "What do you think?"

The doors to the outside opened and the breeze pushed the strong aroma of coffee across the lobby to them. A cop pushed a cart filled with boxes of doughnuts and cups of coffee through the doors. Another one followed right behind. The carts rumbled their way to them across the linoleum floor.

Rabe stood up and turned to Cullinane.

"If these guys think that's the way to go," he said "I'm behind it all the way. However we play it out, I just want us all to stay cool, let him talk, and keep our eyes on the ball. It's just going to take as long as it takes."

Nobody had anything to add to that.

269

"I'll tell him dinner's here," Rabe said, "and remind him we are too. Grab anything you like. No charge."

Katz didn't wait to be asked this time, and headed back down the stairs with him.

Bohlinger sat slumped in his chair, head down. They walked to him and waited for him to look up. When he didn't, Rabe bent down to see his eyes closed and hear his heavy breathing. He shook him by the shoulder. Bohlinger lifted his head, labored to open his eyes, and bounced back in his seat when he saw Rabe peering in at him up close and personal.

"Son," Rabe said. "Go upstairs and grab yourself a coffee. But before you go, call dingledick and put him on the speaker."

Bohlinger dialed Khaalis up and dragged himself to the staircase without waiting for an answer. BJ's voice came over the line.

"Hello," she said. "Who is this, please?"

"This is Deputy Rabe," he said. "I want to talk to Mr. Khaalis."

"All right, hold on, sir," she said.

They heard her mumble something and Khaalis mumble something back. She came back on the phone.

"He says he'll be down in thirty minutes," she said.

Rabe's face flushed.

"Please let me talk to him," he said, struggling to keep an even keel.

They heard more mumbling, then Khaalis.

"You don't like to be messed with, do you, huh?" he said. "Neither does Khaalis."

"I have your coffee," Rabe said, "and your doughnuts."

"Excellent," Khaalis said. "Put it on the elevator and send it up. No tricks, do I need to remind you? Anyone's on there, they're coming back down dead."

"It's coming up, all by itself, no problem," Rabe said. "So let's talk about when you're coming down, okay?"

"I need my dinner first," Khaalis said.

"Okay," Rabe looked at his watch. "It's just about five o'clock."

"Give me a half an hour," Khaalis said.

Rabe and Katz looked at each other.

"A real half hour?" Rabe said. Or one of your bullshit half hours?, Katz thought.

"Khaalis is offended," he said. "He is just as trustworthy as you, Mr. Deputy. When he says a half an hour, he means it, just like you, huh?"

"Mr. Khaalis," Rabe said, "I've got the three ambassadors sitting down in the lobby right now, just waiting for you. I've got a Deputy Attorney General and the U.S. Attorney here. They're ready to start talking, right now."

"Then let them talk," Khaalis said. "Let them talk about how they will bring me the wolves I want. Maybe in time for dinner, huh?, so Khaalis can carve them up and feast on their flesh. They can talk about that while they wait for Khaalis."

"Hamaas," Katz said. "You've made your point. We get it. The Chief told you we made a mistake. Can we get on with it now?"

"Mr. Katz," Khaalis said, "your Chief said it took him such a long time to get all his people together, isn't that right?"

"Yeah," Katz said, "that's right."

"Then that's my story too," Khaalis said. "It's taking me a long while to get my people together too."

"What people?" Rabe said. "We agreed it'd just be you."

"Khaalis did not agree to anything, Mr. Deputy," he said. "You said that, he did not."

Rabe flushed again and started to say something, but he didn't. Katz took his cue and held his tongue too.

"Perhaps Khaalis will call you," he said. "In a half an hour."

The phone clicked off.

Rabe turned to Katz, redder than before.

"We need to talk to Cullinane," he said, "about Plan B."

32

Back at the table, Rabe filled them in on the call.

"So we're right where we were," Earl said.

Rabe looked to the ambassadors.

"So, Plan A is what you gentlemen were talking about." He turned to Cullinane. "Should we take a stab at a Plan B?"

Cullinane shook his head slowly.

"Every alternative I talked over with the mayor and the Feebies back at the command center wasn't a Plan B," he said. "They were more like Zs, what we'd have to do if nothing else worked."

"Such as?" Flaherty asked. Cullinane sighed.

"We could drop some SWAT guys on the roof," he said, "and have them come down the stairs and bust in the doors to the conference room, or they could crash in through the roof or maybe the windows, because they painted them over, and surprise them."

"That sounds like a good start," Flaherty said.

"Yeah," Cullinane said, "but it's the run-up that's the problem, not making noise that might tip them off or spook them into doing something. That rules out choppers to drop them down. It also rules out the stairwells. Every time we sent someone up above the second or third floor early on, they saw bad guys looking down at them, so that's a no go too."

"Do we know they're still there?" Flaherty said.

"No," Rabe said. "But that's a lousy gamble. If they are there and we come up, that gives them way too much time to alert the rest of them, and then it's over for the hostages and the OK Corral for us. Everyone loses."

"But what if they're not?" Flaherty asked.

"If they're not," Rabe said, "and assuming they don't show up while we're getting up there, we also have to hope they're not in the hallway."

"They've been there both times I've gone up," Katz said. "Rifles and shotguns pointed right at me."

"But they knew you were coming both times, didn't they?" Flaherty asked.

Katz nodded they did. Flaherty turned to Rabe.

"So this time they won't know," he said. "What if we came up by the stairs or even the elevators, and no one was out there?"

"Those are huge ifs, Mr. Flaherty," Rabe said. "But let's play that out. We take the elevators, that bell's going to ding when the doors open. If there's a way to get rid of that, I don't know it, so that's one more if. But okay, let's say they don't hear it, it's going to take another five, ten seconds to cross the lobby to the conference room, whether we take the elevator or the stairs. Best case again, they don't hear us and we bust in. Then what? All hell breaks loose and a lot of innocent people get shot. And that's the best case."

"I got you, I do," Flaherty said. "But let me just play devil's advocate. What about pumping gas in there, through the windows or the air ducts?"

Gas coming in through the vents, Katz thought, just like the camps. They'd all die of fright, if nothing else.

"Another huge if," Cullinane said. "Assuming we could get it in there like you say, or maybe we could even fire it in from across the street, there's still no telling how much time they'd have to wipe everyone out before we had a chance to charge in there."

"Our folks across the way say they've got an arsenal up there," Rabe said. "Plus, what they're carrying up there already."

"That's knives and swords and machetes," Katz said, "plus the guns."

"Plus the people at the Islamic Center and the District Building," Rabe said. "We've got to coordinate three buildings really tight and, even if we do, we can't be sure who's where or who knows we're coming," Rabe said.

"Okay," Flaherty said, "What else have we got? What are we not thinking of?"

Cullinane surveyed the table. No one had anything to say.

He looked down the table to the ambassadors and spread his arms wide.

"No pressure," he said, "but Plan A's all we got. We got nothing else."

They each nodded their agreement. Cullinane turned to Rabe.

"We gotta get him to come down here, sooner than later," he said.

Rabe looked at his watch.

"The last time I talked to him was just about five," he said. "He gave me the usual half an hour business, so let me call him in about five minutes, show him we're taking him at his word."

"He's got his coffee and his doughnuts," Cullinane said. "Maybe he'll be more amenable now."

Rabe stood up and stretched.

"I'll go downstairs," Rabe said, "check in with the guys at the elevator and across the street, then I'll ring up his Highness."

He headed for the steps and Katz got up to follow. Rabe waved him off.

"Sit this one out, Mr. Katz," he said. "Take a load off. If I need you, I'll send Bohlinger up to get you."

He disappeared down the steps.

Over the next hour, he came back three times, with the same report every time: He says he'll be down in half an hour. The only thing different was the name he bestowed on Khaalis. At 6 he was The Load, and at 6:30 he was the Royal Come Spot. Whoever he was, he wasn't coming down.

Katz went down with Rabe for the six o'clock call and got his hopes up when BJ answered and told him Khaalis was on another line. Rabe pushed the speaker button.

275

"Can you talk?" he asked her.

"No, no I can't," she said way too brightly. "Let me take a message."

Katz pictured her writing down God knows what this time.

"Is he coming down anytime soon?" Rabe asked her.

"No!," she said with emphasis, "I'm afraid not."

"He must trust you by now," Rabe said. "Can you talk sense to him?"

"No," she said, "I'm sorry, sir. That's not possible."

"I don't want you to put yourself --" Rabe said, but stopped when Khaalis said something in the background.

"No," he heard BJ say to him. "It's not Mr. Aziz. It was a reporter, but he hung up."

Her voice came back louder.

"Hello?" she said, "hello? He's gone."

They heard her hang up.

After the 6:30 call, Katz felt himself starting to fade. The adrenalin that peaked when the ambassadors arrived was all drained by now. As seven o'clock approached, the main thing he felt was drowsy. Any other place, any other time, he would have said what he felt was bored. He couldn't even call up the energy to scold himself for being so jaded.

Seven came and went without Rabe making a move to the steps. When Katz caught his eye a few minutes after and pointed to his watch, Rabe shook his head slowly and said "His turn," then put his walkie-talkie on the table, tipped his hat over his eyes, and folded his hands in his lap. Cool Hand Luke, Katz thought.

He looked over to Silbert and Flaherty. Every once in a while, they'd say something quietly to each other, but not for long. It struck him that without Khaalis' madness driving them to talk, they really had nothing to say to each other. He knew his place was to speak when spoken to, so he stayed as quiet as the rest of them.

He turned to the ambassadors at the other table. They kept up a running stream of chatter, mostly in Arabic. It didn't bother him that he couldn't understand it. Unless he was Liz Taylor, none of them would have much to say to a Jew anyhow, and he'd have even less to say to any of them. Other than the fact that they hated Israel, the only thing he knew about Egypt was what they told him in Hebrew school: the Pharaohs held the Jews in bondage and made them build the pyramids. But he found out in college that he didn't even know that because the pyramids were built 3000 years before there was a Jew. He'd just read in the Post that the U.S. was about to start brokering peace talks between the Israelis, the Egyptians, and the Palestinians. He did know what that was: a joke.

He knew even less about Pakistan, even with Khan's thirty-second history lesson on the phone yesterday, and the only reason he knew anything about Iran was from his days in law school. A couple of days a week, he used to eat lunch with his buddy Rick Edelman in Lafayette Park across from the White House. Every day, they were serenaded by what they called the Iranian Marching Band, a few dozen guys with paper bags and pillow cases covering their heads. They'd march through the park shouting something, usually some kind of call and response thing that reminded him of soul music, except it was in Arabic. The only English they heard was "Down with the Shah," followed by something unintelligible, which they pretended to translate out loud, singing out something like "The Shah is a motherfucker!" He remembered Edelman yelling to them, "Hey, fellas! We don't mind you having a civil war, just do it in your own country!" Probably not a good conversation-starter with Zahedi anyhow.

He spotted parts of a crumpled-up, stomped-on Daily News lying across the lobby and got up to get it just to kill some time. He pulled out a few sports pages and threw the rest onto the table. Flaherty and Silbert pulled some of it to themselves. Rabe didn't move.

Katz' eyes drifted to an article that set him back.

"Whoa!" he said. "That is strange."

"What's strange?" Earl said.

"Jabbar's playing against the Bullets tomorrow night," he said.

"Oh, my God," Earl said. "Here?"

"No," Katz said, "L.A."

Rabe kept his eyes closed, but he said "Thank God for small favors."

"What do you mean?" Flaherty asked.

"He means Jabbar owned the house where Khaalis' family was killed," Earl said. "If the game was here, we'd have to call it off, for his own safety if nothing else."

"Khaalis'd probably want us to bring him here too," Cullinane said. "Why not?"

Flaherty was lost in thought for a few seconds, then he said "We don't have a basketball team in Pittsburgh anymore, not since the Condors went under."

"I never heard of them," Earl said.

"ABA," Flaherty said.

"I never heard of that either," Earl said.

"American Basketball Association?" Flaherty said. "We had a few franchises, but none of them lasted."

"You had Connie Hawkins, right?" Katz said.

"We did," Flaherty said. "Back with the Rens in the early '60s. They folded, then we had the Pipers, but they moved to Minnesota. Then they came back a year later, but nobody wanted to see them, so they changed their name to the Condors, but nobody wanted to see Condors either, so they died, probably five years ago."

"You have something in common with D.C.," Katz said. "We lost a team to Minnesota too, except it was baseball and they didn't come back. Then we got another team, but they left and went to Texas, and now we got

278

nothing. Six years and counting. Not that I'm bitter or anything."

"It's criminal," Cullinane said. "The Nation's Capital without the national pastime."

"We do have baseball," Flaherty said, "the Buccos, but everyone's favorite team these days is pretty much the Steelers."

"No Superbowl this year," Rabe said, his eyes still closed.

"That's all right," Flaherty said. "It's only sporting to give someone else a chance."

"You used to hate Bradshaw," Katz said, "now you love him."

"Winning two Superbowls will do that," Flaherty said.

"I hate our quarterback too," Katz said, "although it's really the coach I hate, not Kilmer."

"Billy Kilmer?" Flaherty said. "Old Furnace Face?"

"Yeah," Katz said. "I grew up near Philly and I loved Jurgensen when he was the quarterback there. Then I move down here and I get to root for him all over again because he's a Redskin. Then George Allen gets hired as coach, and he puts Kilmer in! Over Sonny! I quit rooting for them that day."

"Sonny's been gone three years," Rabe said from under the brim of his cap. "Get over it."

"Nobody could throw a ball like Sonny," Cullinane said.

Rabe opened his eyes and looked at Flaherty.

"So we got one other thing in common," he said.

"What's that?" Flaherty said.

"We both hate Dallas," Rabe said.

His walkie-talkie squawked alive.

"Base to Rabe," Katz heard Bohlinger say.

Rabe pulled it to his face.

"Go ahead, Base," he said, "this is Rabe."

279

"The woman's on the line, with Khaalis?" Bohlinger said. "She wants to talk to you."

Katz hurtled down the stairs on Rabe's heels and ran to the table. Bohlinger was on his feet, reaching the receiver to Rabe in both hands.

"She says Khaalis has something to tell you," he said

Rabe grabbed the phone. Bohlinger pressed the speaker on.

"This is Rabe," he said.

"I'm sending a woman down," Khaalis said, then paused to hear something BJ said in the background. "A Mrs. White."

Rabe gritted his teeth. Katz felt the way he looked. What would have been welcome news a day ago depressed them both now.

Then Khaalis said, "And I'm coming with her."

33

Katz slapped Rabe on the back and even exchanged a happy nod with Bohlinger.

Rabe was all business.

"We're ready for you," he said. "You can come down right now. We're on one."

"Just you and the others you said, correct?" Khaalis asked.

"That's all," Rabe said. "Just us. And just you."

"Just me," Khaalis said, "and Mrs. White."

"You bring her down," Rabe said, "and we'll walk her out to the medics, so no one else has to come into the building."

"And no guns," Khaalis said.

"No guns, no weapons of any kind. You too," Rabe said.

"All right," Khaalis said. "We're coming down."

Rabe waited until the phone clicked, then pointed to Bohlinger.

"You call across the street and tell them he's on his way down," he said. "Tell them they've got to keep an eye on anything going on up there and let you know asap."

Bohlinger saluted and reached for his walkie-talkie.

Rabe and Katz scrambled back up the steps. Rabe headed straight across the lobby and out the doors. All eyes were on them. Rabe waved to the first officer he saw, and met him just a few steps outside the door.

"He's coming down," Rabe said, "now. So I want everyone back and out of sight pronto. No one comes in."

He unhooked his gun belt and handed it to the officer.

"You need me or Cullinane for anything, you call Base, all right?"

The officer saluted but Rabe was already headed back through the door. By the time he got to the tables, everyone was standing, facing them.

"He's on his way," Rabe told them. "Wait here. Katz, come on."

Katz followed him briskly back to the elevators. He saw the light blink on over the door on the left and heard the bell ring. They ran to it and got there just as the doors pulled back.

A slim, short blonde woman stood before them, haggard and trembling. Khaalis stood behind her in a long brown trench coat over a blue windbreaker and lifted his left arm towards the open door. The woman stumbled forward and fell into Katz, clinging to him, grabbing his arms so hard they hurt.

Khaalis stepped out behind her and looked at Rabe. He offered his hand.

"Mr. Deputy Rabe, I presume?" he said.

Rabe gave his hand a quick shake, then pointed to Khaalis' waist.

"I am," he said. "That's got to go."

Khaalis looked down at the steel chain running through his belt loops. Katz followed his glance to Rabe's beltless waist. Khaalis unhooked the chain and handed it to Rabe.

"Sorry," he said. "Forgot."

Rabe gathered the chain in his hand and slid it to the wall next to the elevator.

"I need to make sure that's all you forgot," he said.

Khaalis lifted his arms. Rabe patted down his chest and pockets, then circled around him, knelt down, and slid his hands up and down his legs inside and out. Right out of the manual, Katz remembered.

"Okay," Rabe said.

He got up and came back to Mrs. White, still clinging to Katz. He laid a hand on her shoulder.

"Ma'am," he said. "Mr. Katz here will walk you out to the policemen on the streets. They'll get you to a medic and a hospital if you need it, okay?"

"Can I call my husband?" she asked. "He, he --".
She couldn't finish, awash in tears.

Rabe motioned to Katz to take her out. He unpinned an arm, wrapped it around her frail shoulders, and held her close as they moved slowly down the hallway and out through the revolving door. As soon as they were on the sidewalk, two medics ran to them and gently took her from him.

By the time he made it back to the table, they were all taking their seats. Khaalis was in the middle chair to his right, Zahedi, Khan, and Ghorbal across from him, just like Rabe wanted. Cullinane sat nearest to the door next to them, Flaherty on their other side. Silbert sat across from him, and Rabe sat between Silbert and Khaalis. Katz took the open seat on Khaalis' other side.

Hamaas looked beat. Dark rings etched deep into the soft skin below his eyes. A brown stubble and random curls of hair dotted his cheek above his beard. His deep brown eyes, always so full of fire, were now only full of strain, wet, weak, and bloodshot. He could use some deodorant too. He seemed more like a captive than the captor, Katz thought.

"Well, first, we appreciate you coming down," Cullinane said.

Khaalis shrugged.

"You wanted to talk to me," he said. "Go ahead. Talk."

Khan smiled.

"We want to talk to each other, Hamaas, and listen to each other, so that we might understand each other better, no?" he said.

"You want to teach me the Koran, Mr. Khan?" Khaalis said. "Don't bother. I know it better than you."

Khan kept smiling.

"I know you know it, Hamaas, better than any of us," he said. "We are not here to compete with you, or convince you of anything. We know better, trust me."

Ghorbal jumped in.

"We just wish to take the time to hear you," he said. "Hear what you believe --"

"I have told you all what I believe!" Khaalis interrupted, "what I've told everyone who has called. You have heard me, I know that. You are on my phones, listening. Have you not been paying attention?"

"We have been paying attention," Ghorbal said quickly, "close attention, but --"

Khaalis leaned towards him and slapped the table hard.

"No!" he said, "you have not! Or you would not need to ask me what I believe! I believe what you must believe, huh?, because the Qur'an says it is so. What even Mr. Katz and the Yehudis upstairs must believe because the Qur'an says it is from their Torah. 'And we ordained for them in that Torah, a life for a life, and an eye for an eye, and a nose for a nose, and an ear for an ear, and a tooth for a tooth, wounds equal for equal'! What could be clearer?"

Zahedi flipped the pages in his Qur'an until he found what he was looking for.

"But, khalifa, pardon," he said, "there is more to the quotation you say. Allow me. It continues, 'But he who shall forgo it out of charity will atone thereby for some of his past sins'. The Prophet says to us, if you look past these desires for revenge, you will make atonement for your own sins. You see that, you know that too, do you not?"

"I am not here to atone, Mr. Zahedi," Khaalis said. "I am here to do the justice the Qur'an commands of me!"

"But still, Hamaas," Zahedi said. "Your conception of what it commands may not be complete, shall we say? Please allow me to tell you a story, a personal story that my grandmother shared with me about her husband, my grandfather, when he was killed, slain at the hands of others."

"Enlighten me," Khaalis said.

"My grandfather was a leader of his tribe and his tribe was often at war with the other tribes in his area. He went to one of those tribes to make peace, and he was sharing a water pipe with one of their leaders, mounted on his horse, when one of the enemy tribesmen shot him with a rifle, through the heart, and killed him. The wars between the tribes went on for many years, but at long last, the rifleman who shot my father was captured and was to be executed. Before he was, he was brought back to my grandmother so that she could see the man who killed my grandfather, her husband. And do you know what she did? She looked at him and she looked at the leader of her tribe and she told him that she had forgiven him and asked the leader to spare him."

Zahedi sat back and spread his hands to Khaalis.

"So you see?" he said. "When we suffer a tragedy like my grandmother suffered, like you have suffered, we must have the capacity to forgive."

Khaalis let his gaze linger on Zahedi for a minute, then turned towards Cullinane.

"Is this what you brought me down for, Mr. Chief?" he asked. "To hear stories from fools and whoremongers?"

Khan reached across the table and laid his hand close to Khaalis' arm.

"Hamaas," he said, "khalifa, if I may. Let us talk about your demands, eh? One at a time. We are here together to talk, so let's talk about what's really on your mind, why you are here, eh?"

Khaalis looked at him like he was the biggest fool at the table.

"Is this a secret to you too, Yaqub, Mr. Ambassador?" He took in the table. "Has no one been paying attention?"

Khan raised his hands.

"It was a rhetorical statement, Hamaas. We well know you want the murderers brought to you."

"You would have been home by now in your pipe and your slippers," Khaalis said. "And I would be in paradise."

285

"But, Hamaas," Khan said, "forgive me. The word of the Prophet is not so clear, so unambiguous in this regard."

"What could be clearer?" Khaalis said. "I am entitled to my revenge."

"That is not so clear as you may picture it," Khan said. "Shari'a law does permit revenge, even demand it in some circumstances, but it is not for you, or any victim, to take his revenge. That is for the state."

"If the state is a Muslim country," Khaalis said, "I agree with you, Yaqub. But this is not one, and look at what happened here when I turned to the courts for justice – nothing!"

Katz and Silbert caught eyes but kept quiet.

"The animals who did these unspeakable acts," Khaalis went on, "still draw air – and the government houses and feeds them! That is not justice! And the animals who sent them here to do their bidding still run free, mocking me with their gloating!"

"Hamaas," Khan said, "this is as you say, I concede. You look to the courts for justice if they follow shari'a, but – if they do not, revenge is still not yours to take. It is Allah's. As it is said, 'If a man kills a believer intentionally, his recompense is Hell, to abide therein forever, and the wrath and the curse of Allah are upon him, and a dreadful punishment is prepared for him'. Surah four, surely you know this."

"Taking hostages," Zahedi said, "Hamaas, it is against the very soul of Islam. An innocent is an innocent. If you want revenge, it must be taken against the one who has done the wrong."

Hamaas banged the table again, this time with both hands.

"They won't let me!" he screamed in pain.

The table broke into a loud babble of voices straining to outshout each other, making their points to the air, no one giving an inch to the other. Cullinane got to his feet and tried

286

to restore order but he fell back in his chair, outnumbered and helpless.

Katz listened to the din swell, then recede only when the ambassadors gave up first, one at a time, Ghorbal, then Khan, then Zahedi, none of them a match alone or together for the Khalifa at full throttle, standing, spitting, pointing, accusing.

"Why are you helping the police here?" he demanded when he had the floor all to himself. "Is that the law you now respect? Not the law of our people, our forefathers, the Prophet, Allah?"

Tears filled his eyes and streamed down his cheeks. The rage that pinned Katz to his seat felt like it blazed from every pore of Khaalis' body.

"Why are you not helping me? Me?" he screamed on. "Why have you never helped me? Has anyone of you – has anyone, ever, anywhere – endured what I have had to endure? Is there no end to my trials, my suffering, now even at the hands of those who profess to love Allah?"

He fell back into his chair and clasped his hands to his eyes, trembling, muttering, the stench of his sweat filling the air.

Katz thought he had heard everything Khaalis had to say, but this time was different, like he knew he was at last hemmed in, powerless, overwhelmed by what he finally knew to be true. But the words that rung in his ears were not Khaalis'. They were Abdul Aziz', when he told him that Hamaas was beyond Job, alone among all in his suffering. Only now, Katz felt, did Hamaas, for the first time, finally accept that that was his fate.

Cullinane was the first to speak again.

"Let's take a break," he said. "I'll grab someone to bring in some coffee and doughnuts." He looked at his watch. "Why don't we regroup at 8:30? That's ten, twelve minutes from now."

Flaherty stood up first.

"Where's the bathroom?" he said.

Rabe pointed back and to the left. Flaherty nodded and disappeared around the corner.

Zahedi and Ghorbal stood up and walked together into the lobby. Katz watched them draw close and talk to each other quietly in Arabic again.

"Let me know if you need to go too," Cullinane said to Khaalis. He pointed to Rabe. "One of us will walk you back there."

If he heard him, Khaalis gave no sign. He sat back in his chair, looking past Khan, lost in his thoughts.

Katz got up and headed for the men's room. When he rounded the corner, he saw two pay phones hanging on the wall. He dug into his pocket for some change, pushed two nickels into the slot, and dialed up his place. Marty picked up on the second ring.

"Hello?" she said.

"Hey, it's me," he said.

"Oh, God," she said, "I've been dying to hear from you. Is it over?"

"No, but he's down here talking, sort of."

"What do you mean 'sort of'?"

"It got a little heated, and Cullinane just sent everyone back to their corners to cool off."

"Who's all down there?" she asked. He told her. When he got to Flaherty, he told her he was going to be the new Deputy AG.

"Whoa," she said, "that's interesting. Have you told him you're going to be working for him?"

"No," he laughed. "Nobody's really had much time for chit-chat."

"Just asking," she said. "Sorry."

The last thing he needed was her to get her nose out of joint. She must have sensed it too.

"I am sorry," she said. "You've been on my mind all day. How are you doing?"

"I'm doing fine," he said, "I guess, as well as can be expected. It's been a long day, a long two days. I've got to get back there. Let me go."

"I'll be here waiting for you," she said. "Wake me up if I fall asleep. I can't wait to hear how you were the hero of the day."

"Okay," he said. "I love you."

"Love you too," she said. "Get back to me."

He hung up the phone and hit the head.

When he got back to the table, Khaalis and Khan were standing together behind Khaalis' seat. Both of them had their hands in their pockets, chatting casually like they were old chums. Katz walked past them toward his seat, but hung back a few feet so he could see them but Khaalis couldn't see him.

"My first preacher was from Pakistan." Khaalis said. "I studied with him for thirty years. A very learned man."

"Who was he?" Khan asked. Khaalis told him, but Katz couldn't make out the name. Khan nodded like he knew who he was.

"The Hanafis are the school of love," he said. "The school of pardon."

Khaalis' eyes welled. Khan laid his hand softly on Khaalis' back.

"Come," he said. "Walk with me."

They walked together back down the hall. Flaherty walked to Cullinane.

"Should one of us go down there with them?" he asked.

Cullinane looked to Rabe. Rabe watched them disappear around the corner. By the time he turned back, Cullinane had made up his own mind.

"Let's let 'em talk," he said. "I'll hang down by the corner just in case."

"Ten-four," Rabe said. "I'll check in downstairs and across the way."

He headed for the stairs and Cullinane headed off in the opposite direction. Katz took his seat. Silbert nodded to him, then leaned over.

"Can I tell him?" he asked, loud enough for Flaherty to hear.

"Tell him what?" Flaherty asked. Katz had the momentary fantasy that Marty somehow managed to pull this off in the last five minutes.

Silbert looked over his glasses at Katz. Katz shrugged.

"Of course, sure," he said. Silbert looked across the table to Flaherty.

"He's coming to work for you," he said, "at Main Justice."

"Oh, really?" Flaherty said to him. "Where?," he said to Katz.

"Criminal," he said, "Fraud. I'm going to be Deputy Chief."

"Oh, terrific," Flaherty said. "Congratulations. When do you start?"

"I don't know yet," Katz said. "They told me it depends on whether Thornburgh signs the papers before he leaves tomorrow."

"You'll probably be there before I will, officially at least," Flaherty said.

"You'll be confirmed in no time," Silbert said without a trace of irony. "The Democrats own the Senate."

"Well, whoever gets there first," Flaherty said to Katz, "give me a call and we'll set up a time to reminisce about how well we got this thing over with, hopefully."

"I will do that, sir," Katz said. "Here's hoping."

By the time they all sat back down together, it was just past nine.

"If I may," Khan said to Khaalis. Khaalis extended his open arms.

"Hamaas and I had a very nice talk," Khan said. "Not surprisingly, we did not agree on every single thing, but I think we found what you would call common ground. Stop me if I have already got it wrong, Hamaas," he said.

"I will tell you when you have erred," Khaalis said.

"I have no doubts," Khan grinned. "So what we agreed on is that Islam is a religion of compassion, that our faith holds dear the notions that all men, Moslems, Christians, Jews, whoever, must forbear from spreading mischief or creating fear in the minds of hearts of anyone. Do we agree or do we not agree, Hamaas? Let me know."

"In normal circumstances, in times of peace, yes," Khaalis said, "but not here, not now, in this time of war. In war, there is no compassion, no justice without the sword."

"So," Khan said, "this then is where we begin to differ, because this is not a war, Hamaas. You are not fighting a war, a jihad, eh?"

"Do not pretend to tell me what I am fighting, Mr. Ambassador, huh?" Khaalis said. "There is no other name for my actions against the infidel, the apostate government, the thieves at the so-called Islamic Center, the wolves who slaughtered my children. What name would you give what I wage against them all? I am a soldier, we are soldiers, prepared to die, all of us! Jihad is all it can be!"

"Hamaas, it does not matter what I would call it, or what you would call it," Khan said. "It is what the Qur'an calls it, and it does not call that aggression jihad. A true

Muslim does not wage war for revenge, only to maintain the peace and put an end to mischief in his community."

"It is true, Hamaas," Ghorbal said. "When we are vindictive, we transgress against Allah."

"May I please?" Zahedi said. He traced his finger from right to left across the pages of the Qur'an before him. "In English, 'And fight in God's cause against those who wage war against you, but do not commit aggression for God does not love aggressors'. Your war, Hamaas, if you call it that, would be permitted against those who seek to destroy us and our faith, but for no other reason."

"Spare me your great spiritual lessons, Mr. Zahedi," Khaalis scoffed at him. "I would rather hear Mr. Katz or Mr. Silbert expound to me on the lessons of the holy Torah than to hear you so reverently quote the Qur'an. You profane it by reading it. Enough from you!"

"Hamaas, please," Khan said. "Let us not personalize this. We are here to talk to you, to enlighten you when it is appropriate, and to be enlightened by you. The Ambassador's point is a good one. You know Ash-Shura, verse 40, of course."

Zahedi flipped the pages in his Qur'an forward.

"Ardeshir," Khan said, "it is not necessary. I know it and Hamaas does too. An attempt to requite evil may also become an evil, but whoever pardons his enemy and makes peace, his reward rests with God, for He does not love evildoers."

"I am not an evildoer, my friend," Khaalis said. "I am the one to whom evil was done, repeatedly and from the bowels of animals not fit to be called Muslims, or even humans."

"There can be no doubt of that, Hamaas," Khan said, "you are a truly holy man. But, when you give in to the sweet temptation of revenge, as delicious as it might taste, it is the same evil as the evil done unto you. Perhaps this is harsh, but you no doubt counseled your flock the same thing many times, I'm sure."

"I have counseled them to kindness and justice, of course, always, but also to abide by Allah's will. You must ask yourself, Yaqub, would Allah truly deny me the opportunity to slay these evildoers? Why would he not applaud it?" Khaalis asked.

"Hamaas," Ghorbal interjected, "you have a right to ask that as no other man perhaps has that right. Who has been injured so grievously as you? But the word of God, the divine will, calls upon us to follow his compassion even in these circumstances. The same surah that Yaqub quoted to you goes on to say that those who oppress others and behave outrageously on earth, they offend all that is right, and will be made to suffer grievously."

Hamaas shook his head.

"Compassion, peace, I hear you say to me over and over," he said. "You counsel me to abide by the courts of this country, but they are Godless courts that cannot take the revenge I demand, did not take it, will not take it. You deny me the power to take revenge and counsel me to leave it to Allah's grace. Well, where is your compassion for me, huh? Where is the peace you wish for all humanity but not for me, huh?"

They all sat quiet for a long minute until Khan leaned forward and reached his hand out to Khaalis again.

"Hamaas," he said quietly, "Islam is not such an easy faith, eh? Perhaps if it were, the whole world would be our brothers. But this is what it is and this is who we are, the two of us, Mr. Ghorbal, Mr. Zahedi. As it is said, if one is patient in adversity, and forgives, this, then is indeed something to set one's heart upon. This is who we are, who we must be if we are to follow the will of God. I know you know this, and I know how hard it is for you to bear this now, of all times. But so it is."

Katz waited for Khaalis to answer but he sat silent. The room felt like gravity had tripled in an instant. No one moved until Zahedi leaned across the table.

"Hamaas," he said, "I know you think me an infidel of the worst order. I am not quarreling with you about this. So be it. I am not the world's most religious man. I am weak and I will pay for my sins. But I do know one thing, one thing I have done to offend you, and I want to atone for that now, to you."

Hamaas flicked his gaze from the table top to Zahedi and held it there.

"I sit on the Board of Directors of the Islamic Center, as you know, and you know as well that we secured a great blessing of millions of dollars from the Sheikh of Sharjah in the UAE, the Emirates. This is what I wish to apologize to you for, not for receiving the money, but for failing to share it with you. Please, accept my apologies for that mistake."

"And mine," Ghorbal said. "You have played such a major role in spreading the word, inspiring so many people, persuading them to see the wisdom of the Qur'an, you should have shared in that bounty. It was not only ours to keep, but yours as well. I truly, humbly apologize for my part in denying it to you."

Hamaas turned his head to Khan.

"What more can I say than what my brothers have said, Hamaas?" he said. "It was a grievous mistake by all of us, by the Board, by Dr. Rauf. We should have been magnanimous and shared our bounty, for he who gives to others and is conscious of God, that is the true path."

Hamaas lifted his eyes to the ceiling. Katz didn't know if he was waiting for Allah to inspire him or thinking about the eighth floor.

Earl leaned into view down the table.

"Hamaas?" he said. Khaalis turned towards him.

" I want you to know," Earl said, "we did everything we could to bring those bastards to justice. There wasn't a stone we left unturned, a lead we didn't follow. I know you know that, but I want you to hear it from me, personally. We combed every inch of 16th Street to find the crap they threw out the windows when they ran from you. We went to Philly to find those guys, every one. We went to Florida to bring back Griffin and Christian. We went to hell and back to chase these guys down and convict them."

Khaalis wagged his finger at Earl but looked the other way, towards Katz.

"Not Griffin," he said. "Not John Griffin."

Katz was dying to remind him of what Abdul-Aziz reminded him of, that he had called off the cops from going into Hamaas' home to grab the unregistered guns, but he couldn't make himself do it. It was too much like grandstanding, not his style, even now. He let Earl answer him.

"Hamaas," he said. "We tried. Four times we tried. The jury let him go, not us."

Katz knew that Amina might've put him behind bars if she testified at either of the last two trials, but he also knew that Earl wouldn't remind Khaalis of that either.

Khaalis looked away from Earl and back to the table.

They all sat silently. Katz felt they had shot their last shot. There was nothing more any of them could say. Either Khaalis felt it was in his heart to let them go, or he didn't. They had come to the end of their road.

Ghorbal broke the silence.

"Hamaas," he said, "perhaps a gesture of good faith, eh? Would you release thirty hostages, maybe, just as a sign that we are making some progress, no?"

"You've made your point," Rabe said. "We all understand."

Khaalis stared straight ahead at Khan. Khan returned his stare, but said nothing.

After another eternity, Khaalis spoke.

"Fine," he said. "I will release them."

295

"Ah!" Ghorbal said. "The thirty?"

"No," Khaalis said. "All of them."

34

Katz wasn't sure he heard that right. He looked to Rabe who looked to Cullinane.

"So you'll release them all?" Cullinane asked. "I just want to --"

"All of them," Khaalis said. "You heard me right."

"Do you mean all of them here?" Silbert asked, "or everywhere?"

"Everywhere," Khaalis said. "I will release them all, everywhere, each place, all of them. Is that clear enough for all of you?"

Khan was the first to his feet. He pushed himself up off his chair and extended his open arms to Khaalis. Khaalis stood and reached across the table to clasp his hands, then Khan circled it to embrace him. One by one, each ambassador hugged him and nuzzled him on each cheek. When they were done, Katz shook his hand and the rest did too.

"This calls for a celebration," Zahedi said.

"Let's get everyone out first," Cullinane said. "We can celebrate then."

"Let's talk about how we should go about this," Rabe said. "Mr. Khaalis is going to have to make the first calls, I think, make sure his men don't think we're setting them up."

Khaalis took his seat again before he answered Rabe. Everyone else stayed on their feet.

"First things first, Mr. Deputy," he said.

"I thought that was first, Mr. Khaalis," Rabe said. "What am I missing?"

"We need to talk about what happens to me," he said.

"Mr. Khaalis," Earl said, "that's going to be up to the courts. My office is going to have to present this to a grand jury and then take whatever they wind up charging you with to a court for trial."

Khaalis waved him off.

"You are way, way ahead of me, Mr. Silbert," he said. "I mean now."

"That's what the Deputy was saying," Cullinane said. "Let's spend some time talking about how we're going to go about it."

"You're missing my point, Mr. Chief," Khaalis said. "I mean there is still the matter of what happens to me."

Cullinane cocked his head.

"What do you mean?" he said.

"I mean what I say, Mr. Chief," Khaalis said. "If I release these people, what do you plan to do with me?"

"Mr. Khaalis," Cullinane said, "you and your men have kidnapped over a hundred people in three different places. You've held them hostage for the better part of two days, for all kinds of demands. One of your men – maybe a few of them – shot people in the District Building. One of them died and two others were wounded. So, what we plan to do with you and your people is arrest you for all of that, then it's up to Mr. Silbert and the courts to figure it out from there, just like he told you."

"Then that is something we need to discuss before anyone is released," Khaalis said.

"You've lost me," Cullinane said, his cheeks reddening. "What do we need to discuss?"

"The terms for my release, I would put it," Khaalis said, "in return for theirs."

Cullinane and Rabe exchanged glances that Katz could read as well as they could. Cullinane planted his thick index finger into the table across from Khaalis.

"Your release is not on the table," Cullinane said. "You're not going to be released. You're responsible for this, all of this, and the next place you're going is jail."

Khaalis folded his hands and shook his head.

"Mr. Chief," he said, "as long as we hold these people, everything is on the table."

"Mr. Cullinane, Hamaas, if I may," Khan said.

"You may not," Khaalis said. "You have done your job, Yaqub, you and Mr. Ghorbal and Mr. Zahedi, you have played your part in this little drama. Khaalis has agreed to release the hostages. Now, it is for the others to play their parts. You have no further business here. It is for me and the authorities."

Khan started to answer but Rabe cut him short.

"Mr. Khan," he said, "give us a minute to talk this over please."

He and Cullinane walked back down the hall. Silbert, Flaherty, and Katz fell in behind. At the corner, they huddled up.

"What in Christ's name is going on here?" Cullinane said. "This guy is out of his skull if he thinks we're just going to hold the door open while he walks out of here."

"You know that and I know that," Rabe said, "but the problem is, this guy *is* out of his skull."

"Can you throw him a bone?" Flaherty asked. "Something, anything, to get this thing over with?"

"Like what?" Cullinane asked. "A limo to the jailhouse?"

"I think he is right about one thing," Rabe said. "It's time for the three of them to go. They did what we wanted. I don't think it does anybody any good to keep them around at this point. It's all police business now, him and us, period."

"Anybody see anything wrong with that?" Cullinane asked. No one did.

"Okay," he said. "they're gone. Then what?"

"He's the khalifa," Silbert said. "He's the leader. Maybe give him some concession we don't give anyone else so he can keep his pride."

"What?" Cullinane asked. "What do we give him?"

"I don't know," Silbert said. "We can take him home so he can say goodbye to his wife before you book him, something like that."

He looked at Katz.

299

"Can you think of anything?" he asked. "Something that might mean a lot to him but nothing to us?"

"Maybe let him make a statement that we can okay before he gives it," Katz said. "Let him enlighten the world one last time before he leaves the stage. He loves to talk, loves the spotlight. Maybe that'll do it."

No one else had anything.

"I got a bad feeling about this," Rabe said, "just going down this road at all."

"I do too," Cullinane said, "but this is where we are. I'm ready for any other ideas, good, bad, let's have 'em."

They all looked to Rabe. For once, he didn't have a better idea than everyone else.

"All right," he said. "Let's play it out, see where it goes."

"Okay," Cullinane said, "let's go say adios to the ambassadors or however the hell you say it in Arabic."

They followed him back around the corner. Khaalis was at his seat, smoking a cigarette. The ambassadors, huddled in a group, stood across the table from him.

"Okay," Cullinane said to them, "we're going to talk to Mr. Khaalis alone now, just us. You fellas have done more than enough to get us here. I can't thank you enough."

"Are you sure?" Khan said. "The job is not yet done. We would be pleased to stay to the end."

"I have no doubt about that, Mr. Khan," Cullinane said, "but I think we have to carry it from here."

The ambassadors looked from one to the other, then Khan raised his hands in acceptance.

"Then so be it," he said. "We will take our leave."

"I'll get a cruiser to take you back to your embassies or wherever you want to go," Cullinane said. "We all truly appreciate everything you've done."

"Mr. Chief," Zahedi said, "will you walk us to the door so that we may have just a word?"

"Of course," Cullinane said, and walked them through the revolving door onto the sidewalk.

Katz and the rest of them took their chairs again. Khaalis watched Flaherty flick a glance at his watch.

"What time do you have, Mr. Other Deputy?" Khaalis asked.

"It's ten ten," he said, "give or take a few minutes."

"Am I holding you up?" Khaalis said. "Do you have another appointment?"

Now Flaherty's cheeks flushed.

"No, Mr. Khaalis," he said. "I'm here for the duration, as long as it takes."

Khaalis took a long drag and smiled, then crushed the butt under his heel.

In a few minutes, Cullinane came back to the table.

"Mr. Chief?" Khaalis said, "can you get Khaalis another pack of Benson and Hedges? And some coffee?"

"I'll take care of it," Rabe said, and placed the order on his walkie-talkie.

Cullinane took his seat and gave it one more shot.

"Mr. Khaalis," he said, "I want to ask you one more time. Let's get this over with, now. You release the hostages, then you and your men go to jail. You'll get a lawyer, you'll get all the due process you want, you'll have your day in court. What's the sense in prolonging this? That's how it's going to end up."

"Mr. Chief," Khaalis said, "you're talking turkey to me, isn't that what they call it? Then let me talk some turkey to you, huh? I am the khalifa, to these men here, to the men at the Islamic Center and the District Building. They have followed my every order, my every wish, with no regard to their personal fate, all of them. Why? Because their khalifa ordered them to. They gave their allegiance to me. What would it look like to them if their commander just went to jail at once, huh?, with no acknowledgment by anyone that this was something worth fighting for, dying for?"

Cullinane looked like Khaalis might as well have been talking in Arabic.

"Mr. Khaalis," he said, "with all due respect, I have no idea what you're talking about. What do you possibly expect us to do about that?"

"Show a little respect, huh?" Khaalis snorted. "Would you tell the Pope or Billy Graham they weren't entitled to some dignity? No, their followers would protest, rebel, cause great agitation and roiling of the populace. I deserve the same respect."

Cullinane looked to Rabe for some help. Rabe nodded to Katz.

"Hamaas," Katz said. "How about this? How about if we give you one last opportunity to tell the TV guys, the radio, the newspapers, everyone, whatever you want? We'll give you that shot, you say everything you want to say, then we put you in the squad car and take you home so you can say your goodbyes to Khadyia before we take you away. You're still the khalifa and you had the last word. What do you say?"

"Where are my cigarettes?" Khaalis said. "That's what I say."

"They're on the way," Rabe said. "How about it? Do we have a deal?"

"I like it," Khaalis said. "That's good."

He took a deep drag from his cigarette and exhaled it across the table.

When the last wisp of smoke cleared his lips, he said "Then what?"

Cullinane threw up his hands and leaned forward. His complexion surged from white through pink to crimson.

"Then what what?" Cullinane said. "This isn't a game show. There's nothing behind the other door. Your men come down, everyone goes free, you make your statement, and you go to jail. That's it, end of story."

A policeman came through the door and stopped. They all turned to look at him. He held up a pack of cigarettes in one hand and a cup in the other one.

"Coffee and cigarettes," he called out.

Katz looked at his waist. No gun belt. Rabe waved him forward.

The cop crossed the lobby and laid them both in front of Khaalis, then turned around and left. Khaalis pried the lid off the cup and took a smell. He pushed the cup to Katz.

"Go ahead," he said, "take a sip."

"I'm fine," Katz said. "I don't need any."

"I don't care if you need any, Mr. Katz," Khaalis said. "I just want you to taste it first."

"Mr. Khaalis," Rabe said sharply, "there's nothing in there but coffee. You have my word. Drink your coffee. The cigarettes will kill you first."

Khaalis pushed the cup away and took his time firing up a cigarette, then looked to Cullinane.

"You're playing with me, Mr. Chief," he said. "There's plenty more you can do. What would you do for Billy Graham, I ask you again, huh? Take your time. Think on it."

"What is the point of all this, Hamaas?" Earl said. "Any way we cut it, you're going to have to go to jail for all this. You had to know that coming in."

"I didn't know that, Mr. Silbert," Khaalis said. "Khaalis expected to die here a martyr, content to pass on to paradise after killing the heathen swine you would bring to me. So don't tell me what I know and I don't know."

Flaherty cleared his throat. They all turned his way.

"Mr. Khaalis," he said. "Can I talk to my colleagues one moment?"

Katz waved a hand at him through the haze of smoke hovering over the table.

"Talk," he said, "talk. I'll be right here."

303

They walked back down the hall. Flaherty stood with his back to the table.

"I'd have to run this through channels," he said, "but maybe I could see if the Attorney General would be willing to talk to him, hear him out. Not make any promises, but just listen to him for five, ten minutes to close the deal. Is that worth a shot?"

Katz had an answer to that and he bet Earl did too. Rabe said what he was thinking.

"That can't happen, sir. The President got on the line with some kook holding a hostage in Indiana or somewhere yesterday, and he shouldn't have. We let every Tom, Dick, and Hamaas talk to some bigwig every time they take a hostage, it'll never stop."

"Well, what else do we have?" Flaherty said.

"Jesus Christ," Cullinane said. "I hate this shit."

"We're almost there, Chief," Rabe said, like he almost believed it. "Let's just keep playing it out, keep him talking. This is the hardest part, no doubt."

"So, what do we tell him?" Cullinane said. "What's behind the door?"

Earl ran his hands back over his hair.

"Maybe we can do something about the bail," he said.

"Bail?" Cullinane said. "You're seriously going to give this guy bail?"

"Maybe we could set it at some ridiculously high amount," Earl said, "tell him we're giving him a chance at scraping it together rather than giving him no bail at all."

"Maybe the ambassadors could help him there," Flaherty said. "Put their money where their mouths are."

"If they'd done that in the first place," Cullinane said, "we wouldn't be here. If I'm thinking that, he's going to think it too."

"What'd they want to talk to you about, by the way?" Rabe asked, "when you went out the door."

Cullinane shook his head.

304

"That Zahedi?" he said. "He asked if he could throw a little reception for us back at HQ when we get everyone out. You believe that?"

"I like his confidence," Rabe said.

"Guy earned his reputation, I guess," Cullinane said.

"Okay," Rabe said, "let's get back there and give it a whack. I don't want to leave Monty Hall alone with his thoughts for too long."

They took their seats at the table. Khaalis lit another cigarette. Katz saw the coffee was lower in the cup and Hamaas was still alive. He couldn't decide if that was a good thing or a bad thing.

"So what do you have for Khaalis?" Khaalis said.

"Let's talk about bail," Earl said.

"Let's talk," Khaalis said. "You first."

"First of all," Silbert said, "you should know the courts never grant bail to anyone who's committed a crime where someone's died."

"That was your fault," Khaalis said, "not ours."

"How do you figure that?" Cullinane said.

"Your men attacked my men," Khaalis said.

"Where do you get this stuff?" Cullinane said.

"Abdul Muzikir, Abdul Nuh," Khaalis said. "They were holding the hostages. No one was hurt, then Nuh saw your policemen crawling down the hallway with their guns and their rifles. They fired over their heads to warn them. The ones that got hit just came off an elevator at the wrong time. Their bad luck."

"Mr. Khaalis," Silbert said, "you'll have the chance to make your case in court. You have my word. Let me finish what I started to say. Ordinarily, we always oppose bail in murder cases and the courts never permit it, but, in this case, to bring this to an end, I'm willing to ask the judge to set bail. It'll have to be a very high amount, but if you can get the money, maybe from the ambassadors or someone else, you'll be able to go home."

Khaalis dropped his cigarette to the floor, ground it out, and reached for another one. He gave no sign of answering so Earl went on.

"I don't know if any of your men can make any amount of bail, but I'm willing to ask for it – for the ones here and at the Islamic Center. I can't do it for the ones at the District Building, the ones who did the shooting. No judge would grant it anyhow. For the rest, I'll ask for the same bail as you."

Khaalis leaned his head back and blew a smoke ring into the air. He watched it spread until it drifted apart and vanished.

"All right," he said. "What else?"

Cullinane banged his fist on the table.

"There is no what else!" he roared. "We're giving you one last shot at the microphones, he's giving you a shot at bail, there is nothing more to give you! We're done!"

"Really, Mr. Chief," Khaalis said. "Do you want the blood of a hundred dead Jews on your hands because that's all you're willing to do for Khaalis? Dead civil servants, dead Moslems? All because you were so unwilling to yield, so unbending? It's your choice, Mr. Chief. Khaalis will be dead and gone, a happy martyr, and you'll be left holding the bag, huh?"

Cullinane slapped the table with both hands and muttered something. Katz couldn't make it out but he had a pretty good idea what it was.

Cullinane stood up and pulled his cap from his head. He rubbed his scalp with his other hand, then said "I gotta get some fresh air," and headed for the doors. When he went through, a couple of officers approached him. Cullinane shook his head, repeatedly.

"This might be a good time to check in upstairs," Rabe said.

"That's another good idea, Mr. Rabe," Khaalis said. "Where's the phone?"

"Not you," Rabe said, "us."

He turned to Katz.

"I'm going to sit with our friend here," he said. "Go down to Bohlinger and see what's what, okay?"

"You don't have to hide things from me," Khaalis said. "Khaalis knows you have men across the street. I wave to them from the window all the time."

He turned to Katz too.

"Go, Mr. Katz," he said. "Go check with men across the street, but I can tell you already. My men are under strict orders to do nothing. Yet."

35

"What does that mean?" Rabe said. "'Yet?'"

Khaalis shrugged.

"It means they are to do nothing now," he said.

"How about later?" Rabe asked. "Are they waiting for some sort of signal from you? Or did you put some kind of time limit on this?"

"Will you allow me to talk to them?" Khaalis asked.

"There's no way," Rabe said.

"As Khaalis figured," he said. "So he had to make some plans in advance, just to protect himself, a contingency, huh?"

"What's the contingency?" Rabe asked.

"We are not there yet, Mr. Rabe," Khaalis said, "so you need not worry about it. You will know when you have to worry, believe me."

Rabe stared at Khaalis grimly, then turned to Katz.

"Get down there and get a read on what's going on," he said. "Check in with everyone."

Katz went down the stairs. Bohlinger was on the phone. Two cops with headphones chatted down the table. Each of them had the earphone closest to the other one flipped up. They both turned to look at Katz, then went back to their conversation.

Bohlinger hung up the phone.

"Who was that?" Katz asked.

"Nobody," Bohlinger said. "Personal."

"You hear anything not personal from anyone upstairs?"

Bohlinger shook his head, slowly. Katz walked over to the other two.

"You guys hear anything?" he asked.

They shook their heads no too. He went back to Bohlinger.

"Can you call the guys across the street?" he asked him.

Bohlinger hesitated.

"Rabe's orders," Katz said.

Bohlinger handed Katz the receiver and dialed the phone. They picked up in half a ring.

"Wright," Katz heard.

"Hey," he said, "this is Jake Katz, the guy who came over with Deputy Rabe last night? He asked me to give you guys a call to see what you see over there."

"Nothing," Wright said, "except the head guy still isn't back."

"He's down with Rabe and Cullinane," Katz said. "They're trying to get him to give it up but it's not going real well."

"So what's that mean?" Wright asked.

"It's hard to tell," Katz said. "Wherever it's going, it's getting there slow."

"Well, you tell Rabe, we're ready for whatever he wants to do," Wright said.

"Will do," Katz said. "Nothing else I should tell him?"

"No," Wright said. "Every once in a while one or two guys go out, but they come back in five or ten minutes. They might just be going to the john, catching a smoke, I don't know."

"Okay," Katz said. "I'll let him know. Call base on the walkie-talkie if you need him. They'll get him on."

"Roger that," Wright said.

Katz hung up and headed down the hallway to the back elevators. Two of the three cops Rabe sent down stood next to the stairway door just past the elevator lobby, their M-16s leaning on the wall between them. When Katz rounded the corner, they started to come to attention, then relaxed again when they saw he wasn't Rabe.

"What's up, guys?" Katz called to them. "What do you know?"

The black cop said "Nothin', man." When Katz got closer, he saw his name pin said Hylton. The other one's said Malloy.

"They pop their heads out time to time, check us out, but that's all," Malloy said. "It's quiet."

"Where's the other guy?" Katz asked.

Hylton pointed to the door.

"In there," he said, pointing to the stairwell. "We're taking fifteen-minute shifts."

Katz nodded and opened the door slowly. He winced when it squeaked. The cop was about halfway up the first flight. He turned to Katz and put his finger to his lips. Katz came through the doorway, then clicked the door noiselessly back into the frame behind him. The cop tiptoed back down the stairs. They shook hands.

"Jake Katz," Katz whispered. "Rabe sent me down to see what was going on."

"Tommy Ciccote," he whispered back. "Not much. One of those clowns's pushed the door open a couple times and looked down, then popped his head right back out. The last time, Malloy waved at him," he chuckled. "Dude didn't wave back."

They looked up the stairwells. Pieces of broken furniture seemed to be about two or three levels up. A lot more crap was up above.

"You see any way up through all that?" he asked. Ciccote shook his head.

"I'd hate to be the point man," he said. "You get up to six, seven, it's all clogged up. They'd be pickin' us off like ducks in a barrel."

That seemed about right to Katz.

"Okay," he said, "you see anyone moving up there, let the guy at the desk know, he'll let us know."

"Ten-four," Ciccote said, and popped quietly back up the steps two at a time.

Katz told Bohlinger all was cool, then headed for the front elevators. The door to the stairwell was propped open with a doorstop but no one was around. He wedged himself through the doorway and looked up to see three cops strung out on the stairwells above him. The one on the second floor landing came back down to him. He looked familiar.

When he got to the bottom, Katz saw his name tag. McGillicuddy. Now he placed him. He was Floyd Krebs' best buddy from Philippi, West Virginia, who came to D.C. with him to be a big city cop.

"Hey, man," Katz said. "I'm Jake Katz. I used to be with MPD. I was Floyd's partner?"

It took McGillicuddy a second to make the link, then his eyes brightened, and he wrapped Katz' hand in both of his and treated his ears to the same hillbilly twang he hadn't heard since the last time he talked to Floyd.

"Hey, man! Sure, I remember you, the Philly Jew boy!" he said. "Floyd saved your ass, didn't he?"

"Yes, he did," Katz said.

He'd remember that for the rest of his life, but McGillicuddy made him remember what he'd almost forgotten. His mother used to tell him, 'Never forget you're a Jew, because there'll always be some goy to remind you.' She reminded Katz about that the only time she met Floyd, and he heard her again right now.

"Where is he now?" Katz asked. "He still on the force?"

"Oh, shit, no!" McGillicuddy said, "he had enough of this place, with all the spooks and what not. It was too fast for him. Oh, shit, but he would have loved this here today, wouldn't he? A building full of A-rabs just rarin' to get blown up! That woulda been right up his alley, wouldn't it?"

311

Oh yeah, Katz thought. And a bunch of Jews to boot? A perfect day for hunting. He saved your life, man, he struggled to remember, and changed the topic.

"Sure would've," he said. "Hey, Rabe asked me to check in with you guys, see if anything was going on he should know about."

"Nah," McGillicuddy said, "every once in a while, we see a raghead pop out. He sees us then he pops back in. I'm just dyin' for him to point his gun down here so I can send him back to Africa in a box."

"Well, don't do anything until you let Rabe know," Katz said. "You see anything you're worried about, you let the guy at the desk know asap, okay?"

"All right, chief," McGillicuddy saluted. "I'm goin' to tell Floyd I saw you again. I'll tell him you said hey."

"That'd be great," Katz said. "Tell him I think about him all the time."

Just a little more clearly now, he thought.

He stopped by the tables to check in with Bohlinger and the others one more time, then popped into the men's room. He locked himself in a stall, dropped his pants, and took a seat. He was so clenched up it took him a few minutes even to make water. He figured it'd be Tuesday by the time he got anything else out, so he zipped back up and went to the sink to wash his hands.

He looked in the mirror and hoped it was distorted. His tired red eyes stared back at him, some of his hair matted to his forehead, the rest of it spiked off his head at random angles. He shaved this morning, but now he had an eleven o'clock shadow, going on midnight. Splotches of bare skin on his neck reminded him of the zits he suffered through as a kid. His face was beyond drawn, haggard and pale like he'd been left to starve in a cellar somewhere. He could hear his mother now. *Gottenyu! Zunelah!* What have they done to you? If she even recognized him.

He splashed water on his face but when he looked for the paper towel dispenser, he saw it was empty, so he wiped his face with his suit sleeve. The cloth was already wet and stiff with sweat and reeked of tobacco smoke, Benson and Hedges specifically. He took one more look in the mirror and tried to pat his hair down but it was useless. He swung the door open and made his way back up the stairs, hoping it'd be the last time.

He swiveled back to the table and saw Flaherty and Earl head to head in conversation. Khaalis was pacing a tight circle down the hall, his head wreathed in smoke as always. Cullinane and Rabe stood between him and the elevators, their arms crossed against their chests. The clock over their heads showed it was just about 11:30. When Rabe spotted Katz heading for them, he said something to Khaalis. Khaalis ground his cigarette out and kicked it to the wall, then made his way back to the table. He didn't look at Katz as he went past.

"Everything's still cool down there," Katz told them, "and across the street. Every once in a while, one or two of his guys poke their heads out into the stairwell, but that's it."

"Okay," Cullinane said. "We're throwing him another bone." He turned to Rabe. "You want to run it past him?"

"No," Rabe said. He looked at Katz. "He goes for it, he goes for it. He doesn't, we'll just keep tryin'. We ain't done here, I'm afraid."

They came back to the table and took their seats. Cullinane sat across from Khaalis.

"Okay," he said. "We'll do everything we said we'd do before. You make your statement, you go home, you pick up your things, you say goodbye to the wife, then we take you downtown and we set bail for you. We'll also let you keep your swords, your knives, your machetes – everything but the guns, okay? You can walk away with all of that.

And we'll ask the judge for bail on your men here and at the Islamic Center. What do you say? Do we have a deal?"

Khaalis leaned back and launched another smoke ring into the haze already engulfing them. He leaned forward and tapped the ash onto the pile of butts filling the ashtray.

"You keep mentioning my men," he said. "Khaalis has not demanded anything for them. They knew the consequences of what they were getting into. They are soldiers. They will take the punishment they must take to serve their khalifa."

After a day and a half of murder, terror, threats, and intimidation, Katz didn't know why this betrayal of his own men hit him so hard, but it did. He somehow felt sorry for them, the misguided souls who followed him, trusted him to lead him, but now were his victims as much as anyone else who survived whatever this wound up being. Would they have followed their khalifa into hell if they knew he'd sell them down the river – or send them up the river – without a fight or even a care? He thought he was prepared for all of Hamaas' highs and lows, but this was a new low.

Rabe looked to Katz and slowly shook his head. Khaalis stubbed his butt out and reached for the pack. He held it upside down until a cigarette slid out, then lit it and watched the perfect circle of his smoke ring drift across the table again.

"And why no guns?" he said. "You didn't grab them last time when they weren't even registered. Now they are, so why now?"

It was the first time Katz ever heard him even hint that he knew anything about that. Abdul Aziz said he knew but that he'd never acknowledge Katz for it, much less thank him. True to form, he didn't even look Katz' way.

"Mr. Khaalis," Earl said, "last time you were the victim. This time you're not. You've used those guns in a felony, a serious felony, a felony murder. We cannot let you hold them. You have to understand that."

"But Khaalis doesn't understand," he said. "Forgive me for being such a simple man but the swords, the knives, the machetes, they too were used in what you say is the same crime. Why is Khaalis allowed to keep them but not the others?"

Earl started to answer but Cullinane cut him off and he was hot.

"Goddamn it!" he screamed. "Are you serious? We're only letting you have the swords because we're at our goddamned wit's end trying to end this thing! Nobody wants you to have one lousy thing you can use as a weapon, trust me, but we're willing to give you this just to get this over with! Is that so hard to understand?"

Khaalis smirked.

"Mr. Chief, you sound like you have had enough of Khaalis. Don't you want to have your puppets drive you home and tuck you back into your beddy-bye already? If you are really so anxious to get this all over with, you have the power to do so right now. You – not Khaalis! – you! You make all of these so-called concessions to me and you pull your hair out and you scream at me each time I tell you it's not enough. You can stop Khaalis from driving you crazy now, right this very second, huh? You can bring me those five animals and watch me slaughter them one by one!"

Cullinane didn't answer. He couldn't answer. Katz watched his nostrils flare as he pulled long deep breaths through his nose and tried to get himself back on as much of an even keel as he could. Rabe didn't take his eyes off Khaalis.

"Hamaas," Earl said, "that's not going to happen. You need to take that off the table because none of us here is ever going to agree to it. Period. The only thing we're going to talk about with you is the terms of how you're leaving here now. You can see how repugnant it is to everyone here, but we're willing to work with you on that, just that. Let's get the deal done and get everyone here out, including you."

Khaalis reached for yet another cigarette, then changed his mind.

"Mr. Deputy Chief," he said to Rabe. "What time is it?"

Rabe shot a glance at his watch.

"Just about eleven fifty," he said. "It's almost tomorrow."

"Khaalis needs to use the bathroom," he said.

Cullinane fell back in his chair. He ran his hands back over his hair again and pushed himself up and with a grunt that sounded more like exasperation than effort.

"I need to vomit in the sink," he said and pointed to Khaalis. "You can come with me and watch."

He didn't wait for Khaalis to join him. When Khaalis disappeared through the door behind him, Rabe turned to Katz.

"What a miserable fucker," he said. "This is all about him, all of it. It's got nothing to do with Islam or his men or the movie or anything else. Me, me, me, poor me, that's it, that's everything."

Katz nodded. Rabe was right again. This was Hamaas' giant cry of pain. Everyone had to suffer if he did, and no one would stop suffering until he did. A cold chill clutched him. The crystal clarity of it all was obvious to him now. Martyrdom was Khaalis' only way out. All their talking, all their deals, all their concessions, they were for nothing. It was all a sham, just another act in the script Khaalis had written to end his life. Katz felt real fear for the first time in a long time. He looked down the barrel of that gun at the Howard again and prayed just as hard this time.

The floor was quiet. The lights in the ceiling were darker somehow and the light angling from the street was harsher. The squawk from Rabe's walkie-talkie just about sprung Katz from his seat. Rabe grabbed it off the table and brought it to his lips.

"Rabe," he said.

316

"This is Base," Katz heard Bohlinger say quickly. "The guys at the back say those fuckers are spraying all kinds of shit down the stairs!"

"What kinds of shit?" Rabe said.

"Gasoline, they said that's what it smells like – hold on a minute."

They heard a voice in the background. A frantic voice. Bohlinger came back on the line.

"It's fucking paint thinner!" he yelled into the phone. "The fucking cans are bouncing down the steps!"

Katz heard a set of footsteps growing louder, running. He heard someone bang on something like it was a steel drum, over and over.

"They're throwing the cans down empty, Chief!" Bohlinger screamed. "Both stairwells! They're torching this fucking place!"

March 11, 1977

36

Katz bolted out of his seat but he didn't know where to go, where to turn, what to do. He heard a door swing open to his right and watched Khaalis come out of the men's room, Cullinane right behind him.

"Mr. Khaalis!" Rabe called out. "Get your ass down here. Cully, hold it right there."

Rabe ran past Khaalis down the hallway. Cullinane stood and waited for him with a confused look on his face. Katz watched it turn to shock, then flush again as Rabe told him the news.

Khaalis strolled to Katz, then followed his eyes to look back to the two of them. He watched for a second, then turned back to Katz.

"Does Mr. Deputy have a problem?" he said.

"Like you don't fucking know," Katz said. He looked at his watch. 12:02.

Rabe and Cullinane were running to them now, then Cullinane ran past them and out on to the street. He ran through the cops on the sidewalk to a patrol car at the curb and threw himself into the passenger seat.

Rabe grabbed Khaalis by the elbow and sat him back in his seat.

"You know exactly what's going on, so I don't have to tell you, right?" he said to him.

"What?" Khaalis said. "What do I know? I'm here with you. Tell me what I'm supposed to know."

"Your boys are raining shit down the stairways, paint thinner and gasoline," Rabe said. "They think of that all on their own? I don't think so."

"Mr. Deputy, I had nothing to do with that," Khaalis said, as sincerely as Katz ever heard him. "I'm here with you. What could I tell them? How?"

"Right," Rabe said. "They just snapped all of a sudden, after thirty-some hours, right at the stroke of midnight? Stop with the bullshit, Mr. Khaalis! Enough already!"

That was as hot as Katz ever heard him. Cullinane ran back through the door. He was redder than Rabe and out of breath.

"The Fire Department's on the way," he said. He pointed at Khaalis.

"You. We're done with this shit. Now. One hair on one person gets touched or burned or anything from this point on, you're never seeing the light of day again."

Khaalis leaned back in his chair and reached for his cigarettes. Rabe swatted them away from him. Khaalis tucked his head into his chest and actually managed to hold his tongue.

Katz heard sirens not too far away, horns blaring below their wail.

Khaalis lifted his head and looked at Cullinane.

"You have my terms, Mr. Chief," he said. "You have the power to end all this right now. You, not Khaalis."

Earl circled behind Rabe and Katz and went to Cullinane's shoulder.

"Let's talk, quick," he said. "One minute."

Rabe's walkie-talkie buzzed again. He flicked it on. "Rabe. Go."

"The stuff's stopped coming down, at least round back," Bohlinger said. "But it reeks to high heaven in there. One match, chief, that's all it'll take. What do you want us to do?"

The wails grew louder, filling the air.

"Hold fast," Rabe said. "I'll be back in a minute. Let me know what's going on at the other stairs. Out."

He followed Earl and Cullinane back down the hall, Katz and Flaherty just behind.

"I ought to handcuff his ass to the table and let him burn in here with everyone else," Cullinane said.

"Chief, it's your call," Silbert said, "but I think we need to wrap this up, quick. God knows what he told them, or if he told them, but it doesn't really matter at this point. If he planned it or those guys just went stir crazy, it comes down to the same thing. We need to get this over with now."

"So what's that mean?" Cullinane said. "Give him the deal he wants?"

"Yeah," Earl said. "We can jam him up with all kinds of restrictions and conditions at the arraignment, but for now, we get him out of here and these people out of here, alive."

"So we give him everything we said and let him walk out of here?" Cullinane said. "That's what you're telling me?"

The sirens wound down to a dull roar close by. Bright lights danced through the window. They turned to see two fire engines pull to a stop right in front of the building.

Rabe spoke into his walkie-talkie.

"Street, this is Rabe."

"Street," Katz heard.

"Tell them to stand down outside till further orders,"

"Ten-four," Street said. The phone cut dead. The lights kept swirling around them like a strobe in a disco.

"What's the option?" Earl said to Cullinane. "Do you want to face the mikes and the cameras tomorrow and tell them why you let a hundred people burn to death, plus whatever happens to the people at the District Building and the Islamic Center? He may walk out of here, but he's going to be strapped tight into his house until the trial and then he's going to jail, forever. I'd rather explain that."

"And we can guarantee him the judge will let him go home, not slap his ass in jail?" Cullinane asked. "There's no way he's letting anyone go if we can't."

Silbert thought about that for a second, then pulled a small black leather address book from his inside suit pocket.

"I'll call Judge Greene now," he said.

Judge Greene was Harold Greene, the Chief Judge of the Superior Court. He was short and pudgy with big tortoise shell glasses, and as smart as they came. Katz knew he had a lot to do with the big civil rights laws getting passed when he worked at Justice for Bobby Kennedy in the early '60s, but one day early on, when he asked Earl why he had a German accent, Silbert filled him in, *lantzman* to *lantzman*. He told him Greene was born in Germany, but fled the Nazis with his family in the late '30s, when he was a teenager. They went through half of Europe together before he wound up in an internment camp for a year, then made it to the U.S. His heart was as big as his brain but he could be a real stickler for procedure too.

Rabe asked what Katz was thinking.

"Is that on the up and up? Will he go along with that?"

"Never done it before," Earl said, "but only one way to find out."

He dug into his pants pocket.

"Oh, Christ!" he said. "Does anyone have a dime?"

They all dug into their own pockets. Flaherty pulled his hand out first and dropped two nickels into Earl's hand. Earl ran to the pay phone.

"'For want of a nail, the kingdom was lost'," Flaherty said, "isn't that how it goes?"

Katz didn't know and didn't care. He walked to the pay phone until he got close enough to catch Earl's eye. Earl crossed his fingers. Katz crossed his fingers back, then folded his arms across his chest, too tense to even sweat.

Earl shot him a thumbs up.

"Your honor?" he said, "this is Earl Silbert. I hate --"

Katz saw him look quickly at his watch.

"12:15. I am terribly sorry to call you this time of night, but --"

He paused a few seconds.

"That's exactly what it's about," he said. "The men holding the hostages upstairs have started throwing all kinds of flammable things down the stairwells. We're one match away from a fire, so we need to end this now before anyone else gets killed."

He stopped short and listened again.

"We've been doing that, for hours," he said. "He's agreed to let everyone go, but he won't do it until we let him go on his own recognizance." Another stop, then "I know, believe me, but this is where we are. We're willing to go along with it, figuring we can tie it up with so many conditions, he'll be locked up soon enough in any event. But we need to guarantee him you'll go along with it --"

He waited, then said "I know . . . I know . . . I know."

Katz could guess everything Greene was saying. Due process, unconstitutional, his decision, not Earl's. Silbert rolled his eyes at Katz and spun his index finger around and around. Katz felt a tap on his shoulder. He turned to see Rabe, grim and anxious.

"What's the story?" he asked. "What's he saying?"

"Not sure yet," Katz said.

They looked at Earl and saw him wince, then raise his hand and teeter it back and forth, the universal sign for maybe.

"Yes, of course, your honor," he said. "I understand. Of course. I wouldn't expect that. I just wanted you to know what you could expect to hear from us."

He hung up the phone.

"He said he'd take it under advisement," he said.

"That's not good enough," Rabe said. "We need to tell him it's a done deal."

"He'll do the right thing," Earl said. "He knows the stakes."

"Then that's what we'll tell him," Rabe said. "He's going to okay the deal."

"But that's not what he said," Earl said. "I can't tell him that."

"You won't have to," Rabe said, and headed back to the table. Earl threw Katz a quizzical look, then hurried to catch up, Katz right behind.

When they got back, Khaalis was the only one sitting, smoking another B&H. They joined Cullinane and Flaherty standing across from him.

Earl started to say something but Rabe reached out and laid a hand on his arm, then nodded to Cullinane. Katz watched Rabe squeeze Earl's arm. Earl said nothing.

Cullinane pulled out the chair across from Khaalis, folded his arms on the table, and leaned in as up close and personal as he could.

"So, here it is, Mr. Khaalis, our final offer," he said. "We will take you out of here and drive you home. You can get changed, cleaned up, kiss your wife, whatever you want to do. Then we will drive you to the courthouse and the judge will release you on your own recognizance – with the usual conditions. Then we will drive you back home and you can stay there until it's time for all the court business. That's it. That's our deal. Take it or leave it. It's all we can do."

Khaalis took a deep pull on the cigarette, swallowed the drag, and tapped an ash onto the stack of butts in the ashtray.

"How does Khaalis know the judge will release him?" he asked.

"We just talked to him," Rabe said. "He said he'd do it, if that's what it took to get this over with."

Katz flicked his eyes to Earl. Earl kept his trained on Khaalis.

Khaalis nodded and pursed his lips.

"Ah, the grand American justice system you all so revere," he said. "Equal justice under law! Civil rights! Wonderful words, so noble. The big curtains, the big courtrooms, all the majesty, the splendor. This is all for show, huh?, keep the people sedated with all the ceremony and the oaths."

"Mr. Khaalis," Cullinane cut in. "Enough. No more speeches. Let's end this now. Keep yourself from another hundred murder charges."

Khaalis shook his head and Katz's heart dropped dead.

"So now Khaalis has the power, he gets the deal, huh?" he said. "Khaalis knew this in his heart but now he really knows because this time it works for Khaalis. Is this not the game you play, the rules you bend when it suits you?"

No one answered this time.

Khaalis ground the cigarette out in the ashtray. Butts and matches spilled onto the table.

"So now that we all know," he said, "I accept your corrupt offer."

Cullinane slapped the table with both hands. Katz groped for the back of the nearest chair and held on for dear life. Rabe dug into his pocket and threw three dimes on the table in front of Khaalis.

"Your turn," he said. "Make the fucking calls."

37

Khaalis called the eighth floor. It rang a long time before someone picked up.

"Adam," he said. "It is over. You tell the others. Tell them to lay down their arms upstairs, then come down the elevator."

"Which one?" he asked Cullinane.

"The back ones," Cullinane said. "To one. Give us five minutes to get someone back there."

Rabe took a few steps towards the door and got on the walkie-talkie.

"Street, this is Rabe," he said. "I need about a dozen men to go to the rear elevators on one. The bad guys are coming down, unarmed. It's all over. Out."

"You just come down, with the others," Khaalis said into the phone. "I will call them myself. Ma'a salama."

He hung up. A string of policemen decked out in full SWAT array filed through the doors and double-timed back to the elevators. Their bootsteps echoed off the walls.

"I'll go back with them," Rabe said to Cullinane, then led them down the hall.

Khaalis reached for the phone again.

"Hold it," Cullinane told him. He unclipped his walkie-talkie and spoke into it.

"Street," he said, "this is the Chief. I want you to call our guys at the District Building and the Islamic Center and let them know Mr. Khaalis is about to call his men there and tell them to come out and surrender. Tell them they'll be coming down the elevators at the District Building and walking out the main gate at the Islamic Center with no weapons. When you get 'em, you 'cuff 'em and book 'em by the book. Copy?"

Katz heard something scratch back out of the phone.

"Then," Cullinane said, "you're going to call the Command Center and tell them we don't want any news of this to leak out until we have all the bad guys out of here. I want the Mayor to know that personally and you tell him it's from me. The last thing we need is a bunch of reporters mucking this up now. You copy that?"

"I copy," Katz heard loud and clear.

"Out," Cullinane said.

"Now," he said to Khaalis, "you call the others and you tell them to do just what I said."

Khaalis made the calls.

When he was done, he turned to Cullinane.

"Khaalis has done his part," he said. "Now you do yours."

"I'll do it when everyone's out safe and sound," Cullinane told him.

He picked up the walkie-talkie again.

"Street, this is the Chief again. I'm going to need some cruisers asap. The first one is getting Mr. Khaalis the hell out of here, back to his house up 16th. We're going to stay with him until everyone's out of here, then we're bringing him back down for the arraignment sometime tomorrow – sorry, today. Don't even know what day it is. As soon as I see them pull up, I'll bring him out. The rest are coming down in a few minutes and they're going to the jail. Book 'em as usual. Copy?"

"Copy" squawked back one more time.

Cullinane kept his eyes on the street. A patrol car rolled up in a few seconds. He turned to Khaalis.

"Let's go," he said.

He turned to Katz.

"Come on," he said. "You've earned it."

Cullinane held Khaalis by the elbow and pushed him through the door and across the empty sidewalk to the cruiser. Katz followed right behind. A cop on the street grabbed the back seat door and swung it open. Cullinane pushed Khaalis' head down and the rest of him into the seat.

The cop slammed the door shut and saluted Cullinane, a wide smile on his face.

"Good job, Chief," he said.

Cullinane saluted him back and walked around to the driver's side. The window slid down.

"Flashers on," Cullinane said, "but no sirens, no horns, no letting anyone know he's there until you hear it's okay from me or the Mayor makes an announcement. You got it?"

The cop threw him a salute and slid the window back up. In a couple of seconds, they whipped around Scott Circle and disappeared up 16th.

Katz turned to see fire engines swing wide around the corner and crawl to a stop down 17th St. He saw a phalanx of ambulances and police cars come up all four lanes of Rhode Island, lights flashing and blinking like it was Christmas gone crazy. A sea of cops, medics, and firemen filled the sidewalk in an instant.

Cullinane waved a captain to him.

"I got some guys in there now waiting for Khaalis' men," he said. "When they clear the building, I need a couple teams of SWAT guys to take the stairs up to eight, front and back, make sure they didn't booby-trap the place or leave us any other surprises. There's all kinds of stuff in there and they've sprayed it all with gasoline and God knows what else, so you need to be careful. The hostages are in a conference room on the part of the eighth floor they're redoing. You need to sweep that too. If and when I get the all clear, I'll send up another bunch of guys to help you get 'em all down."

They swapped walkie-talkie handles. The captain saluted and ran back to the throng of cops behind him.

Cullinane waved Katz to follow him back into the building. By the time they got back to the rear elevators, the cops were cuffing and frisking five guys. Four of them were clean, but Abdul Razzaq, the one who'd been so ready to blow him and Blotnick away, was filthy with all kinds of knives. One of the cops showed Cullinane a switchblade, a straight razor, a stubby knife, and a Swiss army knife. Two cops marched each of them to the doors.

The captain Cullinane talked to passed them, a squad of SWAT men just behind. They headed up the steps.

Cullinane turned to Rabe.

"They're going up both sets of stairs to make sure they didn't leave us any presents. Once we get the okay, how do you want to handle the hostages?"

"More cops," Rabe said, "and we're going to need medics too. I know all of the folks upstairs just want to go home, but some of them, most of them maybe, are going to need a doctor to check them out first."

"Okay," Cullinane said. "but a lot of their families've been keeping a vigil at the Gramercy next door, or the church up 16th street, the Foundry? We ought to let 'em know when they're coming down."

"Okay," Rabe said, "then let's just walk them over to the Gramercy when they come down. We'll let the people at the church know to come over and get them and we'll pull the buses around to load the ones that need to go to the hospital."

"Sounds good," Cullinane said. "I'll call the Mayor's office once they're all down so he can put out the good word. Anything else we should be thinking of?"

"Can't think of anything now," Rabe said. He turned to Katz. "Mr. Katz, anything we forgot?"

What Katz had to add went without saying, but he needed to say it anyhow, not because they needed to hear it, but because he had been a cop too, and he knew he sometimes needed to hear it himself.

"When they bring them down," he said, "just remind them to treat them all with a lot of care. They've all been through hell."

"Well said, Mr. Katz," Rabe said. "We'll tell 'em to treat them like their own mothers and fathers."

Then they waited. Katz glanced at his watch and counted the hours since he got up a little before seven. His brain told him it was eighteen hours but his body said it was eighteen days. It all whizzed by in a blur, but it was a day he knew he'd never forget. He wanted to call Marty, tell her all about it, but he remembered Cullinane telling the cop to keep it under his hat till the Mayor said it was done, so he stifled the urge.

He walked back down the hall to Earl, who was pretty much splayed out in a seat across the table from Flaherty. Katz had never seen him look anything less than immaculate but now he looked like he'd been on an all-night bender. His sparse hair fluttered off his head, a patchy beard was visible, his skin was sallow, his glasses were smudged, and his eyes were heavy and ringed with dark circles. He looks like I feel, Katz thought.

Flaherty, on the other hand, was still crisp and clean. Maybe the less responsibility you had, the better you looked, Katz mused.

"So what's the drill?" he asked Katz.

"They're just waiting to hear it's okay to come up," he said, "then they're going to go get them."

Katz looked to Earl and felt compelled to ask him if he was okay.

"I'm fine," Silbert said. "It's been a long day."

"Three days," Katz reminded him.

"You guys did a great job," Flaherty said. "Getting this done with no one else shot or hurt, that's a hell of a job."

"Hold your applause," Earl said. "Let's wait till we see what's what upstairs and everywhere else."

"Fair enough," Flaherty said, "but how you handled this screwball, brought him down to earth? No words can describe it. It was a clinic."

Silbert threw him a salute.

331

Katz heard Rabe yelling down the hall. He turned to see him waving to them.

"Let's go!" he shouted. "We got the all clear."

They cleared the table. Katz somehow found the energy to run down the hall. Rabe held the elevator door for him and he wedged his way in.

"Take the next one!" Rabe yelled over his shoulder to Silbert and Flaherty just before the doors shut.

The trip up this time didn't seem nearly as long as the ones Katz made before. The doors pulled open and Katz turned to see just the SWAT cops in the hallway. The captain Cullinane recruited on the sidewalk hurried over to meet him as he got off the elevator.

"It's clean," he said. "We're just getting them up and on their feet now."

He pointed to the conference room and Cullinane headed that way, Rabe and Katz at his shoulders, the rest of the troops right behind.

When Katz cleared the doorway, he was disoriented by all the light. Bare bulbs dotting the ceiling threw a harsh glare on the room and everyone in it. He saw a thousand things he hadn't seen in the dark smoky haze that filled the place before, blood stains and streaks on the concrete and the walls, an ocean of paper cups, plastic plates, doughnut boxes, bread crusts, soda bottles. He saw a few cops kneeling by the door, tagging rifles, shotguns, revolvers, knives, and box upon box of bullets. He looked to the right to the tarpaulins. They were strewn across the floor now, just in front of the line of wooden boxes he'd mistaken for the workers' equipment. Rifle snouts nosed out of each box.

He turned back to take in the scene as policemen and medics helped men and women to their feet from one end of the room to the other. They weren't hostages anymore, just the people they'd been their whole lives before Wednesday morning. Sobs, cries, and even laughs carried to him from every direction.

He edged and picked his way through them to look for someone to help. He saw faces he remembered and gave them a quick hug or a thumbs up. Medics and nurses laid out stretchers and gurneys and brought up wheelchairs to get the ones going to GW first. Rabe stood with a corpsman doing some triage at the doorway. Katz crossed back to him to see if he could be of any use.

Just as the first stretcher was about to clear the doorway, an older gray-haired man spoke up from the middle of the room.

"Friends!" he called hoarsely, "my friends!"

The room turned to look at him.

A blue and white striped tie was still under his collar, hanging untied down the front of his rumpled white shirt. He pushed his glasses up and raised his arms high and wide like he was trying to embrace them all.

"We have been through so much here together, for the past, what, three days?" he said. "Surely we must thank the police who have come to our rescue and saved us from that madman and his hoodlums."

A cheer with as much gusto as they could muster rose all around Katz.

"But," he continued, "we must also say a prayer of thanks to our adoshem, our God, as well. Please, everyone."

They stopped in their places and sang it together. It bubbled to Katz' lips too, from somewhere he thought was out of reach way back in his past.

"Baruch atah adonoy, elohaynu melech ha-olom, shehechianu, vekeyamanu, vehigyanu, lazman hazeh."

Some of them said it in English.

"Blessed art thou, O Lord Our God, King of the Universe, who has created us, sustained us, and enabled us to be here for this festive occasion."

38

Katz squeezed into the elevator and held his arms tight around the shoulders of two women. The one on his right spent the whole ride down complaining to the one on his left. Her *tuchus* was sore from sitting so long. She was starving. She stunk from the smoke. Her husband would be so *verklempt* he'd probably had a stroke by now, worrying about her. The one on the left took it as long as she could, then stretched up to whisper in Katz' ear.

"He's going to get a stroke when he hears she's coming back," she said.

Katz tucked her head into his neck and tried not to laugh out loud. At one, he walked them slowly to a cop at the front door who told them he'd take them over to the Gramercy. The lady who whispered in his ear blew Katz a kiss. Katz shook a finger in her face.

"You be good now," he said and watched them shuffle down the block.

The street and the sidewalk were clear but, when he turned to go back inside, he saw a pair of headlights streak across the glass, then another one. He looked back and saw one of the reporters he'd seen the first day jump out of a car and run to him. A film crew set up at the curb.

"Are they out?" the guy called to him. "Is it over? What can you tell us?"

"Nothing," Katz said. "The Mayor'll let you know."

The guy had a mike in his face now but Katz pulled the door shut and hustled back across the lobby. He stopped in front of the cops leading another group out.

"The press is out there," he told them. "Tell 'em you have to get everyone to the hotel and can't say anything until the Mayor does."

He got a nod from the guy in front and backed out of the way. They headed through the doors and kept moving.

More reporters, more cameras, more lights filled the sidewalk. He ran to the elevators and went back up.

When he got out, Rabe was listening to a medic at one end of a stretcher holding a heavy woman with white hair and glasses on a chain lying on her chest. She looked like she was sleeping.

"She fainted," the medic said. "We were helping her get up, and she just keeled over."

Rabe nodded, then saw Katz.

"The press is down there," Katz said. "The Mayor say it was over?"

"No!" Rabe said. "Shit! I'll let 'em know."

He yanked out his walkie-talkie.

"Base!" he said, "this is Rabe. Tell the goddamned Command Center that somebody goddamned leaked it because the press is all over us already!"

He clicked off and yelled at someone on the elevator.

"Hold that goddamned thing!" he said. They did. He got on and turned back to look at Katz and shake his head until the doors closed.

Katz headed back to the conference room and squeezed back in through the crowd coming out.

Some of the hostages were still on the floor, most of them with medics. Katz headed to a woman still lying on her back, another woman kneeling over her. When he got there, he saw the woman on her knees was BJ. He knelt down next to her and touched her elbow.

"Hey," he said. "How're you doing?"

She turned to see him.

"Mr. Katz!" she said and threw her arms around his neck.

He held her back tight. The woman on the floor back smiled up at him weakly and patted his thigh.

"I don't want to interrupt you," he said. "Can I help here?"

"I think she could use a wheelchair," she said. "What do you think, Shirley? Should I get you some wheels?"

Shirley nodded and closed her eyes. Katz got a medic's attention and made like he was pushing a wheelchair. The medic ducked into the hallway and headed back his way with a real one. The three of them got Shirley to her feet and into the chair, and the medic pushed her to the door.

"Hey, so," BJ said, "did you get my little note?"

"I sure did," Katz said. "That was unbelievable."

"And did it help?" she asked.

"Absolutely," he said. "We didn't miss a word after that. And we shut him up in a hurry when it got to be too much. You did good, real good."

She gave him a mock curtsey.

"Glad to be of service," she said.

"You ready to go?" Katz asked.

She surveyed the room and Katz did too.

"There's Lillian," she said, pointing to a woman sitting on the floor waving at her. "I told her we'd get her out of here alive. Let me go get her."

"Sure," Katz said. She watched her go to her, then plop down on the floor and hug her hard. He felt a hand on his shoulder and turned to see Rabe.

"That was quick," Katz said.

"I never made it out," Rabe said. "They need someone to ride with the ones going to the hospital," he said. "You up for it?"

"Sure," Katz said. "Where do I go?"

"One of the buses is coming around to the front of the Gramercy. You can meet him out there."

"Got it," Katz said.

He moved for the door but stopped when he felt Rabe's hand squeeze his shoulder. He turned to him.

"Good job, Mr. Katz," Rabe said. "I just want you to know I appreciate everything you did."

Katz patted his shoulder.

"You did everything," he said. "I was just happy to watch. I never saw anyone so --"

Rabe squeezed his shoulder again, and pointed to the door.

"That's enough," he said. "Go get 'em to the hospital."

Katz smiled and saluted, and headed for the elevator.

When he hit the sidewalk, he saw three white Metrobuses edging their way around the TV trucks and cars suddenly clogging the street. He beat them the half-block down to the Gramercy. The driver of the first one popped his door. He was a heavy-set white guy with white hair, glasses, and a heavy Southern accent.

"You in charge here?" he asked Katz.

"Not hardly," he said, "but I'm going to ride with you down to GW Hospital. You're going to take the ones we know need a doctor. The rest of them have families waiting for them at the Foundry Church who need to come down here. Can you arrange that?"

"I got it," the driver said and picked a microphone off the dashboard.

"Dispatch," he said, "I'm heading over to GW Hospital in a few minutes. The other guys need to pick up relatives who're waiting for them up at the Foundry Church. You know where it is?" He waited for Dispatch to tell him he didn't. "Up 16th, about two, three blocks north of the Circle. It's two minutes from here. Right. I'll let you know when I'm at GW. Roger."

He hung up the mike.

"I'm ready any time you are," he said.

"I'll be right back," Katz said and crossed the sidewalk to the Gramercy. He saw the captain Cullinane buttonholed on the street after Khaalis gave up, and headed his way.

337

"We got a bus out there ready to take the ones to the hospital," he said.

"Roger that," the captain said. "I'll start bringin' 'em out."

Katz headed back for the bus, but stopped when he heard a siren coming up Rhode Island from his left. Why is there always someone who doesn't get the word?, he thought, and walked back towards the B'nai B'rith.

When the car pulled to the curb, he saw the patrol car peel to the side, and a Caddy with diplomatic plates stop in the middle of the street. A tall man got out of the back seat and buttoned his suit jacket.

"Mr. Zahedi?" Katz called to him.

Zahedi turned to see him and broke into a beaming smile. He walked quickly to Katz and embraced him.

"Mr. Katz!" he cried. "I am so happy to see you, and to see that the hostages are free! Free at last, is that not what Dr. King said?"

Katz didn't know where to start.

"Yes, they're out," he said finally. "I didn't expect to see you back here."

"Of course I had to come," Zahedi said. "Mr. Khan has gone to the Islamic Center and Mr. Ghorbal has gone to the District Building to see them all out. This is a wonderful ending for all of us!"

"It is," Katz said. "We owe all of you a big debt for everything you did."

"It was all of us," Zahedi said. "A wonderful team effort, no? So tell me, is Hamaas still here or is he in the jail?"

"Well," Katz said, "neither. He's home now."

"Home?" Zahedi said. "I don't understand."

"He's there until later this morning," Katz said, "then the police are bringing him downtown to be charged."

"And then to jail, eh?" Zahedi said.

Katz really wanted to end this conversation.

338

"I've got to head back to the bus," he said. "I'm going with some of the hostages to the hospital."

"Ah!" Zahedi said. "I will come with you!"

"I can't let you come to the hospital," Katz said.

"Of course," Zahedi said, "I meant to the bus."

They headed back down the sidewalk in silence until Zahedi turned to him.

"I am afraid I do not understand your American justice system," he said. "In my country, in Iran, he would be dead before he left the building, deal or no deal."

Katz had a sinking feeling in the very deepest pit of his stomach. He was grateful for the chance to ignore it when the first stretcher wheeled out of the Gramercy. He clambered up the steps of the bus and helped the man on it to a seat just behind the driver.

The hostages came out two and three at a time, each group escorted, carried, or wheeled by cops and medics. Zahedi posted himself at the door to the bus and excitedly shook everyone's hand as they came on board, embracing the ones who could walk, congratulating them all for making it through. There wasn't one of them who didn't look at him queerly. They had no idea who he was, or why an Arab was so happy for them.

Katz saw Cullinane try to make his way to the bus through a herd of newsmen and cameramen. The last of them trailed him to the door, jabbing his mike in his face.

"I got nothing to say now," Cullinane said. "Beat it, I'm begging you."

His walkie-talkie squawked.

"Cullinane," he said, then listened to what Katz heard too.

"Chief, the Mayor just announced they're free. Get ready for the vultures."

"Good to know," Cullinane said, watching them gather. "Appreciate the heads up."

The guy with the mike stuck it back in his face.

"Call the Mayor's office," Cullinane told him. "They can't wait to talk to you, evidently."

The bus driver poked his head out of the door.

"We're pretty full up now," he said to Katz. "I'm ready whenever you say."

"You riding with them?" Cullinane asked.

"I am," he said. "Rabe asked me to."

"All right," Cullinane said and patted him on the shoulder. "You done good. Thanks for the help."

He headed back to the B'nai B'rith without waiting for Katz to answer.

Katz scooted up the steps of the bus and found an open seat almost at the back. The driver threw the bus in gear. Katz leaned his head against the window and checked his watch. 2:28. The bus turned onto the circle and pressed him against the side. He closed his eyes and felt himself sliding into sleep until church bells woke him up, clanging a joyful noise. They were coming from up 16th Street. The Foundry, was all he could think before he closed his eyes again.

39

Katz felt someone tugging his shoulder.

"Marty," he murmured, "stop."

"Sir, we're here," he heard. "Wake up please."

Marty's voice wasn't that deep or that Southern.

He squinted to see the bus driver standing over him.

"We're here and there's a whole lot of cameras and reporters out there. You need to tell me what to do," he pleaded.

Katz pushed himself up and looked out the window to see George Washington sitting on a horse. He rubbed his eyes and looked out the window on the other side. Dozens of people filled the driveway in front of GW Hospital. The bus was parked right in front of the emergency room just across from Washington Circle.

He checked his watch. 2:38. He had ten minutes of sleep. Up and at 'em.

"Okay," he yawned. "I got it."

He made his way down the aisle and waited for the driver to open the door. The horde pressed closer to the bus. He had no authority to tell them what they could do or what they couldn't do, and he had no idea what he should tell them anyhow, but he was the man standing on the steps so he had to say something. The driver pulled the doors open. The crowd drew even tighter but they shut themselves up to hear what he had to say. He'd been asking for mercy for three days and that finally worked so he figured he'd try it again.

He held up his hands.

"I need to ask for your cooperation here," he said as loud as he could without screaming. "There are a lot of people on this bus who need to see a doctor as soon as possible. I'm asking you to let us get them through here so they can get what they need as soon as they can."

Something Rabe said came back to him.

"Treat them like you'd want your mothers and fathers to be treated, okay? We're going to start bringing them off now so please, no questions, and make a little room here. I appreciate it."

"What about you?" a man's voice called out. "Can we talk to you?"

"I'll give you what I can," he said, "but only off the record." He'd been an AUSA too long to give them anything else. Then he saw the cavalry ride to the rescue behind them.

"Okay," he said, "please make way for the doctors."

They turned to see a squad of doctors and nurses run out of the entrance, pushing and pulling gurneys, wheelchairs, and IVs, and parted to let them through.

Katz stepped down and they took over. Some climbed onto the bus and others stayed on the ground, gently wrapping blankets around the people who could walk, seating others in wheelchairs, lying some on gurneys, and getting them all inside as fast as they could. It was like a military operation. He'd never been prouder of his alma mater.

He kept the press types at bay till the bus was cleared, then gave them a few dozen variations of "No comment," "You'll have to talk to the Mayor's office about that," and "I really don't know" until they gave up and left him alone with the bus driver.

"You ready to go now?" the driver asked.

"Absolutely," Katz said and collapsed into the front seat. "Can you take me home?"

"I just got a call from dispatch to take you to MPD on Indiana."

"Really?" Katz said. "I thought we were done."

"I don't know what to tell you," the driver said, "but that's what they told me."

He thought about taking a cab straight home, then gave up himself.

"Okay," he said. "I surrender. Let's go."

In ten minutes, the driver eased to a stop in front of headquarters. The first floor was lit up and so was the fifth, where the top brass' offices were. A detective who recognized him shook his hand at the door, and waved to another cop to let him in. Katz had no idea who wanted him where for what, so he punched the elevator button for five and figured he'd ask when he got there.

He stepped off the elevator and thought he might still be asleep, dreaming the sight of Rabe holding a wineglass and talking to Ghorbal, resplendent in a tuxedo and a red bow tie. Zahedi somehow appeared at his side and handed him a glass of red wine. He sported a tuxedo too.

"Mr. Katz!" he said. "I'm so glad you could join us. We're just about to start."

Katz felt like he was tumbling down the rabbit hole head over heels.

"Didn't I just leave you at the Gramercy?" he asked.

"Yes," Zahedi said, "what, an hour ago?"

Katz strained to understand what he couldn't believe was really happening.

"What is – what are, how?" he managed to get out.

Zahedi laughed and rested a hand on his arm.

"This is a celebration, Mr. Katz, of the release," he said. "It is our honor to serve you."

Katz tried to formulate a single coherent question.

"How did you pull this off in the last hour?" he asked.

"Ha!," Zahedi laughed. "I didn't. You must remember, you excused us around eleven." He looked at his watch. "More than four hours ago. We have been working on this since."

"But Khaalis didn't give up then," Katz said. "How could you be so sure we'd have something to celebrate?"

"We are Muslims," Zahedi said. "We are people of faith!"

He laughed again and tugged Katz by the jacket sleeve down the hall and around the corner to the Chief's conference room. There must have been fifty people gathered around a table covered in white linen that stretched from one end of the room to the other. Waiters and wine stewards shuffled among them with trays of hors d'oeuvres and drinks. The glow of three lit candelabras shone off place settings of fine china all along the table.

Katz remembered a Marx Brothers movie where Groucho asked someone "Who're you going to believe, me or your own lying eyes?" He couldn't believe what he was seeing and he didn't believe what he was hearing until he turned to see someone actually was playing a violin next to the door. He touched the wall to make sure it was real.

He turned at the sound of someone tapping silverware against a glass. It was Zahedi.

"My friends, please," he said, "let us be seated."

"Jake!" he heard from across the table. He saw Silbert waving him to the seat beside him. Katz circled the table and sat down.

"Holy God," he said, "are you really here? Is this really real?"

Earl pinched his own cheek and squeezed Katz' forearm.

"It must be," he said, "but I don't believe it either."

They took in the scene. Zahedi sat at one end of the table, Cullinane and the Mayor in the seats closest to him. Down the table, Katz recognized Sterling Tucker, the chairman of the City Council, and all of the cops, but there were plenty of people he didn't know. A waiter filled his glass with wine. Zahedi rose to his feet and lifted his glass.

"My dear friends, let us raise a glass to the release of the hostages." They all raised their glasses. A few of them whooped and hollered.

"This is a wonderful occasion," he said, "and we, Ambassador Khan, Ambassador Ghorbal, and myself, are so proud to have played a small role in bringing this terrible ordeal to an end. There are many people who share in this tonight so let me introduce you to each other."

He started with the Mayor and worked his way down the right side of the table. The names meant nothing to Katz. The meal meant nothing to him. He just wanted to lie down and close his eyes. He leaned over to Silbert and pointed to the table.

"Do you think he'd mind if I just crawled up here and stretched out?" he said.

"You might want to stay up another few hours," Silbert said.

"Why?," Katz said. "I'm not hungry, whatever he's serving."

"Not for that," Earl said. "Khaalis' arraignment is at 5:15, a.m."

Katz heard Zahedi call his name. He lifted his glass, then waited for Earl to take his turn in the spotlight. When it passed, he turned back to him.

"Are you serious?" he asked.

"Absolutely," Earl said. "Greene's going to hear it himself."

"Why so early?" Katz asked.

"We want to get him in and out of there before anyone knows," Earl said. "Plus, the sooner we get him under house arrest the better. I'm starting to hear some people aren't so happy about the way this ended."

A waiter set a salad in front of Earl. Katz waited for him to put his down before he said anything else.

"Who?" Katz said. "Who's not happy?"

"DOJ," Silbert said, "the White House."

"How can DOJ be unhappy?" Katz asked. "Flaherty was in it every step of the way."

"He's the one who told me," Silbert said.

Katz scanned the room.

"Is he here?" he asked.

"Nope," Silbert said. "I'm trying not to read anything into that."

Katz pushed his salad plate away from him.

"What were we supposed to do?" he asked. "They were about to set the place on fire!"

"You know that and I know that but no one else seems to give a damn," Silbert said.

"Would they be happier if we let him kill a hundred people?" Katz said.

Earl played with the salad with his fork. Katz sat and stewed.

"Can we lay it out at the arraignment?" he asked. "Spell it out so everyone knows we had no choice?"

Earl shrugged.

"We can try," he said, "but we don't have all the facts yet and I don't want to blow the case by saying something that might come back to haunt us if we can't prove it. The most important thing is to convict him and put him away for the rest of his life. That's what we need to focus on."

He sounded like he was trying to convince himself. Katz didn't need convincing.

"We had no choice," he said and shook his head. "This is a whole lot of Monday morning quarterbacking and it's still Friday."

"Well," Silbert said, "we did everything we could. Go home and get some rest as soon as you can. You did a great job."

"Who's presenting the case?" Katz asked.

"Me," Earl said.

Katz understood why he wasn't doing it. Leaving aside the fact that he really might be hallucinating by then, he was a witness now, not the prosecutor. But he was surprised to hear Earl would do it himself. The U.S. Attorney didn't usually get down in the ditches like this, and there was an office full of guys who could probably do it a whole lot better only because they did it every day. Earl must have known what Katz was thinking because he answered the question Katz was still figuring out how to ask.

"This is a huge deal and I'm the U.S. Attorney," he said. "I'm not going to ask anyone else to stick their head in this noose. I can handle it."

"Well, I'll be right behind you," Katz said. "I'll be there."

"You don't have to," Earl said. "I'll see it through."

"I will too," Katz said. "Plus, it gives us both an excuse to get the hell out of here."

He looked around the table. Cullinane and Rabe were already gone. He wiped his lips with his napkin and threw it on the table.

"I'm out of here," Katz said.

Earl tossed his napkin on the table.

"I'll be right behind you," he said.

40

Earl walked Katz to his car in the Federal courthouse garage and handed him the keys.

"I'm going to stay here," he said, glancing at his watch. "The hearing's in a little over an hour and I can use the time."

"You want company?" Katz said. "I'm happy to help."

"I know," Earl said, "but I'm fine. Go take a shower for both of us."

He offered his hand and Katz shook it.

"You did a hell of a job," Earl said. "I picked the right guy."

"Thanks, Earl," Katz said. "Yours is the only opinion that counts."

"At least for the next two weeks," Earl smiled. "See you in an hour."

He disappeared up the steps.

Katz climbed into the driver's seat and headed home. He couldn't find a legal space on East Capitol so he did a uey at the corner of 16th and parked it at the corner. He figured he was safe. Ticketing the U.S. Attorney's car would take a lot more balls than parking it there.

The place was dark when he came in. He didn't expect Marty would still be up waiting for him, so he pulled off his shoes and tiptoed back to the bedroom. He circled the bed to her side to give her a kiss, but she wasn't there. He flicked on the lamp and saw the empty bed, still made. He looked for the little love note she'd usually leave on his pillow but it wasn't there either. He tried to put two and two together. She had no idea if or when he'd be coming home so she stayed in her own place. Wouldn't be the first time. He got it. He headed for the shower.

By the time he came out, it was almost 5. All he wanted to do was lie down and wake up sometime late, like

Sunday, but he knew he had to be there with Earl for the final act. He got himself dressed and out the door.

The car was where he left it, unticketed. He drove back to the courthouse and pulled into Earl's spot. He let himself imagine what it would be like to be the United States Attorney for the District of Columbia. He enjoyed the feeling until he remembered everything Earl had gone through to be it, and what he had to do this morning. He got out of the car and hustled out of the building and over to Judge Greene's courtroom on the second floor of Building B a few blocks away.

Earl was at the counsel's table, Flaherty sitting next to him. Katz came up behind them and tapped Earl on the shoulder. Flaherty spun to see him and popped up out of his seat.

"Hey, Jake," he said. Katz followed his good buddy's lead.

"Hey, Pete," Katz said. "Good to see you again."

"You get any sleep?" Pete asked.

"Nah," Katz said. "I stuck around for the dinner, then Earl let me take his car home so I could at least get a shower." He handed Earl the keys. "Thanks, dad."

"I took a shower too," Silbert said, "in the sink, but I don't think it's going to help till I get out of these clothes."

"Come sit with us," Flaherty asked, then remembered his place. "If Earl says it's okay, of course."

"Katz," Silbert said, "take a seat. That's an order."

Katz took the seat on the other side of Flaherty.

"You got it under control?" he asked Earl.

Earl took a peek at the gallery behind them. There were only about eight or ten people but all of them had notepads and pencils at the ready.

"I do," he said, "but if either of you have something to add any time, slide me a note."

Katz looked over to the defense table. Tim Morrison and Silas Wasserstrom, a couple of public defenders Katz

349

recognized, flanked Khaalis. Khaalis wore a blue windbreaker and sat quietly, staring at the table.

A large black marshal poked his head in from a door behind the bench and looked their way, then at the defense. No one at their table paid him any attention until he came down and leaned across it into their faces.

"You gentlemen ready?" he said. "The court is."

"Can we have one more minute?," Morrison asked him.

"You have till he comes out," the marshal said and came to the prosecutors' table.

"Are you gentlemen ready?" he asked.

"We're ready," Earl said.

The marshal went up the steps on their side and back through the door.

Katz knew his role. He pulled a pen and a legal-size yellow pad out of his briefcase and scribbled "Khaalis hearing 3/11/77" at the top.

The door behind the bench opened and Judge Greene came out. They all rose and sat back in their seats after he took his.

"Good morning, everyone," he said.

They all said their good mornings back. He flipped a file open, then looked to Earl.

"Mr. Silbert," he said, "are you ready to proceed?'

Earl stood.

"I am, your Honor," he said.

"All right," the judge said, "but before you do, I need to make a statement for the record about an unusual aspect of this proceeding."

Earl sat down. Judge Greene spoke to the gallery behind them.

"Mr. Silbert called me earlier this morning, when he was negotiating with Mr. Khaalis about the release of the hostages at the B'nai B'rith Building, the Islamic Center, and the District Building, and asked me to approve Mr. Khaalis' release on his own recognizance in advance in order to facilitate his release of the hostages. In view of the hostages, I agreed to his request. Mr. Silbert, have I stated our conversation accurately?"

Earl stood again.

"You have, your honor."

Greene turned to the defense table.

"Does the defense have any questions about that conversation?" he asked.

"We do not," Morrison said.

"Then I'll hear from the government," Greene said.

"Thank you, your honor," Earl said. "First, I'd like to read the complaint charging Mr. Khaalis with one count of armed kidnapping."

He recited the complaint and the maximum punishment, life in prison, and handed the paper to the clerk, who handed it to Greene. He took a few seconds to scan it, then looked back to Earl.

"Very well, Mr. Silbert," he said. "And what do you have to say now about what the court should do with Mr. Khaalis?"

"First, your honor," Earl said, "with respect to the point you raised about Mr. Khaalis' release, he does face a serious charge here, but under the Bail Reform Act, the defendant's ties to the community are an important factor the court must consider in weighing his release."

He picked up a file from the desk and opened it.

"The bail report shows that he lives with his family and has lived in his house for six or seven years. He also is an officer of a corporation that sells jewelry in the District of Columbia."

He slid the file back onto the desk.

"In addition," he continued, "the defendant negotiated on a continuing basis with government authorities, and early this morning agreed to the peaceful surrender of himself and his colleagues and associates, and the release of hostages

351

numbering approximately 125. In view of the release of the hostages without violence and the peaceful surrender, the United States has agreed, with the approval of the court, on the conditional release of the defendant pending his indictment and arraignment thereon."

Greene turned back to the defense table.

"Does the defense wish to say anything to the court?" he asked.

"Only that we fully concur in the government's rationale," Morrison said.

Greene looked back to Earl.

"The defendant may well qualify for release," he said, "in view of his community ties, stable residence, and lack of criminal convictions. The bail agency has recommended personal recognizance. But, the court is also mindful of events in the city in which the defendant has had considerable significance."

Katz held his breath. No one made a sound.

"However," Greene said, "as I said at the time, the court was not in the position to second-guess the government authorities on that question, so it will go along. But the court will impose conditions."

He addressed Khaalis.

"Mr. Khaalis, as I've said, the court will release you on your own recognizance, without requiring you to post a money bond, until such time as a grand jury returns an indictment against you, at which time I will reassess this order. Until then, you must abide by the following conditions. You may not leave the District of Columbia without the approval of the court. You must appear at the Metropolitan Police Department on Monday morning for fingerprinting and booking. You'll bring your passport with you and surrender it to the Department. You may not even travel anywhere inside the District of Columbia without the approval of the police department. You may not keep or possess any firearms, or engage in any unlawful conduct, and you may not communicate with any of the persons who participated in this act with you."

He looked to Silbert.

"Does the government request any other conditions?" Earl stood. "No, your honor," he said.

The judge looked to the defense.

"Does the defense wish to be heard about the conditions of Mr. Khaalis' release?"

"No, your honor," Morrison rose and said. Greene looked back at Earl.

"I am also ordering both the prosecution and the defense to make no comment on this case or the events that transpired to anyone at any time in any form without the approval of the court. Is that clearly understood?" the judge asked.

Silbert said it was. Morrison did too. Judge Greene peered down at Khaalis.

"Mr. Khaalis," he said, "this condition also applies to you. Do you understand it and agree to abide by it?"

"Yes," he said softly.

"Do you understand and agree to abide by the other conditions I have imposed on you?"

"Yes," he said again.

Judge Greene turned to Earl, then to the defense.

"Mr. Silbert, gentlemen, anything else?"

When they all said no, he said "Then I order the defendant released on his own recognizance subject to the conditions I stated." He raised his gavel and rapped it once. "This proceeding is adjourned."

Katz and the rest rose to their feet. When the door behind the bench closed behind the judge, Katz fell back into his seat. He looked at his watch one more time. 5:35, fifteen minutes after it started.

The clerk came down the steps to get some information from Khaalis. He watched him give it to her, then get up and say a few words to his lawyers before he turned to the gallery. Katz looked back to see Abdul-Aziz come up through the gate to greet him. They clasped hands and exchanged kisses on the cheek, then crossed behind him and left the room without even a glance at any of them.

Earl gathered up his things, then stood with a groan Katz had never heard come out of him before.

"If you gentlemen don't mind," Silbert said, "I'm going home now to get a little sleep. Strike that – a lot of sleep. Jake, can I give you a lift?"

"I thought you'd never ask," Katz said. "God, yes."

"How about you, Pete?" Earl asked. "Drop you anywhere?"

"No thank you, Earl," Flaherty said. "I'm supposed to call the Department for a car, then get over to Bell's office as soon as he gets in so he can hear all about it, this morning, last night, everything."

"You want a ride somewhere else?" Earl grinned.

Flaherty grinned back.

"I'll let you know what he says," Flaherty said, "if you don't hear it yourself. Jake, we'll be in touch."

They shook hands all around and Flaherty left. Katz saw Allan Frank, a guy he knew from the Star, waiting behind the gate to the gallery. Everyone else had gone.

"Hey, Jake, Mr. Silbert," he said, "can I talk to you fellas a second?"

"We said everything we had to say, Allan," Earl said. "That'll have to do."

"How about off the record?" Frank asked. "There's an awful lot to ask about."

Earl looked at Katz. Katz played the trick he conjured up two long days ago. He turned his back to Frank and said to Earl quietly, "This may be a shot at getting our side of the story out."

Earl nodded and turned back to Frank.

"Off the record," Earl said. "I'll tell you what I can."

354

"Thanks," Frank said and came through the gate. "Why just one count? Why not a hundred counts?"

"It's just a holding charge," Silbert said. "When we get to the grand jury, there'll be a lot more."

"Okay," Frank said, scribbling on his pad. "And how about the other guys? Are they walking too?"

Earl grew red.

"No one's walking, okay?" he said. "Khaalis is going no place until he's indicted, and then he's going to jail, forever. The rest of them are being arraigned this afternoon. I don't know what we're going to recommend until I get the bail report, but I assure you, anyone charged with murder or armed kidnapping is not walking."

He gathered up his papers, stuffed them into his briefcase, and snapped it shut.

"Anything else?" he asked.

Frank looked at Katz for a little help but got nothing. He turned back to Earl.

"Mr. Silbert," he said, "you got to understand. There's a lot of people out there who aren't going to be able to figure out why a guy who killed people and held the city hostage for three days gets to go home like nothing happened. I'm giving you a chance to explain it."

"I've given you all I've got to say," Earl said. "You'll hear more when we've got more to tell you. We did everything we could to save those people's lives, keep those guys from doing anything worse than they did when this thing started, and it worked."

He jabbed a finger at Frank.

"*That's* the story you should be writing!"

He picked up his bag and left. Katz ran to catch up.

"That was good, Earl," he said. "That's exactly what he needed to hear."

Earl pushed open the door to the stairway down to the garage. He looked back at Katz, flushed and still pissed.

"Want to bet he didn't hear any of it?" he said. "The story those fuckers are going to write is 'Khaalis walks', not 'Hundreds saved', trust me."

He looked down at the ground and shook his head in disgust before he raised it to look at Katz.

"You want a ride?" he asked. "Come on. I'll drop you off."

Something held Katz back, maybe the need to think about all of this in broad daylight, maybe the need to let Earl just go home and lie down.

"No, I'm going to walk," he said. "I could use the fresh air. Get some sleep. I'll see you Monday – if that's okay."

Silbert managed a laugh.

"God yes!" he said, "if I'm in by then. Get some sleep. You did us all proud."

He headed back to the courthouse and Katz headed home. He strained to sort out the million thoughts careening through his brain, but the fuzz of sleeplessness kept him in a fog all the way back. In fifteen minutes, he was at his front door but didn't remember a step of the way. He threw off his jacket, walked back to the bedroom, untied his shoes, and laid back on the bed. See you Monday, world, he thought. It was the last thing that crossed his mind.

41

He didn't know a bus even had backup beepers but they grew nearer and louder every second. He screamed he was back there but the driver couldn't hear him and he was too low to show up in his mirrors. He was stuck in the pit, up to his chest in mud, and his legs wouldn't move. All he could hear were the beeps, over and over, harsher and harsher. Earl stretched for him, yelling at him to take his hand but it was all he could do to touch his fingertips. He screamed so loud he screamed himself awake.

The phone was ringing in his ear. He dropped his right hand on his sweaty chest, his heartbeat nearly bouncing it off. He struggled to get a grip and finally made himself roll over and pick up the receiver.

"Yeah?" he said, "hello?"

"Jake, are you up?" Earl said. "I'm sorry if I woke you."

Katz closed his eyes and prayed this was a bad dream too.

"What time is it?" he asked.

"It's two o'clock," Earl said. "Think you can get yourself over here by three?"

Katz heard himself ask a question you never asked Earl.

"Why?" he said.

"We're meeting to talk about the bail requests for Khaalis' guys," Earl said. "Moultrie's doing the hearing. It's at five."

Katz forced his eyes open.

"Okay," he said, "I'll be there."

He yawned a mammoth yawn.

"Did you get any sleep?" he asked Earl.

"Two hours, maybe," Silbert said. "Flaherty woke me up with a phone call. Said he just got back from a meeting with the AG who chewed his ass out, up, down, and sideways about letting Khaalis go. He wanted to give me a heads up that the shit would be flowing downhill like it usually does, only faster."

"Ugh," Katz said and sat up. "Sorry to hear that."

"Yeah," Earl said. "It's not going to be pretty. I've already heard from two Council members. It turns out Nadine Winter's son was one of the hostages at the District Building."

"Oof," Katz said.

"Let me make sure I get this right," Earl said. "She was 'absolutely appalled' we let him go home. Everyone's life is in jeopardy, unquote. And I also got a call from Julius Hobson asking me how in the world I could let a murderer go."

"I don't get it," Katz said. "Would they rather be pulling a hundred bodies out of the B'nai B'rith this morning?"

Earl sighed.

"Anyhow," he said, "we need to talk about all this before we go see Moultrie. See you at three?"

"I'll be there," Katz said and hung up.

He walked over to the little black and white TV on a stool at the end of the bed and flicked it on. He turned the dial to all four stations but there was nothing on about the siege. He turned it off and walked back to the radio and punched up TOP.

"We talked this morning with Chief Robert DiGrazia of the Montgomery County Police Department," an announcer said. "WTOP asked him to give us a little insight into why the District might have allowed Mr. Khaalis to return home last night, rather than go to jail. Here's what he had to say."

"I don't know what the situation was," DiGrazia said. "I wasn't there. It's difficult to second guess these things, but my feeling is that if we're going to short-stop this sort of stuff, we've got to be tougher. Promise them anything to get the hostages out of there, and after they're out, don't even give them Arpege. The number of hostage cases around the nation is growing. The power of suggestion is very strong. The more we show we're tough with them, the quicker we get it off the front page."

The announcer came back on.

"And we talked to a number of you who expressed the same concerns."

Katz heard a young woman's voice.

"That was the stupidest thing I ever heard of," she said. "I was so mad. It's just going to happen again and again until the big shots put an end to it. There isn't a law anymore."

He flicked off the radio and headed for the bathroom.

At two fifty-eight, he walked into Earl's conference room. He was the first one there. He pulled out a chair but stopped when he saw Marty come through the door.

"Hey!" he said. "There you are." He looked to the door to make sure no one else was coming. "I missed you this morning," he said softly.

She walked around to the other side of the table and took the seat farthest away from him.

"We'll talk about that later," she said without looking his way.

Earl came in with Mark Tuohey, Teddy Loomis, and Hank Schuelke just behind him. Tuohey and Loomis were AUSAs in the Felony I trial section. Schuelke had tried the murders of Khaalis' family with Katz. They all took their seats.

"Okay," Earl said. "I think we're all assembled. Let me make sure everyone's up to speed. Moultrie's set a bail hearing at five for the eleven other guys who held the hostages. We need to come up with a bail request for each of them, so let me go over the bail office's recommendations, then get your thoughts."

He flipped open a file on each guy, hit the high points, then pushed it around the table. Everyone took notes except Marty. The gist of the situation was that some of the guys had priors, some didn't, and all of them had lived in DC for a while. The bail office recommended varying amounts for each of them, except for recognizance for the three guys at the Islamic Center, who had no priors and didn't hurt anyone. Katz was surprised to read they were brothers.

"So," Earl said, "what do you say? Start with anyone you'd like."

"I think we need to set a high bond for all of them," Schuelke said. "Anything less than twenty-five K or so is going to be seen as just a slap on the wrist."

"The guys with the priors," Tuohey said, looking at his notes, "I show them as Latif and Salaam at the B'nai B'rith? They ought to get more, fifty maybe? And the guys at the District Building where the people got shot – Muzikir and Nuh? – they ought to get the most."

"So what's that?" Earl asked. "Fifty? Seventy-five?"

"Earl," Marty said, "with all due respect, fifty thousand for a murder of an innocent victim? And the people they shot who're still in the hospital who might die too? And a councilman, Barry? That's way too low for them."

"Marty," Earl said. "I'm with you. We can ratchet them up."

"I'd do more than ratchet," she said, a little more heat seeping into her voice. "I'd go with a hundred K across the board, all of 'em."

"Wait a minute," Tuohey said. "All of them? Are we using a cookie cutter here now? What're you talking about, Marty?"

"I'm talking about a situation," she said, "where the public is pissed because the fucking murderer got home before the hostages did!"

"Whoa, whoa, whoa," Katz said. "Khaalis didn't murder anyone."

"Maybe not," Marty said, staring at him with an ice cold fury, "but the guys he controlled did. He's responsible and he walked. Now we're going to let his cronies walk? Shame on us!"

He squinted back at her like she couldn't be serious but he knew in his heart she was. And he knew in that moment it would be a long road back to her heart again.

"Okay," Earl said, "let's take it down a notch. No one's walking for anything. They're all going to be behind bars when we get through with them, for a long time. Let's keep our eyes on the ball."

"Earl," Marty said, "right now people think we've already lost our minds because we let Khaalis go home. Do we want them to *know* we have by letting these clowns go home too? What does that say to the next fuckups that want to try this? Do whatever the fuck you want because nothing's going to happen to you, that's what. We can sit here and rationalize it all we want but all anyone's going to think is that we're a bunch of weak sister idiots for putting a whole lot of murderers and kidnappers right back on the street."

"She's got a point," Loomis said. "Why should we take the fall for it? Let's go in guns blazing and ask for the max and let Moultrie take the heat for knocking it down. He's the one with the fifteen-year appointment."

"Jake?" Earl said. "What do you say?"

Katz didn't want to give Marty the satisfaction of agreeing with her but what Flaherty told Earl was on his mind first and foremost.

"I agree with Teddy," he said. "If they're going to wind up getting lower bail anyhow, let Moultrie set it. We've taken enough heat for doing the right thing. Let him share in the joy."

"You know the bail act requires an individual assessment, right?" Tuohey asked him. "One size does not fit all."

"I got it," Katz said, "but I'm pretty sure they didn't write the thing with this situation in mind."

They all looked to Earl. He took another look at the files.

"Okay," he said. "I'm persuaded. A hundred thousand each?"

He looked at them in turn. No one made a sound.

"Going once? Going twice?" he said. "Then that's what we'll ask for. Marty and Mark, I'd like you to sit with me. Jake, Teddy, Hank, feel free to come and watch."

Marty bolted immediately. Katz decided not to chase her and headed to his own office. He made a half-hearted stab at refamiliarizing himself with his files and his calendar, but mostly he stared out the window and let the thousand images of the last three days flow through his mind, right down to the final scene, watching Marty stalk out of the room and maybe his life. At five to five, he headed back to Building B.

Marty sat next to Silbert, with Tuohey on her other side. Two public defenders sat with the eleven defendants, surrounded by looked like about twenty U.S. Marshals standing in the dock and maybe another thirty behind it. Katz picked his way through them and took a seat next to Schuelke in the front row behind the prosecution table.

Earl nodded at him. Marty turned back to see who he was looking at, then turned back to stare at the folder in front of her. Katz took a look back at the gallery behind him. He recognized about two dozen reporters but there must have been more he didn't. The place was packed and noisy.

A tall guy with long reddish-blonde hair waved at him from behind the defense side. Katz waved back and went over to give him a handshake. Tim Murray was the first bail officer he ever met when he started at the USA's. He had a wicked sense of humor and never failed to give Katz a serious dose of shit whenever he could for offenses real and imagined. He looked at Katz with amazement.

"Is this right, counselor?" he asked, pointing at his two-pronged file folder. "Are you seriously asking his honor for one hundred thousand dollars bail for each of these gentlemen – well, I wouldn't necessarily call them gentlemen, they're more like giant pains in the ass, but still my question remains – are you fucking serious?"

"That is the case, sir," Katz said. "You have not lost your senses."

"Then you have lost yours," Murray said, "because that is fucking crazy. There is no way Moultrie is going to go along with that, for any of them. He is somewhat familiar with the actual law, you know."

Katz smiled.

"I believe that is a part of our nefarious plan," he said.

"Oh," Murray said, seeing the light. "I get it. Let the judge take the heat for being the pussy, instead of you guys. Why would I ever think higher of you?"

"Just so you don't totally give up on us," Katz said, "you might remember that people died in this thing. That may still mean something to even a jaded soul like you. Who's posting for them, Bonabond or one of the other outfits?"

Bonabond was the main bail bonds provider for black defendants. The others were the Black Man's Liberation Army and the Black Man's Development Front.

"None of them," Murray said, "Bureau of Rehab."

The Bureau of Rehabilitation was an arm of Lutheran Social Services and usually cherry-picked its clients, which meant that almost all of them were white.

"How'd that happen?" Katz asked.

"None of the brethren wanted to go near these guys," Murray said. "Afraid of what they were getting into."

Moultrie appeared in the rear door. Katz tapped Murray on the chest and made his way back to the other side. He waited for Moultrie to sit, then took his own seat.

363

Judge H. Carl Moultrie was a black man in his early sixties with a full gray and white tufted afro who came on the bench a little after Katz started with the USA. He respected the rule of law, and demanded the same of everyone in his courtroom, especially the lawyers. He was not a man who put up with b.s. of any sort from anybody. Katz got the uneasy feeling this would not be the USA's finest moment. It didn't take a minute for Moultrie to end all doubts.

"The court is here to set the terms of release for the eleven defendants who have been charged in the takeover of the three buildings downtown that ended last night," he said. "Under the terms of the District's Bail Reform Act, each defendant is entitled to an individualized review of the conditions of his release."

He lifted his head to look intently at Earl.

"I had presumed, until I read the Government's filings in this case, that the Government was also familiar with the terms of the Act. Am I mistaken in that regard, Mr. Silbert?"

Earl stood.

"No, your honor," he said. "You are correct."

"I see," Moultrie said. "I was confused because you have asked that the same large bail amount be set for each of the defendants. Am I correct about that too, Mr. Silbert?"

"You are, your honor," Earl said. "We are asking that each of the defendants be held in lieu of $100,000 bail. If I may continue, your honor."

"Go ahead, Mr. Silbert," the judge said. "I am very interested in hearing what you have to say."

"Thank you, your honor," Earl said. "These men and their leader, Mr. Khaalis, imposed a reign of terror on their hostages. My office intends to pursue felony murder indictments against all twelve defendants in this case. As I'm sure you know, your honor, a young radio reporter was struck by bullets fired by the defendants at the District Building shortly after they took it over last Wednesday.

364

Other persons were kidnapped and injured by the defendants at the B'nai B'rith and the Islamic Center. It is our intention to present this matter to a grand jury as soon as we can. Until we do, however, the terms of the Bail Reform Act require you to consider the defendants' threat to the safety of the community in determining the conditions of their release. In light of the severe threat they have already posed and likely will pose again, we are asking the court to set the very high bail we requested."

"All right," Moultrie said, "I hear what you are saying to me, although I'm not sure I fully understand it. Perhaps it will be clearer as we proceed. Who would you like to begin with, Mr. Silbert?"

Earl picked up the first file in front of him.

"We'd like to begin with Mr. Abdul Al Qawee, your honor."

Katz watched the man he recognized as the second gunman at the Islamic Center walk to the bench, his hands cuffed, with a Marshal on either side. Katz guessed he was the middle brother. Earl sat down and Teddy Loomis stood up.

"Your honor," he said. "As you know, the Government is requesting Mr. Al Qawee to post a $100,000 bond for his release. Your honor, if I may –"

"You may not, at least for a minute, Mr. Loomis," Moultrie said. "I am still confused, I guess. Maybe you can clear a few things up for me."

"Certainly, your honor," Loomis said.

"Mr. Al-Qawee was at the Islamic Center, is that correct?" the judge asked.

"It is, your honor."

"And I don't see anything in your papers that he harmed anyone there, is that also correct?"

"To the best of our knowledge, your honor," Loomis said, "but, as you can appreciate, the investigation is just beginning."

"I understand, Mr. Loomis," the judge said, "just bear with me a moment. And I don't see that Mr. Al-Qawee has committed any prior criminal offenses, or am I mistaken?"

"You are not mistaken, your honor," Loomis said. "Mr. Al Qawee has no criminal record. Again, we have not completed --"

The judge held up a hand. Loomis stopped talking.

"And, again," Moultrie continued, "please correct me if I'm wrong, it looks like Mr. Al-Qawee is a resident of the Washington metropolitan area, and has been for a number of years. Is that the case?"

"It is, your honor," Loomis said. "He resides in Wheaton, Maryland."

"With his brothers and his parents," Moultrie said. "Is that the case?"

"As far as we know, your honor," Loomis answered.

"As far as you know," Moultrie said. "So please explain this to me so that I can fully grasp the Government's position on Mr. Al-Qawee and the rest of these defendants. We have covered all of the issues that the Bail Reform Act says I'm supposed to consider and, for the life of me, Mr. Loomis, I don't see what I'm missing. Please explain to the court why the Government is requesting a one hundred thousand dollar bond for Mr. Al-Qawee?"

"Your honor," Loomis said, "Mr. Al-Qawee and the other ten defendants before you were linked in a conspiracy to occupy these three buildings by force, and they will all probably be indicted for murder at the District Building. As a result, your honor, we believe that a very high money bond is required to ensure the public safety."

Moultrie peered at Loomis for a good long while.

"Even though Mr. Al-Qawee himself did not harm anybody," he said to Loomis.

"Correct, your honor," he said, "this was a conspiracy knowingly entered into by Mr. Al-Qawee and each of his confederates."

Moultrie kept peering at Loomis, but it seemed he wasn't any closer to finding what he was looking for. He turned to Silbert.

"Mr. Silbert," he said, "just so there will be no misunderstanding on part of counsel, this court is not considering these defendants as part of a group. Do you have any further arguments to provide on this score in addition to the ones Mr. Loomis provided?"

Earl rose.

"No, your honor."

"All right then," Moultrie said. "Mr. Silbert, Mr. Loomis, Miss McAdoo, I am sure you appreciate that judges find themselves in positions where they must adhere to the law. Judges are sworn to uphold the law as it exists. We don't make the laws. We just carry them out. And that's the case here, all right?"

Silbert and Loomis nodded. Marty didn't. Moultrie went on.

"The D.C. Bail Reform Act, like it or not, *requires* me to release defendants who have strong ties to the community when there is no strong likelihood they'll flee, The citizens may want to change that. The judges can't, all right? So now that we totally understand each other, I am going to release Mr. Al-Qawee – and his brothers, Mr. Rahman and Mr. Rahim – on their own recognizance to the Bureau of Rehabilitation. Does the Government have any questions or quarrel with that now?"

Earl said "We do not, your honor."

"All right then," Moultrie said, "let's motor through the rest of them, shall we?"

In the next fifteen minutes, he set bail for the two men at the District Building, and four of the six men at the B'nai B'rith at $50,000 each. Because Abdul Latif and Abdul Salaam had prior convictions, he set theirs at $75,000. When he read the last of his decisions into the record, he looked to the defense table.

"Gentlemen, I understand that you requested r.o.r. for everyone other than Mr. Latif and Mr. Salaam, but, under the law, the court has to weigh in the safety of the community. In my mind, a $50,000 bond is warranted for that reason. Do you wish to be heard on that?"

They looked at each other and stood together to say no in unison.

Moultrie turned to Earl.

"Mr. Silbert," he asked, "anything?"

Earl said "No".

"In that case," Moultrie said, "this hearing is adjourned. The defendants are entrusted to the custody of the marshals."

They all stood until he disappeared back to chambers. Even before the door closed, the reporters raced for the phones, the marshals surrounded the defendants, and the lawyers gathered up their files.

Katz came through the gate and offered a hand to Earl.

"All things considered," he said, "not too bad."

"We did our job," Earl said. "That's all anyone can ask."

He reached over to shake Tuohey's hand, then Marty's.

"Good job all. Take the rest of the day off," he grinned. "I insist."

"Dubliner, anyone?" Tuohey asked.

"I'm heading home," Earl said. "Next time."

"In a minute," Katz said. "I need to talk to Marty first."

"See you there," Tuohey said, and headed out the door with Earl.

"Marty," Katz said. "Can we talk about this?"

She rolled her eyes.

"Here? Now?" she said, "I don't think so."

She put a lot of energy into stuffing her pad and papers into her briefcase. Schuelke was still gathering his things and chatting with Loomis so she had no easy way out. She threw the bag's strap over her shoulder and waited, her gaze on the door.

"Then when?" Katz asked. "Would you come back home with me tonight? Please?"

She turned to him, more to hide her face from Schuelke than to look at him.

"Jake," she said, her eyes down, glistening with tears, "I can't. Not tonight."

"Tomorrow night then," he said.

"No, no, no," she hissed through clenched teeth, "not tonight, not tomorrow, not ever. I can't. You really let me down, Jake."

"Marty," he whispered, "it's a – it's not even a case, it's just a call on a thing that happened, a judgment call. We're more than just a judgment call on something that's not even about us, aren't we?"

Schuelke got his things together and turned to Marty to congratulate her. When he saw her face, he thought better of it. He nodded to Katz, picked up his briefcase, and made his way out the door with Loomis.

Marty called after him.

"Hey, Hank, are you guys heading for the Dubliner?"

He stuck his head back in the doorway.

"We are," he said.

"Well, hold up," she said. "I'll come with you."

She faked a smile at Katz and hurried out to catch up to them.

Katz heard the stair door slam.

He heard a grunt and looked to the defense table. A marshal locked the cuffs on Abdul Nuh's wrists behind him. Another two marshals took him and Abdul Muzikir by the elbows and pulled them back to the door to the prisoners' entry. They disappeared and the door closed behind them. There was no one left in the courtroom.

Katz picked up his bag and headed home. It was over.

September 6, 1977

42

It was no use. Katz couldn't keep his eyes off him. He had to watch Harry Alexander, just like he had to watch one of those dazzling metal pinwheels when he was a kid. He'd push the button and send it whirring and sparking and just stare in utter fascination. Even the pinwheel got boring after a while, but Harry never did. Dismaying, irritating, appalling? Absolutely. But boring? Never. He lived to hear the gasps, Earl once said.

Now, Harry was center stage again as Hamaas' lawyer, waiting for him in the dock of the same court where he was a judge, until last year. He decided not to seek reappointment, mostly because he knew that wasn't going to happen anyway. In the words of the public censure he got a few years back, he had a habit of making "intemperate and injudicious remarks tending to downgrade litigants, witnesses, counsel, court officials and others appearing before him." Or, as they put it in the USA's office, he was a total asshole. Happy hour at The Dubliner was never happier or more crowded than the day he left.

Harry wore his blackness on the sleeve of his robe. Katz once had the displeasure of trying a weapons case before him where he got on a white cop because he didn't call a black witness "Mrs." Katz tried to cool things down by asking for a continuance but Harry threw it out rather than let the cop testify. He routinely threatened to throw witnesses and lawyers in jail because they pissed him off about something trivial, ridiculous, or both. Katz couldn't count the number of times Alexander called him and every other AUSA that appeared before him a racist. It was like watching trains wreck every day, except these wrecks could be reversed on appeal, and almost always were.

Harry didn't change after he left the bench, mostly because he lived by the credo 'once a judge, always a judge'. It didn't go over too well with Nick Nunzio the first day of the case. When Harry insisted that he call him "Your

Honor," Nunzio told him "There's only one judge in this courtroom." When he wouldn't stop, Katz had the pleasure of doing the research that backed Nunzio up. Even then, Harry cut it out only when Nunzio called him into chambers and read him the riot act in private.

But otherwise, he kept right on being Harry. Nunzio told him more than once to stop shaking his head when he was talking. He told him he'd hold him in contempt if Harry asked him more time to drop Hamaas' bail and let him out on o.r. Once, after Harry let him know he resented Nunzio sustaining so many of the government's objections to his questions, Nunzio told him the cure was to "keep the good ones and get rid of the bad ones."

Katz and Harry were about the same height but Harry's physical presence was way bigger than his. Whether it was his deep megaphone voice or the fact he was just about as wide as he was tall, Harry was a force of nature you always felt in the room. Some people might have called him short and squat, but to Katz he was a *bulvan*, built just like his father.

Katz always suspected Harry secretly wanted off the bench because the robe hid his suits. He prided himself on his wardrobe, usually topping a $500 custom cut with a matching fedora. Katz had no doubt that his elegance and his command of the language were all his way of sticking his chin out and showing the world how much he'd overcome to get where he was, but one man's pride was everyone else's arrogance, pomposity, and egotism. He commanded respect and admiration, but no one had to like him, and few did.

In July, Katz got his first chance to spar with him face to face when Harry cross-examined him about what Katz said he saw when he went to the eighth floor each day of the siege. On direct, Tuohey established that he saw people with their wrists and legs bound, some in need of medical attention. He got to tell the jury about Bortnick reeling around the room and the stacks of guns he saw the last day.

He thought he did a good job laying it all out, but after Harry got through with him, he wasn't so sure. He was even less sure when he read the transcript.

"Q. Did you ever see Mr. Khaalis tie anyone up?

"A. I saw many people tied up.

"Q. That's not what I asked you, Mr. Katz. Did you ever see Mr. Khaalis himself tie anyone up?

"A. No.

"Q. Thank you. Did you ever see Mr. Khaalis himself strike anyone?

"A. No.

"Q. Did you ever see Mr. Khaalis refuse to let anyone leave the conference room?

"A. No.

"Q. In fact, during the three days, didn't Mr. Khaalis release a number of people who he believed were in need of medical attention?

"A. People were released, but I can't say that Mr. Khaalis released them, no.

"Q. Doesn't the government's indictment charge that Mr. Khaalis was the mastermind, the person responsible for the alleged takeovers?

"A. Yes.

"Q. Then doesn't it stand to reason that Mr. Khaalis was the person responsible for the release of the so-called hostages, or is it your contention that Mr. Khaalis was only responsible for the bad acts the government claims occurred during the so-called siege, but not the good ones?

"A. I don't have a contention. I'm only telling you what I saw, and I didn't see him release anybody."

"Q. Let me get my list of the people Mr. Khaalis released.

"MR. TUOHEY. Objection. No foundation has been laid for counsel's statement that Mr. Khaalis released anyone.

"THE COURT. Sustained.

"Q. Very well. Let me ask Mr. Katz if he is aware of the following people being released. Mrs. Thelma Bronstein?

"A. I don't know that name.

"Q. Mr. Phillip Silver?

"A. I don't know that name either.

"Q. Do you recall a woman and a man coming off an elevator on Wednesday morning?

"A. Yes. I do.

"Q. How about Mr. Henry Siegel? Do you remember him being released?

"A. Yes.

"Q. How about a Mr. Melvin Blotnick?

"A. Yes.

"Q. Mrs. Evelyn White?

"A. Yes, I remember Mrs. White."

Alexander took every opportunity to make sure the jury knew that Katz had every reason to lie because he was an Assistant USA, he worked for Earl, and he was a colleague of Tuohey's. Nunzio sustained every objection every time Harry went in that direction, but it didn't matter. He'd planted the seed with the jury just by asking. The damage was done. Katz spent three and a half long hot hours on the stand. By the time he was done, you could have wrung him out like a sponge.

He felt he let the office down but, in the end, it didn't matter. On a Saturday in late July, after two-and-a-half days of deliberation, the jury found all twelve defendants guilty of one hundred and thirty-nine counts. Khaalis was convicted of murder in the second degree, and twenty-four counts of armed kidnapping and assault. The jury found him innocent of one count of felony-murder.

Sentencing was today. Katz and the rest of the filled courtroom waited for Nunzio to come out and deliver justice to all of them. He tried to take stock of everything that had happened since the hostages were released. Almost none of it was good.

The one bright spot was that all the drama over letting Khaalis go home ended three weeks later. He showed up for a preliminary hearing on April Fool's Day and Earl gave Greene a policeman's affidavit saying he heard Hamaas tell Abdul-Aziz, "I'll kill all 200 people today, they are going to pay for it. I'm going to kill for it." Nobody had any idea who he was talking about but it was good enough for Greene to lock him up pending the grand jury. He said the threats themselves weren't enough to revoke him, but because they didn't stand alone, he couldn't say they were "simply idle words". Hamaas had been locked up ever since.

The DOJ job just up and vanished. He didn't hear anything the week after the hostages were freed, so he called Flaherty to see what was up. Flaherty promised he'd get back to him, but never did. Katz called him a few more times but all he could do was leave a message. After a few weeks, Earl asked him when he was heading to Justice. When he told him the story, Earl said he wasn't surprised. He'd picked up that Flaherty was having his own problems – "drowning in a sea of Georgians," he put it – so it might not be doing Katz much good to have him in his corner anyhow. Between that and his intuition that DOJ might not want to look like they were rewarding anyone who had anything to do with Khaalis walking, he stopped calling and no one ever called him.

Earl told him he was sorry as hell but he couldn't take the Deputy job away from Riordan. He promised he'd make it right, but Katz wasn't holding his breath. Marty attached herself to Riordan like a leech. Katz wasn't sure if she really loved him, or even liked him, or whether she just knew his prospects now seemed infinitely better than Katz', but he had the luxury of not caring either. They never talked about it but she didn't have to tell him what he'd known all along: she wasn't one to hitch herself to a falling star. In some small way, he felt sorry for her because she was in a job in an office in a profession where her merit and ambition weren't enough. She still needed a man to be her ticket to the top and that man wasn't him anymore. Lonely Boy had never been lonelier; he'd been in solitary ever since Marty left.

Before he could feel even sorrier for himself, Tom Wallace squeezed in next to him. He was wearing a black sports jacket with thick gray pinstripes, a white shirt, and a black tie.

"Hello, my man, I figured you'd be here," he said.

They exchanged a shake.

"I saw you a few times hanging around the back of the courtroom," Katz said. "Here for the finale?"

"Couldn't miss it," Wallace said. "I don't think it's gonna be a happy ending though, at least for Mr. Khaalis."

"Here's hoping," Katz said.

"How'd you survive Harry?" Wallace grinned.

"Did you see it?" Katz asked.

"Every second," Wallace said. "You took a mandatory eight count once or twice, you know, but you made it to the final bell. That's better than most."

"Give the devil his due," Katz said. "He's a damn good lawyer when he drops all the preening and the bullshit."

"Aw, now, give his honor a break," Wallace said. "He's a good man despite all that hoo-hah. Does a lot for the community."

"You know him?" Katz asked.

"How could I not?" Wallace said. "Everyone knows Harry. Plus, he talks to me a little when there's something I need to know. Which reminds me."

He reached into his jacket pocket and pulled out a pocket-size billfold. He flipped it open and gave Katz a look at his shiny silver Detective's badge.

"Whoa!" Katz said. "That's fantastic! How'd that happen?"

Wallace pocketed the badge.

377

"You know your man Rabe?" he asked.

"Yeah," Katz said.

"Turns out he's my man too."

"Well, how about that?" Katz said. "At least something good came out of all this. Congratulations."

"Thank you very much," Wallace said. "And you? How goes it?"

"I don't know," Katz said. "Okay, I guess. I think I might just be a little burned out."

"Oh, yeah?" Wallace said. "You lookin'? Ready to make some real coin?"

"No," Katz said. "I don't know. Maybe. I might. We'll see."

"Well, as long as you're sure," Wallace laughed.

A marshal stood up in front of the bench.

"All rise," he said.

They rose and waited for Judge Nunzio.

Nunzio, a stocky dark-haired man in his mid-forties, had on his game face. He sat down and they did too. A string of marshals led the defendants through the prisoners' door. Khaalis was at the head of the line, his hands cuffed before him. He looked a lot more relaxed and a little puffier than Katz remembered. Harry shook each of their hands as they made their way to the seats behind his table, then the cluster of marshals blocked Katz from seeing any of them.

Nunzio reminded everybody what they were there for, then turned to the defense side.

"Before I proceed to sentencing," he said, "I will provide each of the defendants the opportunity to address the court. Mr. Khaalis, I will hear from you first."

Khaalis rose to his feet and folded his arms across his chest. He looked at Nunzio and spoke in a quiet firm voice.

"This is my country," he said. "Allah will judge us all and it is a country on the road to self-destruction. And you can use my help. I won't apologize for standing up for the respect and character of my faith. It was a good deed.

378

Today, America is in very, very grave trouble and no one seems to listen. No one seems to understand. Many times in this world things go beyond the stage of writing letters or even seeing someone face to face. Somebody has got to take a stand. Hamaas made a stand. And I'm going to keep that stand. That's all I have to say."

He sat down and stared at the bench below Nunzio.

"Very well," Nunzio said. "Mr. Nuh?"

Abdul Nuh stood up. He was stocky and well groomed, with a broad face and a full black mustache.

"I concur with everything that my leader Khalifa Hamaas Abdul Khaalis has said," he said, "and bear witness to the death that what my leader said is truth."

All the rest gave Nunzio variations on the same theme – undying fealty to their Khalifa and to Allah. When they were done, Nunzio asked them all to stand.

"The crimes of which you have all been convicted are serious offenses," he said. "You kidnapped and held hostage more than a hundred and twenty people at three locations for nearly two full days. Your criminal conduct caused the death of Mr. Maurice Williams at the District Building and the subsequent death of Mr. Mack Cantrell at a hospital, and crippled another man, Mr. Robert Pierce. You inflicted numerous other injuries on many other innocent persons over the course of your conduct. In determining your sentences, the court has also weighed in that you held the entire city hostage for three days, terrorizing not only your hostages, but their families and many other citizens of the District of Columbia as well. The sentences I am handing down today are intended not only to punish you for your reprehensible conduct over the course of those three days in March, but also to make sure that no one ever contemplates perpetuating such acts and wreaking such havoc in the future."

He reached for a sheaf of papers and looked at the top one, then looked at Abdul Muzikir, a well-built young man with a full Afro.

379

"Mr. Muzikir, please stand," Nunzio said.

Muzikir stood. All during the trial, he sat with a smirk, shaking his head every time a witness accused him of shooting or striking anyone. He wasn't smirking now.

"I am sentencing you to seventy-seven years to life in the penitentiary for killing Mr. Williams and crippling Mr. Pierce." Nunzio said. "I am giving you the maximum penalty of all the defendants because the evidence showed that your shots struck Mr. Williams. I did not find your testimony credible when you stated that Mr. Pierce must have been hit accidentally by the spray of pellets from your shotgun when you fired back in self-defense at the police. I do find credible, and compelling, the testimony of many of your hostages who said you shot Pierce at point-blank range as he laid bound on the floor. You may be seated."

Nunzio flipped the paper over and asked Khaalis to rise. He stood, scowling, with his arms still folded across his chest.

"Mr. Khaalis," Nunzio said, "I am sentencing you to forty-one to one hundred and twenty-three years in the penitentiary. You were the unquestionable planner, leader, and decision-maker of the siege and everything that happened during it at all three sites. Although I believe that you also bear responsibility for the deaths and severe injuries sustained by the victims at the District Building, the Government did not indict you for directing a conspiracy to hold those victims hostage, so my sentence cannot and does not include punishment for those acts."

Katz did the math. D.C. law required a defendant to serve the full minimum sentence before he was eligible for parole. Hamaas was 55 now, so he wouldn't be eligible till he was 96. Nunzio made sure he'd spent the rest of his life in the penitentiary.

Nunzio made quick work of the rest of them. Abdul Nuh got the next longest term for his role at the District Building, forty-seven years to life. Khaalis' accomplices at the B'nai B'rith were next. Abdul Salaam and Abdul Razzaq got forty to one hundred and twenty years. Abdul Adam, Abdul Latif, Abdul Shaheed, and Abdul Salaam got thirty-six to one hundred and eight. The brothers at the Islamic Center got the shortest sentences. The two older ones, Abdul Rahman and Abdul Rahim, got twenty-eight to eighty-four years each. Abdul Qawee got twenty-four to seventy-two.

When he was done, Nunzio put the papers in a folder and turned to Earl.

"Mr. Silbert, as you know," he said, "I have no control over the Federal Bureau of Prisons' disposition of the defendants, but I will ask them to send each defendant to a separate prison."

Earl nodded. Nunzio looked to the gallery.

"There being no further business before the court," he said, "this court stands adjourned."

Katz watched him leave the bench. The marshals surrounded the defendants until a pair flanked each of them. Katz craned his neck to try to get a last glimpse of Khaalis before he disappeared through the prisoners' door but couldn't. Inside a minute, they were all gone.

Katz wended his way through the crowd to the prosecutors' table. He shook hands with Khaalis and Tuohey and gave Marty a nod. He turned to join the tail of the crowd leaving through the rear of the courtroom and shuffled his way to the back and out.

It was just about noon. The sky was gray when he walked over earlier but it was clear now. He stopped at the corner of 4th and Indiana and raised his face to the sun. The heat caressed his face. He closed his eyes and shut out all thought. He took his time opening them again, and crossed the street, a little slower. It was the first time he could remember enjoying himself in a long time.

He stopped in the men's room just to forestall the inevitable another few minutes, then slumped his way to his office. He circled the desk and sat in his chair and looked at the pale lime walls surrounding him. Six months ago, he couldn't have told anyone what color they were but now it seemed he stared at them every day. Each time he did, the same question came to his mind, a little quicker each day.

"Am I going to be here the rest of my life?" he thought.

He'd started thinking the room was really a box, set in place over him, marking his limits, like a cage at the zoo. He used to joke that the waitresses at Barney's a few blocks away on Pennsylvania were so old they built the place around them, but he didn't think it was much of a joke these days. Until a year or so ago, he hadn't even started looking, much less thinking about making a move, but then Marty made him think about it and he started shooting 171's, the Feds' job application form, to a few places. It was just the next step on the career path, he thought then, but, ever since those three days in March, it took on a little more urgency. The split second he was on the top of the wave felt great, but then it crashed on him. Now, the work was still okay, but he was beginning to feel more and more that until somebody retired, got fired, or died, he was going to be doing it until the day he retired, got fired, or died, maybe by suicide.

One look down at the case folders, messenger envelopes, and pink "While You Were Away" slips swamping his desk cleared his mind and sent him back to work. He picked up the slips and started sorting through them, until he heard a rap on the door and looked up.

It was Harry Alexander. He got to his feet.

"Your honor," he said. In court was one thing but in your office was another.

"Mr. Katz," he said, beaming a broad smile. "May I?"

"Please," Katz said, and met him to shake hands in the middle of the room. A lot of D.C. lawyers, especially the 5th Streeters who made their living representing defendants who couldn't afford anyone better, were always roaming the halls, looking to strike a deal or get a heads up, but Harry wasn't one of them. Katz couldn't remember ever seeing him back here.

He pointed to the two brown wood chairs in front of his desk.

"You want to sit down?," he asked him.

"No," Harry said. "I just wanted to say hi, take a minute of your time."

"Okay," Katz said, "what can I do for you?"

"A little birdie told me you might be looking to make a move," Harry said.

"What? Who?" Katz asked, truly shocked. Then he knew who, before Harry could tell him. Wallace.

"Okay," Katz said. "Never mind. I know who, but I told him I was just thinking about it. Maybe."

"Okay," Harry laughed. "But when you're ready to do more than just think about it maybe, give me a call. We'll have lunch, or grab a drink. I've seen you in action enough to know you're the real thing, Mr. Katz. I think we could do a lot of people some good. Plus, I enjoyed our little sparring match."

"I didn't," Katz laughed. "But thanks for the compliment, your honor."

"Call me Harry," he said and waved a large index finger in his face. "I only let a few people do that, you know, so be properly impressed."

"Okay, Harry," Katz said. "But, really, you need to know it was just something I told Wallace because I hadn't seen him for a while, just catching up, you know. I haven't given it a lot of thought, really."

"No problem," Harry said. "When and if you do, give me a call. No rush."

He extended his hand and they shook.

"Have a good day, Mr. Katz," he said.

"Jake," Katz said.

"Jake," Harry said, and left.

Katz went back to his desk and sat back in his chair. He picked up the phone slips and leaned back. He took in the lime green walls one more time. This time, he didn't finish the thought. He jumped out of his seat and ran to the doorway.

"Harry!" he called, "hold up a minute."

This book is a work of fiction, but I based it as closely as I could on the actual facts of the murders at Mr. Khaalis' home and the takeover of the three buildings in D.C. Jake Katz, as well as Marty McAdoo, Tom Wallace, Officer Bohlinger, and the other police officers, medics, and lawyers I invented to meet the needs of the story exist only in my mind and on these pages Every other character is a real person who played the role ascribed to them in the book. In a few cases, I changed the names of real persons to protect their privacy.

I researched and wrote *Siege* over 18 months. During that time, I made numerous trips to the Washington Area Federal Records Center and D.C. Superior Court to review trial transcripts, U.S. Attorney's Office files, police interviews, and Mr. Khaalis' medical records, and interviewed many participants in the hostage crisis and a number of other persons involved in prosecuting and reporting the event. Although I made up much of the dialogue, some of it, particularly Hamaas Khaalis' orations and threats, is taken verbatim from media interviews and trial transcripts.

Jake Katz was my surrogate for several real people who did not appear in the book, but need to be recognized for their substantial contributions to resolving the real hostage crisis. They are MPD Captain Joseph O'Brien, who investigated the 1973 murders, and developed a personal relationship with Mr. Khaalis that was indispensable during the 1977 negotiations; Patrick Mulaney, an FBI psychologist, and Dr. Steven Pieczenik, a psychiatrist working with a State Department task force on terrorism, who were instrumental in advising MPD about how to respond to Mr. Khaalis' volatility during the negotiations; and Douglas Heck, a State

Department official who facilitated the MPD's use of the ambassadors during the crisis.

Special thanks go to the many people who helped me throughout this effort, including:

- Earl Silbert, who was the United States Attorney for the District of Columbia during the siege;
- Henry Schuelke, one of the Assistant United States Attorney (AUSA)s who prosecuted the murderers of Khaalis' family;
- Mark Tuohey, who prosecuted Khaalis and his accomplices for the hostage-taking;
- Retired D.C. Superior Court Judge Truman Morrison, who was the public defender assigned to represent him at the hearing following the release of the hostages;
- Tim Murray, who was on the pretrial services staff of the D.C. Superior Court and went on to become Executive Director of the Pretrial Justice Institute;
- John Hanrahan, a Washington Post reporter who covered the murders of the Khaalis family;
- Dr. Abdullah Khouj, Director of the Islamic Center;
- Robert Reed, archivist at the Washington Area Federal Records Center in College Park, Maryland;
- Alicia Shepard and the staff of the D.C. Superior Court Criminal Clerk's Office; and
- The Washingtoniana Special Collection of the Martin Luther King Library in Washington, D.C.

I also relied on Washington Post, Washington Star, and New York Times articles on the murders and the siege, and the accounts of two survivors of the siege: Paul Green's book *Forgotten Hostages* and Diane Cole's article *39 Hours: The Siege Remembered* in the May 1977 National Jewish Monthly. Kareem Abdul-Jabbar's *Giant Steps* provided excellent insights into Mr. Khaalis' beliefs and personality, and Imam Feisal Abdul Rauf's *Moving the Mountain* and Tarek Fatah's *The Jew Is Not My Enemy* were also helpful. One of my most important sources was Muhammad Asad's *The Message of the Qur'an*.

I also want to thank my daughter, Annie Tevelin, who provided me invaluable assistance in bringing this book to publication; Polly Hanson, for reaching out to Chief Cullinane on my behalf; Gary Klein for his several acts of friendship; Greg Brady, for his help and memory; Leslie Williams for her creative graphic design skills, and more than all of the above put together, Sandy Tevelin: Muse, wife, love of my life.

Hamaas Khaalis died at the Butner Federal Correction Institution in North Carolina on November 13, 2003. He is buried in Lincoln Cemetery in Suitland, Maryland, a short distance from the graves of his family.

Made in the USA
Middletown, DE
21 August 2015